T0000307

PAGES OF MOURNING

A Novel By

DIEGO GERARD MORRISON

Two Dollar Radio
Books Too Loud To Ignore

Two Dollar Radio
Books too loud to Ignore

WHO WE ARE TWO DOLLAR RADIO is a family-run outfit dedicated to reaffirming the cultural and artistic spirit of the publishing industry. We aim to do this by presenting bold works of literary merit, each book, individually and collectively, providing a sonic progression that we believe to be too loud to ignore.

TwoDollarRadio.com

Proudly based in
Ohio
TURTLE ISLAND

 @TwoDollarRadio

@TwoDollarRadio

/TwoDollarRadio

Love the
PLANET?
So do we.

Printed on Rolland Enviro®.
This paper contains 100% sustainable recycled fiber, is manufactured using renewable energy - Biogas and processed chlorine free.

Printed in Canada

 100%

PCF

 BIO GAS ENERGY

PERMANENT

All Rights Reserved

ISBN⇢ 9781953387400 : *Library of Congress Control Number available upon request.*

Also available as an Ebook.
E-ISBN⇢ 9781953387417

COPYRIGHT⇢ © 2024 BY DIEGO GERARD MORRISON

SOME RECOMMENDED LOCATIONS FOR READING:
Pretty much anywhere because books are portable and the perfect technology!

AUTHOR PHOTO⇢ Courtesy of the author

COVER PHOTO⇢ Photo by Benjamin Child on Unsplash.
COVER DESIGN⇢ Eric Obenauf

ANYTHING ELSE? Yes. Do not copy this book—with the exception of quotes used in critical essays and reviews—without the prior written permission from the copyright holder and publisher. Without limiting the rights under copyright reserved above, no part of this publication may be reproduced, stored or introduced into a retrieval system, or transmitted, in any form or by any means.

WE MUST ALSO POINT OUT THAT THIS IS A WORK OF *FICTION*. Names, characters, places, and incidents are products of the author's lively imagination, or used in a fictitious manner. Any resemblance to real events or persons, living or dead, is entirely coincidental.

Two Dollar Radio would like to acknowledge that the land where we live and work is the contemporary territory of multiple Indigenous Nations.

"Inventive and thrilling… an impressive achievement."
—PUBLISHERS WEEKLY, STARRED REVIEW

"*Pages of Mourning* by Diego Gerard Morrison is a bitingly funny novel about family, loss, grief, and creativity steeped in the food, drink, literature, superstition, and magical realism of Latin America. *Pages of Mourning* is a standout novel of 2024."
—CAITLIN BAKER, ISLAND BOOKS

"The world that emerges from this crafty 'universe of dust' is lit everywhere with empathy and insight."
—LAIRD HUNT, AUTHOR OF *ZORRIE*

"One of those rare books that emerges from the clashing of several schools of literature, filled with sad young literary men and women, tortured by art and life and their creations."
—FERNANDO A. FLORES, AUTHOR OF *VALLEYESQUE* AND *TEARS OF THE TRUFFLEPIG*

"*Pages of Mourning* is not magic, but magisterial realism."
—FORREST GANDER, AUTHOR OF *THE TRACE* AND *BE WITH*

"At once bookish and political, this novel crossfades between times, places and states of being…"
—GABRIELA JAUREGUI, AUTHOR OF *FERAL*

"Diego Gerard Morrison has written a glorious kaleidoscope of a book in which the roads to artificial paradises lead to hell. When the dead are as restless as the living, how do we mourn them?"
—MÓNICA DE LA TORRE, AUTHOR OF *REPETITION 19*

"Diego Gerard Morrison masterfully intertwines individual and collective trauma through the lens of magical realism. A literary masterpiece, *Pages of Mourning* illuminates the complexities of existence with haunting beauty and profound insight."
—SHIRIN NESHAT, DIRECTOR OF *WOMEN WITHOUT MEN*

Also by Diego Gerard Morrison

Myth of Pterygium

PAGES OF MOURNING

BOOK I

No Magic in Realism

2017

A GRAY WINTER DAY, CLOUDY YET SOMEHOW GLAR-ing, snow melting in puddles on the street, brisk wind leaping off the Hudson River, while inside Andromeda Coffee, Chris waits for me behind the fogged-up window, sipping a latte, its cap of foam catching on his Daliesque whiskers, scarf still around his neck although he has removed his coat, fingertips protruding from fingerless wool gloves—a calculated piece of attire suited to the performative look of asceticism he brings to his pro-bono editing tasks, which is his excuse to sneak out of his job at a venerable publishing company on 8th Avenue, not, indeed, all that far from Andromeda Coffee, where, with a fair amount of hesitation, I creak open the door and bob my head to the barista to let him know I'll have the same as always, enjoying the sensation of being cocooned by warm air as I step inside the café.

Chris's red pen rests on the marbled tabletop, having left enough of its ink on the stack of pages in front of him for me to sigh nervously as we greet with a clash of curled fists. As I take a seat, a sense of déjà-vu arrives with my double espresso spiked with rye whiskey in the freckled hands of the barista, its ashy scent rising from the cup in fleeting twirls of steam.

"*No Magic in Realism,*" Chris reads from the cover page of my manuscript. "Bit stiff for a title, isn't it? It's like if García Márquez called his novel *Uncertain Feelings in an Ordinary Year.*"

I run my hands through my hair and knit my fingers behind my head. "Nothing more than a working title at this point."

3

As he turns the page and I spy all his red effacing lines, my breath goes out, slow and sore, while his pen dabs at the page edge again, the felt nib leaking red ink like bruises spreading over my ego.

"So, this woman, Oedipa," Chris says, referring to my main character. "She's ready to flee, leave everything behind." He returns his eyes to mine, rapping the table with his pen. "But a crow that is *camouflaged in darkness*," he quotes directly from the page, "keeps pecking at her window, right?"

"Right." I slurp my rye-loaded espresso, then put the cup back down on the table and watch the foam disperse, first into continents, then into islands.

"And you want the reader to believe this bird is no accident, like it's there to stop her, to communicate something to her?" He doesn't wait for me to confirm this time. "This makes her a touch nervous, but it also makes her curious, second-guess herself, makes her question if she should really take off, leave her known life and her family behind." He lifts one page from the stack and skims over more words. "A very obvious way to introduce tension." He pauses to look straight at me, then returns his eyes to the page. "But let me tell you, writer," he whistles sarcastically, "the writing is just not up to par."

I click my tongue and give him a slow nod.

"She seems to resent her curiosity, her delusory leap, even feels sorry for herself. Of course, birds are no messengers, right?—she's *almost certain of it*," he quotes the text again, lingering on every syllable.

With my hands around the warm cup, I allow my shoulders to sag and hold back a groan, knowing the worst might not have even started.

"Her *freshly dyed black bangs are like the wing of the crow*," Chris continues, adding a one-handed air-quote. "So, there's a moment of identification, like the woman and the bird are one and the same. You want us to wonder what is making her go, but also what is suddenly holding her back." He has a sip from his coffee.

"Sounds like a vague summary, yes."

4

"Naming your character *Oedipa* makes me think of Thomas Pynchon's *The Crying of Lot 49*. It's a loaded name and brings its own associations. Which is a bad start for a writer without a track record. To be honest, I kept reading only because you're my friend."

I sink further into the warm fabric of my chair, looking at the dry remnants of espresso along the inside of the porcelain cup. In my mind, I cross out the name *Oedipa* and replace it with the anonymous acronym, *O*.

He unrolls the scarf from his neck and sips his coffee through embouchure-parted lips. "Then you have a nice detail here: *Once we disappear, our kin remain uncertain and expectant, forever awaiting our return?*"

A slight rush of joy kindles in my chest.

"I like how the affirmation becomes a question. Nice way to convey doubt and unreliability—made me keep reading; you're not a complete lost cause." He reaches over and gives me an overfamiliar clap on the shoulder. "I like her *expiring breast implants*, it's a good characterization. Finally, I partially see her."

My arms folded, I give a backward nod at the page, "You want to use a green pen for the good bits?"

He doesn't look up, instead skims down the page, and I remember that green ink pens are as rare as Chris's reasons to put green ink on my text. I turn away, half ashamed, half offended, and notice that the café has emptied during the lunch hour. Only the barista remains, witness to the stripping of my pride, beside the silver La Marzocco espresso machine while texting on his phone, appearing not to listen, but very obviously listening.

"If you cross out the whole *darkness in camouflage* business, the bit of the bird against the night's backdrop can be good too," Chris says. "How it's like a black-on-black minimalist painting, how the black square of the night-filled window caught in the white contours of the wall is like a page of mourning in a newspaper—really good, exceptionally ominous." I expect him to applaud sarcastically, but he just adds, "First engaging image so far."

I roll my eyes and catch the sun-drenched fog of the winter day through the window.

"But, again, the overstated question is dreadful: *is there a message you come bearing?* Seriously? Does this bird have extreme cognitive abilities?" Chris asks and curls his lip—a gesture of contempt he'd find overdone if it appeared on a page. Widening his eyes, he adds, "Now, *that* would be *very* Magical Realist"—he pauses, chuckles—"for a text that wants to make Magical Realism shatter."

My breath could be perceived as a sigh of pleasure, but it's all frustration. "I get it, it's naïve, it's clichéd. It's also untrue—birds don't bring messages. They fly around, looking for food, or else just the south, for that matter."

His face congeals for a second, a bad sign, then his eyes shrink to a wince, perhaps trying to express that sarcasm belongs to his position in our power structure. As he stares at me, the day seems to darken behind the window, removing the kindling aura of light around him, killing my concentration, almost taking me far from Andromeda Coffee. His voice, though, is enough to keep me grounded—"Let me ask you, writer, isn't the point of Magical Realism having the dead come back, not the living take off?"

The coffee machine hisses and gushes sudden laughter, and the barista next to it looks at his phone with the subtlest hint of a smile. His shift ends soon, when he'll likely walk across town to his second job bartending at the Widow's Walk, his daily calendar comprised of pouring coffee and booze—or in my case coffee *with* booze—in order to afford rent in New York City.

Tapping my fingers on the table, I turn back to Chris. "Now that you mention it, you might be right."

"Of course I'm right," he cuts in with a raised hand.

"Don't give me that shit, don't act like you have the narrative all figured out," my voice louder than I had intended, earning the barista's sidelong glance.

"OK," he says, his palms open and upraised, like I've pulled a gun on him. "Just remember, a narrative like yours should be sliced open by certain death, not constrained by the endless possibilities of life."

"I know, I know, then I can endlessly collapse her return, which is the same as collapsing the genre."

He nods. "Sorry to break it to you, writer, but there don't seem to be many narrative possibilities in this literary cul-de-sac you've gotten yourself into." He puts the manuscript back together after that, clearing his throat, apologetically, perhaps, and then there's the sound of glass shattering, as if the barista has dropped one of his tumblers behind the counter. The clouds darken further behind the window—a sudden change in the light that makes my eyes flutter and focus, this time fully removing me from Andromeda Coffee, far from the corner of Hudson and Jane.

I jerk upright at my desk, my mouth tacky like I've been caught in this daydream for ages. Through the window, the snow over the Hudson is gone, and all I can see is Mexico City in all its paradox, its old colonial facades next to modern high-rises—all of it a shifting mirage. The glaring light of a Word document in front of me has dimmed, the computer's automatic energy saver akin to the sun-drenched New York fog.

I've crash-landed back in my reality, residing in a studio provided for me by my writing fellowship. Around me, bathwater-thick air, polluted too, a desk and a mattress on the sloping wooden floor, a Word document with a ticking cursor beneath my first chapter, a bitter Nescafé spiked with Jim Beam bourbon in a styrofoam cup, and a dog-eared paperback copy of Juan Rulfo's *Pedro Páramo*.

Lost in my coffee, trying to stay in the world of my daydream, a picture rises in my head of Oedipa—now O—framed by the window casting her reflection, which Chris might think is masterful. As far as I'm concerned, I've nailed her as a character, but I have nailed nothing more: the present is always expiring, which accomplishes the stiff forward linearity of time appropriate for a novel looking to shatter Magical Realism as a genre. Her black hair like the wing of a crow is a decent visual, expanded by the imperfection of the spider vein in her nostril. But, as a whole, the scene is too vacuous and still, Daydream-Chris is right about that. My Magical Realist parody needs action and motive. What makes her leave and consign us to forever wait? Is the return of someone who has disappeared the same as having someone back from the land of the dead?

"It seems like you have no clue why she leaves. Hell, I don't think you even know what happens to her after that, let alone why she never returned," Chris would say through a Cheshire Cat grin, my imaginative failure, as always, a source of pleasure for him.

"You might be right."

Nodding, he would get up from the table, coil his scarf around his neck and fling his coat over his shoulders. The door would creak open, but he would turn to me before leaving. "Where do you go from here? Do you kill her off? Does she live?"

The last of my cold coffee slides bitterly down my throat. "I have no clue, you said it yourself."

"I'd say you better take full advantage of this fellowship, writer. You can't move on until you figure out what happens to O."

I pack my things and walk through the door Chris would be holding open for me. Once outside, I can't make out his final words—they are no more than a Rulfian murmur—and I try to breathe against the heat in the air, to feel the trampled snow beneath my soles, but find instead only the crunch of a shattered Coca-Cola bottle on the sticky tarmac of Calzada de Los Misterios. Looking up to see if I can spot Chris walking ahead, headed for Reforma, I fail to assimilate my daydream at odds with this all-too-real haziness.

The sun has burned off the early cloud-cover and the sky beams a clear blue that defies all sense of realism. The streets are riddled with car exhaust, busted plumbing fumes, street-stall smoke. All those tedious molecular assailants that glue the corners of my eyes, that itch on my skin, that turn my mouth to a swamp, enough to make me wish I could really teleport back to the winter of New York.

The walk takes me up Reforma and its rotundas, its sinking and skewed monuments, its colonial buildings with walls meeting at odd angles in the style of a vorticist painting. Then a backstreet leads me into la Colonia Juárez, a neighborhood full of forlorn theatres and Art Deco columns coated in bubble-font graffiti—AMORIRNOHAYHUIR—under which a homeless man sleeps in a heap of crusty blankets. Only his head is left uncovered and his face is still and solemn. As I walk past him, though, he comes to life—his bloodshot eyes flick open, and he cups the palm of his hand, "Algo de algo, vivo muerto de hambre."

Stopping in front of him, I clap my pockets for change. There is nothing there, so all I can give him is a shrug.

"No le hace, we're all feeling it." He rubs his marbled eyes, then lowers his body to the ground, ready to sink back into a dead sleep.

Further ahead, blocks of absurd conglomerates of disjointed businesses—a vulcanizadora, a pet grooming shop, a cantina, a print shop, a pulquería, a 24-hour brothel with glaring red neon—all of them sharing walls, and in front of them, endless taco stands stationed under plastic tarps. There are untold rations of shredded pork sizzling on hotplates, noses and ears behind a foggedup vitrine, the overused, clichéd sign featuring an exultant naked pig bathing in a cauldron of boiling oil. Booming loudly over this hiss of frying food, the music cross-fades between narco-corridos, cumbias, and pop blown in from the world's real capitals. I sit at the counter of a stand and order one quick taco—campechano with a sprinkle of cilantro and the barest drizzle of salsa verde to go easy on the stomach, hoping to dodge the sure and impending revenge of Moctezuma.

Folded in front of me beside the plastic plates and grubby napkins, are the tabloids with their now routine headlines, VIVOS SE LOS

LLEVARON, VIVOS LOS QUEREMOS: PARENTS OF THE 43 MURDERED STUDENTS MARCH TO THE CITY, DEMANDING THEM BACK ALIVE.

I can't avert the eyes of the students in the newspaper, and wiping my mouth after my first bite, the napkin soaked by salsa verde run-off, I read the familiar story: almost three years since their disappearance, the parents of the forty-three docent students from Ayotzinapa are demanding that the government return them alive—this, then, has become the narrative of the country, where the number of forced disappearances has risen to the hundreds of thousands, sparking the cruelest of waits.

"Sound familiar, writer?" Chris says—my mind conjuring him out of a cloud of greasy smoke.

I nod, "Way of the country."

The taquero in front of me, flipping tortillas over his hotplate with pinched fingers, responds as if I were talking to him, "México, eh? The mystical country where everyone gets murdered, but where we can't find the bodies."

I nod, a shiver running down my spine, and turn to Chris, whose shrug is so fervent that he disappears, leaving me to finish my taco while leafing through the tabloid—there's no black mourning page for the missing students in there, nor for any of those who have gone missing. *In Mexico, nobody ever dies,* wrote Juan Rulfo, *we never let the dead die.* All we are ever left with are blank pages—white space symbolizing the possibility of their return.

When I get to Rose's building, I sit on the patio in the shade of a century-old jacaranda tree. Some of its unseasonably shed blossoms are scattered underfoot. While some of them remain purple, others are decaying, transitioning to the brownish color of rot.

Rose is nowhere to be found, so I spread out my work on the marbled table, which for a second is hard to tell apart from the one in my Andromeda Coffee daydream.

My head is fried from the walk over, so I flip through notes I took yesterday on *Pedro Páramo*, my spidery handwriting reading: *The dead won't die here—the dead are kept alive through active verbs.* Some of it's good, or at least better than I remember, and I'm almost excited to flip open my laptop to compile the notes and perhaps add a question on whether the past tense is the right device to lend a *lively deadness* to Magical Realist characters. Before I can, though, I hear the clatter of footsteps on the tiled floor, followed by the thud of Rose's body on the chair in front of me. She stoops forward to lean over my notes, her gray hair dangling over the furrows on her forehead.

"Does the *literary drought* live on?" she asks, like she did all throughout my MFA in New York and my early days as a writer. Ever since she pulled the strings to get me this fellowship, she's been anxious to read my work, this weak attempt at a novel, even if only to see that I'm producing something to be turned in at the fast-approaching first session with my fellowship advisor.

Placing my elbows on the table, shielding my notes from her, I say, "It does. It lives on."

"Even though I got you a fellowship and a studio? One would think they would spark some motivation. It's the writer's dream, is it not, the closest thing to Bohemia?"

I nod heavily, digesting her words; Rose is the closest thing I have to a mentor and a mother. After my mother left, my father shipped me off to Cuernavaca to live with Rose during the school term. According to him, it was for my education; according to Rose, it was for his convenience and my safety.

"Well, then, let's hope for a cloudburst," she says, "and maybe less sulking."

I lift my head and study her face. There's something of a resemblance to my mother there, even if they're only step-sisters—the fish-hooked smile I've seen in pictures, the drooping eyes—some resemblance to O, even.

"I hope you're ready to split soon," Rose says, staving my gaze and leaning back in her chair.

"Where are we going?"

"Meeting Nayeli." She pauses for effect. "*Your fellowship advisor,* the famous writer. Then she's reading at SOMA tonight, we can't miss that."

Nodding, I pack up my mess against a rare gust of air that sweeps in, under the flurry of jacaranda leaves slowly falling to our feet.

The cab ride is sweltering, and I feel like the shredded pork sizzling on the hotplate at the taco stand, my pores seeping grease-thick sweat to the point where not even the open window brings relief. My stomach is turning too, probably due to that indigestible street taco.

Rose also shifts around, detaching her back from the clammy seat, pulling a handkerchief from her purse to dry the sweat beading on her forehead.

"Give it to me straight, honestly," she says. "How's the work *actually* going? You've been in the literary trenches for quite a while. You must have some progress to report."

I want to tell her that the trenches are not solely literary, she should know as much, but only say, "Not great. Every time I leave the studio, the ideas pop up, somewhat. When it comes time to write the ideas down, they vanish. The place is so lifeless inside, as lifeless as my story."

"But that's sort of what you're looking for, no? The *polarization of action with inertness,*"—mimicking my style of writing with her voice—"*the ocean between them as big as the gap between life and death, real and artifice, the material and the specter.*"

I run a hand over my pockets, feeling for my pen and notepad and she looks at me with another one of her lopsided smiles, "You want to write that down?"

"Yeah, it wasn't bad."

She sticks her hands into her purse and pulls out a notepad and a pen with a tip on either side, one red, one black. "I've heard these are useful."

Taking the pen from the red side brings an image of Chris to my head.

"Now you can jot down the *crucial details of this as-yet unborn narrative with infinite potential.*"

"Keep talking like that and you and I should swap jobs," I say, although of course she wouldn't need to—as the accomplished novelist that she is, Rose is already the founder and director of the Under the Volcano Fellowship. Her clout reached so far she was able to offer me a spot in the program, even if my writing doesn't match the fellowship's repute.

"You don't actually *have* a job remember?" Rose says.

"I thought the writer's job was to write."

"Exactly." It takes her some seconds to rid the sarcastic grin from her face. "You'll love Nayeli's house, the neighborhood, so unlike the Mexico City you know. Maybe it'll serve as inspiration for you to finally put pen to paper."

From what I've heard from Rose, Nayeli hasn't dealt with the everyday struggles of the city for a while. By the time her first book was published to great acclaim—an appropriation of the Greek Myth of Aspalis placed in the context of the Mexican Drug War and the rise in femicides—there were no more rungs left to climb at the top of the writer's ladder; she was safe from the city's bovinities, wrapped in a frock of fame, cash, and political militancy, all of it happening before she hit thirty, an age I have already surpassed, without showing any promise of success, having to ride in taxis or peseros from one edge of the city to the other.

My stomach clenches again from the taco, but I manage to contain myself until we exit the cab beside Nayeli's house.

Once we're on the cobblestoned street in Coyoacán, the lack of transition from the jammed avenue to the sound of water over rocks, to arching palms and weeping willows, volcanic rock and village calm, makes me dizzy for a second.

"You were right," I tell Rose, "I feel very much transported to García Marquez's Macondo here. Might need that notepad in a second."

She gives me a mild shake of the head and presses firmly on the buzzer.

After a few seconds the gates rattle and we push open the door, letting daylight creep into a dark and dank foyer, illuminating tiles on the wall with Aztec images on them, a representation of what might be El Mictlán.

The light intensifies as we step onto the patio of a large Art Deco house, where Nayeli's footsteps echo from the depths. Her face seems utterly un-aging, way below thirty, and she is outrageously slim too, her upper body lanky under a plain white t-shirt, while her lower body is covered by a wide woven skirt with geometric patterns. Her black curls swing over her oval, almond-colored face with every step she takes in our direction, and once she's close enough, I can see the jarring, unusual deep black color of her eyes.

When she reaches us, there's a flurry of embraces. Hugging Rose and meeting my eyes over her shoulder, she says, "You're the one I've heard so much about." She smiles and grips my shoulder with icy fingers. "Yet another writer of promise," she adds, but it doesn't sound like she means it.

"You know writers," Rose says, "they can stay potential forever."

I hum nervous laughter and follow them through a doorless archway into the living room, where light spills over a black leather sofa, a beige corduroy settee, and an oversized desk that looks like a single slice of a monkey-ear tree, and which holds a computer, books open face down, and a few manuscripts without a single trace of red ink—every object arranged in a neurotic manner.

"We should have a drink. I think gin and tonics are in order," Nayeli says, veering around a table already set for three, and out of sight into the kitchen.

"Sounds good," Rose says loudly, but then peering sideways at me, she whispers, "you better go easy on the booze."

I nod my agreement even though I want to wave her away.

After reading my submissive gesture, her sight lingering on me for some seconds, she turns back towards Nayeli's desk. "Now this is a proper place to live, quite the writer's dream."

"Right," I say, although I'm not so sure. The place feels as uninspiring to me as my own childhood home. There's no family narrative to be read from the décor—no pictures with loved ones, no human element, and the similarity is enough to cast a gloom over me, but not one so dense that the coppery tang of gin-loaded tonic water can't get rid of it.

"Food's almost ready, mole negro," Nayeli says, handing me one of the cocktails. "I ordered in. Deadlines don't leave me any time to cook."

Rose looks at me in silence, then follows Nayeli into the kitchen, allowing the time needed for me to down my gin-and-tonic in a few gulps, thinking both the fizz and lime might help soothe my gut.

"Can you help us uncork the wine?" calls Nayeli from the kitchen. "Needs breathing before imbibing."

"Got a bottle in mind?" I shout back.

"Any one you like."

The pitch of her voice is *operatic*, and for a second, I wonder if I should write that down, but instead head straight for the wine bottles. The one I choose looks pretty august, but that just means the cork crumbles as soon as I sink the screw into it. As I manage to pull the stub out of the neck, a few of its many pieces fall into the wine.

In the kitchen, the microwave beeps and Nayeli walks to the table, wearing oven mitts and holding a fuming platter of mole negro. She pauses her stride for a second and laughs at the sight of the destroyed bits of cork—a laugh loaded with subtext.

"Just about managed." I display the largest chunk of remaining cork between index and thumb.

Behind Nayeli, Rose emerges from the kitchen too, basket of tortillas and bowl of refried beans in hand, and shoots me a look that full-on portrays embarrassed ire.

"The alcoholic tends to be over-eager," Rose says.

Nayeli widens her eyes and my chest floods with cold.

"He's had some issues with it before, that's all," Rose says.

Nayeli slowly nods, and I attempt a chuckle, hoping to lighten the mood, to which neither of them reacts. Instead, they place the food on the table.

Still standing, and eager to blend into the nonchalant action, I decant wine into our glasses—bits of cork like driftwood flowing in the stream.

Reaching over the food to pour into Rose's glass, I calculate the height wrong and a belt of wine hops from the glass onto the white tablecloth. Nayeli stares at the stain for more than I would like, and says, "Don't worry about it."

I turn to Rose, who looks at my empty glass of gin and then at me. There's no option other than to pull my chair back and sit to stave off her gaze.

The first sips of wine hit me hard, since I'm already knocked about a bit by the gin-and-tonic I gulped down in such haste, not to mention my spiked coffee earlier in the afternoon. As we serve food onto our plates, I'm wary of Rose's eyes beside me, even though she seems absorbed by Nayeli. When the dizzy spell fades, I tune into their conversation.

"Fellowship's going good," Rose says. "But you know young writers, they just want to gloat in attention rather than do the actual work."

"Young writers dream, don't they?" Nayeli says, turning to me.

"I'm not that young, and I'm more into realism than dreams."

"Realism, dreams," Nayeli says. "It's all literature, no?"

Before I can respond, Rose cuts in, "Realism, dreams—it's all useless blabber, the point is putting words on the page, which he doesn't."

Nayeli nods with a full mouth, a half-chewed blob of food making her cheeks protrude monstrously. After swallowing she says, "So, how am I to advise someone who doesn't write?"

"It'll come," I say. "Hopefully—in the fullness of time."

"Take note," Rose says, pointing with a backward thumb at Nayeli's desk. Then turning to her, she adds, "So how is your new book coming along, anyway?"

Again, Nayeli nods, picking out the bits of cork from her wine glass, and placing them over the stain on the tablecloth, which swells and reddens. "New book is going well. It's a stark deadline, though, if I want it out in time for the third anniversary of the events in Ayotzinapa."

Slicing through my food, I realize I'm nodding as Nayeli speaks, to what, I'm not so sure. "A book about the forty-three murdered students," I say, trying to stay a part of the conversation. "A story ripped from the headlines."

Nayeli pauses, wets her lips with wine, not once blinking—like she's underlining my statement of the obvious. "Forty-three monologues, one by each student, speaking from beyond the grave, or wherever they are held captive—depends on what you want to believe. Something that can leap beyond the narrative and be politically useful."

Rose and I nod in silence, pausing our meal.

"Mexico, yeah?" Nayeli says. "The magical country where we expect the dead to waltz right back."

A cold sensation washes over my face, which I try to mask with a long sip of wine.

"Speaking of magic," Rose says, now pointing at me with her fork. "He has his opinions about it." Her smile seems to suddenly go from wry to morbid.

Nayeli's stare doesn't give much away. "Is this for your fellowship project?"

Rose seems to enjoy the question. She rubs her hands together in delight, and it's as though the heat emanating from all the friction goes straight to my face.

I finish chewing a tough piece of chicken drowned in mole negro, washing it down with more wine, wondering if Nayeli knows that I'm Rose's nephew, that she played a big part not only in me getting into an MFA program, but also this fellowship. I turn to Rose for help but she turns away. "It's a novel." I lay down my cutlery over the plate like Nayeli did when she spoke about her book. "A novel that sets out to discredit Magical Realism as a genre. The narrative is hyper realist. The idea is to situate Magical Realism within the literary canon it belongs to, as opposed to being a pseudo-canon of its own."

"And that canon is…?" Nayeli probes, performing a sort of sitting bow, while Rose mimics a drumroll, which makes me wonder if she is as tipsy as I am.

"Fantasy," I say, and quickly add, "and there is nothing wrong with fantasy."

Nayeli's nod is slow, her expression blank, and Rose seems to cringe in her chair.

"And how do you plan to write a novel that can express that?" Nayeli says. "What can you do—just say *These things aren't magical, they're just what they are?*"

I have yet another sip of wine which empties the glass. "I guess the epiphany has not yet fully dawned on me."

"I see," Nayeli says, impaling a chunk of food with her fork.

"I want to build everything up so it seems like the dead are about to return, but collapsing it over and over, keep the reader waiting, endlessly, to no avail, Godot style."

Nayeli nods and winces, allows for some time to pass. "You mean, exactly like the story of the forty-three murdered students." She pauses. "Only here, in the real world, it's their relatives who wait to no avail, not just a mindless reader."

Her words force a sigh down my throat, and before I can tell her that I have experience with loved ones who have disappeared, Rose turns to me with a gentle shake of the head—is she trying to censor me, or has the damage been done and the gesture is more akin to the thumbs-down of a Roman emperor?

"Seems like I beat you to writing that book," Nayeli says. "No, wait," she lifts an index finger, "it's our nightmare of a country that beat you."

A long silence grips us after that, which we try to fend off with a few mouthfuls of mole negro.

When she finishes the last bit of food, Nayeli joins her fists under her chin with her elbows on the table. Then, locking eyes with mine, she says, "Look, you have to be careful on many fronts. Even though it might seem farcical, Magical Realism is a device that helps people in this country think about death. Think of it the way atheists think of mass—it's a ritual that carries very little meaning, but that probably grants people a lot of peace."

I hum in affirmation and finish the last droplets of my wine before pouring myself some more.

Rose turns to me, stopping her mole-laden fork on the way to her mouth. "More wine?"

I stop the high-pour at half a glass. My face is a version of Chris's gambler's reticence, but it needs real resolve to keep it that way.

"Where are you from anyway?" Nayeli asks me. "Haven't you observed the rituals of death here. You *are* Mexican, aren't you?" She smiles again, and there is definitely something self-righteous about the position of her lips.

I stay silent, the breath out of my nose long and distinct.

"He's from a place called Comala," Rose says, in a voice that's stifling laughter, but when she sees my face, she looks down at her plate of food. Yes, *Comala*: the setting of Juan Rulfo's iconic work *Pedro Páramo*—that Magical Realist novel that seems to have symbolically constructed the harsh reality of Mexico and the people it has forsaken. Even though it was published in 1955, the book has become a recurring mirror of the country's crises both past and present. Comala serves as the archetypal, tireless realm where the ghosts of all the dead and the missing are tossed together, where their voices refuse to be silenced.

Nayeli widens her eyes and places a hand over her mouth, finding it hard to quell the laughter. "Are you serious?" She turns to Rose as if looking for confirmation, and Rose nods still facing her plate, letting a slight laugh spring from the back end of her throat.

"But not Rulfo's Comala," I say. "Just another lost Mexican pueblo."

"But that *is* Rulfo's Comala," Nayeli says and chuckles. "Goodness. And your parents, are they from there too?"

I nod, then shake my head. "My dad's from here, my mom's an American expat."

"And they gave you *that* name?"

I nod in resignation.

"Aureliano from Comala?" Nayeli says, as if she has stumbled upon a fortune—a writer and living pun who through name and hometown is the dissonant confluence of two iconic works of the magical realist canon, *Pedro Páramo* and *One Hundred Years of Solitude.*

Rose releases the laughter she was trying to hold in—a dam breaking. When it recedes, she says, "One of a kind, your parents."

"No wonder you hate Magical Realism," Nayeli says, laughter catching on her words. "You had me wondering how you got this fellowship with *that* proposal, but I'm sure you had them at *Aureliano from Comala.*"

Before she left, Nayeli popped open another bottle of wine without any difficulties. She had to leave early to prepare for her reading, insisting we stay in her house for as long as we'd like. Most of that time, though, has me stuck on her feeble Art Deco toilet. Nayeli's jeers loud in my mind, I imagine a scene with my mother in our Comala kitchen—one that, like every one of my daydreams starring my mother, is entirely a fictional creation. In it, the window frames the volcanoes, who have a new cap of snow and tower over a low embankment of clouds, while she fixes up a yucca, eggplant, and plantain salad, half-watching whatever is playing on TV.

"I can't believe you didn't put your foot down when he suggested my name."

"You win some, you lose some," she replies, tasting the dressing with her finger.

"But I'm a living punch line."

"It's real easy to change your name these days. You can probably do it online."

Behind the window, a crow lands on my mother's bird feeder, nibbles at the seeds, and shits on an empty spot of the tray.

In my daydream, I'm trying to make out its peck against the window, but the only sound is that of Rose's fist banging against the bathroom door.

"Bowels empty yet, Aureliano? We'll be late for the reading."

As the cab rides over the elevated freeway, I look out the cruddy window. The silhouettes of buildings vanish in the cloud of smog like ghosts from a previous time, and, down below, people walk endlessly through the haze.

As soon as we are dropped off outside SOMA, Rose knocks on the blue metallic door of the large colonial building that houses the arts programs and which hosts her fellowship's literary events every Wednesday night.

"Look, I'm sorry about all that at Nayeli's. Hope it didn't get you down or anything—writers must develop a thick skin."

Before I can reply, the door clicks open and a guard demands my credentials and a signature on a full register sheet with red ink scribbles.

"Being here'll clear your head," Rose says, leading me in. "And hopefully inspire you."

Going up a low flight of stairs, my head throbs and I burp mole negro, a taste that rapidly coats every nook of my mouth. I'm also afraid the wine didn't get me drunk enough to be sociable without the usual touch of anxiety. Rose is as poised as ever, though, enjoying the auratic power of being the director of the renowned Under the Volcano Writer's Fellowship, guiding me with her quick stride down a gauntlet of people with identities just as ghostly as characters from *Pedro Páramo*, only the ones here are far too neoliberal, sporting fake spectacles, impossible hair-dos, and self-drawn tattoos promising late-age regret—disguises befitting the quirky yet stylish cliché of the contemporary artist. Some of them are taking selfies to immortalize the occasion—pictures of themselves passed through filters of unnatural tones—and hanging them on social media. Before I find myself judging them, I wonder how they are different from the cryptic author I'm studying, who projected an identity by cropping away the worst of himself, whose primary mark on the world is his own literary work, comprised of only two books, all of it afloat against the backdrop of an enigmatic author-portrait. I find myself wanting to jot down *Rulfo as a social media addict*, but Rose would scold me if she saw me. Following her deeper into the crowd, within the buzz of voices on the patio, I spot both fashionable and failed items redeemed as chic through sheer force of irony—onesies, pajama-length shirts, old people's sweaters, hoodies with the printed faces of Selena, Zapata, and Marilyn Monroe. My own clothes—all-black jeans, boots, t-shirt—are somewhat expensive, but nameless, and I'm not sure if that means I've tried too little or too hard.

Rose introduces me to the other two recipients of the fellowship, one man and one woman around my same age. "Hola infrarrealistas," Rose tells them, and they both smile, Rose's flattery reflected by their rosy cheeks. While the woman looks like an Emo, with straight black hair like O would have, and which matches her clothes and the rings beneath her eyes, the man looks like a Mexican version of Tom Waits on the cover of his album, *Closing Time*, with salon curls descending to bushy sideburns. I dry my palm of its ever-present moisture and shake their hands, which are cold and wet from the beers they're holding.

"The Tom Waits of La Gran Tenochtitlan," I say, holding the man's gaze, and I'm immediately left wondering where I got the bravery from. He nods with a grin, and Rose seems to widen her eyes in surprise.

"I think that's a compliment," Mexican Tom Waits says.

"Yes, yes," I say. "Of course. It's a compliment." Trying to mask my embarrassment by keeping my gaze on his, I wonder whether what he was going for with his curls is rather a resemblance to a young Roberto Bolaño.

Beside me, the Emo stares at Mexican Tom Waits, raising her brows high, while Rose's laugh is whinnying, almost desperate. Without any excuses on my behalf, she drifts off to greet other people and leaves me with my two peers, who swig their beers in unison.

Hoping to avoid an awkward silence, I ask, "Where can I get my hands on a cold one?" and blush at the way my Spanish is studded with outdated slang in a way that my English used to be when I first moved to New York.

They point with their bottles toward a makeshift bar at the end of the patio, where the phrase *Miércoles Literario de SOMA* is written in chalk—perhaps suggesting this evening was a sufficient weekly dose of literary socializing to run up the numbers on the pedometer.

Mezcal and Dos Equis Lager are the only available options, as though the beverages were not refreshments so much as tokens of some rarefied circle of internal reference, whose sub-categories include the *patriotic choice* of mezcal or the *humble choice* of beer, neither of the two options seemingly aware enough to settle upon, and I don't resist buying one of each.

From my vantage point I spot Rose. She's in the middle of the crowd, talking to two women, faculty probably, both of them, as Rose, in their late fifties. When I reach her, she breaks off from them with a rehearsed one-liner and a smile. She takes from my hand the mezcal I'd already started drinking, and stares at me with unblinking eyes.

"You've had some wine, some gin—and that's just the drinks I've seen. I'm not here to pull you out of your sick again. You're my nephew, or godson, or whatever, I know, but I have my limits."

"All right. Calm down."

"No, no. Doing that once was one too many," she says, guiding me into a room full of folding chairs, which is as muggy as the shadeless corners on the streets at midday, and where a projector exposes a black screen against the front wall with the title *"Drug War Aspalis"* above Nayeli's name.

When the room is full and the audience equipped with drinks, a loud, scratchy tapping of the microphone signals the start of the reading, and in the rush of the last people taking their seats, heat blooms from foot to head, enough to make me miss the Hudson's wintery breeze again.

Nayeli comes through the doors and heads straight to the podium. She has changed into torn black jeans and a white t-shirt with an altered Mexican flag on it—where the traditional green and red stripes have been replaced by a stark black—a design that became popular after the abduction and murder of the forty-three students, and which has now come to symbolize our mourning country. She looks over the audience, but instead of making direct eye contact with anybody, her eyes hover. After waiting for the final crowd noise to settle, she detaches the microphone from its base, and, bringing it close to her mouth, opens with a statement about fiction as a fallacy in contemporary Mexican culture, where the misuse of drama within the themes of our recurring violence does nothing but a disservice to the possible solutions—an argument I'm unsure I can immediately agree with.

Rose looks at me, her face slightly askew, and hisses, "Don't make that face. What have you accomplished to own those rolling eyes?"

Even after I look away, I feel her grumpy look linger on me, and it takes Nayeli more than half an hour to dissect the concept of a sub-genre that must blur the lines between journalism and fiction, appropriating the advantages of fictional narrative while at the same time utilizing the unavoidable urgency of reporting on current events. She reaffirms her thesis from the opposite point of view, too—journalism in and of itself can no longer capture the resolve to ail the current events that mar our country, it's the dramatic tension of fiction that should color the news, while stressing that the paradox resides in the fact that the country no longer needs fiction or metaphors to make everyone fully aware of our hellish zeitgeist. She addresses current examples whose media narratives have failed, beginning with the murder of the forty-three docent students from Ayotzinapa, then moving to our now standard desensitized reactions when learning of forced disappearances in the country, and culminating with the rise in femicides in Mexico City's metropolitan area—every case she mentions is enough to cause a choking sensation in my throat, the constant thought of my own narrative, of O, her disappearance.

Nayeli reads from *Drug War Aspalis* after that, her appropriation of the myth interspersed with real testimony, words spoken first hand by those who are searching the country for their missing kin.

When she folds the book shut, a silence follows. Then we are drowned in applause. Students and teachers mob her, while others run to the bar, converging around it like a flock of crows over roadkill.

After hanging around the patio, post-reading, Rose goes home and Nayeli's admirers leave. Perhaps looking to maintain her post-reading high, Nayeli invites us fellows for a drink. Eager to impress her,

Mexican Tom Waits is quick to suggest the most obscure club he can think of. There's a crowd at the entrance, and Mexican Tom Waits is trying to talk our way in. As we wait, the Emo can't withstand another awkward silence and has a go at a seemingly casual yet cunning conversation.

"Aureliano, right?"

"Yes," I nod, hands deep in my pockets.

She nods too, *"One Hundred Years of Solitude."*

I curl my lips and nod again. Yes, there's also that cornerstone of South American literature mixed into my life, strongly enough to have given me my name.

"I guess it's all good if you don't have to live through them." She turns away and advances in the direction of Mexican Tom Waits, who appears to be slipping a bribe into the bouncer's open hand.

Beside me, Nayeli shifts her gaze downward, but not quickly enough to hide the faintest trace of a smirk. I'm almost expecting her to spill the whole Comala business to our comrades, but luckily, Mexican Tom Waits summons us to the door. We cut through the jittery crowd into the underground nightclub.

After stepping inside, the door thumps shut behind us. The air immediately thickens, and the music's bass vibrates the walls. The club's interior is truly ravaged, the exposed brick walls boasting their durability, their resistance to endless upheavals, releasing a slight yet noticeable asbestos smell. Two DJs are elevated behind a pulpit, blasting a fusion of cumbia, house, and reggaeton.

Before she left, Rose insisted I should stick around, to get to know Nayeli better, and to get on her good side—she's a famous writer and now my advisor, and I should see that as an opportunity.

It's really hard to speak with her, though, as she is still being fawned over as the star of the night by the other fellows, fully gloating in a post-performance, semi-glamorous indulgence. I linger at some distance, feigning indifference, mostly making my way to the bar to avoid standing aimlessly in her vicinity.

Again, only Dos Equis Lager and mezcal, only this time the mezcal is sold in three-ounce collectible bottles with labels hand-drawn by an artist who is allegedly famous, allegedly in the house, and allegedly not ripping us off.

From the bar I can see that Nayeli is in conversation with the other two fellows. Mexican Tom Waits is doing most of the talking, though, his arms flailing all over the place as he speaks. I get drinks for them and head over, but as I'm reaching out to hand them around, Mexican Tom Waits refuses his with an open palm.

"Not up for a binge here." His face glares under the shifting nightclub lights. "I'll rue the hangover come morning. One must make time to write."

"Ah, the voice of past experience," the Emo says.

All the while, Nayeli doesn't offer any expression, just divides her glances between them both as they speak.

"I do have an idea, though," Mexican Tom Waits says, in a voice both suave and pretentious. I try to look around the place to avoid staring at his face for too long without speaking, but when I turn back to him, he pulls out the smallest Ziploc bag I've ever seen from his shirt pocket, slanting his eyebrows invitingly, while wiggling the bag and dispersing the dust inside it. "Who shall be partaking?" he says, lacking the vocal scratchiness of the real Tom Waits, which would make anything impossible to refuse.

Nayeli leans in to take a closer look, then looks away. "What is it?"

I get an urge to make a joke about it being SOMA, but resist, and instead wonder if Nayeli would consume drugs after devoting her oeuvre to chastising the violence that comes about through their distribution.

Mexican Tom Waits informs us it's pulverized Oaxacan shrooms, then dips a wetted fingertip into the bag, sucks on it, and spreads it over his gums.

As if sensing my thoughts, Nayeli ends the brief moment of awkwardness by offering validation: "It's not like anybody is killing each other in this country over magic mushrooms." She takes the bag and drops some of the dust into the tiny bottle of mezcal I just gave her, swishing the liquid around and shooting it down in a single gulp.

The way she went about it, so unfazed by our presence, has the Emo doing exactly what she did, then handing the bag to me to do the same. After downing the smoky, shroom-spiked beverage, I stick the bottle of mezcal once intended for Mexican Tom Waits in my back pocket.

Then comes the nervous wait, but also the cheeky stares, the false symptomatic assault, until the flickering lights on the walls intensify in pitch and tempo and I find myself staring at the spectacle for longer than I should. Mexican Tom Waits is staring at me with uplifted brows as sweat gathers beneath my hairline, an experience to which he seems immune, given that his curly thatch is so thick as to look waterproof.

"Are you feeling it yet?" I ask him.

"Relax, man, show some patience," he says, and beside him, Nayeli smiles smugly, with her eyes shut, like she wants to underline my naïveté. Right next to her, the Emo is swinging her head to the rhythm of the music, showing the first signs through the sway in her perception, and as I listen more closely, the music seems to magically rise in volume, from one second to the next, the bass puffing air against my neck.

Nayeli's eyes seem overtaken by large pupils that look like black pearls, which inspires a mental image of O, the blackness of her hair like the wing of that crow.

Time and shame break open, and I wind up dancing, which I never do, convinced that my awkward movements will be forgiven by the larger mass performing this common ritual. My t-shirt darkens with sweat, and while I'm thinking about how this is supposed to be enjoyable, there's a newfound suspicion creeping under my skin. I feel myself checking back over my shoulder, as if I expect someone coming, there, behind, sensing their return, but when I turn back toward the group, all I see is a flicker across Nayeli's black eyes.

While people around us loop and leer, the shivers go from delicious to paranoid, and I whirl at every noise. The initial euphoric rush is long gone, and I'm suddenly desperate for solitude. I head to the bathroom, shoving my way through the prancing crowd.

The lights inside the bathroom are at first flat and white, with a rattle and a buzz coming from the old bulbs. The ice on the urinals is melting into diluted pee, releasing an all too familiar tang.

Another buzz and a flicker of the bulbs has my own stream of urine breaking over the ice, the fluid bearing a striking resemblance to the amber hue of the rye whiskey I used to down with Chris, and as one of the bathroom stalls pops open, sending a flood of white light my way, I'm temporarily transported to the moment when Rose broke through the door of Chris's apartment. Later that night, when I was back to my senses, she told me what the scene had looked like, leaving me to imagine it from her perspective: how behind the open window the moonlight wavered on the Hudson River's surface, its waters whipped up and frothing, how the bottle of rye had tipped over, how she pulled me out of my own vomit. She said that was the last straw—her excuse to bring me back to Mexico, offer me this fellowship even if I didn't deserve it, back to the narrow crossroads of here and now, to the twitching lights, to the automatic flush of the urinal before me.

The dance floor is in turmoil. While Nayeli is nowhere to be found amidst the bluish wink of slow-motion lights, Mexican Tom Wait's laughter reverberates loudly above every other sound, setting off a draft that ripples across my skin and stimulates my bowels. I rush back to the toilets, maneuvering through the dissonance of rapid dancing that appears somehow magically slowed down, no longer knowing if street food, mole negro, or pulverized shrooms are to blame.

Hoping the drug is finally dissipating, my body languishing, I ghost out the back entrance to the empty street, shutting the door on the noise of the party, leaving me to face the distant bark of dogs, the occasional car zipping past, a moment where everything seems slowed down, although perhaps it's just a contrast produced by the heart-attack rhythm of my pulse.

Above me, the sky is hazy, blanched by the light of a full moon. I down the bottle of mezcal I had in my back pocket in one long gulp and walk home through the empty street. A few blocks ahead, I toss the bottle over the fence of an abandoned lot and hear the glass shatter—like that coffee tumbler in my daydream, like that Coca-Cola bottle in actual life.

Returning to my studio, the visions behind my eyelids are like Kandinsky paintings, like brightly colored tree-rings that are also like sound echoes or the concentric ripple of disturbed water. I lie on the floor until a glare forces me to open my eyes to the early morning sun climbing like a halo over the water tanks on rooftops.

Knowing sleep won't come easy, I put on some coffee, add the final drops of bourbon to the mug, and spread out my work on the desk.

Enjoying the rare silence of the early morning, I zero in on stripping *Pedro Páramo*—polestar of Mexico's literary canon and of my own writing, tireless resonance box of the voices of the departed—looking to find the ways in which Rulfo's scenes of magical realism are cunningly constructed, and how the story of O's disappearance might find a way to undo them.

Once I down the first mug, the sweat starts to flow, and I feel my heartbeat shaking the pit of my stomach. The booze-laden caffeine sparks nicely in my head, though, and soon builds to a Balzacian-rush with which I pinpoint Rulfo's tricks as if Chris had marked them with his red pen, my new notepad ready beside me.

'Rulfo's Comala is so hot, people who die come back from hell to get their blanket.' A literary device in which the natural and vernacular use of diction veils a set of supernatural laws—opacity rendered through limited and unreliable points of view. Writer setting reader up for a

world in which natural rules cease to apply. The first acknowledgement of the dead coming back to perform active verbs.

Honking rises from the crossing of Reforma and Calzada de los Misterios. To stay on track, I swig from my coffee, but it's too late, the noise shakes Chris's ghost loose in my mind, holding a frothy latte in a large mug with the words "Andromeda Coffee" on it. He leans forward to look at my handwritten notes, much like Rose, but the breaking light on the window makes him vanish, freeing me to continue my work. Uncapping my pen with a shaking hand, I add:

Misdirection: the preferred deployment of the magical in the Latin American tradition is the return of the dead. Realism as the guise of fantasy.

Through the window, sunbeams bounce off the line of parked cars. My pupils are still pinned, so the glare makes me wince and return to the page. The note finished, I lean back on the chair and yawn at the ceiling, rubbing my eyes before opening my novel. The white space of the virtual page and the laptop fan combine to transform into a breeze off the Hudson River. I attempt a new scene by cropping and crossing out aspects of Rulfo's paragraphs, looking to strip away the trickery and the magic from his words. The scene might become the night O chooses to take off:

The sky is filled with ~~fat~~ stars, ~~swollen from the long night~~. The moon has risen ~~briefly and then slipped out of sight~~. It is one of those sad moons that no one looks at or pays attention to. It has hung there a while, ~~misshapen, not shedding any light~~, and then gone to hide behind the hills. O walks away sure that nothing and no one can see her...

After reading them over, the lines aren't hideous to me. Encouraged, I try to expand on the scene:

... There is not a mild current of air; ~~only~~ the ~~dead, still~~ night fired by the dog days of August. ~~Not a breath other than her own. She had to suck in the same air she exhaled,~~

~~cupping it in her hands before it escaped.~~ She feels it, the warm breeze, in and out of her nose, ~~less each time,~~ and all around her, ~~until it was so thin it slipped through my fingers forever. I mean, forever.~~ She needs to control it, her breathing—if it flows in too quick, she might want to turn around to what she is leaving behind...

"Seems too stale," I tell Chris, reading the paragraph over.

Chris nods as if in pain. "Look, writer. The question is, can *you* even hear her, do you understand her motivations? There's no point in writing if you can't listen to your own character. Seems like Rulfo had a keener ear for his characters, no matter how dead they were. Not that there's any point in comparing the two of you."

His words make the coffee shakes smooth out and recede, lending my body an overwhelming heaviness. Heading straight for the sink to toss out the cold remains of my coffee, I ask Chris if at least the "Realist" voice is coming out right, or if it's the only voice I have, but he has nothing to say—as a matter of fact, he's no longer there.

Sitting by myself, I try to channel his cold editorial eye while sorting through words that are like enneagrams of my internal state.

The noise of morning rush hour sifts into my studio, and in the peaty updraft of my dumped-out coffee, I recall better mornings than this one, mornings with no rush hour, no street sweepers, no barking dogs, just the lush shirr of grasshoppers in the hills around my childhood home in Comala. I banish the recollection, though, since it feels trite to me, pseudo-tropical, auto-exoticizing. If only sleep would come, but the yawp of a water-vendor from the street like an opera singer with a two-word aria that runs, "El Aguaaaaaa," makes this yearning impossible.

EVERYTHING I WROTE SEEMED RELUCTANT TO FIT A coherent narrative when I went back to revise it, the words only good enough for another one of Chris's magical bashings, so I deleted the file.

Nayeli seems almost relieved to hear I have nothing to turn in, allowing her to focus on her forthcoming book. She has been overwhelmed with it all, with the date of her release fast approaching—the third anniversary of the disappearance of the forty-three students from Ayotzinapa.

While she plans for a reading at El Monumento a la Revolución—the location where the commemorative march will begin—I have remained passive, trying to crawl out from the hole I fell into after ingesting Mexican Tom Wait's magic mushrooms. My inability to write has also placed me in a role more akin to Nayeli's assistant rather than a fellow under her advisement, which leaves me frequently imagining our contrasting creative production like cities as seen at night from the heights of an airplane window——mine dead and dull like Comala, utterly dark save for a few weak lights; hers illuminated and beaming like New York City.

As I sit beneath the shade of El Monumento a la Revolución, staring out in the direction of Avenida Juárez, my *Pedro Páramo* paperback open face-down on my lap, Nayeli power-walks in my direction, forty-three paper sheets in hand. Her new book is written in short fragments, forty-three in total, one for each murdered student. Each fragment is called an *effigy*, and is composed as a first-person soliloquy from the point of view of each of the students. When she is close enough to me and her thin shadow is lost within the larger shade cast by the monument, she says, "Can you get over here? I need your help."

"What can I do you for?" I say, attempting to sound so tired I'll be deemed useless to her.

She doesn't buy my act, or chooses to ignore it. "I'd like you to read one of these, so we can figure out the range and the reading positions." She forces one of the sheets of paper into my hands.

Tossing my book aside, I meet her glance. "Can I do it from here?"

"Not really, no—the readers won't be slouching in the corner as you are now. Just think of the energy on the night of the march. It wouldn't hurt you to try and match it, please."

She adds that for her reading, she has cast forty-three students from the teacher schools in Mexico City, all of whom on the day of the reading will march from the Angel of Independence to this spot where we are now, candles and soliloquys in their hands, standing single file overlooking the crowd, opening with the name of one murdered student and then read, one by one. Nayeli will then close with a brief text—an epilogue to the book—before we all join the march led by the parents of the murdered students. As I take my position on the highest part of the platform steps, a few feet ahead of the monument's slanted shadow, Nayeli skips down the decline, taking her position at the lowest point.

"I'm ready for you," she screams up, the echo of her voice bouncing off the vaulted roof of the monument. "The idea is to be able to proclaim, not just mindlessly read. You're addressing people hungry for justice. Show me some passion, if you have it in you."

I breathe in—shoving off a sudden and absurd stage fright—and stare out into the distance, to the smog hanging above the valley and the strip of haze wobbling the horizon. I then level my sight upon the page, and scan the text as best as I can before I begin.

"*Abel Garcia Hernandez,*" I stammer—the bolded name of a dead student sending shivers down my limbs. I clear my throat. "*Abel Garcia,*" my voice squeaks, and when I look up, Nayeli is already climbing the steps in my direction.

She nabs the sheet of paper from my hand. "Go stand down there."

I walk down the decline—wondering where she gets the resolve from to embody the voices of dead people—and turn to her, placing an open palm on my forehead to shield my eyes from the sun.

"*Abel García Hernandez,*" she reads, her voice steady, rising over the soundscape of the city—the strings of honking, the mechanic lullabies of the organilleros, the yap and whistle of the camote vendor—"*father of two, son and husband, student and future teacher, farmer of Ayotzinapa's land. I got on a bus to never come back, to be caught in a flurry of bullets, as if caught in the midst of arrowing rain. You'd say that I'm stubborn, that I'm wrong to blame bad luck, that I live in a land where destiny forgets me. Yet here I stand, for even if half dead, I cling to the wind with my nails, I walk blindly in the dark. These chills that course through my body are the frigid threads of the night. I'm the tail of the lightning bolt, the spinning tornado of the dead. Someone must still be out there to hear my voice, my muted screams like the wind in your ears. Or am I nothing but human loss? This land is flooded with people like me, people like us, the wandering dead—alive I was taken, alive I'm wanted back.*"

She looks up after that, and I can't tell whether her eyes are defiant—deep in character—or seek my approval.

"So?"

"Perfect." I hold my thumbs up for her. "Very Rulfo."

"What do you mean, *very Rulfo?*"

"I just meant the orality if it, the language sounds reinvented, soaked in traditional speak but reaffirming our everyday reality."

She gives me a puzzled look, a mild shake of the head.

"Not a single one of those missing students would speak like that, but never have their words felt so genuine. The mystery of it—I suppose it's exactly the way the dead would speak."

She nods, half-satisfied, it seems—even though what I said was utter bullshit—and shuffles through her pages, readying herself to have a go at the next effigy—the voice of one more lost soul.

After the recitation of each of the forty-three texts and an impromptu editing session on site, the afternoon dims behind El Monumento a la Revolución. The sky burns an amazing vermilion, synthetically intensified by the high levels of pollution.

Once Nayeli waves me off, I head to my studio up Insurgentes, walking as slow as the cars caught in its endless stream of traffic. On every other lamppost on the sidewalk are missing person signs—of the forty-three students and more anonymous faces—images that could well be the cover for Nayeli's book. There's one of a woman that looks like O, too, which I tear from the post and stop to examine. Are they really all expected to return? Surely Nayeli doesn't buy all this rhetoric, but she does know that for some people being dead is not a permanent condition—that they can wreak more havoc than the living can.

I neatly fold the poster of the missing woman and slide it into my back pocket.

Farther ahead, past a chunk of sidewalk torn open by the ever-spreading roots of a gum tree, I find announcements for the mandatory simulacrum commemorating the earthquake of 1985, which claimed thousands of lives in the city alone, with black-and-white images of a fallen building, of rubble over a marquee that reads *Hotel Regis* with cars crushed underneath it. Every year on the anniversary, the authorities hold an emergency drill where citizens are required to exit their homes when the seismic alarm sounds, and stand outside on the sidewalk until the alarm goes silent and the all-clear is triggered.

Closer to my neighborhood, I make out the metallic stutter of jackhammers, a continuous pecking sound that loudens with every step. Gradually, the view in front of me becomes a universe of dust.

Half the sidewalk on Calzada de los Misterios already turned to rubble, I find yet another flyer announcing tomorrow's mandatory earthquake drill taped to my door, as if everyone in the city needs even more reminders of the endless threats that assail us.

Once inside my studio, the jackhammer racket is slightly muffled behind the frail walls. I toss the missing person poster of the black-haired woman on my mattress, and head for the desk, where, spurred on by Nayeli's writing and the crumpled image of the woman on the missing person poster, I flip open my worn copy of *Pedro Páramo* and run my fingers over the sallow texture of its pages. The bookmark takes me to the scene of Miguel Páramo's death, told first hand by Eduviges, and then secondhand by Comala's townsfolk. In my notebook I jot down:

Secondhand and colloquial commentary as an additional layer of ambiguity.

Through my window, beams of streetlight expose airborne dust hovering in my room from the demolished sidewalk. A brief pause by the workers is a parenthetical second that aims futilely at silence, where I try to imagine the rattling of the keyboard, the incarnation of words on the page, the sound of every strike being a letter, every compounded rattle a sentence.

As the dust begins to settle, it shapes the silhouette of Chris sitting in front of me, the haze adjusting the setting to something that might resemble Andromeda Coffee.

"I know I've said so before," Chris says. "But just calling someone '*O*' is too Kleist, too Bataille."

What is meant as a sardonic laugh on my part comes out as a cough, the dust of the battered sidewalk tickling my throat. Allowing my mind to sink further into the daydream, I manage to evoke the figure of Andromeda Coffee's barista making his way towards us from my useless kitchenette, the place where I keep the daily quart of bourbon.

He slides the usual spiked coffees across the table and lifts the bottle in his freckled left hand, "This shit, really?"

"Yeah, well, you can't find rye in these latitudes." I have a fiery sip that sinks down my gullet. "Next best thing."

In front of me, Chris has a sip from his coffee, too, and then taps the table with his red pen. "Focus, writer. You won't even get one decent paragraph if you keep babbling with this guy."

The barista retreats, taking a swig straight from the bottle. I have another sip from my coffee and then force my fingertips to hover over the dusty keyboard. Chris picks up the missing person poster from the mattress and holds it before his eyes. Then, placing it on the table, he says, "Nayeli. She's arrogant, that one, but she does tend to nail it. You know why that is?"

"I sense the question is rhetorical."

"She understands that mature writing is unafraid of the notion of death."

I meet his eyes. Behind him, the dust looks like a persistent crackle of electricity, refusing to make its way to the ground.

Perching his glasses on his forehead and hunkering forward, making sure to maintain emphatic eye contact with me, he quotes Thomas Pynchon at me to make his point: *"When we speak of seriousness in fiction, ultimately, we are talking about an attitude towards death—how characters may act in its presence, or how they handle it when it isn't so immediate.* Look. You're writing about death here, or teasing the subject, at least. The reason it's falling short is that you have no clue what death means, or even what having lost a close loved one feels like. You've written this to understand your mother, why she fled. Maybe you want to understand your own feelings too, who knows. Only an idiot could look past this thing of *O for Oedipa.* Very on the nose."

I look at him, determined not to blink despite the dust accruing along my eyelashes.

"If you, like the rest of this country, avoid the prospect of death, of real mourning, how do you expect to write about it?"

The following morning, I wake to more drilling, to more dust filtering in through the window.

The quart of bourbon I drank makes it now feel like the jackhammers are cracking open the back of my skull.

My mouth dry like wool, I head straight for the tap and let the questionable water of the city gush into my mouth, all over my face and the nape of my neck.

Knowing I'll need more than one cup of coffee to look half-respectable for another one of Nayeli's rehearsals, I set out to buy a large Nescafé on the corner.

As I set foot outside, the jackhammers are suddenly silenced and the dust begins its sway to the ground. The sidewalk on Calzada de los Misterios is completely fractured and the huge hole in the street emits a stench of wet dirt and human feces. An odd silence befalls the city as well—an expectant silence—and while purchasing a large Nescafé in a styrofoam cup, the seismic alarm goes off, a wail that comes in ominous waves. After a second of panic, I recall this is only a simulacrum. A modest number of people pour to the street, mostly from offices and government buildings, and as I begin the walk back to my studio, a medical crew performs a mock rescue in the middle of the street. The whole performance calls to mind the few memories my father shared with me of the original earthquake on this day in 1985, how the city shook for well over a minute, the cracking sounds of walls, the debris dropping from the ceilings, the roar and hiss of toppling buildings, the life-long arm injury it gave him, the voice of Jacobo Zabludovsky caught in a mix of panic and exhilaration. "You were with your mother," I remember him telling me. "It was impossible to know how you had fared."

After more than a minute, the alarm goes silent, the jackhammers begin pounding the ground again, and the traffic resumes on Reforma.

Back inside my studio, I pour the miserable dregs of bourbon into my coffee and flip open my laptop. With gritted teeth, trying to concentrate, I begin to type:

This town is not filled with echoes...

No, I jab backspace...

Echoes are not trapped behind the walls, or beneath the cobblestones...

Better,

...When you walk, you'll never feel like someone is behind you, stepping in your footsteps...

No. I slam the computer shut while the relentless noise continues outside, and wonder why O wants to leave everything behind. Where does the assurance come from? How am I to know? Am I infallibly leaving myself no other option with my writing but effacement, the loud rattling of the deletion key?

Defeated, I shut my eyes and place my forehead on the desk, overwhelmed by the drilling, picturing how I delete my way, word by word, to a blank page, with Chris clapping in front of me and Andromeda Coffee's barista raising a celebratory tumbler overflowing with rye.

Remaining still like this, before finally arriving at what might resemble peacefulness, letting the spiked coffee do its work, I feel my desk begin to rumble against my forehead. I look up, hesitant, hoping for things to slow, but rather than things slowing, the room starts to move at an alarming pace—the floor of the studio performs what feels like a balancing act while the wall to my left draws an irregular, diagonal crack. Pieces of drywall shower to the floor—it *is* shaking, it's not a hallucination, nor is it the skewed perception that comes with my drinking. Beside my books and computer, I feel myself fall. The empty bottle of bourbon shatters next to my mattress, but there's no daydream to wake from this time. Through the walls, I can hear people screaming, a baby crying, an overpowering roaring sound, rapid footsteps rushing to safety. The roof, it creaks and it groans. Fearing it might give, and holding the closest wall for balance, I stumble outside, where it seems like two worlds exist, one vertical and one horizontal, and are merging into one another. Bricks fall from the sky, or from the roofs of buildings, rather, shattering to little rocks on the cut-open street, barely missing people who rush out in their pajamas and bath towels. Peering upwards, at undulating electricity cables and the frail branches of tired trees, I run to what seems like one of the few intersections without anything towering above it, the wide crossing of Calzada de los Misterios and Reforma. The streets are crowded now, with people covering their mouths, holding their palms firmly over their chests, some crouching to the ground for something approximating balance. Then there's an explosion, and a thundering pillar of smoke shoots skyward, but after the first panicked sight of it, I realize it's the billowing debris from a collapsed low-rise building. Dust masks the scene for what feels like minutes, and all I can do is rub my eyes while my body goes cold. When some of the dust settles, rendering yet another fuzzy and particulate scene, I find myself, along with every other person there, staring in the direction of the collapse. "No, no, no, se cayó," a woman screams, rushing to the scene, her body swaying side to side like a drunkard's, while stray dogs bark in every neighborhood, near and far, and as the earth comes to a halt, I can hear it, the wail of the same seismic alarm I heard only minutes before. Only a moment of complete stillness follows, of incredulous faces, of people faced with the dissonance of this earthquake occurring on the exact same date as the famous earthquake of 1985, all of us searching for meaning, fearing that past and present might be uncertain, as if they could shift and rearrange, a trickery of time that seems confined to the pages of *Pedro Páramo*. Then everyone on the block rushes to the fallen building, to the shroud of dust and debris, the mountain of rubble it has become, piles and piles of stones, just like those that Pedro Paramo transformed into when he died. The sounds that replace the seismic alarm are the yowl of ambulances and police helicopters hacking the air, a whole brigade of them, sweeping the city overhead. As I run within the moving throng, I know I'm trying to overcome my own body, the shaking of my legs, the dampness and cold of my feet. Before the fallen building, an old woman covered in dust stands on the hammered sidewalk, staring at the rubble, frozen, as though hoping for its resurrection—like she is staring at something beyond what the eyes can see.

An hour has passed since the earth shook, and there are only civilians—still no emergency personnel—on top of the rubble, removing chunks of shattered concrete from the fallen building in a frenzy.

My mind is a daze, my hands are already scratched with thin abrasions and there's dried blood on my forearms crusted with dust.

Traffic has flooded the streets, people rushing to get home, most of them frantically calling on their phones to discover the fate of their loved ones. They turn on their radios to full volume so everyone can hear the news reports of the earthquake.

Mental ruminations about Chris spin in my mind, his suggestion that O might already be dead. As I pick up a heavy piece of concrete with metal rods sticking from it and haul it to the side, I wonder if what I'm doing now is something akin to what I've been doing all along with my failed novel—trying to unearth those that might already be dead.

Taking a step forward over the cumbersome piles of concrete, I hear something from the depths, what might be a hiss, an airless voice, or a gas leak. I crouch down, slowly, attempting weightlessness, and place my ear against the fissures. Again, there's something like a breath, a trailing sibilance. With a new dose of adrenalin streaming through my body, I begin lifting more rubble and dragging it to the side. "Aquí," I yell, trying to reflect the desperate urgency of a potential survivor trapped underneath me—the slivers of light, the puffs of oxygen creeping in. I find myself yelling again, the one word repeated in quick succession, "Aquí, aquí!" and turn to people rushing my way over the rubble, all of them cautious, on tip-toe, as if the weight of their bodies could sink the collapsed building farther into the earth. The men and women who join me are all as covered in dust as I am, which showers from their heads with every step. Immediately, they lift more slabs of concrete, as I do, but one of the men who is lagging behind screams hoarsely for "Silencio." We stop in our tracks, halt our breath. He yells out again, in the direction of the street, where a substantial crowd has gathered.

A deeper and rattling "Silencio" accomplishes the feat. The man holds a closed fist up in the air and the city falls into a deep and eerie silence—

—As no sound rises through the rubble, we begin again removing parts of the fallen building while the drone of merged voices returns to the street. Police are arriving now, cordoning off the whole block and directing the few cars trapped in traffic out of the way. In the distance, I can make out army trucks, men uniformed in camouflage and holding heavy artillery, circling the block.

Underneath the clamor, I catch what seems like a stifled voice fighting through many layers of debris, and I'm not the only one this time. The man that called for silence locks eyes with mine. We crouch over the rubble and the man yells for silence again, curling his fist, lifting it, holding it still. I do the same, feeling the rapid pulse in each one of my clenched fingers—

—"Dónde estás?" The man directs his words to the pockets of trapped life beneath us. Again, we lock eyes, giving each other a slight nod of the head, lacking more words. Policemen and soldiers are starting to demand civilians get off the rubble so that they can take over the scene. But right then, there's a muffled scream, one of intolerable pain, sifting upwards through the cracks. "Ahí estás!"— There you are, there it is, a sign of life. "Silencio, aquí está!"—

Another cry, "Aquí estoy,"
"We're getting you out,"
"Get me out!"

—Police and soldiers have taken notice and begin climbing the site, rushing to where we are and demanding that we move away. The man who called for silence smiles feebly at me, offers me his dry hand, and I can feel how it won't stop trembling. I follow him to the street, to the point where the rubble ends and the pavement begins.

We get another call for silence, a louder one, this time booming from a loudspeaker. The soldier talking through it lifts a curled fist just like the man did before, who, still standing beside me, curls and lifts his own, his sight shot downwards, eyes shut. The whole crowd follows his example—

Cries of life.

Louder.

—Soldiers clear the rocks, and the screaming from beneath becomes even louder.

After several minutes, members of the rescue team Los Topos, the grand heroes of the earthquake of 1985, thirty-two years ago on the dot, rush onto the scene.

We live through more pockets of silence, of lifted fists, through alarmed bloodshot stares, through the hearsay of more collapsed buildings across the lacustrine area of the city.

Los Topos drill the rubble; they whisper through the layers.

Hours seem to drift by to the point where the crimson sun is now low in the sky and the shadows of swaying palm trees stretch long and distorted on the street.

Time gives, it seems to slow, but then the breakthrough comes—a girl is pulled from this massive tomb. As she is carried to safety in the cradled arms of a soldier, she smiles, expansively, setting off a heavy flutter in my chest. All around me there is thunderous applause as the girl is reunited with her mother, who climbs over the rubble to embrace her. I only realize I'm weeping when my tears have streamed down my hands, breaking up the dust on them like a river pushing through drought-plagued land.

The man beside me pats my back. "History repeats itself, doesn't it?"

I can only nod, failing to make eye contact with him.

"We're back in 1985. The past has overtaken the present."

"If only that were true," I say, but when I turn to him, the man is no longer there, he has slipped through the cracks in the crowd.

THE DAYS FOLLOWING THE EARTHQUAKE HAVE BEEN bleeding past, time I've spent trying to make myself useful, volunteering to transport medical equipment from one fallen building to the next, bringing food for medical workers at collection centers, running tired eyes over endless sheets of paper with the names of those who lived in buildings and haven't been accounted for—the wait for the missing to be accounted for runs on, with nothing happening in between, a delay that with each passing second diminishes the chances for those still trapped underneath the rubble, waiting for life, waiting for death.

When night falls upon the valley, and the lights all across the city glimmer bright and tremulous, I head home, but instead of writing, I live-stream the evening news on my computer with the daily quart of bourbon, knowing the shakes I'm getting are more related to my drinking than to the unrelenting aftershocks.

For two days now, the main story in the news has been about a girl no older than seven, Frida Sofia, trapped in the rubble of a fallen primary school in the south of the city, who is communicating with rescue brigades and giving real time accounts of how many children are stuck, their conditions, and possible routes of escape. Beyond the school's gates, teary-eyed parents, television crews, Los Topos, all stare at the pastel-blue building under the hazy-gray sky, at the taller stories still intact, but crushing the lower levels, where the children had been in the middle of class when the earthquake struck.

With every passing day, the story seems to be running into inconsistencies—Frida Sofia's descriptions of locations and the names of the other children next to her have subtly morphed. Independent media outlets have caught on to the fact, leading to a deluge of stories questioning the authenticity of Frida Sofía herself. Some of the more sensationalist networks have likened the story, and the figure of Frida Sofía, to El Chupacabras of the mid-'90s: the bloodthirsty creature sinking its fangs into cattle in every nook of the country, and who would soon be preying on human blood. That story was eventually accepted as a myth as much political as it was fictional, aimed to distract the population from the assassination of a revolutionary political candidate, the devaluation of the currency, a tri-national trade agreement, the insurgence of the Zapatistas in Chiapas and the overall authoritarian nature of the regime of the time. The question now: what can the government be hiding by creating Frida Sofía and having Televisa shove her story down the tube in every home of the country? The first rumored presumptions suggest that it's related to diverting attention away from cases of corruption connected to building permits and construction laws, briberies accepted by government officials to allow the development of buildings in areas where seismic fractures run underfoot.

Needless to say, the parents of the forty-three students from Ayotzinapa have been collaterally damaged the most. The story has been buried in the media, and so have the questions about the flawed criminal investigation. The protest scheduled for the third anniversary of their disappearance has been cancelled and replaced by a city-wide vigil for the victims of the earthquake, both the one in 1985 and the one that struck on its anniversary mere days ago, brought together by a common date in the calendar. Nayeli's grand reading has been cancelled too, of course, despite her book *43 Effigies* being hot off the press.

When the news goes to commercials, and the image begins to freeze, falling victim to my poor Wi-Fi connection, I close the browser window and am left staring at my latest attempts on my novel. It's not hard to imagine O as someone trapped beneath the rubble, but somehow, still, the words will not come. I fold my laptop shut and drink myself into a stupor—the only way sleep arrives these days.

The evening of the vigil, the sun refuses to fully drop behind the city skyline. At eight pm sharp, the street-lamps light up even though the final rays of sunlight shoot vermilion gashes across the sky. In this twilight, there is a glare from the artificial lamps over sidewalks, a haunting of sulfurous smelling smog as the smoldering air rises spectrally from the pavement adopting a human form—the crepuscular collective ghost of the country.

Heading up Reforma, through a corridor of blackened Mexican flags hanging from balconies, I find yet more faded posters, faces and names of the missing now doubled on every lamppost and wall—the new additions of people lost beneath the rubble.

Everywhere around me, the sounds of the city have fully returned—the roar of traffic, of accelerating motors, the mechanic shrill of bulldozers working through the fallen buildings. The weak edifices that managed to remain standing, but that are too damaged to house their inhabitants, have yellow caution tape wrapped around them and black plastic tarps hanging from their rooftops—a shroud of shame and mourning.

The night fully descends when I reach the corner of Reforma and Bucareli, where a sea of people awaits, once due in support of the forty-three students, now assembled to remember those lost in the earthquakes—thousands of people walking down Bucareli with candles in their hands.

Past a block of abandoned houses, a woman is handing out candles and puts one in my hand. "Récele a los suyos," she says. "Pray for those that you have lost." While I subtly nod, it seems like she notices my body trembling. She takes my hands and brings them closer to hers so she can light my candle, which flares up in the shape of a quivering raindrop. "Réce por los que siguen ahí debajo," she finishes, looking away, already putting a candle in someone else's hands. All those trapped beneath the rubble come to mind again, snatched from their lives in only a moment. Cutting through the crowds, narrative possibilities assail me, and I'm silently cursing myself for having left pen and notepad at the studio. Full of a self-conscious shame, I wonder if O, in my ruin of a novel, might fall victim to a disaster like this one, that her pending return could be forever built-upon and collapsed, and that tragedy having cut her life short, leaves her kin awaiting an impossible return. Could she have fled the earthquake while others assumed she perished under the rubble? Might her return give her the qualities of a ghost in the minds of those who survived?

While all this might tread over territory of promise, it's throwing me off from the real heart of the matter—why she flees in the first place.

"No need to be so loyal to the truth, writer." What seems like Chris's voice sifts through the hum of the crowd. I turn every which way, but nothing. "Last time I checked, Magical Realism was still fiction?"

I rub my face, trying to keep my sight straight ahead and quiet his voice by ignoring it, focusing instead on the slow stream of bodies.

A few blocks ahead I find Rose and Nayeli, their elbows locked and holding lit candles in front of the orange walls of Café La Habana, both of them, as if by previous agreement, wearing t-shirts with the blackened Mexican flag on them. While Rose subtly purses her lips as I approach, Nayeli seems distraught, her sight fixed on a faraway distance. She doesn't even meet my eyes, and as soon as I'm next to them, they take steps to join the march. I position myself next to Rose, who immediately lets out a loud sniffing sound, then leans close enough to smell my neck.

"Fuck's sake," she whispers, peering straight at me, "I thought you were working on the booze thing. I'm getting drunk just by standing near you."

I try shushing her and turn to Nayeli, who is either still in a daze, or playing dumb.

"That shit is oozing from you again."

Knowing any attempt at defusing the situation is gone, I say, "I didn't know I had a bloodhound for an aunt."

"That's what keeps you from writing."

Nayeli turns to face us both, then restores her gaze forward immediately, a swift movement which sees the flame of her candle burn out and give off a string of smoke until it fades to invisibility. "The writing," she says, "never happens when I'm drunk. I've never been sold on all that Lowry bullshit."

Despite her being a big Lowryphile, Rose nods, lifting her brows, while Nayeli pulls out a lighter from her pocket to light her candle anew. She shields the flame with a cupped hand and turns to me. "And you'll be needing to turn in some pages soon. Your reading is fast approaching. I know of many talented writers who would kill to be in your position."

Rose keeps nodding while looking ahead, as if my lack of literary output was a reason for her to be offended.

"Look around you," Nayeli tells me. "Dreadful as all this is, take advantage of it. Reel in some inspiration."

"I'm sure he slept through the whole thing, drunk as he always is," Rose says.

In a flood of rage, I want to tell her about the fallen building next to the studio, about the voice that crept through the cracks, about the girl that returned to life, pulled from the rubble. I remain quiet, though, looking ahead like Nayeli, at a crowded Avenida Bucareli with a myriad of quivering flames.

"I mean, very Magical Realist, is it not?" Nayeli says. "Two deadly earthquakes on the exact same date! Call me gratuitously poetic, but to me it seems like the clock was wound back, that the ghosts were living among us and knew their fate."

Rose inhales deeply next to me, and inside my head, only there, I think I hear Chris's voice again, "See what I was talking about, writer. *She* gets it."

I subtly glance around, hoping I haven't summoned up his figure, and catch Nayeli cocking her head. "There's your novel for you."

While Chris seems to have gone mute, Rose's laugh is like a clap of thunder. Quickly stifling the outburst, she becomes solemn.

I follow her lead and turn to Nayeli. "I'm sorry about your book."

Nayeli stares ahead. Rose rubs her upper arm, the one locked to her elbow, and on that cue, there's a reverberating sound a few feet away—"VIVOS SE LOS LLEVARON, VIVOS LOS QUEREMOS"—a minor contingent within the crowd chanting on behalf of the forty-three murdered students. The slight echo fighting its way through every other sound gets Nayeli's attention immediately. Still locked to each other's elbows, Nayeli yanks Rose in the direction of the chants. Rose waves goodbye, and even though I can't really make out the words she's mouthing, to me they look like *cut it out with the booze*

Once I've lost them, the crowd comes to a halt at the intersection of Bucareli and Avenida Chapultepec. A woman standing dead in the middle of the procession asks for a minute's silence for the victims. The quiet, while being symbolic and potent enough, is still filled by sounds near and far—soaring airplanes, ambulance sirens, indifferent barrio chatter—but loudest of all, Chris's voice back in my head.

"What Nayeli understands, and you haven't fully grasped, my dear writer, is the bottom line of this book you keep consulting." He lifts a copy of *Pedro Páramo* from beneath his arm. "The subtext— the political commentary that earns its admiration—is that the real ghosts of this country are those people forgotten and forsaken by history. Nayeli knows, for instance, that she can't let forty-three students from Ayotzinapa become ghosts, she can't allow the government, our collective memory, to toss them into the forgotten realm of a symbolic Comala. *Where* did O go? *Why* did your mother leave? Why hasn't she ever returned? I mean, the seed of conflict *is* there."

I'm fighting the urge to cry. "Not now," I say, loudly enough to draw a few stares. I keep my face down and try to remain still, looking to fend off his voice, and notice that my candle is guttering, that not even my hand shielding it will keep it alive.

The woman beside me seems to sense my trouble and runs a hand over my back, which is hot and damp with sweat. She smiles when I turn to her, her cheeks dimpled in the feeble light. "I lost people in '85, and I lost people this time around."

Nodding, holding back the storm surging inside, I watch while my candle dies. In the distance, way beyond the crowd, the lights of the city tremble like all the candles around us—a mirage of all the earthquakes this city has lived through, past and future.

Above it all, the sky is dark and impenetrable—the deep black of a traditional mourning page.

The woman takes the dead candle from my hand and places it on the ground. "The past," she says, "you can't run away from it. You have to confront it before you can fully embrace the future."

IT TOOK OVER A MONTH TO GET THE FELLOWSHIP back up and running, and for the city to regain a sense of normalcy. The scismic alarm went off a few times from the stronger aftershocks and additional earthquakes with epicenters in Oaxaca and Guerrero, but whose ripples haven't been felt as far as Mexico City. The worst effects caused by these tectonic shifts have mostly been panic attacks, but there was also a case of a broken ankle—a man who leaped at the alarm from his first-story balcony. Paramedics have been treating cases of tachycardia, delirium, and PTSD, while the news reports there has been a rise in alcoholism as a result. As I hear the story about it on the radio, I turn to the litter of Jim Beam Bourbon quarts I'm collecting over the kitchenette's counter. The empty bottles hint at the passing of time and so does the diminishing level of whiskey in the bottle I have in hand, which I wet my lips with every passing minute. This linear unfurling of days means that the deadline looms large, that there must be something on the glaring white of my electronic page in exactly two days, the unavoidable date of the next *Miércoles de SOMA* event, where I'll have to read from my nonexistent novel, along with the two other fellows.

Outside, the sites of the fallen buildings are yet another sign of forward progress. The rubble has been fully removed, and some of the spaces have become open lots for sale, voids in the city's grid, bookended by buildings that, time and again, endure the endless tremors. There's also more and more vegetation growing in the cracks of the cement—ivy, daisies, bougainvillea, embankments of weed and grass.

Within the walls of this studio, though, there is no growth or progress of any kind, words are not sprouting from the rubble of this novel, and worst of all, there seem to be less and less signs of life. The white page beams its blinding light, and seems to be summoning me to a blank slate—exactly what this city refuses to become.

On the day of my reading, the constant buzz of my flip phone makes it flutter across my desk—it's Nayeli calling, over and over, and declining her calls is not putting her off. When I finally grow impatient enough to answer, she begins speaking over the line before I can even say a word, telling me I have to be early for the *Miércoles de SOMA* reading, that she wants to look over my text, perk it up if needed. What she doesn't know is that during this latest alcoholic binge, all I've managed to do is arrange a mix of my writing and Chris's words into a page-long villanelle, a single poem, hoping its inherent circular structure and vague relation to the use of time in Magical Realism is enough to get away with.

Rose *did* hear about this idea during a brief phone call, but she immediately rebuked it: "It's a fellowship for a *novel*"—her voice got livid through the phone—"don't be getting clever on us." Then, after a loaded pause, she added, "You do know the risk I'm taking selecting my kin as a fellow."

It's hard to tell if she'll see humor with what I've put on the page, so I look over the document once more, confirming the proper placement of each stanza and the compulsory rhymes.

Wetting my lips with my spiked Nescafe, glancing over at the clock in the screen's corner, I realize I don't have much time before setting out, so I begin a final rehearsal read.

When I'm done with it, Chris's voice rises in my head: "Quite the gamble you're taking there, writer."

"Don't even fucking start." I slam my computer shut, grab the printed copy of my villanelle, down my spiked coffee, and flag down the first cab that swings by on Calzada de los Misterios.

When I arrive at SOMA, I'm sweatier than everybody else, including the bartenders yelling behind the makeshift bar, and I'm not sure if this is related to my hangover, or the second thoughts I'm having about my impending reading.

The patio hosts the usual drinking party, while inside the small auditorium, there's a blue projection screen the size of the wall and an overpopulation of chairs. Nayeli is nowhere to be found, though, nor is Mexican Tom Waits or the Emo.

My anxiety is mounting with every passing minute, and I have to buy a beer to soothe the palpitations and maybe help my hangover, which is as much physical as it is emotional. I then lean on one of the patio walls, full of dread, knowing the clock silently ticks on its path to seven— the deadly seven, sure to strike with a pang. A few minutes later comes the announcement that the reading will begin, and bodies flood into the auditorium.

The three fellows—Mexican Tom Waits, the Emo, and I—are summoned to a folding table used as a podium, with name placards and water bottles on it, amidst the weak sound of applause. In the front row, Rose is sitting next to Nayeli—who is avoiding eye contact with me—and the two other advisors, Mexican Tom Wait's and the Emo's respectively, two men in their mid-forties, I'd say, one of them obviously tall even though he is sitting down, with wild gray shoulder-length hair; the other is dressed all in black, too, a mirror image of his apprentice, black hair with a metallic sheen like O's and my mother's trapped in a face-stretching ponytail—both of their presences, it seems, nothing other than ornamental. When the noise dies off in the crowd, which settles like the dust motes outside my studio, Rose is called to address the audience. She stands, folder in hand, and puts on reading glasses. She takes the microphone from our table and blows on it to confirm it's working. She welcomes everybody to the reading, to have a glimpse of the works in progress of this year's three literary fellows. She reads our bios in order of appearance, Mexican Tom Wait's first, the Emo's second, and lastly mine. She then reads out a brief description of each of our projects—Mexican Tom Wait's quasi-dystopia, tracing the literary scene in the Mexico City of the near future, is a text strongly reminiscent of Roberto Bolaño's *The Savage Detectives* but with what Rose calls *a futuristic glow*; the Emo's text, a collection of short stories, offers the much needed feminist touch in the male-stilted fellowship program. Titled *Pink Crosses,* and narrated in the first-person singular perspective of dead women, it investigates the rising number of femicides in the country, a problem that factors into the crisis of forced disappearances. "Lastly," Rose says, trying hard to avoid a smirk, "Aureliano Más the Second is working on a novel that seeks to resituate Magical Realism as a genre in contemporary Mexican culture, drawing its parallels to Fantasy and Surrealism"—a line that earns me a weak, diplomatic applause.

Rose returns to her seat after that and Mexican Tom Waits picks up the microphone. Offering no more than "Buenas noches," he sets off with the opening scene of his novel—a rather moving third person omniscient narration of a city in ruin, of endless earthquakes and poor water supply, but whose main characters, a gang of young poets obsessed with the past, attempt to rescue the Mexican Literary Scene by reviving its old literary landmarks. He runs on, level-voiced, for a full chapter, ending with a scene where the gang of poets is standing in the way of the demolition of Café La Habana, known for hosting Bolaño and more of the Infrarealists, perhaps also hinting, metaphorically, at the Student Massacre of 1968.

When he flips the last of his pages over, and thanks the listeners, a mighty applause rises from the crowd, a rattling sound with celebratory whistles. Right in front of me I spot Rose and Nayeli, along with the two other advisors, rising from their chairs to offer a standing ovation.

Mexican Tom Waits seems caught off guard by such a response. He blushes and bows his head, then tries an arrogant wink and a grateful adjoining of his hands. I only realize I'm not clapping when the Emo flicks my elbow. I begin clapping immediately, and I'm the last to cease the applause.

Mexican Tom Waits hands the microphone to the Emo. My mouth has gone completely dry by now, so I grab the bottle of water in front of me and sip from it.

The Emo opens by saying her collection of stories is dedicated to the work of Rosario Castellanos and to every woman murdered by the hands of gender violence in the country, from Ciudad Juárez to Ecatepec. It gets her an initial thundering applause and a few wails of encouragement scattered throughout the audience. She turns to me briefly with what I can tell is a glance of nationalistic pride and of an inspired political awareness. Only then does the glaring certainty of my failure at this reading sink in. I down the remainder of my water in a long, desperate gulp.

She begins her reading, and as her voice scratches through the speakers, I scan the crowd, where faces begin to look both riled up and impatient.

Her voice gently streams throughout the room and she reads with a naturalness and grace, supported by significant pauses, that grab the full attention of the attendees. In the front row, her tutor nods at her every line, slow and assertive, encouraging her on. Her text has to do with lives lost and the potential of the lives that could have been—something, perhaps, not too dissimilar to what I've been attempting since I joined the fellowship program.

Though her text might seem gratuitously poetic, too abstract, and a little over the top, I find myself liking it way more than Mexican Tom Waits's, and I join the loud applause that ripples throughout the auditorium when she is finished with her story.

"Gracias totales," she says, putting away her pages, followed by a slight nod rather than a bow.

A mild hum rises in the room after that. There's the sound of shifting legs and bodies, the clink of empty beer bottles as they are placed on the floor. But then the sound dies off, suddenly and completely. The room is all glaring eyes, all of them pointed in my direction. The Emo has to tap my forearm with the microphone so I grab hold of it.

The impatience of the crowd seems palpable now, where a few pools of light on cell phones glimmer in the room. The heavy shroud of doom that fell over us with the Emo's reading has me now fearing it might be impossible to lift it from the crowd.

"Thank you," I say into the microphone, I don't really know why, wincing at the loud shrieking of the speakers, which makes me hold it even farther away from my mouth, feeling how my temples bead with what I hope is imperceptible sweat.

"Do I sound OK?" I ask, leaning into the microphone again and looking up, spotting a few uplifted thumbs from the sea of heads. I look over to Rose and Nayeli, hoping for gestures of encouragement, but they hold their gazes locked straight ahead.

"As Rose mentioned," my voice a bit cracked, "this project is to do with the collapse of Magical Realism within contemporary Mexican culture. What I've done for tonight's reading is arrange the paragraphs I'm working on into lyrical notes—prose turned into the circling motions of a villanelle."

During a brief pause, I spot Rose wringing her hands together, briefly shooting a worried side-glance at Nayeli. She then casts jittery looks my way, her face washed in a grim pallor, while Nayeli, to her side, is staring at me pistol-eyed, which is to say, staring at me with pupils as round and dark and threatening as the barrel of a gun.

The silence becomes so deep that it makes it impossible to tell if I've confused the crowd before I've even begun. Getting my pages ready and clearing my throat, I scan the crowd once more: At the very back of the room, I fabricate the fleeting image of Chris, his face as defiant as Nayeli's, as worrisome as Rose's, frowning to the taste of his mezcal.

I lower my eyes to the page. The words on there seem familiar, and I feel that if I focus, I might deliver them properly, and put an end to this. But as soon as I speak, I feel the rasp and whine of my vocal cords, wavering, utterly fearsome, *"Empty, soundless landscape, the world seen through a haze."* In the silence of the room, my cracked, amplified voice seems desolate. *"Spectral scenes where all is formless."* The podium feels cold, distant, the only warm part of my body seems to be my forehead, which is now surely pearling with sweat. I get the urge to toss the pages into the crowd, storm out, drown myself in a sea of whiskey, flee to New York.

At the back of the room, Chris reappears, shaking his head, and gesturing with his hand slicing across his throat repeatedly, coaxing me to give up.

Somehow, though, I carry on, I take the plunge, Nayeli's eyes on me, fixed and unblinking, my voice breaking, as if the words were coming from someone else's body: *"Outside there is no texture, not a hint of distant light..."*

After spending some time in the bathroom and then downing three shots of mezcal under the dappled moonlight on the patio, feeling my sweat go cold under my clothes, I spot Nayeli talking to Mexican Tom Waits and the Emo at the opposite end of the gathering.

It's not hard to guess what they're talking about by studying their gestures. What is hard to guess, though, is if during my absence they're contrasting their successes to my failure. While I fear this is the case, the worried eyes of the crowd during my reading return to me—Rose trying hard to smile while showing too many of her teeth, demonstrating horror, rather, as Nayeli concernedly shook her head while biting on her nails.

Quite drunk now, I find myself judging them and their readings too, being put off by their conceited demeanor, let alone their own drunkenness. Even so, I find myself walking to them knowing I must wear the mask of normalcy and belonging if I want to keep this fellowship, which is, really, the only thing going for me in my life.

When I'm close to Nayeli and the fellows, I can already hear Mexican Tom Waits's criticism: "These fucking readings, eh." I can only see his backside, the curls on his head, and half of Nayeli's face behind him. "Like the listeners can take away anything from something like this. A fucking reading of a text in tatters."

As I hear this, I know for certain he is talking about my text, my performance, the big letdown of my makeshift villanelle.

"It speaks ill of the program and the other fellows," he says, his mezcal overflowing with his hand gestures, dribbling to the floor, leaving there what look like raindrops.

The Emo is the first to spot me behind him, and eyes me with a curled lip of concern, widening her eyeballs at Mexican Tom Waits, like a heads up, but I halt my stride to allow him to carry on.

"And all this Magical Realism stuff," he says, oblivious to the Emo's overdone signals. "Don't even get me started with Magical Realism."

Nayeli smirks and chuckles, but then meets my eyes behind Mexican Tom Waits's frame. I can tell she's trying to adopt a position that doesn't come naturally to her in the moment—a fake nonchalance even though she clearly harbors feelings toward me, as if my reading reflects poorly on her as my advisor. What is not completely clear is if she is now—with the reading behind us, and after a few heavy-handed servings of mezcal—half-enjoying my fiasco.

"Oh hey," she says and slips her hands in her trouser pockets, "That was... nice and quirky, you don't hear that every day." Then turning to Mexican Tom Waits, she adds, "What were you saying about this whole Magical Realist stuff?"

Mexican Tom Waits turns to me and half-startles, spilling more of his mezcal. "So, you're writing a novel out of that?"

"Yes, that's the idea."

"But you know what?" Mexican Tom Waits says, pointing his drink at me. "What you're doing is futile, it's all a caricature."

A simmering bile rushes to my throat, it lingers there, but I do my best to nod as if I agreed with him, which, in fact, I somehow do.

Nayeli looks at me, then at him, surely knowing she has kindled a flame that can only engulf me and which everyone else is impervious to.

"We all know Magical Realism is horse shit, there's no need to restate it, less so in the length of a novel," Mexican Tom Waits says.

I nod again, thinking I might still be thick-skinned when it comes to blunt criticism, but getting a mild urge to whack him over the side of his curly head.

"So, I guess you both agree," Nayeli says.

"It's so obvious," Mexican Tom Waits says, "that I don't see how one can pursue the subject." With a nod of his head while fixing his half-open eyes on me, he adds, "It's horse shit, I swear."

"Sure," I say. "If Rulfo wants to write about zombies in Comala, it's not Magical Realism, it's zombies in Comala."

He clicks his tongue and winces at me, which makes me unsure if he is—as I am myself—considering a swift jab right between the eyes.

"I don't know if I'd go as far as that, but Magical Realism sure is the cheapest mode of perception of our identity. I mean sure," he pats my shoulder harder than I would like with his mezcal-dribbling hand, "you're on the right side of the issue, but why even talk about it, it's yawn-inducing, we all know it's absolute horse shit."

The heat in my throat breaks into a sweat all over my body, and I can feel the Emo giving me what she must think is a reassuring rub of my shoulder. This prompts Mexican Tom Waits to look away for a second, then at his empty glass. He leaves us for the bar where he gets a refill.

"He's had too much to drink," the Emo says, and walks to the bar to catch up with him.

When they are far enough away, Nayeli turns to me. "Don't take that personally, it's meant to be constructive. And you do need the feedback, which is why you have an advisor you're supposed to workshop pages with before presenting them publicly. But you chose not to, which is why this is awkward."

Only at that very moment do I realize that the last thing I want to do is socialize, to be on the receiving end of Nayeli's resentment. I'm only here trying to guard appearances, when what I really want is to drink myself to death, take it up a notch, like I did in New York.

With my vision lost, I find myself mumbling to myself, "Zombies in Comala"—which would really make a good title for my novel.

"Let's not make a big deal of this," Nayeli says. "Just carry on with the work, forget this night ever happened. One can only rise from ashes."

Trying hard to suppress a response, I look away from her and spot Rose, who is glancing over to us, but caught in a conversation that doesn't allow her to break free. She is trying to mouth something to me, gesturing to come to her, but all I do is avert her eyes, gulp down the last of my mezcal, and let the empty glass fall to the floor—as if the sound of glass shattering could mark the end of this nightmare.

Nayeli widens her eyes and her mouth and stares at me like I belong in the nut-house. I turn away from her and head out the door to the empty street, where I find the solitude I had craved all night long.

I walk the empty streets in a drunken trance. The slanted light cast from light poles makes my shadow fold over walls and buildings until it disappears within the intense interior glare of the neighborhood OXXO convenience store, where I wander inside to buy a bottle of whiskey. Not even able to find the now-religious quart of Jim Beam Bourbon, I have to settle for a full-sized bottle of Famous Grouse, which I conceal in a paper bag as I step outside.

"If you could only get some rye," I whisper against the nighttime quiet.

Why did you think you'd find any answers here? hiss the shuddering leaves of a lone tree on the sidewalk.

There is nothing here to find, I think, deep in the hollow of the empty street, until the silence is, of course, filled by Chris's voice.

"Yeah, why *did* you come here?" He appears beside me, but shadowless, dressed all in black, matching my stride, red pen caught in the curled fist of his fingerless gloves.

"The fuck if I know," I say, and when I turn to him again, he has vanished.

Farther ahead, there's a missing person poster with a woman on it, whose face gently morphs into O's. As I approach to peer at it in more detail, the wind is moving its rugged texture to the point that her lips come out with the words, "To find *me!*"

Startled beyond belief, I uncap the bottle and take a first swig of whiskey, which makes the image on the poster cease its motion. I rub my eyes, hard, and when I focus my vision, O is no longer there.

Taking another gulp from the bottle, the booze now gallivanting nicely through my bloodstream, I descend into the San Pedro de los Pinos Metro Station, which is empty, somewhat cold, impossibly odorless, and rather unrecognizable without its commuters. As I look around to get my bearings, Chris appears next to me again.

"How could I have not seen it earlier?" he says, as we step onto the downward escalator. "You know why your novel fails? Or should I say *your villanelle?*"

I fail to find a response, so I glue my mouth to the hole of the bottle, tilting it up full swing.

"You have collapsed every conflict into a single character. One person cannot bear the burden of solving your narrative, of tying up every loose thread."

A chill slides down my torso despite the warm feeling the whiskey had instilled in my gut. When we reach the platform, I lose him, and from afar I can see the train gliding towards me. Even though I can't see him, Chris's voice still reaches me from somewhere in the vicinity: "You know that line Lowry once wrote? The one about the subway trains, how the wheels over the tracks seemed to always communicate with him. How they first said *womb*, then *tomb*, then both in quick succession, over and over again. Funny, isn't it?"

As the train's doors open in front of me, I pull in a long breath, deep into the base of my lungs. The lights inside are migraine-inducing, and I find myself walking towards them, not once looking over my shoulder, holding on to one of the greasy poles.

The doors beep, announcing they are slamming shut, but right before they do, Chris manages to fit his slim figure onto the train. He reclines his back against the door, and clinks coins between his fingers.

The train pushes forward with a clack and a whine, and is immediately swallowed by a tunnel, voicing Lowry's haunting words. Chris walks past me and stands in the middle of the train, feet wide apart for balance, and from seemingly nowhere, holds up a stack of pages.

"Here, here for the literary lovers," he says playing the part of an experienced underworld vendor. "This red ink-stained manuscript is the work of this fine writer." He opens up a palm in my direction while I gulp down more whiskey. "A tale of damnation, a work in progress, but above all, his inner denial, his very own attempt at closure—it's yours for twenty pesos, for twenty pesos it's yours."

The empty train comes to a screeching halt at Tacubaya Station. Once on the main level, with only the remnants of the day's activities—closed stalls, idle garbage on the floor—Chris is out of sight. I hurry to the Pantitlán-bound train, past the fans spraying mist, trying to catch up with him, but it's impossible. All I can do is wait for the next train and get to the studio to sit facing my tale of damnation, my work in progress, my inner denial, my very own attempt at closure.

When I get to the studio, the window in front of the desk is open and a draft of air creeps in. Over the surface of the desk, my copy of *Pedro Páramo* is open, the wind shuffling the pages as if a ghost was still looking for clues in its words.

The bicolored pen Rose gave me is also on the desk, next to the red ink-stained manuscript, but I feel unbearably drunk, tired, heavy, and Chris isn't rushing to my aid. I lean my head on the desk and shut my eyes—a sort of death, as it tends to happen in life.

A swollen bulk of self-loathing, I wake to the rosy glint of dawn with a sharp pain in my gut, my face over the red ink-stained manuscript. The Famous Grouse bottle has rolled all the way to the wall and left a puddle on the floor. I immediately place it upright and have a sip, which sets my stomach on fire.

Oozing whiskey from every pore, I run to the bathroom and vomit over the white porcelain of the sink, and after wiping my mouth, I go to the kitchenette in dire need of potable water, of which there is none. The tap in the kitchen releases no more than a brownish string of liquid and all that is left to be had is the final pour of Famous Grouse, which I try to avoid by sitting at the desk, facing away from it, looking out the window.

Calzada de los Misterios is deserted, evanescent almost, with garbage flying about in the momentum of early morning wind. The city bears a dark appearance of finality, and dead in the middle of this hell-scape, Rose is walking in the direction of my door, dressed in a long black parka with a large purse hanging from her shoulder. Fully resigned to my fate, I leave the door to the studio ajar, and wait for her to come in.

She looks around the place before locking eyes with mine. She glances over to the clutter of empty bourbon quarts over the kitchenette's counter. "Why the hell did you leave last night?"

"I was trying to sober up."

"By drinking more?"

"Temptation is always there."

"I thought you'd come a long way, from *that*." With a backward thumb she points to some abstract place that symbolizes New York. "No one died this time. And no one left."

Before I can respond, the garbage truck swings by on the street, collecting overnight remnants. I hear it stop and the tolling of the garbage man's bell. When it journeys away and the ruckus ends, I breathe in, still unable to find any redeeming words.

"Look," Rose says, "you have to get to the bottom of this." She pauses, shakes her head. "At first I thought this was about Chris, but it has to run deeper than that."

I feel my jaw tightening, a heat-storm welling in my chest.

"Are you even listening?" She comes over to me and shakes me by the shoulders. "Are you?"

I nod and can feel the pressure on my temples as she shoves me back and forth.

"I can only do so much." She lets go of me and takes a few steps back in resignation. "You can't write because there's a rock of repression inside you."

I try rubbing my eyes, as if this could sober me up.

"This whole thing of writing about your mother, it isn't working, it's not bringing her back," she says with a fair amount of spite.

"Yeah, no shit."

"Time to face the music." She pulls out a stack of pages from her purse, awkwardly folded in half. "I once attempted what you are trying now. You think I don't miss her too? She was the closest thing I ever had to a sister." She tosses the pages over the desk. "See if this can give you any answers, any clues—you might even get to know her better."

I unfold the pages to find a cover sheet that reads *Snake Skin: Brief Passages in the life of Édipa Más*. Just running my eyes over the title, over her name, makes a cold feeling wash over me. "History repeating itself yet again, is it?"

"It's a failed novel like yours. Takes place in Comala, too. Deals with our beloved who fled."

"All fiction?"

She shakes her head. "I guess what I'm trying to tell you is that if you want to know more, you should go find your father. You and I, we're searching for her in a fictional world. Go find out, please, get some closure, something." She pauses and breathes out. "You'll probably be stripped of the fellowship anyway. Nayeli's pissed. Just take the money you got for it and go."

I look up at her, feeling an urge to protest, but just swing my neck back down.

"What's the point of living like this?"

I rub my face with both hands. "I'll get to my unfinished business in Comala."

"There you may be able to hear her better." She tries offering a smirk but fails, then turns and heads to the door like Chris would. "You're no longer under my wing."

Through the dusty window, I watch her walk away, not once turning back, with the assurance I might need to travel there, to *that* place.

When she vanishes past the corner, ghost-like, resembling a character from Rulfo's seminal novel, I spread open her failed novel over my desk, running a finger over my mother's name.

A dust of truth rises from the text with every turn of the page, and I can only hope to find something that might permit me to re-shape this past, even if what I learn doesn't promise closure or the possibility of a hoped-for future.

BOOK II

Snake Skin:
Brief Passages in the Life of Édipa Más

1970s–1980s

THE HISS OF A BURNING MATCH, THE RUSHING, VAN-
ishing smoke, the sweetness of its smell. The viscous sway of the
flame, its elusive dance. But oh, how it catches on the blades of
grass, on the dry leaves. How it turns the wind's whisper to a roar,
how it paints the scenery a hellish hue—but above it all, oh how we
fear it.

Evelina's first memories were infused with the smell of burning
smoke, its gritty texture coming over the horizon, where the Pacific
Ocean seemed to fall over a cliff. Those memories were full of fire
and fleeing: the Santa Ana winds had blown in a hot wheeze, fueling
flames that in her mind's eye rose into the shape of a rogue wave,
swelling unannounced, blazing across the dry land. Her recollec-
tions, gritty as the smoke-filled horizon, allowed one image to drift
to the forefront, as if pushed by the ocean breeze towards clearer air:
her being dragged to the trailer home, the paper-dry texture of her
father's hand on her wrist, the roar and snap of the wildfire burning
through the bush. Then it was all framed by the rearview mirror, an
image retreating: the flames, a Martian-orange sky, the glint off the
Southern Californian ocean at the far end of sight, filled with mist
and sunshine, the one place she ever thought of as home.

Scraping deep at her unconscious through the years, Evelina
unearthed the memory of her father's Ford pickup whinnying like an

injured horse as it stormed through the Californian desert, ploughing inland, struggling as it dragged their trailer home uphill, barely beating the wildfire's dash across the dry land. And oh, how that trailer home rocked as it traveled at high speed, how every object inside it shook, her father's paintings especially, their expressionistic desert landscapes turning frenetic in their vibration, their brushstrokes almost coming alive. Their new destination—her new home—was the high desert town of Sunfair, full of looming, monumental rocks and Joshua Trees lit by the incandescence of endless dusk. Vultures hung in a blood-red sky until night came and cloaked the desert molten-black. Sunfair was the first place she ever thought of as a ghostly land, and that she would later realize as a type of place that repeated itself across latitudes. It was a vague swath of time she spent in that haunted desert landscape, a time of silence and paralysis, but that somehow carried her infancy into adolescence, bringing a whole lot of pain and little rewards, the former in the appearance of her father's new wife, whom she was forced to call mother but to whom she felt no sense of kinship, and the latter in the shape of an older step-sister, who would come to slice open that world, so that the new one that emerged, if ghostly still, felt imbued with possibility.

The second time she fled wasn't from a wildfire, but from that haunted desert landscape. Rose, her step-sister, jerked open the door of her trailer home, allowing for a quick injection of cold air into the cabin. Once having flicked open her eyes and turned her head to scan her surroundings, Evelina thought she heard Rose whisper something along the lines of "now or never," but what she succinctly caught was the word "nowever," which was good enough for her to ram a few clothes into a plastic bag and head out, doubtless, under Rose's wing, swept up in her apparent urgency, her sure pace and noiseless movements. Both their parents had passed out in the adjacent trailer home, after a night of drinks and dope, of painting the ghostly sunsets of Joshua Tree on canvases strewn on the sandy ground next to bottles of cheap scotch. Rose was heading out, now or never, however. this could be Evelina's only chance. In a second, she knew she had to go through with it, come what may. Outside, the night was an indigo-blue, lacking stars but framing a full moon in the middle of the sky, reflecting on the sand. There wasn't the slightest hint of fire, nothing yet following after her, and she only realized she was fleeing as she listened to her own footsteps, following Rose's, quickening through the sand, rendering her sight shaky but yet clear enough to walk around the coiled figure of a sleepless rattlesnake: could she make out the hiss, the rattle, the sheepish warning? Could that perfect circle formed by the reptile's coil symbolize rebirth? The complete silence, the animal's stillness, spurred Evelina on, poised, her body piercing through the biting chill of the high desert night. Further ahead, a set of headlights moving swiftly, in a straight line over the plateau, then bombing down the steep descent to Sunfair, making a sound like wind roving in the distance. Rose sprinted toward the lights and Evelina looked up at the sky: was the hollow black around the moon a symbol of her exile?

A succession of hitched rides and buses took them past the border. The only real moment of uncertainty had come when the customs officer shifted eyes from her passport to her face, silent, uneasy, but the stiffness in her every limb relaxed as the man voiced the word "Bienvenidas." Evelina arrived in Mexico, chaperoned by Rose, either a girl or young woman seventeen years of age. It did feel like escape, like having torn free of something, leaving it behind.

The long roads, the pitch-black nights of transit, moments spent reading Rose's books beneath the dim oval light cast by the bus's overhead lamp: *Under the Volcano, The Labyrinth of Solitude, El Llano en Llamas, El Gallo de Oro, The Letters of Remedios Varo.* But the one that sang to Evelina most had been at the bottom of the pile, forgotten, still more Californian than Mexican, *The Crying of Lot 49,* where she found her improbable relation: a woman braving a world of men, braving her own existential exile, forever looking for the clues to her own liberation, always compelled onward by the idea of the ocean. Oh, how Thomas Pynchon's San Narciso reminded her of her childhood and its vague yearnings, like little stabs at the unconscious that bled out as images of the glow of the sun over the Pacific. Would she ever find her own San Narciso, her own archetypal place of freedom? She knew as she read that San Narciso was both everywhere and nowhere, the place where things fall into place. But could she avoid falling off the deep end, avoid yet another fire, yet another hot, dry, dead-still place like Sunfair?

The metronome of waves pounded the Sinaloan coast off the town of Mazatlán, a deep and entrancing lull, allowing Evelina's body to lie in an almost pleasant weariness on the terrace of El Motel La Impermanencia. The ocean breeze blew the smoke from Rose's joint into Evelina's face, drifting in the direction of the bluffs, utterly green ridges with dry yellow foothills that transformed into cliffs and led into the ocean. "Those hills," said Rose, "they're overflowing with poppy and cannabis, the best in the world." She extended the joint in Evelina's direction, who turned to see the burning tip of the roach, and faintly shook her head. "That shit our parents smoke, day after night, it comes from these hills. There's money to be made down here." Evelina felt a childish sting, a naive tremor, running warmly across her upper body, but that gently soothed when she focused on the waves pummeling the shore. The sun was warm on her face, and she loved the sound of each upsurge and its break over the sand, as if each wave was the same as the last.

Come sunset that same afternoon, after lunch at Mar Vista, Rose had another joint caught between her lips and a pair of scissors in hand. "We have to go through with it, make a full escape. It won't do us any good to half-ass it." Not fully grasping Rose's jargon, but knowing the scissors were intended for her hair, Evelina nodded. "Your dad could be after you, or he might have reported you as missing. I'm not ready to be charged with kidnapping." Rose performed a cutting motion with the scissors, which let out a squeal of sharpened metal, before running a hand through Evelina's cascading blond hair. "Still want to go through with it? Really get away? Let the past be the past?" Another nod of certainty and then Evelina felt the screeching edge of the blades against her skull, icy. Rose had cut through the first strand, which fell onto the terrace's wooden planks, swirling with the breeze. Looking at her hair on the floor, Evelina found it somehow foreign to her already, and thought of the snake again, the one she saw the night she left, the scaly diamonds on its back and their moonlit glimmer, the crusty old skin it would one day leave behind. Evelina adored her new appearance immediately and stared at her reflection in the windows of their room out of the corner of her eye. Once Rose had gone back inside, Evelina sat among her hair, turning back the pages of Pynchon's novel to the scene where Oedipa, "perverse," is laced by a Remedios Varo painting with the girls with the "spun-gold hair, prisoners atop of a tower." She had forced her emancipation, and now she was where that painting had been created, this place called Mexico, among her own fallen gold-spun locks, prodding herself forward, breaking identification with the past. She shut the book after reading the scene, and stared once more at the Pacific's circular cadence, its resilient if not stubborn sound. She realized that she was already likening that view to the memories of her Californian childhood. Rose stepped out onto the balcony again and lit another joint with the delicious, rasping sound of a burning match. "Did you have to cut that much?" asked

Evelina, dangling the longest strand of severed hair she found on the floor. Rose dragged a puff of smoke. "Yeah," she said, exhaling decorous, fleeting rings. "Perfectamente necesario."

The bus to Guadalajara turned inland and uphill, reminding Evelina what it felt like to part from the ocean: everything suddenly became hot and dry, dead-still, creating a sensation that lifted goosebumps all along her skin. The sound of waves was replaced by the droning engine of the bus, which swayed—dangerously it seemed—with every turn on the road, causing the world to tremble beyond the glass of the window. They passed through Badiraguato, San Ignacio, and Culiacán, straight onto a road that cut through the cliffs and the marijuana fields. The smell was vaguely familiar at first, like the smoke from Rose's joint that blew into her face, but it was all around them, pungent, sifting through the poorly sealed windows. They came to a halt on a federal road, behind what looked like an already endless line of cars, and through the windows, Evelina spied what felt like yet another flashback to her early childhood but which was not her childhood, more like an eerie, distorted relative of her memory: a vision of flames sprawling through fields, catching on marijuana plants, fire flailing and leaping, as soldiers with torches walked among them, burning everything so as to leave no trace. The flames rose and swelled, like a rogue wave, she thought, as they advanced through the bushes. To Rose's dismay, Evelina left her seat, walked down the aisle. Stepping out onto the pavement, where she could feel it again—that heat, its swelter—the dryness of her face slowly breaking into a sweat. Then the traffic jam loosened and the bus rolled wearily forward. Evelina took a deep breath, smelling the burnt gasoline, the weed, but above all, the erasure. She spun around on her heels to find Rose waving her back in the direction of the already moving bus.

The image of flames dissolved into the horizon through the back window and the smell of smoke was lost with the bus's momentum. They journeyed further inland into more nameless country, where the only sense of direction and reality came through green road signs at highway crossings: Victoria de Durango, Tepic, Comala, Puerto Vallarta, Petatlán, Papanoa, Tomatlán. Come night, they descended upon the endless, blinking lights of Guadalajara. In the bus window's reflection, Evelina's face was deeply shadowed, unrecognizable, her newly shorn hair almost invisible in the feeble light. Dogs barked, invisible, too, in the depths of the night.

The lodging that best suited Rose's extremely meager finances was a three-story colonial building on Calle Morelos, Hostal El Efímero, off the Plaza de Armas, where they were fortunate enough to get bunk-beds in a private room with a balcony. Evelina did not sleep the night of their arrival. She sat on the balcony overlooking Guadalajara's lights, dangling her legs over the edge between the railings, mimicking the pendulous, ever-returning motions of the old clock inside the room, digging up an old memory with her father, canvases rolled in his hands, as they stood on a hilltop that overlooked the distant lights of Los Angeles. Had they been in Cahuenga, San Fernando, she could no longer tell, just another Kinneret or San Narciso, here and elsewhere, the transient settings of her Californian youth. The lights in Mexico alternately blurred and focused in the impossible distance as they had then with her father in the city of angels. Guadalajara lay dormant, in the pose of a coiled snake. The few sounds below came from rats sifting through garbage bags in the alleyway, while stray dogs raced through the street. Then, she sensed it like water coming to a boil, a slight simmer at first, then a fuller effulgence: taxis crawling through the cobblestone streets, the shutters of kiosks in the plaza opening for business. A navy-blue line appeared between buildings, clear and distinct, reminiscent of brush strokes on some of her father's paintings, then slowly rose into the sky, brightening. Homeless men and women emerged from under blankets and store porticos. In a flash it all lit up, as daylight flared onto buildings and flat concrete and tree leaves in the plaza. It was all noise and bustle as the city awoke, and Evelina sat there, watching. The morning had opened into something other than the endless expanse of Californian deserts, and she vaguely felt a part of it, too, dangling her legs over the balcony on Calle Morelos, where underneath, the cafes and restaurants were opening, the shoe-shiners were setting up camp, and the lottery vendors nagged at the people pacing by on the sidewalk. Farther away, dead in the middle of the plaza, the central fountain came to life in leaps and spurts of water. Behind her, Rose had woken and was smoking a joint over her pillow, readying her journal and her pen.

El Mercado San Juan de Dios was all hustle and noise, a three-story resonance chamber that amplified every voice inside it, every sales pitch, every transaction, every unrelenting haggle: voices merged, looped together, echoing left and right like ghostly murmurs or lost languages, not one word decipherable, a cacophony that spoke within her, the interior dialogue of her yearning, so that Evelina herself became a resonance chamber: through her pierced those words, some she held, but there were no sentences formed. Blinking slowly, again she felt consumed by it, and felt a cold tremor in her abdomen, a slow tectonic ripple. She had never swum in a sea of people this vast, their voices piled onto one another, creating a sound like high tide rushing back towards the ocean, washing against the sand. A dizziness came to her and it took Rose yanking her elbow to get her past the spice section, beyond the shamanic healers and their ever-burning candles, away from the fruit stalls with their tangy smells of fermentation, and to the rows of the butchers, their floors tarnished by the offcuts of dead chickens and cows, the smell of blood pungent, hanging in the staleness of the air. Rose led Evelina on with a hand on her lower back, firmly, past a taco stand where a man was trying to feed the remnants of his food to an emaciated stray, who sniffed and grazed at the food with his tongue, but then turned away, looking to scavenge elsewhere. The man swiveled on his squealing stool to face Evelina and Rose, eyes awfully bloodshot, snorting with laughter. "Perro no come perro, señoritas," he said, and then whistled a universally lustful tune. "What did he say, that man?" Evelina asked Rose, who hastened forward, then replied: "He said, dogs don't eat dogs." When they got to the alleys full of pirated clothing, Rose pulled open her purse and handed Evelina a wad of money. "Buy whatever you can get with that; you're still short of a full transformation." Rose eyed her up and down. "Get rid of all that cowboy denim. And those boots, there are no snakes in the city, remember, show us your gorgeous calves." The coiled figure of the snake revisited Evelina, and she reimagined the sight of its old skin left over a smooth slab of Suntair rock. Standing in front of a wall full of clothes, she managed something akin to sign language with the vendor that was made up mostly of pointing and displaying the fanned bills Rose had given her. In her mind, as the vendor desperately showed her the clothes she picked, bringing them down from the higher parts of the wall with a hook attached to a pole, she leafed through Rose's books in her mind, through their female characters, and it dawned on her that she really couldn't make out a clear image of Oedipa Maas in *The Crying of Lot 49*, let alone what she wore. The one scene that rushed back to her was that of Oedipa playing strip Botticelli in a San Narciso motel, wearing everything she had on her, giving her the appearance of a beach ball. With the vendor's yaps loud in her ear, which distinctly rose over the unearthly chatter all around her, Evelina began trying items on over her clothes. She had to start anew, that much was clear, and was ready to leave the market wearing black leggings, a sky-blue button-down shirt,

Aviator sunglasses as fake as they were wide, and an oversized black blazer. Rose returned, eyeing her up and down again, giving her what Evelina now knew as her signature sarcastic laugh. "I didn't know I was traveling with a glam-kitsch Debbie Harry." Evelina frowned, silent and inquiring, but got no response. Rose wiped the shoulder pads of Evelina's new blazer with her palms, and then started toward the glare of daylight at the end of the corridor. As they were about to exit the maze, Rose a few steps in front of her, Evelina spotted an empty stand, guarded only by a broken radio. Pins of all kinds cluttered a wooden board, and on its bottom left corner was one of the rattle of a snake, reflecting sparkles of the interior lights. She ran a silent hand along the board and snatched the pin in one movement. Before exiting onto the street, she had it hooked on her new blazer's left lapel.

Rose insisted on lunch at Motor Hotel Americas, where she had scheduled an appointment, the one reason, she said, they were passing through Guadalajara at all. At a poolside table they were fed ceviche and tortas ahogadas: food soggy and spicy that was hard for Evelina to swallow without her nose running. She enjoyed the feeling of being able to mask her tears behind her new sunglasses, even though they resulted from spicy food and not sorrow, as the concept of having this veil appealed to her, taught her how to bluff, to perfect a face void of expression. She also enjoyed the dimmed glimmer her sunglasses gave the water in the oblong pool, as if life could always be rendered through endless shades of gray. It seemed like a sudden and foreshadowing life lesson. She voiced these thoughts to Rose, who was taking sips from her tequila while throwing nervous looks around the hotel patio, and had to ask her to repeat what she had said. When Evelina did repeat her thoughts, after a long pause and a mouthful of her torta ahogada, a pause meant to convey the slightest offense, Rose replied: "That's what's called opacity, it'll do you lots of good considering the situation you're in." After that, they fell quiet for the remainder of their meal, accentuating the noise of splashing water, of blenders crushing iced margaritas behind the bar, more indistinct chatter flowing in the wind, only gentler, the words half-decipherable, far from the murmurs in the market. Rose kept glancing at the entryway, sipping her tequila. Evelina watched her behind the dark shades, finished her papaya juice, and when she put the highball glass down on the wooden table, Rose pushed the tequila snifter in her direction. Evelina lifted her glasses over the bangs of her pixie cut, winced at the glare from the sky and the sun-winks on the pool water, and took a sip of Rose's tequila. She could taste nothing but its bite, and fought the urge to frown, the sharp vapors stinging her mouth and sinuses. She held her face still, though, motionless, and swallowed. Rose took the glass back, and let out a nervous laugh. "That's opacity, all right." Evelina slid her sunglasses back on her face. When their plates were cleared, the manager of the restaurant asked Rose, by herself, to a private booth inside. She offered no explanation to Evelina as she walked away, escorted by the manager past the brick archway that gave way to the restaurant's dim interior. A complimentary snifter of tequila was placed in front of Evelina for the wait. Why not, she thought, catching her reflection in the windows of the hotel. This new look of hers, was it as visual as it was existential? She sipped the liquor boldly, all the while staring at the motions of the water in the pool, which made her wonder if she still missed the Pacific. Confusion came with every ripple, slight as it was: would she ever settle down again? She finished the snifter and felt a dullness in her face, a slackening of its muscles, and the feeling streamed slowly and gently to her mind, like a river to its delta. It was not exactly a sense of relaxation, she thought, nor was it bravery, it was more a release of her expectations, rather: the thought that, like driftwood, all she could do was let herself be pulled by the currents of chance. She thought of Oedipa Maas again, and almost mouthed the lines she remembered reading, slanted by their italics, *Shall I project a world?*" But her thoughts were overtaken by a far more urgent manifestation of sound, first by Rose's clattering steps on the tiled floor, then by the words—"Get up, fast"—from Rose, then by her own cumbersome steps as she was being dragged away, tugged by Rose's sweat-laced hand. Evelina matched her pace, she had to, looking forward only but imagining wildfire behind her, flames rising, the wheeze and roar of the Santa Ana winds. They were slowed by the hotel's revolving doors, but eventually clambered into the middle of Plaza del Sol and got into the first taxi that would take them, which sped through Chapalita Sur, past alleyways brimming with bougainvillea, under stone aqueducts, running over the shadows of palm trees fracturing the sunlight on the road, then finally into the colonial decay of the Plaza de Armas. Evelina kept quiet, looked straight ahead, picturing orange skies caught in the rearview mirror, and was asked to wait in the cab while Rose got their things, the meter running, the driver smoking a hand-rolled cigarette while leaning on the hood of his car. When Rose came back, she threw their scant luggage in the backseat, over Evelina, and finally they raced away towards the setting sun at the end of Calle Morelos.

At the bus station, daylight was urgently fleeing the main terminal, a darkening slab of concrete with the words Terminal Cintalapa perched upon it. Inside, there was a steady hubbub of shifting crowds. "Mexico City at last, is it?" asked Evelina, toneless, trying to catch Rose's attention, who, craning her neck to and fro, flicking their tickets against her wrist, waiting for the platform doors of the bus to swing open, could only nod.

Three bus rides over snaking roads, and then two subway trains from Observatorio to the heart of the city. Evelina could now feel it within arm's reach: there was a world out there, swarming with people, a world that had existed parallel to hers, adjacent to the empty expanse of her Californian deserts. Exiting the subway station to the sight of swaying jacaranda leaves, under a night sky infused with refracted city light, Rose was quick to flag down a cab on Avenida Juárez, which seemed to be going around in circles in the vicinity of La Alameda Central, through slums and plusher neighborhoods alike, all lined with Art Deco and neoclassical buildings. Evelina sensed they were close to where they were going all through the ride, but didn't say a word: there was something pleasurable in the loop, something akin to the cycles of the Pacific's tides, and, suddenly, she found herself dreading the moment when the taxi would come to a halt and she'd have to get out. Would she be able to, or would she stay rooted to the seat? The taxi did stop in the middle of Avenida Hidalgo. The driver pressed on the meter and pointed to it, skittish, demanding his cash. Rose matched his urgency, paid him, and led Evelina in the direction of a cream-yellow building: Hotel Regis, its vibrant marquee announced, the ghostly buzz of the city loud in every direction. Another set of revolving doors muted the exterior noise and spat them into the lobby's own urgent sounds: the creaking of hardwood floors, pinging elevators, amplified voices, the shudder of air from the ever-looping revolving doors behind them. Every light inside burned warmly across the ceiling. Evelina lifted her sunglasses on top of her head and winced while adjusting to the glare. Right in front of her, facing the main desk, a posh lady was getting her hair done in a beauty parlor, the strands of her hair caught and swiveled in plastic curlers, smoking an extra-long cigarette while an older lady wearing an apron with the hotel's insignia blow-dried her hair. Right beside the parlor, an entrance to steam baths and a spa, and at the very far end of the lobby, the restaurant and club, Capri, where Rose was leading them and where most of the voices seemed to be pouring out from. "You'll wait in the restaurant while I tend to my appointment," said Rose. "Get some papaya juice and whatnot." The restaurant was packed, and the maître d' told them they faced an hour wait before a table for two freed up, but that they were welcome to wait at the bar. "Go on." Rose nodded Evelina to the bar. "I'll be back soon." The maître d' bowed, extending his arm in invitation. Rose spun in the direction of the elevators, but Evelina tugged at her sleeve. "Were we in danger in Guadalajara?" asked Evelina, and Rose turned to the maître d', who nodded and smiled and played dumb, a gesture that somehow seemed both casual and rehearsed, then returned her gaze to Evelina, nodding. "Was it about your dope?" Rose pulled her away, out of the maître d's earshot. "Look, yes, OK?" Evelina stared straight into Rose's eyes. "Are we in danger now?" Rose immediately shook her head, condescendingly. "Just sit down at the bar, kill some time." She shoved Evelina towards the restaurant again, but Evelina stiffened her body in resistance. "Is this about your dope too?" Rose blew out a strong shaft of air, desperate. "Just go sit, I'll come right back." Knowing there was no more information to be drawn, Evelina stepped into Capri, the maître d' giving her another idiotic if not polite smile. Immediately, though, she became enthralled by the restaurant's beautiful ruckus. She sat at the only empty stool at the bar, facing away from the bartender. She shut her eyes, absorbing the laughter, the clinking glasses, the cutlery shrieking against porcelain plates. Underneath it all, the piano man's slow tune travelled in the thick air while mingling with the fumes of food. When she opened her eyes, there was a man in front of her, which caused a frightening drop in her stomach. His pear-shaped face was close enough to be utterly scrutinized: the dry skin like Sunfair soil, its folds and furrows, the hair graying at the temples, the large nose, the dirty pores like open craters on the surface of the moon, the perfectly trimmed moustache and the clean shave upon his cheeks. His eyes were a mere suggestion behind the amber shade of his Aviator sunglasses. He stretched an arm around Evelina's left shoulder to grab a highball glass the bartender had slid across the wooden surface of the bar, as if the man was a true regular and needn't utter words to get his fix. He took a long sip, down to half the glass, and then it seemed like he noticed Evelina's pin, the snake's rattle on her lapel: "Traerá ponzoña esta niña?" he asked the bartender, self-righteously, who laughed nervously in return, like performing a mandatory response of eternal agreement. The man then vanished into a private room at the far end of the club, allowed to carry on without paying for his drink. The bartender tapped Evelina's shoulder and asked, "What will you be having, niña?" Evelina turned. "Same as him," she said, without hesitation, and the drink was mixed, pushed in front of her. She took a shy, test-sip without even knowing what it was, expecting something like the tequila she had, but which rather tasted like old, perhaps rotten, Coca-Cola. "You have ID?" asked the bartender, and Evelina shook her head. The bartender shrugged, a gesture that generated immediate trust, and which drove Evelina to ask, "What does ponzoña mean?" The bartender pointed at the lapel of his white suit, shook it, then pointed at Evelina's. "Means venom," but before he could explain further, he was called to the opposite side of the bar. Evelina waited, taking slight sips until the ice in her glass diluted, rendering the drink easier on her amateur palate. She admired the dinner party, scanning from left to right the many tables that seemed at once choreographed, like a single gathering, until Rose came back, straight for the bar, where she paid for Evelina's drink, wordlessly, and then led her out the door.

The halls on the top floor of Hotel Regis reeked of cheap perfume, the walls coated in greenish wallpaper with diamond patterns in white, the floor soft and plush, teeming with wine stains. They crossed paths with a group of four young men whom Rose seemed to know. They exchanged a quick farewell of hand waves and winks, needless perhaps, as if they had already said their goodbyes and weren't really expecting, let alone wanting, to run into each other again. Their voices trailed behind them until captured by the elevator's vault, transported downstairs, to Capri, maybe, Evelina thought, while Rose led her to the end of the hall, where a window held an opaque glow. Rose knocked on the door of room 705 three times, paused, and repeated the code. The door clicked and swung open, as if of its own accord, with nobody there waiting behind it. A pungent smell made its way out, dissipating in the hall, and then they were in a small foyer with a replica of a famous Diego Rivera painting of a naked woman holding a large bouquet of arums. A small archway led to an open loft, with velvety couches and leather ottomans scattered like it didn't matter where they were placed, and in the middle of them, a glass table, lozenge-shaped, with five bouquets of dry plants tied loosely with strings of different colors, each with a rolled joint to their side, like the ones Rose smoked all through their travels. Thick velvet drapes—burgundy, they seemed in the dim light—covered every side of the room. Rose threw her jacket over one of the couches, and told Evelina to pick the one she wanted. "We'll crash here tonight; we'll probably get our own room in a couple of days." Evelina knew better than to ask, not about the plush suite, not about the bouquets of dope on the coffee table, or the smell that lingered in the room, which—she only now noticed—was the smell of her travels with Rose, the smell of every room they'd stayed in up until now. Instead of removing her blazer or her glasses from her head, she flicked at the cracks in the drapes, looking for an opening, a window, and finally found her way to a door that led to a large terrace overlooking the park, which was like an enormous patch of black, like she knew the ocean was at night, city lights flickering endlessly beyond it on either side. Once more, she sat on the very ledge, face between the railing's bars, legs dangling in the motion of an old clock. Looking out into the city, reeling in the still-active, haunting sounds of night, the idea sank further in: she had escaped, one life had folded shut and one had flared open, and there she was, fully in the midst of it. She tried to feel as drunk as she could, like the day before in Guadalajara, but it didn't seem to work; she was only here. The footsteps she eventually heard behind her, the heavy breathing, must've been Rose's, who'd be asking her to come in already, to sleep for once, but when she turned, ready to respond, she found the figure of a man, scrawny and tall, a figure made of shadows and dim light, features to be guessed at, but which slightly brightened as he approached and sat beside her, legs also past the ledge. Curls dangled over his forehead and stubble lined his face, thinly, sideburns to chin. A joint burned brightly in front of his mouth as he pulled in its fumes. He then exhaled a dense fog, white against the dark backdrop, which rose in a slow drift. He offered Evelina a hit. "Premium kind," he said. "It'll take you to a dreamless sleep." She took the joint between her fingers, index and thumb, like how she'd seen Rose holding it, then waited, watching how the tip burned to a dead but flimsy black. When she brought it to her mouth, it took another leap of faith to drag in the slightest puff, another come what may moment. She pulled in the smoke and handed the joint back immediately, resisting the tickle in her throat, and exhaled with a slight cough. "My name is Lázaro, and I'm guessing yours is Evelina." She nodded, looking over the city without end, as dark as it would ever get.

Things did not take long to turn interesting. After a few weeks, it became clear that Rose's cross-border journey—the one that had set Evelina free of her haunted desert landscape—had at its roots something both illegal and ambitious in nature. It turned out Rose and Lázaro were running a premium dope-dealing operation, structured like a pyramid to a tightly knit circle of consumers in Mexico City who wanted to avoid having to interact with the burgeoning drug cartels. The route they had taken had been plotted with the aim of researching the state of affairs of the trade along the Pacific Coast, after the alleged merger of several northern drug cartels, based in Guadalajara. Rose and Lázaro believed that the size of such an operation—with the product primarily destined for export to the United States, and with police, military, and legal forces either fully focused on the trade or deeply colluded within the network—would allow them to set up their own scheme, discretely, for a circle of wealthy customers based in Mexico City, providing them with strains that could be found nowhere else in the country, which Lázaro had harvested from South America during his recent travels. While Lázaro was the tip of the pyramid, having risked his rear crossing South American borders, Rose was the second brick in the structure, with the social grace that could lure countless connections. One thing they had to solve, Evelina overheard, was her own situation—Evelina's that is—and while Lázaro believed she should be kept out of the scheme entirely, Rose argued that she deserved a go at it, that one day he'd understand where she had come from, and that she—Rose—could not be dragging Evelina's albeit light weight forever. The agreement they arrived at was that Evelina would become a third echelon, assisting Rose in spreading the web, and earning a modest percentage of money from Rose's share.

Though her next move should have been to lay low and take whatever was offered to her, and though her position in the operation clearly stipulated a certain submission to Rose, Evelina felt with each passing day more drawn to Lázaro. Predictable, yes, she knew as much, and Rose surely thought so too—Evelina could see it in her gaze, in the droll positioning of her lips when she saw them together—that she was not overly pleased that Evelina was attracted to the first male figure that came into this new world of hers. Within a month of arriving in Mexico City, on the top floor of Hotel Regis, which already felt like a more permanent home, her appointed bed in the double room with Rose remained tended and done. The rose petals strewn upon its pillows and over the covers turned dry until they lost their color. The chocolates next to them melted as the sun came through the window, a slow-moving square of light and heat, spilling the chocolate past its paper wrapping, running over the sheets and then solidifying, somewhat, when the sun moved further west and finally out of sight. These were swaths of time Evelina spent in Lázaro's master suite, with the king size bed that remained undone and disheveled. It all suddenly became a routine again, though Evelina didn't seem to mind. Was she even aware of it? What were once her fears, her demons, could have been creeping in furtively, and she didn't seem to pay much attention to the fact. For now, she was one of the three top echelons in the pyramid, tending to appointments in the midst of Capri's bustle or privately in the suite, recruiting both customers and further pawns, while keeping a close eye on Lázaro's and Rose's demeanors, to learn the trade and add a layer to what Rose had called opacity, the poker face Evelina was so eager to perfect. The few trips outside the walls of Hotel Regis came as idle walks along the edge of La Alameda Central, under the evasive shade of the jacaranda trees, down to El Hemiciclo a Juárez, and then east on Calle López, past the red light district to the greenhouse, a large industrial hangar at Puente Paredo Alley, what once was a parking lot, repurposed by Lázaro to house his four exotic sativa strains brought from Colombia, plants growing tall and bushy, sprayed by a flash of perennial LED lights overhead. Every night, as part of this routine, Evelina stared out into the city from the terrace of her suite, legs dangling over the ledge, wondering if there was still something to cling to from the past, from the previous versions of herself, from the lingering shell of her old skin. She stared into the darkness of the park, which had become something like her Pacific Ocean, an anchor, lined on all sides by warm lights.

The mood at Capri was royal, a spinning thread of voices. White-gloved waiters rushed in and out of the kitchen, and the bartender had two barbacks there to help. They mixed and poured endless glasses of white rum and Coke in highball glasses over cracked ice. By then, all the bartenders knew that Evelina's rum and coke should contain much more coke than rum, that she preferred only the gentlest dash of liquor. What they didn't know was that she drank only to guard appearances, that it was something that came with her job. The waiters also knew not to waste any time taking her order, that she'd have enchiladas verdes no matter the day and no matter the mood. Rose had scheduled her an appointment with two potential buyers, and had done so behind Lázaro's back. The Huerta brothers arrived with British punctuality, right at Capri's peak, which wasn't at all common in Mexico, a place that had always forsaken the expectations of time. Just then, as Evelina saw them talking to the maître d', she recalled a line in one of Rose's books and mumbled it, precisely: "In this country the letters telling us a relative is sick arrive long after they have died, that's why everyone thinks we're a ghostly folk," and she lost herself in both the thought and the cadence of the sentence. Evelina readied herself as the brothers struggled with the maître d', whose reticence and resistance never failed to annoy. It took Evelina's intent gaze from her table, sunglasses in place, rattle pin fully visible on her left lapel—the discerning details the brothers were instructed to follow—and a hand motion to the maître d' before he finally permitted the brothers to pass and showed them to Evelina's table. After offering Evelina an unimpressed nod, they sat down, sweaty, removing heavy leather jackets and hanging them on their chairs. Not many pleasantries were exchanged. As Rose had directed, it took no longer than two minutes before their food arrived—Evelina's religious enchiladas verdes, and tacos de escamoles for the Huertas—a gesture they seemed immediately content with, washing them down with snifters of tequila while Evelina softly spoke about numbers, her voice merely an undercurrent within Capri's busy hum. She kept her sunglasses on throughout their meeting, shielding a nervous tick of her left eyelid. She still did not fully trust her face. "There's one way to do this and one way only," she said, once the brothers' plates were cleared and there remained only the miserable puddles of tequila in their snifters. "If you agree to this deal, you can take the paper bag from underneath the table." The Huerta brothers leaned back in their chairs; one of them stroked his chin. "It's a one-time offer.

If there are second thoughts, this lunch is on me and our meeting comes to a gracious end." The brothers exchanged glances back and forth, their own attempt at bluffing, at trying to get Evelina to lower the stakes, maybe, but instead she confidently took out her copy of *The Crying of Lot 49* and trained her eyes on the pages for what felt like an eternity, ignoring their deliberations. The words in Pynchon's novel were, of course, not sticking, so she briefly glanced up to say, "The offer lasts five minutes, of which you've already consumed two." They ran down the clock, the Huertas, sighing loudly, until one of them bent over, lifted the tablecloth, and removed the bag, all in one movement. Evelina returned her eyes to the book, hastily searching for a passage that calmed her, such as one of the scenes where Oedipa Maas drives along a coastline road. The Huertas left, she sensed it more than saw it, felt the absence in front of her, but she kept her eyes on the book, on the runny print of the old page. But then, lifting her eyes for only a second, she saw knuckles on her table, reddening at the bones. She lifted her eyes further to find the man again, his bushy moustache on his plump face. "Ándese con cuidado, viborita," he told her. "You're swimming in a sea of venom here." Evelina knew color had risen to her face, pinkish, felt a burning sensation in her cheeks: the telling gestures Rose would want her to avoid. But she kept still, resilient, eyes on the page, sunglasses in place, until the man knocked on the table with his knuckles again, with finality this time, and turned away due to her lack of engagement. Lifting her gaze over the cover of the book, she followed him until he walked past the idiotic, tired smile on the maître d's face, and left through the restaurant's door.

Legs dangling over La Alameda Central, Evelina waited, barely registering the hiss of voices inside the suite, sifting through the fine cracks between the velvet drapes. The faint trace of dope also flew as far, the distinct smells of each of their four sativa strains, one after the other. The sound of clapping followed, glasses clinked celebratorily, and minutes later there was the sound of the door, leaving only what seemed like the muffled voices of Rose and Lázaro inside the suite. Evelina waited for something like a verdict, waited for Lázaro and Rose to come out to the terrace. When she at last heard the squeal of the terrace door, another silence followed, which was immediately filled by footsteps. Lázaro had stepped out, alone, a glow on his face despite the darker hue of the night. Evelina concentrated on his features, the sharp cheekbones underlined by the patchy stubble. His curls were combed back, with sweat lining his hairline. His gestures, Evelina thought, subtle and opaque, revealed only in the creases of his skin, matched the mystery of his personality, something she couldn't help but be drawn to. She could tell there were dreams in there too, a utopia he was striving for, and she wondered what that was. Above them, a shield of clouds that matched the size of the city. He couldn't avoid a smile, like it was forcing itself on his face, sets of perfect creases on each corner of his lips. He held two bottles of champagne, one in each hand, their glass a deep-green, with beads of sweat rolling down its surface and whose vacuum-sealed corks flew skyward and then headlong into La Alameda Central as they lost upward momentum, prompting a rush of the champagne's foam. They plugged their mouths to the bottles, felt the fizz dancing festively on their tongues. They'd done it, no words needed be spoken, the deal was closed, the money surely already hidden under their mattress. They downed their bottles, both of them, laughter spilling from their mouths. Lázaro screamed out after swallowing, then flung his empty bottle into the park below. They heard it shatter. The sound of the glass breaking, distantly, into what in Evelina's mind was a million pieces, a true puzzle, kindled a rush of adrenalin throughout her body, flowing like sparks. Had she known such feeling before? She picked up the bottle she had drank and hurled it over the balcony like Lázaro had, closed her eyes during its flight, then almost startled as it, too, shattered. She felt it in her jaw, like a force coming over her, turning into a fit of laughter. She fell to the floor, was left looking up at the pinkish underbelly of the clouds. Lázaro was laughing now too, lying next to her, sliding a joint between his lips. He pulled a match from a box with an image of a scorpion on it, but Evelina stopped his hands. "Allow me," she said, and proceeded: the hiss of a burning match, the rushing, vanishing smoke, the sweetness of its smell, the viscous sway of the flame, its dancing motion. It caught on the tip of Lázaro's joint and he inhaled deep. An opal smoke immediately rushed out through his nostrils. Evelina pulled the joint from his mouth, stared at the orange tip, and brought it to hers. She imagined the sound of a wildfire as she dragged in the smoke: the whisper of the wind turning to a roar. And she felt no fear, just more and more of those warm sparkles in her body. Had she known such feeling before? She asked herself anew, silently, like she wasn't herself anymore, like a new version of Evelina had replaced the old her. Slowly, Lázaro began creeping closer to her, planting soft kisses on her neck, which felt ticklish at first, and made her laugh even harder, even as she helped him remove her blazer while he tugged her black leggings to ankle height Little by little, he shushed her laughter, his mouth wet over hers, his breath hot over her face. She knew, as something throbbed and fluttered somewhere deep in her abdomen, that this was a moment of rapture, a coming of age. She pulled him inside her on the stone floor of the terrace, feeling a little pain, but also electricity coursing through her veins. Her body jolting back, she stared at the clouds above her, which were beginning to part, to push away from each other. There she was, becoming full, full of life: a well staring up at the sky.

Rose moved to her own suite with her own terrace, one on the opposite side of the hotel, overlooking the copper dome of El Monumento a la Revolución. Little did Evelina know that it wouldn't last long, that view, the opulence of it, and it was when the sun was half a cinnabar ball above the gleaming dome of the monument that Rose broke the news. "With success come decisions." The operation had grown so steadily, that the dope they were growing in the underground greenhouse could no longer sustain distribution. They could either shift to the cunning abstractions of a Ponzi scheme, luring deals via promise without actually possessing the tangible goods, or continue offering their signature sativa strains to the growing community, which would require additional land and investment. Lázaro had been in and out of Mexico City, looking for secluded land to purchase, where they could grow their sativa, which was really the scheme's distinguishing asset. During this time, despite having all her meals at Capri, Evelina took to the streets, embodying the figure of the flaneur—a concept Rose had recently taught her—and lived amidst the seas of people wandering by foot throughout the city. Traversing the capital's decay like driftwood, engulfed by its noises and its action, the vendors and their echoing calls, the fire-eaters, the fakirs lying on shards of glass at busy intersections, she feared all of it could be snatched from her in an instant, perhaps even more quickly if they were to go through with this expansion. The more product they moved, the more threat they posed to the burgeoning cartel business. Should she follow Lázaro and Rose's lead and keep on embracing change? But hadn't change, its flux, brought her as far as she was now?

The building's shadow poured vertiginously over Avenida Juárez while Lázaro and Rose waited by the car Lázaro had bought, a crimson Chevy Cheyenne purring in the hotel's driveway. A gust of wind swept in and the jacaranda trees towering over the park had lost most of their leaves. The sight of the leave's falling sway induced a chill that made Evelina button up her blazer: was there a hint of finality in the air again, like that fateful night in the desert not so long ago? She flung her bag into the cab of the truck and got in, hesitantly, bundled tightly in the passenger seat with Rose, who wrapped her arm around Evelina's forearm. Words would hardly be exchanged. It was the tightness of Rose's grip that foreshadowed their parting of ways, an inevitable crossroads. They rode like this as Lázaro drove around La Alameda Central, the windows of Hotel Regis reflecting sun-sparks until it all finally disappeared behind the screen of the car window. They headed south, where buildings gradually lost height and prominence, and soon became reacquainted with the Mexican federal road, the solitude of its snaking curves. The air became hotter with every mile travelled, but not dead-still. Cuernavaca, or Quauhnahuac, as Rose referred to it, greeted them with a row of palm trees on either side of the road, "Guard of honor," Rose said, and they could already spot the undulated structure of el Hotel Casino de la Selva down the slope. Lázaro cut the engine when they got to it, as they breathed in the fragrance of the city of eternal spring. "One day," Rose said, as the pickup's door swung open in the burning asphalt of the parking lot, "I'll buy this place; we'll live here forever." She paused, charging the brief silence with what could only be longing, already missing the past few months as much as Evelina was. "Qué Hotel Regis, ni qué la chingada!" Rose finished in her ever-evolving, Lowry-laden Spanish. A final goodbye was offered with resigned glances, and then Rose's hand slipped away from Evelina's, who saw her older step-sister walk down the stone path to the hotel. The image travelled far with her, crystal clear, well past the plains flanked by the two snow-mantled volcanoes, past the cactus-riddled hills of Taxco, past the ghostly wane of Chilpancingo, but only until she caught sight of the Pacific and its indigo dazzle in the gaps between the rolling hills ahead.

More and more road signs, all of them green with white letters: Tecomán, Sayula, Manzanillo, Cihuatlán, Cuixmala, Colima, the already-visited Guadalajara. Then the road signs yellowed and rusted along the coastline, old and ravaged, constantly sprayed by ocean mist: Careyes, Pérula, Chamela. They veered inland toward Tomatlán, their new home, a few miles away from the ocean, in the direction of a ranch called El Comal, which was now theirs—yes, Evelina and Lázaro's, they had somehow become a couple. "Our very own Macondo," Lázaro said, with a crooked smile intending to convey pride. A brief pit-stop for supplies at a roadside store with the words "Abarrotes Doña Meme" painted on its chipped concrete walls: rice, beans, tortillas, assorted salsas, beer, tequila, a box of local fruits. The owner of the store, a dark-skinned woman, Doña Meme, walked barefoot over the sun-stricken dust, her feet protected by callus-conquered soles, tossing a flurry of seeds right outside the store, in the shade of a tall Jatropha tree that housed countless birds, all of them hidden by bushy leaves yet vociferating a unified chirp, melodious, the avian version of the harmony of voices at Capri. One by one they flew down, tiny blackbirds over a litter of seeds, feathered wings dazzling in the sunlit gaps between the shade. Heading back to the car, groceries in hand, Evelina walked through the birds, making them scatter, flurry back up the tree, the shudder of their wings blowing wind and feathers in her face. The birds filled the tree with their screams again, and she heard a laugh behind her. She turned to find a wholehearted smile on Doña Meme's face, who waved her goodbye as the pickup's wheels lifted dust all around her and made her vanish as they picked up speed. After a few more miles of dirt road, lifting a wake of dust that rose like wildfire smoke, they reached a plateau where there spread endless fields and groves. Lázaro parked in front of the old house and its faded blue walls. Evelina got out, slammed the door of the Cheyenne shut, walked around, the ground hot beneath her feet. Her sunglasses were now more than a veil. She removed her blazer, which was coated in light sweat along the inside hems. Beyond the house, an oblong pool with peeling paint stretched before the purple bloom of a low-lying bougainvillea bush. Its dead blossoms swam across the surface of murky water, its mild current languidly pouring from a hose coiled like a snake ready to strike, which made her think of the new word she knew for venom, "ponzoña." She mouthed it, but it didn't even come to a whisper. A few steps ahead the groves began, which consisted of two different types of trees, those that were bushy and stark green, shielding the fruit that grew and dangled within, close to the trunks; while the others were barer, thinner, taller too, like they couldn't hold the fruit gnawing at their trunks. "Mangoes and papayas," Lázaro's voice travelled to her. "Our new cover... very Macondo, told you." She turned to him, unsure of what he meant, a hand on her forehead to further screen her eyes from the sun. From this vantage point it was all within her peripheral vision, this new life of hers, or theirs, but her sight was fixed on the horizon, where the Pacific peeked between the many bays. She couldn't accept to look at what was now her home, neither at the fruit trees in the groves, nor at the torn hammock next to the pool, nor at the fallen bougainvillea over the rippling water. No, she was not looking at Lázaro either; her sight was fixed beyond the dullness of the inland hills, where the vastness of her Pacific lurked. Was she, once more, forced to imagine the ocean as a symbol of redemption?

Lázaro hired one employee, Rosendo, a scrawny man like himself, who matched his height, but whose skin was as dark as the store owner's, Doña Meme, and whose thick moustache reminded Evelina of the menacing man at Hotel Regis. Man of few words—Rosendo, that is—but who managed to work all through the day, fueled by endless cans of Carta Blanca beer, sun striking the rugged blades of his shoulders. He planted sativa seeds under the groves and trimmed every tree to allow for a calculated window of daylight each morning. Evelina followed in his tracks planting oregano around every tree, just as Oedipa Maas had done in Kinneret, and which aided the further concealment of Lázaro's scheme. Deep in the shade of their blue house's interior, a fan whining as it gestured no-no beside him, blowing air against his bare chest, Lázaro began to plot how they would import fruit into the city, while somehow making room for his dope. The trucks would leave overnight, make a stop by Rose in Cuernavaca, and then travel on to Mexico City, landing in the hands of the Huertas, fourth echelon in the chain. Evelina wasn't involved much in the day-to-day operations anymore, just waiting for the money to funnel in, and it did, which she stored in a paper bag in the depths of their freezer. She mostly drove during those days, aimlessly on the desolate two-lane roads. She took the Cheyenne pickup down the coastline, hoping to find a San Narciso to match her new Kinneret, up and down the dry winding landscape. She drove with an unreal sense of freedom, with the salty wind in her face, the sativa plants under the trees, occupying her mind. This was what her life had come to, as if scripted; she hardly remembered ever making a choice: is this what Mexico was like? It just seemed to happen and unfold without any sense of order or logic. She turned around near Careyes, a dramatic U-turn, skidding to the dusty side of the road. The one promise she'd made was that she would drive back to El Comal before sundown, when the dry vegetation lining the coast turned the color of metal, struck by a low-lying sun cut in half by the ocean's apparent end.

The nights were outright silent, which made the engines of the shipping trucks growl louder. The pitch-dark cloak of new moon nights—when Lázaro had decided deliveries would be made; a decision that to Evelina reeked more of literary romanticism than pragmatism—made their headlights all the more obvious. Was there someone out there watching, listening? After delivering shipments in both Cuernavaca and Mexico City, and collecting payment, the drivers waited for sundown before turning back toward the coast. The drivers were all Rosendo's relatives, making a handsome buck in exchange for trading a life of daylight for one of darkness a few nights every month, risking their own skin as well. Evelina saw them sleeping throughout the day at times, next to the wheels of the truck, or on the soft pasture of her oregano. She had to wake one of them once, whose sleep was so deep it resembled death, and whose waking required a spurt of water from the hose in Rosendo's hands. The man woke with a jerk, then his skin drew many furrows like the cracks caused by drought in the land. "Sale pues, cabrón," Rosendo told him as he rose to his feet. "You can sleep when you're dead." Then, turning to Evelina, he said, "His name is Fulgor; he knows where to buy your car." Evelina's recent earnings had fattened so that she struggled to conceal them in the paper bag in the freezer, and she was getting less and less time to borrow the Cheyenne, which was mostly hogged by Rosendo to buy supplies. All this prompted Fulgor and Evelina to drive to Manzanillo, to a lot of stolen cars in its favela-like mazes. Evelina, like Oedipa Maas, drove back to Tomatlán, to her Rancho El Comal, in a black Impala Cabriolet with cracked beige leather seats the texture of snake skin. The sun was low over the ocean, the shadows of palm trees invading the road, the wind blowing madly on her hair. Fulgor, in the pickup behind her, came in and out of sight in the rearview. At the far end of her vision, as she maneuvered through a road she was starting to know by heart, she saw a large structure on one of the rocky bays, looming over the ocean: half a sphere, large and lonesome, looking over the Pacific. She thought of taking the sand road ahead, but there was Fulgor, struggling to keep up with her in the pickup truck, lost behind every bend in the coastline.

She made a habit of visiting la Copa del Sol, which was somewhat of an observatory or meditation retreat: half a concrete sphere at the very edge of the cliff, opened up, so it seemed like you were lying on the bottom of a monumental bowl. It became a private enclosure for Evelina, a place of meditation. The sight could only be directed at the sky while the sound that pervaded was the crashing of violent waves forever sculpting the cliffs below, an eternal process of erosion. How huge this ocean was for her, such an expanse to really become lost in, a promise of untraceability. Looking up, at the swath of sky caught in her span of vision, weakly dimmed by her sunglasses to a gentler if still glaring hue, vultures hung slothfully in the sky. They called them "zopilotes" here, but the sight of them reminded her of the vultures floating over a reluctant Sunfair dusk. Again, the thought came to her: how far she had come, as if pushed by those persistent ocean currents below, helplessly, to wash up off the coast near Tomatlán. Only this time, the memory of her own assertion did come to her, the one moment, lying there on the terrace of Hotel Regis, pulling Lázaro inside her. The electric sensation rushed back to her, warm, in shivering sparkles, but soon, in an unforeseeable twist, she became lightheaded, her stomach rushing to her mouth, her vomit coming like the swell of an ocean wave, there, on the lowest point of the observatory. Over the sound of her sickness, she registered the accusatory cawing of the birds.

On her next visit, the ocean had grown prickly and stirred up a creamy froth with every upsurge. "Mar de fondo," Rosendo had said before she left; she shouldn't go into the water. Such upsurges swelled inside her too, the initial furies of a coming storm. Erratically, she walked near the cliff-edge, looked over to study the arrival of the waves, believing she saw the silhouettes of sharks circling in the water, and felt like dangling her legs over the side, the pull of vertigo calling her. She knew she was pregnant by then, but felt like taking risks: was there something that could efface this life inside her, a child inside of a child? Wasn't the ocean below her image of freedom? Her blood racing, she slowly retreated, successfully repressing the suicidal daze, and stumbled into the observatory, a temporary haven. Once inside, confined by its tall spherical walls, she lay back down over the incline of the structure, shut her eyes, and struggled to recall a moment in her life when she had frightened herself as much as she had just now. Breathing deeply, she concentrated on the persistent sounds of the ocean, trying to match their pace with her every breath of air. Overhead ran the shadows of the zopilotes, flashes of vanishing shade over her eyelids. She fell into a slumber like this and in the vague limbo where the conscious and unconscious blur, she watched as birds feasted on her stomach. She woke up because a wave pounded high on the cliffs below, opening up a hollow. She could immediately tell she was sunburned, as her forehead was warm and throbbing. She ran a hand over her stomach, almost maternally, and glanced up to find that there was no moon in the sky. Flustered, she exited la Copa. She had left it a little late, that much was clear, but she didn't think it would get so dark. Couldn't the expanse of the Pacific possess the light long enough, long after the sun had drowned behind it? Not even the sea glimmered under the starlight and everything in front of her was a shade of black. The only thing she knew for certain was the steady crash of the waves against the rocks, the ocean mist blasting off them. Every step over the soft ground unsettled her as she remade the path from memory, avoiding the invisible cliffs on either side. The full acclimation to the living world only arrived when she overheard indistinct voices down the path, voices she must pass to get to her car. Even in the dark, she could feel eyes on her, and caught what she thought were the words: "Ándese con cuidado, viborita," just as she was getting into her car. Was it a fabrication of her mind? The steering wheel still held the lingering warmth of the day, but her hands were immediately laced with cold sweat. Feverish, she flipped on her headlights and saw the men between the dry tasajillo branches on the side of the road, drinking from beer cans over the hood of their cars. She sped away in reverse, lifting dirt in front of her, the men growing smaller in the fuzzy scene, until she was lost in the dust storm kicked up by her Imapala's raging wheels.

Ándese con cuidado, viborita: the words had something of a catchy quality to them, a cadence, utterly rhythmic, like the perfect title for a book. Evelina's previous self—the Hotel Regis version of herself—had enjoyed the phrase, it had brought a thrill to her body, a new-found excitement, yet, somehow, here on the coast, the expression was clad with menace. Either way, the words had latched to the inside of her skull, so that they could sieve through to her consciousness unannounced and spark threatening thoughts. It was having heard the expression both in the altitude of Mexico City and at the sea level of this desolate coast, by different sets of mouths and with no variation, that loaded them with what Rose called subtext. Ándese con cuidado, viborita: it had become some sort of an adage. But could it really be a warning? Could the words be passing on, mouth to mouth, marking a clear path from the city to the coast?

The wind blew an emphatic whisper through the groves, the shadows of trees stretching and flailing over the grass. This was her new spot of meditation, inside the confines of her ranch, where the fragrance of oregano was pushed to her by the wind, and, even if much fainter, the ocean was still audible beyond the hills. Granted, she was no longer concealed by the structure of the observatory, was no longer racing along the coastline road, it had all been traded for this new concept of security. The skin on her nose and forehead was peeling, swaths of it lying idle on the grass, and a new, paler skin already shone from within. She ran a hand across her abdomen, felt a slight trembling inside it, this life inside hers, which, surely, at some point, would seek its own liberation. Time was marked by this bump, which gained in volume with each passing week, even if the ocean waves forever hinted at a consistent loop. As the wind withdrew from the groves, she heard the ocean more clearly, every wave lapping at what was left of her dreams, if there was such a thing, at their indecipherable codes, and she pictured them wearing down, like the cliffs, battered and eroding, falling into the ocean.

For Lázaro it was all part of the balance of normalcy, the foundation of their new life: a successful enterprise, a life partner, a roof over their head, and, of course, offspring, the final piece to the puzzle. There was nothing too disconcerting about it. Evelina's surge of emotions was, to him, a result of her pregnancy, tantrums that would wane, an outpouring of hormones that would recede once the baby came out of her body. She had two months to go, but the weight was getting more burdensome to carry. It was unfathomable to imagine that the baby could grow even more, for there seemed to be no more space inside her. A shortage of space was also evident in Lázaro's shipments to Cuernavaca and Mexico City: the container trucks could no longer hold the supply needed to satisfy the demand, and anger was beginning to simmer beneath the higher echelons of the network. If they had more product, they could sell it; demand had once again outpaced production. Lázaro called for a meeting at suite 705 in Hotel Regis, which, to Evelina's surprise, he had kept all along. When he told her that he would be spending the night in Mexico City and come straight back the morning after, Evelina responded with a loaded tone she tried to deliver like she imagined Oedipa would: "Bit off more than you could chew?" Lázaro shook his head. "All this, it's for us," he said, "for the three of us," but Evelina would not have it. She crossed her arms, leaned her lower back on the couch. "What if my water breaks?" A threat Lázaro didn't seem to viscerally respond to. "It's not yet time," he said, "and it's only one night." Evelina was afraid, and she told him so, toneless and straight. "There is nothing to fear," Lázaro added, "everything's under control." Evelina stood up straight, turned her back to him, and said, "It's all the money that brings the fear." Lázaro slammed a closed fist on the table, and said, "Would you relax? Would you rather not have money, the car, a house, nice things? Would you rather we live in a motorhome, and our child be born in the desert without a doctor? But she couldn't hear the rest, she was already storming away, supporting her belly by its base. Outside, the wind was high in the groves again, rippling the bougainvillea-littered water in the pool, and the ocean roared loudly between the distant bays. The salty breeze ruined the outer bush of her oregano, reaching the sativa growing under the fruit.

New moon night. Utterly silent. Ocean, wind; a moan, a wheeze. Sleepless, Evelina couldn't sit still. Her baby weighed her down, or it kicked, as if matching her own fury, her own sense of alarm. Lying on the torn hammock on the terrace, she thought of the ocean's mantra: ocean, wind; a moan, a wheeze—as if the sound matching these words could lull her to sleep. The sound, though, both out-side and inside her mind, was disturbed by the hum of a nearby car engine, as headlights bounced along the dirt road. Evelina shut her eyes, waiting for her mind to drift off to sleep, for the hum to end, but the car stopped and pointed its headlights straight toward her house, toward her on the hammock on the patio. It took real intent to lift her weight from the hammock, but she did so as quickly as she could, and, once she was up, hurried toward the lights. "Lázaro," she yelled. But he must still be in suite 705 at Hotel Regis, on the terrace, maybe, looking over the lightless patch of La Alameda Central. She turned back, headed into the house, where the lights shone through the kitchen windows, casting the inside walls of the house a livid blue. Thinking of where she might be able to hide, she hurried back outside, around the edge of the pool. A bundle of nerves, she snuck into the fruit grove, into the brush of a mango tree, her nose thick with the smell of sativa and spoilt oregano. From this vantage, she could still spot the headlights: they shone all throughout the night, and only turned off at daybreak The car veered away after that, before she could get a good look at its make or model, from where it had come, humming until the wind was back, until the ocean was back: ocean, wind; a moan, a wheeze.

During the sleepless nights upon Lázaro's return, her baby kicking madly every hour after dark, there was endless talk about the city, its life, its people: they were too young for the middle of nowhere. Twisting and turning in his midnight sweat, Lázaro was in no mood to listen to her moaning. "Middle of nowhere?" he said. "This is Macondo, our very own. A place as idyllic and magical as the setting in a book." Evelina wondered where all the magic had gone; the place felt lonely and haunted. During Lázaro's one night of travel, he had learned that one of the Huertas had been taken into custody, for one night only, and now the network relied on taking him at his word, that he hadn't spilled any information to the authorities. Put off by Lázaro's anger and anxiety at her side, Evelina pictured the scheme, and their life in Tomatlán, as a house of cards—like Rose had called it—its structure fragile yet somehow still miraculously stable, its pieces well in place. But the one Huerta had become the crack, the card removed to make the structure tremble, left hanging in the balance. "Rome wasn't built in a day, but boy was it burned down in seconds," she said, thinking of those blinding headlights creeping through the groves. "I think someone might be after us." Lázaro only turned in their bed, silently, removing the covers, marking the long hours of the night with drawn-out, growling breaths.

She said the same words every night thereafter to Lázaro's deaf ears—"Rome wasn't built in a day, but boy was it burned down in seconds"—but the fear and worry had to be put on hold to deal with the sudden birth of their son. Water dropped from her body and the dust beneath her captured it, her fluid swallowed by the thirsty land. He was born in a clinic in Careyes under artificial blue light. It took only a single push, like the crashing of a wave, to eject the clotted body: he was utterly silent, he did not cry, the one expression of life captured in his eyes, their darting gray irises, as if he was already looking for a way out, a crack in the door, a slight opening in the window. Lázaro named him Aureliano before any conversation was had: he further needed his obsession with *One Hundred Years of Solitude* to come alive—his own little Macondo, and now there was someone else to pay the price.

Aureliano: so young and a victim to his name already. He slept for long hours, breathlessly it seemed, lifeless save for the flutters of his eyelids. He woke with searching eyes which unequivocally settled upon Evelina's breasts. He sucked on them ravenously, and when she tried to unsuckle him, he would look up, his thin eyebrows slanted to a frown, forever demanding more.

Rose came with gifts, the most exciting being a baby seat for Evelina's car. She had properly guessed at Evelina's postpartum claustrophobia, the tired sight of the bougainvillea in the pool that needed cleaning, the view of the groves behind it. Rose's visit served a double purpose, too: yes, she had been named godmother of the baby, which made her take to the road again—yet another string of buses, taxis, and colectivos, before setting foot on the dusty driveway in Tomatlán—but even while she cradled her godson, her words of caution were aimed in Lázaro's direction. Evelina basked in relief while Aureliano was in Rose's arms, but nonetheless remained wary of their business-oriented discussions: a few incidents of drug-related violence had progressed from the northern strip of the country, south toward Mexico City, for reasons still unknown. Rose theorized that the Guadalajara Cartel had so much money to spare that they were going the useless length of violently clamping down on the minimal insurgencies of competition, although that didn't fully explain why one of the Huertas had been taken into custody by a Judicial Police Officer going by the name of Cancio, thought to be colluding with politicians and drug dealers alike. Operación Cóndor had soared to new heights, too, urged on by the media as much as the D.E.A., and flames were rising as they burned thousands of acres of poppy and marijuana fields from Zacatecas to Sinaloa. The question for Lázaro and Rose that needed answering was whether they should stop their operation, dismantle it immediately, be content with what they had reaped already, let it fall like a house of cards. Or, should they double-down on their investment? After that, Evelina couldn't hear much more. She saw them walk away into the groves, Aureliano still in Rose's arms, eyeing her breasts, while Lázaro gave her a tour, pointing out every tree, every sativa under its shade. Before Rose left the following morning, Evelina had the words on the tip of her tongue: she wanted to come to Cuernavaca with her, leave Lázaro behind for a little while. She wanted to tell Rose about the car that visited while Lázaro was in Mexico City, whose headlights remained on all night, that the cartels or the authorities were already after them, everything Lázaro refused to see. But she couldn't speak. She waited next to Rose until her colectivo rumbled by slowly, careful not to engulf them in a cloud of dust.

The sky pouring down on her with its ubiquitous glare, Evelina drove to Doña Meme's. There was nowhere to park in front of the store, so Evelina left her Impala around the bend and out of immediate sight. Aureliano silent in her arms, she walked along the powdery dirt road. The birds sang their mayhem in the tree, loudly demanding their daily ration of seeds. Right outside the store was a string of parked muscle cars blasting corridos from broken speakers, and a gathering of at least ten men drinking over their hoods. The men passed around caguamas and bottles of mezcal with drowned earthworms whirling inside. As she was about to step into the darkened rectangle of the store's entrance, Evelina heard a sibilant sound, and turned to find one of the drunkards flashing the tip of his tongue through his lips, like a serpent ready to strike. Blood raced quickly in Evelina's veins, and Aureliano's eyes bounced around in their sockets. The sound of the men's wild laughter scarcely muffled once she was inside of the store, where Doña Meme barely turned to her, failing to share her usual smile, and returned her gaze to the television atop the beer refrigerator. On the screen, flames rose high and distinct, and the words Operación Cóndor glared in the text bar at the bottom. "Ahora sí nos va a cargar la chingada," Doña Meme said, and even though Evelina couldn't quite make out the exact meaning of the words, the hollow in her chest opened up to the foreboding of their phonetic. Doña Meme stood, lovingly laid a fingertip on Aureliano's nose, and asked Evelina what she could help her with. Evelina had come to the store behind Lázaro's back, while he had vanished deep into the groves with Rosendo. She asked Doña Meme for baby formula, for she could no longer take Aureliano gnawing at her breasts. She felt guilty, but was desperate, and even tempted to show the woman the ravages her baby had caused to her body: the blood-red nipples, the tenderness along their curvature. Doña Meme didn't say anything, just spooned powdered Leche Nido into a plastic bag, and tied a knot with the corners of the bundled plastic. Stepping out of the store, Evelina averted the eyes of the drunkards, and walked as fast as she could with Aureliano's face tucked against her chest. During her slight dash, she heard laughter behind her again, wild, and she somehow knew that she was at the wrong end of a joke. She drove back to El Comal, jerking backwards to check on her son, whose legs and arms jiggled as they protruded from the safety belts of his seat. It was only when she parked outside her house that she saw the joke at her expense that had sparked such a blithe reaction amongst the drunkards: on her Impala's passenger door, the image of a snake was spray-painted. She felt lightheaded, and a weakness in her limbs. She had to kneel against the car, her back against the spray-painted snake, before summoning the strength to carry her son inside the house.

After scraping off the dry spray paint with a kitchen spatula, Lázaro made little of her account, said it was surely nothing, not cartel toughs blowing smoke but harmless locals who'd had a few too many beers. Tomatlán was safe, he stressed. "Places are not only places, they're a state of mind. It's time you tune in to what's around you." Again, he walked toward the fields, into the groves. Oh, how he clung to this concept of his own little Macondo, with magical flourishes in his eyes, but he was the only one who could see them.

Speeding along the coastline road, the anger relenting and replaced by a sinking feeling that arose as a result of guilt, she tried to see through the layer that hid the magic: the road, silver-lined with plants dead and dry, the ocean racing sapphire blue onto the sand, the sun's glare over the ocean drawn in crimson blades, the idyll of vast distances, the hum and vibration of the road on the wheel in her hands, the cyclonic wind-rush of driving at high speeds, the blissful coo of baby Aureliano, the few hairs on his head lifted back by the forward momentum. Places are not only places, that much she knew, and was trying hard to adjust her state of mind. Up the plateau from Chamela Bay, the smell of manure gripped the air and she spotted flashing police lights and orange cones blocking the road. A gentle press of the brake, and the Impala arrived rumbling at its lower gears, as a policemen flagged Evelina to the side of the road. Jerking her neck back, Evelina peered into her son's eyes, wondering where these images would store in his unconscious, if there is such a thing as repression. The smell of manure had faded, and with the car turned off on the sandy side of the road, the air grew warm and oppressive. Sweat had gathered on Aureliano's head, dew-like, hanging still on his newborn's skin. Evelina broke into a sweat too, but the drops scurried quickly down her temples. In front of her were two police cars and a navy-blue Silverado, more anonymous looking than official, with several figures inside. When a man emerged from the Silverado and approached her, she felt herself shaking her head, sweat dripping down and pearling on the leather seats. "Out of the car," he said, but she kept on shaking her head. The man flashed a badge with the image of the gilded eagle eating the snake, and opened her door. Behind her, Aureliano's eyes darted this way and that, the first time this anxious gesture of his matched the tension of the situation. "Out of the car." But this time it wasn't really a request, as the man had taken hold of Evelina's wrist and wrenched her out of her seat. He shoved her in the direction of the Silverado and opened the glove compartment of Evelina's car, looking over to Aureliano through the corner of his eye. "No no no," cried Evelina. "My baby." But the man kept sorting through the papers in his hand. "Ay Evelina, ay Evelina," the man said, as he read through her Impala's registration. Aureliano's eyes now lingered steadily on the man, his mouth slightly parted. Folding the documents in his hands, the man made for the Impala again, and Evelina cried, "No!" her heart rattling in its cage, assailed by an instinct of motherhood she didn't know she possessed. The man returned the documents to the glove compartment, and shot a paternal smile at Aureliano, then spun towards Evelina. "One too many stolen cars from Manzanillo up this road," he said. "But all seems in order here." He stretched an arm and opened up his palm in the direction of her car. "Ándese con cuidado," he said, adding to her stupor. "Don't go speeding down the road. Think of your baby." Evelina stumbled to her car, the sandy ground underneath her shifting unsteadily. Once behind the wheel, she put the car in gear and the Impala crawled back onto the pavement. She shot a glance at the Silverado as it slid by to her side, where she caught a glimpse of a pear-shaped, mustached face, shadowed behind the glass. Was it him, the same man she saw at Hotel Regis? It was impossible to tell for certain. Ándese con cui dado, the man had said, but he needn't finish the sentence. As she returned her eyes to the road, she realized she wouldn't be able to tell Lázaro about this, because he wouldn't listen. This place wasn't the Macondo of his dreams, and she'd rather spend her energy planning a way to escape this menacing coast. Both hands firmly on the wheel, she steered the Impala to El Comal, racing like a black obsidian arrow along the coastline road.

The trickery of desolation: existence's own opacity. Only wind, only ocean. More and more coos out of Aureliano's mouth, which seemed to voice a stern demand: the milk streaming from her body. He wasn't tricked by the formula, and was already learning to shoot loaded, judgmental stares. His brain is like a sponge, his godmother had said, and it seemed like he had learned something from her during the brief visit. Evelina placed him face down on a towel next to the pool while she dipped beneath the surface. The cold water was the one thing that could soothe the bloody gashes on her breasts. She looked over to her ravenous son, at the groves beyond him, slowly quavering in the haze, how they seemed to be melting in the dry heat.

In bed, Evelina silently begged that it all come to an end, that they leave this place, speed down the road, as far as they could go. The Pacific ran south to the end of the world, did it not? She could sense Aureliano had woken, even though he didn't make the slightest sound. It was the mild currents in the air that she could feel, the quick movements of his limbs like an insect on its back. She picked him up, took him outside, and sat on the torn hammock. Under the pale shaft of a crescent moon, she offered him another try. "Come on, now, be gentle," and uncovered her left breast. Fully plugged against her body, the baby suckled with his gums, and Evelina winced and frowned to the pain. Staring out into the distance she concentrated on the motion of the waves: the Pacific Ocean licking its own wounds. When Aureliano was done he gurgled and sighed, gave her a satisfied coo. She held him in front of her, forced eye contact with those gray eyes: Are you, she asked silently, the one clear boundary to the future?

News arrived later that night through the worried avian wail of the land line. Evelina woke from dreams of screaming birds in the tree outside Doña Meme's, and sprung from bed to check on her baby, who lay still in his crib, but with eyes open and unblinking. It took Lázaro a few pained moans to lift the phone from its base. "Diga," he grumbled into the receiver. There was a broken chirp on the other end of the line, words coming at what seemed a hundred miles an hour and from a hundred miles away. He was only able to relay the news to Evelina after two shots of tequila while sitting next to their pool, running a hand along the soaked bougainvillea blossoms floating over the water: one of the Huertas had gone missing, it had been three days already, he had been last seen at Capri, and never made it home that evening. It was as if he had been wiped off the earth; Lázaro worried he was in one of the clandestine pits he kept hearing about on the news. "See," Evelina said, moving Aureliano from one cradling arm to the other. "This needs to end; sharks are circling, closing in." Lázaro shook his head, poured himself another tequila, heavy handed. He couldn't quite let go of his final wager, his Macondo, his living dream.

Lázaro called another meeting in the suite at Hotel Regis, what was supposed to be the last. Seething in disbelief after Lázaro told her she wouldn't be coming along—that it was too dangerous to bring Aureliano to the city, considering the situation—Evelina moaned about wanting to go live with Rose for a while, saying that she might be safer in Cuernavaca. Even if she knew it wasn't really an option at the time, as Rose would be attending the meeting too, she felt the need to plant this runaway instinct of hers in Lázaro's head. "We're a family now and this is our home," Lázaro said. Before he could continue, Evelina hissed back: "Please don't say this is our Macondo. This is real life, not some book, and the threat to all our lives—mine, yours, your son's—are real." Meanwhile, the sativa trims had been dried and clipped, concealed in boxes with mangoes and papayas, and Lázaro would be leaving come new moon night with Fulgor at the wheel. Before Evelina knew it, the nights grew darker; she couldn't quite fathom how quickly and stealthily the moon had withdrawn from the sky.

Sleep came at intervals and oftentimes Evelina awoke thinking of her father, what seemed like fortuitous images slipping into her mind: brushstrokes in oil, expressionistic and runny, solidified and jagged like the texture of his skin. This time, as she ran a hand over the empty covers to her side, wishing her hand was smoothing over Lázaro's body, the remembrance came at first in the form of her father's voice, then the image spilled over her mind like how the Sunfair night poured across the desert. "Up there," her father had pointed to a row of three stars. "Three planets are in line. This is why the light gets so magnificent. Stars aligned, baby, good time to make a wish." She tried hard, in her bed at El Comal, to see one particular painting of his again—that of a Sunfair sunset blasting orange and pink, a tad more magical than she had ever seen—and wished aloud for the pyramid's destruction. But as she rose to loom over Aureliano sleeping in the crib, she feared she was beyond the point of wishful thinking. Something had misaligned elsewhere, malignant, like air hot and cold merging and swirling into a storm. She was dead in the middle of it, too, there in its eye, knowing this calm would soon be turned to fury.

The nights held on, dragging out longer than she felt they should have. Every sound, near and far, stirred her in her sleep. Cars rumbled slow on the dirt road, and oh how long it took for the sound to ebb, for the headlights creeping into her room to bend away, for her palpitations to soothe, for Aureliano to be full, to stop clawing and nibbling at her breasts. She still had two more nights alone to brave, and she couldn't foresee how she'd get through them.

Slowly, needle-like, she entered the pool, naked, past the coat of bougainvillea on the surface and into the chill of the water. Goosebumps rose along her every inch of skin, but ah the relief in her chest as her nipples were submerged. Aureliano, belly down over a towel on the grass beside the pool, cooed. Just the sight of his moving mouth brought a new sting to her areolas underwater. Drawing a deep breath to the base of her lungs she dove deep, a touch of resentment towards her child stealing upon her. She sat at the bottom of the pool, fighting the upward tug of the water, and scanned the wobbly blue all around her. As soon as she closed her eyes, though, a subtle sound reached her like a distorted vibration, filtering through the water. Was it an ocean's wave? Was it her child? Could Lázaro be back already? Placing her feet against the pool's floor, she sprung upward, exiting the water with a splash of soaked bougainvillea blossoms. She heard it again, clearly now, but it wasn't Lázaro, or Aureliano: it was a rattle, slow and hollow, and so loud it made her shiver. Her face barely above the surface of the water, she spotted the diamond patterns on the glittering skin of the snake. Her blood ran swiftly to her stomach. Slowly, needle-like, she emerged from the pool, lifting her body to the burning tiled floor. The snake she saw in Sunfair the night of her departure flooded back to her, and oh how they looked alike. Skidding slowly like a tectonic plate through the grass, the snake circumvented Aureliano, who cooed, moving his limbs as if skydiving, his stout belly a powerful center of gravity, rooting him to the ground. Evelina knew to take slow, quiet steps, to speak with a smooth voice. Out came the words, unannounced: "Ándese con cuidado, viborita." The syllables matched the pace of a lullaby. "Traerá ponzoña esta niña," she sang, and like a feline mother, she plucked her son by his collar, lifted him up and took a step back. The snake continued its greasy shuffle, its rattle dimming as it sunk deeper into the groves.

The night was a flood of sweat, of full-body rattles, of hissing sounds that were either human voices or reptilian murmurs. Everywhere, she sensed a gliding along the floor.

Lázaro was due back before sundown, but Evelina's anticipation had grown since midday. She somehow thought that by defeating solitude, things would start to regain shape. Defeated by the pain, rather, she tried to feed Aureliano from his bottle of formula, which he shook his head to, and batted away with curled fists. There was no going near the groves anymore; she wouldn't leave the tiled floor, wouldn't place Aureliano on the grass. She waited for the rumbling of the truck, the sight of Fulgor and Lázaro behind the windshield, but when the image vanished, she imagined Lázaro returning by foot on the dusty road. But there was nothing there, and the hours dragged on. While scanning her footing for what might be scaly imprints from the snake, she stepped out onto the dusty road. She looked down the slope, squinting against the glint of sunlight, but Lázaro was just not there. There was only the brown of the road, the lifted dust, the metallic glow of the dry vegetation.

The ocean in the distance went from azure to navy to indigo to a silvery green, then to the color of stagnant water. Its roar remained steady, though, and more ominous than it had ever been.

As the final bloody rind of daylight lingered on the horizon, Evelina's heartbeat pounded in her torso. She could hear a flickering at their gate, and hurried towards it, Aureliano in arms, screaming "Lázaro." But it was only Rosendo who was there. "Not back then, eh, Fulgor and your man," he said, leaning forward, arms stretched and stiff, his hands steady on the gate. He shook his head and turned away, walked into the near darkness.

A sleepless night. The moon already a thin sliver in the sky: the new moon nights had washed away, and Lázaro was still not back. Evelina dragged the landline to the terrace, pulled the cable as long as it would give. She tried Rose, but nothing, and settled on waiting for a call that never came. She sat in the hammock with Aureliano for hours, trying to breathe in the muggy air. Her son flailed at her breasts, tried to reach them with his mouth, his lips mouthing the letters of the word *hunger*, one by one. But her milk wasn't producing as it once had. As the hours passed the pain got worse, matching her desperation, and even on an empty stomach Aureliano didn't but squeal. Looking away from the pain, she offered him the dribbles that his presence still managed to elicit, but her nipples began to hurt at the slightest touch. Nausea came in waves too, as if paired to the sound of the ocean.

A new day brightened to the sound of cackling roosters, to the lazy howl of waking dogs. A gray shimmer along the bay. Slowly, the sun snuck up from behind the house, and the dry landscape gained its full ante meridian color. Aureliano moved in awkward spurts, his thin, almost translucent eyebrows slanted angry and indignant. Evelina's breasts had gone fully numb, and as she tried to feed her baby, milk would no longer stream from them at all. She left Aureliano on the hammock, face up, his cheeks against the fine gaps opening between the fabric's threads. In the dim and cool kitchen, she spooned Leche Nido formula from a plastic bag into the tiny bottle and mixed it with water from the tap. She tried the rubber nipple of the bottle with her finger, and felt her own throbbing and stinging. Staring at a dot of formula like a dewdrop on her thumb, a lightheadedness came to her as if the ground underneath her had shifted. She felt her legs tremble, her balance thrown askew. Was she a bad mother? Was this dawning notion stirring all the turbulence inside? But then lucidity struck with its realist blade: the glass windows shook and blared, the ground had transformed into an all-pervasive tremble, dust deluged from the old wooden ceiling and she could also see it through the window lifting off the road. The tremor bellowed like advancing flames, which told Evelina she had to move quickly. Outside, the bougainvillea bush rustled and released more blossoms into the pool. The early horizon spun, and she found herself rushing to her son, who cooed, angrily, in the swinging hammock. Stumbling with her every step, she took him from under the creak of the terrace's roof and its dislodged cobwebs, and dashed into the grass, where they fell. She looked around for a gliding reptile, but it was the ground that possessed all movement. The water in the pool began swishing sideways and flew out in blossom-packed splashes from either side. The groves shuddered a loud alarm, the fruit letting go of the branches, while the ocean in the distance roared like a lion, until the shockwaves ceased and the earth shook its last spasm. The remaining water in the pool curled and took some minutes before settling back down. The animals quieted. The ocean, treacherous, seemed to have gone back to its usual swells, and in her mind, Evelina saw Mexico City's asphalt gathering in the same motions. Were Rose and Lázaro still there, buried beneath the rubble?

The silence that followed was eerie, dead. Lying down next to the pool, Evelina breathed in, timorously, trying to rid the thought of Lázaro and Rose lost to the cataclysm in the city. She placed Aureliano face down against her body and held the bottle with formula in one hand. She uncovered both her dry breasts and lowered Aureliano's body so he could face them. He went straight for the nipple, and his slightest graze set off a pain that ran like a tender nerve through every node in her spine. Biting her tongue to silence the pain, she slid the bottle's tip next to her breast, and forced it into her son's mouth. He groaned at first, flailed an arm, but was immediately tricked by the steady flow of liquid. She thought of how this parting from her breasts might have meant a step closer toward his future independence. This was the moment, she thought, when, as a mother, she was no longer a biological need, which made Lázaro's image rush back. Maybe it was his turn to provide for Aureliano, the shining light of his Macondo. But he was two nights late: did Aureliano still have a father? Fighting the urge to cry, she turned to face the ocean as Aureliano suckled, begging those currents to wash the thoughts away.

The Impala purred with the first turn of the ignition. Evelina craned her neck to make sure that Aureliano was safe and properly strapped into his car seat. As she drove past the gate and onto the dirt road, Rosendo stepped in front of the car, gesturing with a downward swinging palm for her to slow down. Evelina hit the brakes and when the dust settled upon them, Rosendo went around the hood, placed a hand on the old leather trim of her door, leaning forward. Dust had latched onto his moustache and hair, which still gleamed under the midday sun. "Fulgor," he said. "He's not back." He paused, looked into the distance before resuming: "And I hear of fallen buildings in that bedeviled city where you people hail from. What am I to tell his family?" The instinct that grabbed hold of Evelina was to step on the gas, to leave Rosendo there, but there was something about the pronounced folds of skin, the gestures of his sun-stricken face, which caused her to let the instinct pass. "Lázaro's not back either," she said. "So, I guess that puts us in the same position." Rosendo hissed, leaning further in before retreating. "Está bueno," he said, and backed away as Evelina put the car in motion toward the store down the road. She parked right in front of the tree full of birds, unclipped Aureliano from his seat, and wiped off the dust that had clung to his lashes. Inside, there was a stale quiet, save for the urgent report from the television. Again, Doña Meme failed to offer a smile, only stared at Evelina for an instant, before fixing her sight on the television. She couldn't believe her eyes at first, but as they lingered on the images, she gradually digested their meaning. On the screen, a reporter ran through the streets of Mexico City, which had been reduced to a pile of rubble. "El histórico Hotel Regis," the reporter said, and Evelina needn't hear more. She knew the place by heart, and in the scene, El Monumento a la Revolución peeked its wretched coppery sheen at the far end of the shot, looking over the fallen Hotel Regis. Her senses started turning on her: first, the dry mouth, the smell of ammonia, then the air sucked out of her lungs.

Doña Meme turned to her again, and sprung from her chair. "Ay dios," she muttered, and snatched Aureliano from Evelina's arms. Once she had him steady, she fetched an iced bottle of Coca-Cola from the fridge, which she hissed open with her teeth. Evelina's sight going a dull gray, then black, she fell to the floor collapsing like a struck animal. When she regained her senses, Hotel Regis was still on the screen, or what was left of it—the marquee fallen all the way to the ground, its cream yellow walls now an anarchic mound of rubble over Avenida Juárez. She took slow sips from her Coca-Cola, brought the icy glass against her temples. "Señora, está usté bien? You're pale as a ghost," Doña Meme said, expertly holding Aureliano from a hooked arm. "Sí," Evelina, said, "I'll be taking more formula, por favor."

Memories raced, shifted and merged in Evelina's mind: the noise of Capri, the ever-apologetic maître d', the bartender's high-pour, the women at the beauty parlor puffing out rings of smoke, the jingle of the elevators, the pervasive sativa smell of suite 705, the coolness of the terrace's stone floor, Rose's muffled laughter, Lázaro pushing inside her. An urge to pray came to her, to will Lázaro back. "Let him come back to me alive." She left the house to look out into the distance, though she knew she would find no one there. Color was fading from things once more: from the leaves on the groves, from the rolling hills, from the ocean. Night had fallen again and she was wary of every sound, even those made by the ghosts around her, the previous dwellers of this land.

She thought she slept through a few of the earthquake's aftershocks throughout the night, and woke gripped by a strong if not rare fatalism. Where was the girl who had so bravely come this far? Looking down over Aureliano's crib, she knew that he was grasping for her aching breasts, arms outstretched, even if he knew he would never have them again.

The gate squealed while she was feeding Aureliano on the hammock, the sky threatening dusk. The few clouds were shaded a cream red, composing a beautiful twilight, where everything that happened in front of her, she imagined, seemed half suggestion and half real. The gate clanged against the stone structure that held it upright. Evelina stood, Aureliano in arms, ready to curse at Lázaro for putting her through this wait. But once she turned the corner of her house, past its blue wall, what she saw was a procession of men, guns and machetes in hands, storming onto the property. Evelina held Aureliano as tightly as she ever had, and eyed the men with a terrified suspicion. She stormed inside the house, laid Aureliano face down on his crib, then slowly returned outside. The men marched in front of her and walked into the groves, spreading out in something like a formation, scrutinizing every tree. The man at the end of the line loaded his gun, thumbed back the bolt, pointed with it to Evelina's torn hammock, and said, "Sentada." Slowly, shaky, she did as she was told. All the fear she felt for Lázaro fled her; now, she was gripped by a fear for her baby, and for herself. The man who was guarding her while the others searched the groves stared her down, menacingly. The men in the field slowly returned, as if choreographed, forming a line, advancing like high tide. In their hands they carried branches of sativa, enough to match one of Lázaro's shipments to the city. Evelina's heartbeat pounded even harder when she saw that a man at the far edge of the line clutched the body of a live rattlesnake from his hand, his fingers pressing down hard over the creature's mouth, clasping it shut. The guard shot Evelina a sarcastic look, laughed raspingly, and said, "Se los va a cargar la chingada." He gestured with his hand toward the gate, and the men complied, starting toward the dirt road, tall branches of sativa over their shoulders. The man hold-ing the snake flung it in Evelina's direction; she couldn't repress a wild scream. The snake fell a few feet from where she was standing, where it adopted its coil, and its angry rattle. Evelina retreated slowly, the men's laughter painful in her ears. The snake squeezed into a tighter coil, rattling Evelina away, the conjunctures of its tail right next to its mouth. She had to veer around it just as she had done under the Sunfair moon: was this a symbol for her rebirth? Maybe, but one thing she knew for certain was that it was time to escape. She ran to her son inside the house, and shut every door. No sound came from her, only a stream of tears spilling down her face.

Rare clouds rose above the ocean, marshmallow-like and with ash-gray underbellies, giving the horizon a funereal glow. Even though she knew it was a hazard, she placed Aureliano's car seat beside her in the passenger seat: that's how much she needed her child within arm's length. She drove to Doña Meme's first, and as she walked around the shaded room—the clamor of the birds loud from the branches of the tree outside—she heard more accounts of the earth-quake's damage: 8.5 on the Richter scale, spreading quick oscillations over the prone lakebed of Mexico City, for well over a minute. Hotel Regis was one of many fallen buildings, but perhaps the most iconic. In her mind ran imagined images alongside the ones on the screen: of Lázaro sleeping in the suite, in the bed they once shared, the walls cracking and folding all around him; him falling amongst the rubble, over Capri, maybe, and its subdued morning sounds. She bought formula, that Leche Nido Aureliano once loathed but now drank as his only option, some of which Doña Meme herself mixed with bottled water right there in the store. Evelina got an icy Coca-Cola, too, in a glass bottle, two empty three-gallon plastic demijohns, and a packet of black hair dye. "Would you do it for me?" Evelina asked, and Doña Meme took the packet in her hand, ripped it open, nodded with a creased eye glinting with cheeky if not distrustful amusement. Evelina sat with Aureliano on her lap, gulped down the Coca-Cola's sugary fizz, stared at the images of rubble in Mexico City, that sea of people she loved so much, now awash with destruction. When her hair was done, black and glossy, she kissed Doña Meme's cheek goodbye and drove to the gas station, a feeling of guilt laced with martyrdom crawling upon her.

From the passenger seat of her Impala, under the slanted shade of the driveway, Aureliano was the only spectator. The demijohns were empty again and the gasoline gleamed a waxy trail throughout the groves and grass. Then, the match in her hand hissed, the smoke rushed and vanished. Evelina took in its sweet smell. She saw the flame, skinny and blue on the match, and then muttered, "now or never, nowever," tossed the match to the ground, and as it fell, she saw the viscous sway of the flame, its elusive little dance, and in a flush, it caught on it all, on the dry leaves, the blades of grass, racing through the lines she had drawn with the fuel, crawling up the groves. As the flames rose, she thought of the Operación Cóndor she had seen on Doña Meme's television, but that she had also now witnessed with her own eyes, on the federal road off Mazatlán. She thought of this as her own scheme, Operación Zopilote, she'd call it, if she lived to tell the tale.

The groves burned and crackled, flaring like magnificent fireworks. The parched ground turned black and gray beneath growing mounds of ash. Every tree slimmed and blackened, the remaining mangoes and papayas fell from their branches like tired climbers off a cliff. Evelina turned to face the ocean breeze as it struggled onto El Comal, while, in the distance, like a mirage, the ghostly figure of Lázaro wandered through the road, his eyes studying his ruined Macondo. There seemed to be a cloud of dust surrounding him, moving at his pace. Evelina ran to him, mouth open, her heart pumping a mad cycle. When she got closer, she realized that there was no dust, but rather a cloud of butterflies around him, a cloud which dispersed once she was within touching distance. She ran a hand along his face in disbelief, down his chest, up to his hair, like the blind would to recognize their kin, when she noticed a pronounced tremor in his arm. "Are you alright?" she asked, running a hand over the affected area. "Yes," he responded, "It's just fluttering but it's not in pain." She had been convinced he was dead, yet here he was, his face catching the heat from the fire, his eyes wide in disbelief, watching how the wind made the flames race over what remained of his groves.

The cartels, they came, they're after us, they know; Evelina tested the words in her mind. She still didn't know if she'd lie or come clean, if she would blame herself or blame the goons. "What the fuck happened, Evelina?" Lázaro blurted out, his voice weak under the sizzling croon of his land. "The goons, the cartels," she said, "they came." Trying to buy some time, and finally settling on a half-lie, for wasn't it half a truth as well? "They threatened to kill us, you and me, Aureliano too. They would be coming back, they said, and that we'd better leave this land to them." Lázaro kept shaking his head, wiping the sweat the fire pulled from his forehead. "You'll have to build your state of mind elsewhere." For the first time since his return, Lázaro nodded. "Fulgor is dead, Evelina," he said, "and it was a close call for me." Something stirred in Evelina's stomach. "You know what this means, right?" she asked. "This is the end. Now we become someone else." Lázaro, trying to shake off the flutter of his arm, stared at her black hair with fiery, bloodshot eyes, this inevitable decision already made for him. She could tell he was trying hard to nod, his face burning, his lips parting to the heat of Evelina's flames.

The ground blistered and blackened beneath the flames; the smoke rose in hairy strands. The Impala was full like a pilgrim's wagon. Lázaro tossed everything related to the organization into the flames, the scheme's documents, records, and telephone numbers. From a drawer in the desk in his study, he removed a matte black handgun Evelina had never seen before. Its sight startled her at first, but then the fright dissipated and the logic of it brought her back to the moment. Lázaro stored it in the glove compartment and kissed Aureliano's soft spot on his head. "Time to go," he said. "It can burn all the way down." Where were they going, none of them knew, and Evelina almost reveled in the idea of driving down the coast again, aimless, sleeping in layover motels, disappearing into a new fantasy. As they headed to the packed car, Lázaro's Cheyenne raced into the driveway, lifting a mad cloud of dust. It was Rosendo behind the wheel. He blocked the gates, left the pickup running, and walked straight to Lázaro, eyes bloodshot and creased, as if he had been standing in the smoke for hours already. He took Lázaro by the throat, pushed him all the way against the blue walls of the house. "Fulgor is dead," Rosendo said, his hand like a claw around Lázaro's neck. "Me lo llenaron de plomo," he screamed. "They found his body, on the road, a cartridge of bullets in his chest." Lázaro was clearly having trouble breathing by now, and could barely hiss out his response. "I know, Rosendo," he said. "I know." The admittance fueled Rosendo's fury, like more gasoline had been poured on his inner flames, and he wrestled Lázaro to the ground. With both his hands around Lázaro's neck, he asked, "What am I to tell his family? I brought him here, got him this job, and now he's dead." Lázaro's face was whitening under Rosendo's grip, and Evelina couldn't think of anything other than the gun. She quickly walked to the car, eyed her son in the backseat, gave him a shushing sound, and grabbed the gun. Unsure of how to work the weapon, and guiding her actions more by scenes she had seen on the Western films her father loved, she flicked back the barrel of the gun, which made a clicking sound that didn't capture Rosendo's attention. Evelina went all the way up to him, surprised at her own ease, and placed the cold metal of the cannon on Rosendo's back. "Let go of him, now." Immediately, she felt Rosendo's body loosen. She had to press the gun firmly on his back to hide the tremble of her pulse. Lázaro gasped, long and whiny, while Rosendo raised both his hands and left Lázaro coughing in the dust. He sat against the wall of the house, resigned, looking over to the flames. In that very moment, Evelina felt that maybe Rosendo thought her capable of shooting him, on account of those very flames, like he somehow knew that she had lit the fire, and knew she had this willpower inside. Rosendo burst into tears, but Evelina knew better than to lower the weapon, kept the barrel pointed at him. Lázaro huffed on the floor, his breath slowly normalizing. "Fulgor...What am I to tell his family? They'll lynch me. I'll be nothing more than a heap of bones," Rosendo said, which made Evelina lower the gun, holding it in one hand. "Then you'll have to come with us, Rosendo," she said. "Leave all this behind."

They drove out the gate of El Comal, Rosendo behind them in the Cheyenne, the flames inching steadily toward the blue house. The dust rising from their wheels replaced the view of the smoke, and then they were away, Lázaro's imaginary Macondo behind them. A flock of zopilotes adhered to the wind draft and followed, ocean-bound, barely spreading their wings. Once reaching the federal road, their shadows raced over the pavement, wings open and still. "Where are we to go?" Lázaro asked from the passenger seat, dust still clinging to his hair, looking away, as if seeking answers from the ocean's tide. Aureliano sang a wordless pitch from the backseat, like he was enjoying this climactic turn of events. Taking advantage of the ocean's wind-shafts, the zopilotes sailed ahead of them, cutting over the hills that made the road bend around the bays. The sun was lowering over the Pacific, and once they went around Tenacatita Bay, they came to a scene of carnage: the flock of zopilotes gathered funereal in the middle of the scalding pavement, hounding on the carcass of an animal too disemboweled to be recognized. Is this the fate that we dodged? Evelina thought, feeling something like a vulturous pecking in her chest. As she veered around the massive birds and their executioner-black faces, the Impala wheeled over the roadside, riding over grounded thicket. She could see Rosendo in her rearview, rolling down his window, staring at the feast. Was he thinking the same thing? Evelina stepped on the gas, knowing they'd better get to Manzanillo before the evening fell upon them.

In Manzanillo, topless throngs saw out the end of the day on the roadside beaches, soaking in the shallow froth of the waves. Evelina thought of the many fates her life could have followed. The shy breaking of waves reverberated like an elegiac sorrow through her Looking away, she saw a string of green streetlights and palm trees all down the coastal avenue. She veered into the inland depths of the city, through its steep one-way roads, past Terraplena and Valle Paraíso, up to the neighborhoods of Chandiablo and La Huisachera. They arrived at the lot where she bought her Impala with Fulgor, where, in the cooling heat of the cracked asphalt, they examined the rows of stolen cars, and traded the Impala and the Cheyenne pickup for an ample red Wagoneer with wooden trims on its doors. Evelina's stomach sank, but yet again, she had to go through with it, relenting, come what may. As she finished unpacking her Impala, she knew the dream hadn't lasted long enough, and, before turning away, she caught her own reflection in its windows, her new appearance. She almost didn't recognize herself, with her hair dyed jet-black, the glass on the window distorting her figure into something spectral and transitory. In a flash, she withdrew from this dark haunt of herself.

From the favela-like hills of La Huisachera, they stared over Manzanillo's city lights, over the black depths of the Pacific beyond, over the ever-darker silhouettes of the hills to either side. Tomatlán lay behind the invisible folds of hills to the east, no brushfire smoke in sight. Sharing a joint with Lázaro, Evelina thought she could read his thoughts. She read them on the creases of his skin, on the wrinkles around his eyes, on the uneven curl of his lip. Were they still in danger? Was there really someone after them, and closing in? Was burning everything down enough to keep them at bay, to make them forget? Somehow, she knew of the endurance of rancor and revenge, and finally wondered if their only option was the safe haven of anonymity, of identities lost, something like a burial and then a re-birth. Evelina also knew that in his eyes, Lázaro carried this vanished iteration of Macondo, whatever it meant to him, and that he now might realize that it wouldn't be as easy to just transport it down the road, as a state of mind. Moving the hair from his face with the back of her hand, she asked him, "Do you really think we still have something to fear?" He took a drag from his joint, a sight she'd seen so many times: on the terrace at the now fallen Hotel Regis, whose crumbling he had somehow managed to evade, and in the groves of his Macondo, the light of the joint flaring against the blue walls of their house. After fully exhaling the smoke, he replied, "I'd just like to know if someone is after us, and if so, who they are." Then Aureliano yelled for attention from his seat in the new Wagoneer, but before she could get up and go to him, Lázaro placed a hand over her knee. "We have to find some place to go, Evelina. We can't just keep driving, it's like heading towards a cliff." Evelina moved his hand away, went to Aureliano, took him in her arms, and felt the pain in her nipples as her son snuggled against her chest. Looking down at his face, taking in the sweet smell of his skin, she thought about how far she had come and how much had happened since she had run away from Sunfair with Rose. Living in the Hotel

Regis, negotiating with drug dealers. Living on a fruit farm in the countryside, adrift from friends and family. She had a child now, a boy named Aureliano, who on good days felt like the purest form of abandon, and who on the worst days felt like an anchor and a verdict. She was in a foreign country, where armed men and cartels were threatening her young family. She realized she was in over her head, and that they desperately needed to find an escape, some way to start again.

The following morning, after a long night in the only nameless motel in La Huisachera, they drove further inland towards the state's capital city. It had become clear that Rosendo had overheard their conversation, and it was his idea to take that route. He had even insisted on sitting behind the wheel to direct them there. He knew of a place not far from the city, a place they could purchase on the cheap: he was from around those parts, and knew its workings inside out. "Tomatlán, patrón," he told Lázaro, whose arm hung out the passenger window. "A dry piece of shit. No es más que un infiernillo. Imagine land fertile like a woman's womb." Evelina internally scoffed at this, but Lázaro seemed immediately sold. "It's like heaven, I promise," Rosendo added, "just don't pay much attention to its name."

In a layover motel, Evelina stared from the balcony at a volcano in the distance, its pyramidal rise, a sight she was sure Rose would love, but that felt like a bad omen to her. She argued with Lázaro angrily, and felt she was already facing a dead end, as much actual as argumentative. Her opinions about their family's future were dissolving into the morning mist at the foot of the volcano. She couldn't do much other than to agree to this new life in Comala, knowing the integrity of the fantasy had been forsaken, and that this new life wouldn't be much different from all her lives past, this withdrawal from the ocean to an emotional inland maze. The one condition she demanded was really starting anew, in the full sense of the word, really becoming someone else. If someone was after Lázaro and Evelina, they would really have to look to find them, have eyes set in the present as much as in the past.

At the Registro Civil office, Rosendo scheduled them a private appointment with a notary and clerk. In an office full of black-and-white diplomas hanging on the walls, they chose their new names: Evelina was no longer Evelina, she had become—to her uncontrollable relish—Édipa Más, her name stamped officially with an exaggerated snap. Lázaro followed Evelina's lead, inebriated somehow by this literary flourish, seduced by her chosen surname, finding comfort in its suggestion of vastness and ambition. He accepted his son's maiden name for his, also: "Aureliano Más Primero," he said proudly, his Macondo now alive within him. The clerk shrugged and asked, "*One Hundred Years of Solitude*? Won't be a favorite around these parts. You're sure you don't want to change it to Pedro?" But Lázaro shook his head, certain. Baby Aureliano was at last officially registered, an acknowledged human being: Aureliano Más Segundo, born of Comala, one more person to live among the town's ghosts. To get their new documents, they had to slip la mordida: this country's much obliged and invaluable bribe. After counting the bills, the clerk served up glasses of his top-shelf tequila, and offered a toast for a new life.

The excitement faded, as did the vibrant effect of the tequila, which had rushed quickly to their heads on empty stomachs. They drove past the newly painted, glaring-white walls of Comala's plaza, and ran onto yet another stretch of federal road. "Not far from here," Rosendo said, speeding down narrow alleys, clearly knowing his way around. He had already agreed to the purchase of a coffee farm with Lázaro—Aureliano Más the First, rather—who smiled mindlessly while looking out the passenger window at the eerie pines and Fresno trees, at people with immortal faces walking on the side of the road. The sun had stopped shining through their windows, and the car was struggling uphill, whining with every shift of the gears. Evelina—no, Édipa Más—grew queasy as they turned onto yet another dirt road: "Here is elsewhere," the phrase ran serendipitously in her mind as she patted baby Aureliano's back, trying to express a burp from him. "Here we are, patrón," Rosendo said. "Rancho Los Confines." He swerved onto a gravel path, which crunched dreadfully under the Wagoneer's wheels. Édipa thought it was strangely dark for the time of day, and when she looked at the dashboard's clock, she realized it had stopped. In the driveway, a tall leafless tree loomed over what seemed like an abandoned house. Before getting out, she put on her blazer, the rattle pin tender on her breast, and wrapped baby Aureliano in a blanket. Outside, the wind said "Ahhh" through the empty branches of the tree. "There is no life here," added the rustling leaves of the coffee shrubs in the hills. "Here you'll be alone," wheezed the Fresno leaves beyond them. "Don't," added a final sweep of high wind.

Édipa wandered the forest while the men unpacked. Time seemed to be running in odd directions. Or was it only the weather? A midday darkness dissipated to glaring sunshine parting behind the volcano's swell, and then to a passing sheet of rain. She pictured this water pouring over the ashes she left behind in Tomatlán, sizzling on the ground like meat cooking in a pan, washing over the hot soil, quieting it at last. Then she envisioned that dry ground becoming as fertile as the ground she stepped on here, the growth of a new and greener thicket over what used to be the fields and groves, covering every trace Evelina and Lázaro had left behind. Dots of rainwater began to soak on her blazer, but in a flash the rain stopped. A weaker sun poured over her new home and shone grimly on the rattle pin on her lapel. The hours, she thought, seemed to fade onto the last like a melting goop.

A pack of zopilotes, blackened against the sunset, drew perfect circles in the sky—swinging the wheel of time back, to a past that bore no thresholds, that felt more like a trap. It was as if she had landed back in Sunfair, forever pulled along by a magnet. Walking down the hill, she thought of how this place held no difference between the different iterations of her past, and from the wet, sun-stricken grass rose the steam of remembrance: her father sleeping in the moonlit sand; the lack of stars; the indigo-blue light around the full moon; the first sight of that rattlesnake under its opaque glow. Again, she felt so far from the ocean. Had the time come to sit back in acceptance? Should she just learn to live among her ghosts?

That night, over blankets and sleeping bags in front of a tame fire in the chimney, it was as if he had been infused with life: he had just learned that monarch butterflies wintered in the area, perching high in the trees above the coffee fields; he had seen them while picking coffee berries earlier that afternoon—oh, how quickly he had forgotten the fruit groves in favor of his coffee. To him it was a new beginning, to her it was a step backward, all the while she couldn't quite grow accustomed to their new names. Who would've thought, Édipa Más at last, but it wasn't quite sticking as she once thought it would. She missed her Impala, the lonesome drives along the coastline road, let alone Hotel Regis and Mexico City. The knowledge crept upon her, that a feeling of deep identification comes with action, embodiment, and not merely the abstraction of a name. Lying face up beside her, he spoke of chance, but also of fate, of his escape from death at Hotel Regis. "Places are not only places, they are also a state of mind," he repeated as if he were a toy that couldn't manage more than three programmed sentences, but she couldn't quite disagree with what he said. Other than Mexico City, she had known only two other states of mind, one oceanic, one desert-like, both unforgiving. Why couldn't they go back to the city, the only place she felt free of both? She didn't say a word, though, for he wouldn't listen; he was conversing only with himself. "Just imagine," he said. "Sativa under the coffee's shade, the chance to put things right." Slowly, he crept up on her, kissing her mouth, while her mind shifted seamlessly back to the stone floor of the Hotel Regis terrace, now reduced to rubble. What she didn't feel was the tingling spark throughout her body she had felt then. She couldn't bear the thought of another child, one that would arrive and double the pain, double the promise of abandonment. Once was pain enough. His kisses ran down her neck, but she could no longer take the pressure of his body on her breasts. She pushed him away. He watched her wrap her naked body in a blanket and walk out to the yard, where she glistened under the lively light of the moon. Outside, as the mountain cold blew through her black hair, she exercised self-restraint: oh, how she wanted to shout at the past and push it behind her.

She tossed seeds over the grass, some over the gravel; she made bird sounds; she wanted them to come live in that empty tree.

Rose visited once they made the house habitable, when there were beds in every bedroom, when the roasters were fuming and it seemed like they had been coffee people for years. Rose got to hold her godson in her arms again, but there was a sense of déjà vu, of her arriving solely to talk more about business than to see family. She also came dragging two suitcases full of cash, a sign that their alleged final round of investment had yielded the returns up every brick of the pyramid. As Rosendo prepared mugs of their local Oro Negro roast, Rose guffawed when she learned of their new names. "Aureliano Más Primero," she cackled, and shot Édipa Más a loaded but endearing sideways glance. "Should I be getting re-christened too?" she added, "If I'm following your logic, I should be in trouble as well." Then they went on a walk through the coffee bushes in the hills, which shone under the midday sun, where Rosendo shoved open the branches with red berries on them to reveal the first sativa stalks already protruding from the ground. "So, I'm thinking this means you're giving it another go," Rose said, and the sole utterance of her words shot sparks of rage up and down Édipa Más's body. She tossed her coffee over the grass and stormed down to the house.

Rose suggested they go for a walk, put some distance between themselves and the coffee farm. Baby Aureliano cooed in Rose's clutch, while she kept her sight on the volcano in the distance. "How Malcolm Lowry is this?" Rose asked, clearly trying to perk up her step-sister's gloom, surely realizing rather how Juan Rulfo the setting was. They greeted people who walked past on the road with emphatic nods, while Rose persisted at trying to alter Édipa's mood. "Comala," Rose said, "I thought only ghosts lived here. But I guess people also do." Her words drew no response, and they kept going until they found a roadside cantina, La Eterna de Comala, where they sat to have a beer. The place was empty save for a bartender with his chin in his hand, elbow over the wooden bar, still as a statue, and a server pacing in and out of the kitchen. When they had their cans of Carta Blanca open in front of them, baby Aureliano unblinking in her lap, Rose said, "Sister." She paused, laughed. "I don't even know what name to call you anymore." She paused again and again received no response, no help as it were, no signals of preference: Evelina? Édipa? Sister seemed just fine. "That man of yours, he escaped through a fine crack. He could be six feet in the ground by now, but he doesn't realize his luck. I will be leaving here soon, and sometimes I wish I could drag you with me again." Rose directed her gaze down at baby Aureliano, bounced him on her lap. Even though he was only on Leche Nido formula, he was gaining the weight of a ship's anchor. "We played with fire and it was fun. But the danger is real. It was a gamble, and now I'll be collecting all my chips. You have to think long and hard about what you're going to do, because that man of yours is mad." They gulped their beers until the cans were empty; meanwhile, the bartender hadn't moved an inch. When they left La Eterna de Comala, lightning branched down from the distant clouds, brightening the foot of the volcano. Dust lifted from the road in swirls and Édipa Más flung herself into Rose's arms. Rose shifted Aureliano to her side with a swift movement, and hugged Édipa tight. Deep in her embrace, she could feel her shiver, cry out in pain. "What's wrong?" Rose asked, and Édipa told her it was her breasts. The road was deserted save for two other women carrying buckets full of coffee berries. They let them turn a corner before Édipa showed Rose her breasts. She flung open her lapels and unbuttoned the same blue shirt she got in Guadalajara with Rose. Her nipples were purple and full of scabs, causing Rose to take a step back. "What happened?" she asked, her best attempt at a steady voice. Édipa eyed her son. "He did it," she said, and slowly buttoned up her shirt. "First thing tomorrow," Rose said, "we're going to the doctor." They both nodded in agreement and resumed their walk.

When they turned the corner, the women who had overtaken them had already vanished down the road.

Her breast infection required surgery: thus was the dimension of the harm inflicted by her own son. She had chosen Rose to take her to the surgery, leaving Aureliano to be looked after by his father. "Más vale tarde que nunca," Rose said, and Édipa was forced to pick the size of her breast implants on the fly. She went for the smallest size she could get, and as she was being sedated before going into the surgical room, her grip weakening in Rose's hand, all she could think of were the vermillion tipped breasts of the neon siren on the bar sign in Thomas Pynchon's San Narciso, where the real Oedipa Maas walked into in fictional life.

The recovery happened slowly, with a whole lot of pain, not to mention worthwhile sedation. Rose bought her a television, which blasted sound and image day and night alike. During rare spells of relative strength, Édipa walked to the yard, tossed seeds onto the grass, but the windstorms kept blowing them away. Rose bought her bird feeders, too, and Édipa loved watching the flimsy creatures through the window, picking at the seeds. I'd love to become a crow, a cardinal, a zopilote, even, she thought with a dulled sense of pride, to do away with it all, in a flash, a leap, and a spread of the wings.

When the pills ran out, the drinking started, of the heavy variety, a real coming of age, she thought, a weak excuse she made for herself, for it numbed more than just the pain. The overblown sweetness and subdued sting of a tequila sour grew on her palate, and oh how easy it ran down the gullet. Through blurry eyes she saw how Aureliano went from weak arms to a strong crawl, and there was no longer an easy way to keep him in sight. The hearsay round the house, which wafted in like murmurs that pierced her daze, had it that the sativa had grown sturdy, that it was peeking out from the coffee bush, flowering and seeding. The day came for Rose to leave, as though existence, however lulled, had soared forward into what once seemed like a distant future. "I'm off," Rose said, lying beside Édipa on the purple couch. "I wish I could take you with me." She paused, and one of Aureliano's coos flew away in the air. "You have a son now, just look at him go." Édipa nodded and slugged a tequila sour, watched Aureliano scurry on the hardwood floor out of sight. "I'm heading back north, to try and make a normal life for myself. I'm sorry I dragged you into this. But then again, sometimes I'm not. Maybe this is your fate." Édipa followed her to the gate, weak, walking in a melancholic mood upon the gravel, and said, "This is no different of a trap from the ones I previously knew." Holding on to the dry branch of the tree in the driveway, she saw Rose's taxi arrive before adding, "Sooner or later, I'll find a way out." The dirt road was dry, unstable. Rose waved behind the window, but was soon lost in a cloud of dust rising from the slow turning of the wheels.

She did not like complete silence, and there were no roaring waves here. The rumors had it there were only ghostly murmurs. She kept the television blaring night and day to keep them quiet.

Baby Aureliano was asleep for once, and Aureliano Más the First had taken off with Rosendo in the Wagoneer, looking for more coffee land nearby. "If I'd only known," he had said before walking out the door. "We would've come here from day one, never set foot in

Tomatlán." It really wouldn't have mattered, though, since it was all a fluid loop—no before or after, everything overlapping and happening inevitably eventually—their demons would have chased them down. She wasn't sure if it was the tequila that gave her this clarity, but the thought gnawed at her, made her drink even more. On her television there was the Pedro Páramo movie adaptation on the local channel, in black and white, the one with John Gavin, which opens to credits accompanied by the melodramatic shrieks of a violin as Juan Preciado first enters Comala. Watching the scene, she thought nothing here appeared as dry and as forlorn as the images on the screen, which looked rather more like Sunfair's reddish sand. The one resemblance she did find was that of Rosendo to the buckaroo battered by the dust storm. Lifting herself from the purple couch to mix another tequila sour with the remaining honey and juiced lime, she spotted a bird landing on her feeders behind the window. It had a good look at her, but then flew off due to the clinking sound of the gates. Slowly, she went outside, as though she were expecting this scene before she opened the door to the house and faced it. Three men leaned on the gates, dressed in denim and cowboy hats. As she approached, she fought off a sarcastic laugh. She wanted to say—"Ándese con cuidado, viborita, is that it?"—and couldn't help but feel a wry smile teasing the edges of her mouth. "Qué pasa aquí?" she said, theatrically. "You're not here to toss a snake into the premises, are you? Not here to walk into the fields? Point your guns at me?" She went all the way up to the men, and could smell how they reeked of a hard day's work. The men chuckled in return, entertained, apparently, by her boldness. The one standing in the middle held her gaze with a wild smile, then said, "Nothing like that, chiquilla. Is there someone here in charge we can talk to?" Édipa gave them yet another laugh. The alcohol had added a layer to her bluff. "La patrona aquí soy yo," she said. "The boss here is me," and laughed again, both sarcastic and wholeheartedly. "What is it you might want?" Even though her eyes didn't catch the full subtleties of his gesture, she could tell the man in the middle was losing his patience. "We are here to offer you protection," he said, "on behalf of the Guadalajara Cartel. Coffee is it that you grow here? We love a good mug, especially if it comes from our very hills. We will come collecting derecho de piso, and once you pay it, you will have nothing to fear. So, you better tell the real patrón what I've just told you." She nodded, still smiling, shot her eyes at the gravel beneath her, resisting the raging impulse to respond candidly. She let the men tip their hats goodbye and flash a smile of studded gold teeth before walking away. She stayed in the yard for some time, running her hands over the rugged bark of the leafless tree. Nothing came as a surprise; they were already in someone else's hands. This was the kind of thing that kept happening in Mexico, she thought, the moment you tricked yourself into thinking that this country could be your home. She went back inside, let her body fall upon the couch. The terror of the men's proposition—the same terror she felt in Tomatlán after the menacing headlights that lingered in the driveway overnight, after the men stormed their fields, of having the cartel on their doorstep again—only coalesced after a nap, after the alcohol had run thin in her veins, after a demanding wail of her son from the crib, after those violin shrieks of the movie on the television quieted and faded to a black screen that read "The End."

This time there were no demijohns, there was no Doña Meme, not the half-liberating, half-deceitful coastal drive in a black convertible Impala. There was only a walk along the dirt road, a purchase of high proof mezcal and tequila at La Eterna de Comala, their emptying over the coffee bushes and what they hid underneath. It was all clear in her mind before she felt the friction of the match against the sandpaper strip: the Comala wind blowing just like the Santa Ana winds, a down-whipping swoop from the volcano. She foresaw it, neat and clear: the hiss of a burning match, the rushing, vanishing smoke, the sweetness of its smell. The viscous sway of the flame, its elusive dance, how it would catch on it all, on the blades of grass, on the dry leaves, how it would turn the wind's whisper into a roar. Would Rancho Los Confines burn as wildly as Rancho El Comal? She was about to find out. She turned to confirm that baby Aureliano was still in his playpen, and took the match from the box. After a second's quiet, though, during a moment's hesitation, she heard footsteps behind her, thumping, quickening and loud: she felt a body on hers, tackling her, her face cold against the blades of grass.

When she came to her senses, she was tied to the leafless tree in the yard, her arms pinched beneath countless laps of rope wrapped around its trunk. "It was you, in Tomatlán, was it not?" Rosendo's voice came to her from somewhere behind the tree. She tried to shake the rope around her loose, but couldn't move an inch. "Where is my son?" she yelled through a high-pitched gush of wind. "Your son is fine, Evelina," Rosendo said, still out of sight, "but you—you're crazy—está usted loca de atar." She heard his footsteps quieting as he stepped from the gravel onto the noiseless grass. She sat there, the rope tight on her skin, surely leaving a mark, and time seemed to tease forward. How hard it was to tell time here, the thought revisited her, with the same sort of daylight on either end of the night. Surely the moment had to arrive, a moment filled with footsteps again, be it over gravel or over grass, someone there to set her free. But the ensuing suggestion of movement she felt was a slithering movement. From behind her, a rattlesnake swerved to her side, and despite the opaque glow of a cloud-weakened sun, she noticed that the glimmer of light upon its skin was the same the creature had boasted beneath the full moon of the Sunfair desert, and under the shimmer of the coastal sun in El Comal. Her heartbeat produced a matching rattle, and her blood pumped quickly, from head to toe. The snake shriveled into its coil, hissing and rattling. "Ándese con cuidado," Édipa muttered, but she could say no more—half the body of the snake flung and straightened. It struck so quick it was hard to imagine it had sunk its fangs so deep inside her. Her heartbeat seemed to move down her body and settled, heavily, on the puncture wounds above her ankle. The pain—so deep—circled with every cycle of her blood. How poignant, she thought, that after it had bit her, the snake recoiled into that maelstrom again, both Comala's and hers. She felt herself screaming, so eerie and cold, that Rosendo rushed back to her, heard him say the good old adage, "Ya nos cargó la chingada," and with a single swing of his machete, beheaded the snake. The body, headless, swiveled for several minutes, and Édipa felt the venom coursing inside her, until the reptile's final nerves arrived at stillness. Her eyesight blurring, the air swift and lacking in her lungs, Édipa knew one thing for certain: the pattern had finally been broken: the snake was dead, and she could be too. She felt this subjective reality like a coming darkness, lowering like the black curtain of a night with no moon.

Two nights and two days of gasping for air, of dipping her toes in the sea of the dead, which felt more like quicksand, of waking from dreams skewed by the anti-venom in her blood. In her dreams, she was bitten by the snake in the Sunfair desert, during the fated night of her escape. In those dreams, Rose left her there to perish, and had fled to Mexico by herself. She recovered from the snake bite in the dream, too, as much as in real life, if she could call it that. But in the dream, after her recovery, there had been no sativa, no Impala, no Édipa Más or her long black hair. There was no Mexico at all, and what pained her the most, deep within the well of her womb, was that there was no baby Aureliano either. The pain was so deep that she cried on the ride home from the hospital. With Rosendo's help she got out of the Wagoneer to find the house painted Tomatlán blue, freshly gleaming, even though the town was meant to be all white. She barely had the strength to shake her head, but she did,

141

with all the vehemence she could muster. Past the front door of the house, the snake's head had been dried and stuffed, preserved upon the mantle, the skin spread open and framed, its scales clear, trapped between two sheets of glass, like she needed a reminder that it was the snake who had perished while she lived to tell the tale. But her eyes didn't linger there at all, rather they turned in the direction of her son, who crawled to her over the hardwood floor. She spent three more days with him, holding him close, asking him, "Weren't you the one boundary to the future?" In a way he had been, she could read it in his darting, quizzical eyes, but now an opening to the future had slid wide; the dead body of the snake was proof enough of the fracture in the circle. As she sang to her child in the yard, on that final day, they withstood a passing sheet of strong rainfall, but when the clouds cleared, the remaining light of day burned an ember-orange above the volcano, as if a wildfire was raging behind them. Evelina brought her lips to her son's ears, and whispered one last Comala whisper: "One day I'll come back for you, come what may."

Rose once told her about the concept of Eternal Recurrence: the idea that we live our lives endlessly, exactly the same way, over and over again. She couldn't tell if it was this Nietzschean doom that gave her the courage. What she did know, is that she could not bear an eternity in Comala. She went through with it again—she fled, an empty vessel, now or never, nowever—this time alone. A taxi picked her up at the gate of Los Confines, and as it veered onto the federal road, she had the feeling of traveling in the opposite direction, as if rather than moving away from him she was going straight to her son, a feeling so strong that in every car heading for Comala, she saw herself behind the wheel. She had a final look over her shoulder: there it was, retreating, Comala's singular conflation between the past and the present.

BOOK III

Schrödinger's Cat

2017

THE RED-EYE ADO COACH TO COMALA IS COZIER THAN it first seemed. As it glides through the night, humming along the federal road, I seem to myself suspended, partially nonexistent— life's impostor. If only I could stay on this bus forever, have it drive down an endless road, leaving me simply and idly *here*, with nowhere to land, in the illusory, circular despair of a hangover, awaiting reso- lution and the better feelings that may come with it—then I'd never have to confront the loss of my mother, let alone finish my novel.

After a final rise and fall of the road, though, the bus slows with the rumble of low gears, pulling into the station with an abrupt turn. It comes to a full stop before the illuminated terminal, where the brakes exhale and the vibrating engine dies.

The blue clock by the driver's seat beams 6:00 AM right in my eyes, and then the lights inside the cabin erupt, a bright white, prompting passengers to shuffle down the aisle through air thick with morning breath, grabbing for handbags and boxes, as a curtain of body-heat breaks over me. I've arrived to the town of the dead, where a few feeble lights glitter across the mountainous terrain—the place I've never yearned for, the place my mother fled from, but also the hot- bed of my repression, as I imagine it, not a little self-consciously.

At the coffee stand in the station everything reeks of the past, of stale bread and honey, while the already abandoned tabloids spread open over the tables remind me I'm still in the midst of this country's contemporary wave of violence: VIVOS SE LOS LLEVARON, VIVOS LOS QUEREMOS: PARENTS OF THE 43 STUDENTS MEET WITH THE PRESIDENT AT LOS PINOS.

Flipping through the tabloid, it seems as though the ad on the back not only refers to my own situation, but rather full-on mocks me: BUSCA A TUS DESAPARECIDOS—IF YOUR LOVED ONE HAS GONE MISSING IN COMALA, DIAL 111-ALERTA AMBER.

Up a few blocks there's more of the tug of war between past and present—OXXO, Miscelánea, Pizza Hut, Estética Alicia, Fedex, Registro Cívil, Convento San Miguel de la Mora—as early light peeks behind the hills as I arrive at the town's all-white plaza, its ancient church so white it looks like a cake overwhelmed by icing. In front of the church, I hop into a taxi, and, after a minor jam around the plaza, traffic eases through the bends and ravines on the outskirts of town. Observing the hills as the day brightens further, an overwhelming conflation of distance, rolling and unraveling, sweeps through me, and I find myself testing the sight against my memory.

The taxi turns onto a dirt road, where a woman pushing a wheelbarrow full of animal bones crosses in front of the car without looking, as if it wasn't there. Right behind her, under the early morning sunlight, lies a cemetery of brass and wooden crosses.

In the final stretch towards Los Confines, my mind flashes back to our last goodbye—my father's and mine—which repeats on loop as I head to the doorway that I promised myself I'd never darken—how after a stiff embrace he sat and watched me go, stoic, unmoved, as if I would return come dark. The descending sun struck one side of his face beneath his sombrero, butterflies dancing around him, while in the backdrop, the tips of the volcanoes were capped with snow and towered over a low embankment of clouds.

As the taxi judders slowly over the dirt, engulfing us in the type of dust cloud that rises all over this country, across all time, Los Confines transforms from someplace in my mind from the past, to the thing itself: the rows of coffee shrubs bifurcating the green hills, the leaves the same tint as the silhouetted mountains in the distance, the ground boasting the yellowish tinge of ripe corn. Behind it all, El Volcán de Colima rises precipitously and jagged, like a figurine carved from wood.

Then the "Tomatlán blue" walls, as Rose would put it, peek from behind a line of pine trees.

"Stop here," I tell the driver, handing him the fifty-peso bill over his shoulder. I wait for the dust to settle, and descend to the smell of wet grass, charred oak, roasting coffee beans, and car exhaust.

Reaching the property's gates, I spot the empty bird feeders outside the kitchen window, the Noguchi lamps lined along the roof over the patio, the old Wagoneer parked in the gravel driveway—a car as old as myself. If only my mother could materialize, like Rulfo rather than Rose could write her up. In my mind, I try to script the moment, searching for an exact image of her face, an image informed by Rose's writing, the one visual narrative I built as I read. The image appears at first, whole and recognizable—the black hair, the slender body—but when I try to retain it in my mind, it blurs, floats away like the crows singing "caw caw caw" in the actual sky above me.

The slightest push makes the gates shriek, and I step onto the gravel pathway leading to the front of the house, to its blue walls faded with the cracks of time, strings of moss nibbling at them. In the yard, there's the leafless tree—leafless still—where my mother was tied to, bitten by the snake.

Stepping inside the house, I expect an onslaught of emotion, but the wide living room with stained and sagging purple couches, torn and faded Colombian fique rugs, old coffee equipment, and the framed rattlesnake, all fail to deliver. Had I expected to encounter pictures of our family hanging on the wall, of her, framed like the rattlesnake, to magically appear since I last visited? The truth is there are no preserved artifacts other than the snake skin for me to weave into the present, to match with everything else Rose wrote. A pang of longing stabs into me. "*Snake Skin*," read the title of Rose's failed novel, "*Brief Passages in the Life of Édipa Más*," and here I am, face-to-face not with my mother, but with the skin shed when she left. The regret hangs in the air like Mexico City smog, and the nostalgia it inspires in me, causes me to drop my bag on the hardwood floor and run a finger under the snake's fangs. There rises the sound of footsteps, growing louder, footsteps paired to the sudden and deep beat of my heart.

My father emerges from the hall, his once scrawny figure only slightly thickened in the mid-section, his steps heavy and awkward like a bison's wide stride, feet pointing out diagonally, at *ten-and-two*, he'd say, the light tremor of his arm still present, no matter how hard he tries to shake it off. His morning bathrobe is his cleanest piece of clothing, his jeans underneath smudged with dirt, his silver hair is poorly combed, leaving a few rebellious strands to successfully defy cheap Xiomara hair gel, his thick white beard jutting from his jaw.

"I wouldn't play with those fangs if I were you." He points at the head of the stuffed snake. "People around here would swear it could come back to life and bite you."

The comment, trite as it is, has me removing my fingers immediately.

"Aureliano." He stops some feet away from me, setting off a twitching of my left eye. "Why are you here?"

I came to Comala because my mother won't come back, is what I want to say, *because here I might hear her better*, but the panic has me zoning out, leaving me unable to speak, which elevates the background noises—the shy meow of a cat, voices on the road, the news on TV in the next room—all sounds I would normally filter out, merging but at the same time quite unique.

"Alone as you always are," he says dryly, stroking his beard. "Here I was thinking next time you visited you might have a better half."

Staring at him, I try to take his comments as a reflection of his own loneliness, but also find myself surprised at how he hasn't seemed to have aged during the years that I've been gone.

"Cat got your tongue there, kid?" He squints, but all I can do is look past him, to more empty walls throughout the house.

Has every trace of my mother really been removed? Every trace of me?

"Have you nowhere else to go, is that why you're here?"

"Something along those lines."

He lowers his gaze, peers deep. "Alone and with nowhere else to go." He turns his back to me, following the noise of the TV in the kitchen.

"Sounds familiar, right?"

He turns toward me, and takes a few steps forward, surprised, perhaps, at how quickly this escalated. "Say that again?"

"We're both alone."

He shakes his head and points to my bag. "Get your shit, you can stay in the bungalow for now. You look beat." He turns and starts walking again.

After picking up my bag and catching up with him, he leads me toward the back of the house and out onto the vast yard, where the first monarch butterflies of the season alight in the coffee fields. He points to the bungalow: a small adobe building at the foot of the hills.

"Straight ahead." He taps my shoulder, his most daring show of affection yet.

Even after I've unpacked, the bungalow still feels as grimly minimalist as my fellowship studio back in Mexico City—the splintered wood floor, the desk with the sallow copy of *Pedro Páramo*, the crumple my red ink-stained manuscript has become, now joined together with Rose's novel. There's also a hard mattress on the floor, yet another invitation for uncomfortable idleness under Comala's baking midday heat. The sleep I drift into throughout the day would be an oceanic calm, *oceanic* only in the sense of luminous creatures bobbing around in its black depths: Rose, Nayeli, Chris, and my mother—all of them knocking against my sleep.

Hours past midnight I wake in a puddle of cooled sweat. The moonlight catches the drapes so eerie and melodramatically that I almost groan at the sardonic workings of this setting.

I step outside to the moonrise, a hoary glimmer behind the coffee-lined hills. As I head to the blue house, the wind is high in the leaves and the grassy yard is luminous with dew.

In the living room, a fire is glowing in the chimney. Everything is so still I nearly expect a crow to tap the glass, but the only sound is the charged shifting and snapping of the coals, so I walk from one pool of light to the next, down the hall, over the fique rug, as far as my father's bedroom, where the door is open enough for me to look in and see him asleep, one hand over his stomach, his snore battling the roar of the fireplace in his room, whose light flickers over more empty walls. Fleeting images of either a distant past or culled from Rose's novelistic scenes slice through me: my mother sitting upon the purple couch with a tequila sour, my mother lighting a match for the chimney.

The visions shatter with one of my father's wild snores, and I enter his room. The slight wave of heat from his chimney intensifies once I'm inside, heat that becomes unbearably tropical once I'm tip-toeing to the walk-in closet, where hangers with only a few clothes are lined against the back wall. At the very end of the closet, I find one of the few things she left behind, a dressing table with a mirror triptych above it. Sitting on the stool in front of the table, I encounter endless images of myself in the apparent infinity: endless ghostly me's. Suddenly startled by this treacherous vision, I turn away and head out, running my hand through the clothes lined on hooks. As I'm about to reach the door, my hand comes to a cold and heavy object on the fabric, which upon closer consideration appears to be my mother's rattlesnake pin. I'm tempted to flip on the lights to scrutinize it, but merely running my fingertip over it makes me relieve the coat from the hook, and fling it over my shoulders before stepping out.

Back in the cooler air of the living room, the crackling of the coal is fainter now, but the smell of burnt wood filters through me with yearning, as if she was still here like a sort of smoky matter, caught in the air, drifting into every corner, adopting the shape of every room.

In the kitchen, the walls are struck by the flickering light of the muted TV, where the late-night news rerun has an anchor pointing to a graphic that charts the rising number of forced disappearances.

I look through the cupboards to find my father's bottle of tequila, and steal a long gulp from it, hoping it can help me get some uninterrupted sleep.

Leaving through the kitchen door, nothing reminds me of anything—not the empty bird feeders, not the gliding clouds, not the moonlit flanks of the volcanoes, not even what might be the beak of a bird tapping the kitchen window. I head to the bungalow, my mother's blazer warm upon my shoulders. Above the coffee hills, a silver moon is rising through powdery clouds, and in my mind, I'm replaying the words from Rose's manuscript: *"One day I'll come back for you, come what may."*

Come morning, I realize the bungalow is impersonally equipped for the rare overnight guest, for ghosts like Juan Preciado or myself, searching in Comala for their kin, a room that could well be Eduviges Diada's home—she who hosts the fictional dead in Juan Rulfo's novel—with old folded towels, crusty blankets, and no water to drink. There's not much in the kitchenette either—grinders, coffee-makers, and mounds of locally sourced coffee beans that you'd expect are nowhere to be found. What I do spot, with its metallic red glare over the counter, is a Nespresso machine, and a few capsules of vacuum-sealed coffee sourced from the real coffee capitals of the world. Pressing the buttons on the machine, I get them to wink a vibrant green and make myself a doubled dose of pseudo-fresh Colombian coffee, cursing myself for not bringing a few quarts of bourbon with me.

Once I'm finished with my coffee, I head straight to the blue house, again, parting the film of dew over the grass, and entering to the smell of last night's burned coals.

Following the sound of the TV into the kitchen, I find a basket of pan de muerto sitting on the counter, and dive straight into it. The news draws my attention while I gnaw on the sugar-coated bread. The screen shows images of dead bodies covered by plastic tarps—smears of dry blood across the ground, forensics dressed in fluorescent yellow suits, a ravine with a string of smoke coming from it—where more bodies were allegedly incinerated. A camera-cut is followed by a zoom-in at the mass grave where the dead bodies, some of them dismembered, were found. The shot then shifts to the newsroom, where the same anchor as last night walks onto a virtual blue set. A graphic appears beside him, where he points to the staggering number of deaths claimed by the drug war, the sense of déjà vu strong, the numbers winking an alarming red while he openly pleads with the Mexican government, demanding extreme measures to save the struggling people of Mexico, to legalize drugs, to sign a treaty with the cartels as it had done in the past, to ensure safety for innocent civilians.

The volume then decreases, the green bar on the bottom of the screen showing less color until the sound dies off. I turn to find that my father has snuck in and has the remote in hand.

"Why are you watching this shit?" He walks to his own silver Nespresso machine and fixes himself a Lungo with mechanically frothed milk. "It's like watching those snuff films."

"TV was on."

"TV is always on, one of the few things that rubbed off from your mother." He lifts his cup to sip his coffee, but stops to say, "That and the damned bird feeders."

The mention of her sets off a throbbing in my chest. Through the window, no birds are picking at the seeds, which are slick and black with rot. I reach for a second pan de muerto, and as I bring the pastry to my mouth, sugar falls onto my lap.

My father looks at me. "Take it easy with the bread, you'll be having breakfast with the coffee pickers in a while."

I stare at him wide-eyed, bread in hand. "With the pickers?"

"If you'll sleep and eat here, you'll have to work here, too. You'll pick coffee and make yourself useful." He turns to the muted TV now filled with scenes of the parents of the forty-three murdered students, the one story that, now that the loss and aftermath of the earthquakes are in the relative past, continues to gather momentum, challenging the country's cycle of injustice.

Putting the bitten pan de muerto back in the basket, I say, "It's horrible how all these people just disappear, from one day to the next." Sensible enough for small talk, but really searching for a shortcut to talk about my mother, her own disappearance, about the drug scheme, perhaps, that put her in danger, and ultimately drove her away.

"Innocence is a tricky thing in this country," he says.

"But just imagine," I cut in, dismissing his failure to understand the systemic structural injustice behind the war on drugs. "Try to empathize, and imagine waiting for your mother, or whoever, to come home, and yet never seeing them again."

Another gap of silence comes between us, during which the anchor's mouth rambles on without sound. A heavy current of wind wheezes past outside, rattling trees, shrubbery, Noguchi lamps alike. My father spoons sugar out of a plastic bag and drowns it beneath the foam of his coffee, then dilutes it with a circling motion, making a whirlpool—a Comala maelstrom, Rose would say—of the waning foam.

"I don't know anything about your mother, if that's what you're getting at." He sips his coffee, then adds a bit more sugar, his moustache as coated with brown foam as Chris's used to be. "She could be dead or alive, and all I know is that she isn't coming back, that's clear now. I have no more answers, if that's what you came seeking. She was always on the run, your mother, and she was good at leaving no traces behind."

Trying to shake images of both Chris's daydream and Rose's failed novel from my head, I look away from my father's moustache and back at the TV. "How have you arrived at closure if you don't even know what happened to her?"

"You should treat it as if she were dead, kid. That way, if she ever comes back, it'll be like having someone return from death. Nothing can beat that, I'm sure."

"Yeah, very fitting for a place like Comala," I say, to no response, my eyes now pinned on pictures on the screen of people in different scenarios, people who haven't been accounted for and could be dead, people whose return is prayed for by all of those left alive.

I'm the first to arrive to the communal kitchen where the coffee pickers have their meals. Located next to the coffee roasters and drying beds, continuously infiltrated by the sweet smoke of toasted beans, the space is vast, the ceilings high, the walls covered by patterned ceramic tiles. It has an old brick oven tucked into the back wall, and a hot griddle where a stocky chef and a thinner, younger prep cook perform the tasks, both with braided black hair and dressed in white woven tunics. They offer, "Buenos días," and give me a slow nod.

I sit at a large wooden table in the middle of the room and catch a faint muttering outside, probably the coffee pickers arriving.

The younger woman hands me a coffee in a ceramic mug, a sweet and watery drink they call café de olla, of which I pretend to take swigs from as a sign of gratitude. They check on me as I gulp it down, all the while glancing at one another with unease, unable to choke down nervous laughter.

My silence makes the older cook come closer to me. "Señor, breakfast?"

I nod more times than I can count.

"Huevos rancheros," she says, and gets to work on the griddle without waiting for my approval by cracking two eggshells with one hand and laying the eggs sunny-side up alongside two browning tortillas. Her prep cook chops tomato, onion, and habaneros over a wooden board.

Closing my eyes briefly, I sip my coffee, but then a high-pitched shriek makes me spill it over my chin.

"Be mindful, señor, culebra at your feet," the cook yells, pointing at the ground.

My heart pounding and my lips scalded, I look down, where a snake with kaleidoscopic green and yellow patterns on its back skids toward me from across the cement floor.

I'm on the table in one move, knocking over the rest of my coffee, the farthest from the snake as I can get without having to touch the floor. My vantage point frames the cook, who, having recovered from the initial scare, walks to the knife board and grabs the longest blade and a large wooden spoon. Images of Rosendo beheading the rattlesnake that bit my mother flash through my head, while the cook walks casually toward this one. I'm almost expecting her to say "*Ándese con cuidado, viborita,*" but she only laughs, turning to me at times, while the prep cook, also laughing, but covering her mouth with a cupped hand, takes over at the griddle.

The clamor has attracted the coffee pickers' attention, who now gather at the entrance to the kitchen, witnessing the spectacle, observing me like a circus attraction.

"Be mindful, señor," the cook repeats, "do not come down yet." She walks toward the snake with her weapons of choice, to where the snake has coiled around the leg of a chair and seems to perceive the cook's approach, elevating its head, awaiting an assault. The cook taunts it with the wooden spoon, which the snake thrusts at while the coffee pickers laugh and continue to stare, some of them with crossed arms, others reclining casually against the tiled walls, as though having placed bets in the tussle between human and beast. Although they could be laughing at my very evident lack of virility, directly contrasted to that of the chef's, who, facing the animal, watches it swirl its head around the wooden spoon, feinting her, before going in for the bite. Another flash of my mother comes to me, like a spasm in my viscera—her being tied up and facing such agile movements, defenseless, waiting for the venom to flow into her blood.

The following thrust has the snake biting hold of the wooden spoon, and once it has a steady grip, the cook descends the knife blade with the precision of a butcher, slicing through the hose-like body with a whack.

What seemed to be headed for an epic battle ends pathetically, blood spewing out and running along the cement floor, which prompts the chef to return to her station and rinse the blade under water. She then tosses my overcooked eggs into the trash and starts again. Just like Rose wrote, the remaining nerves in the body of the snake remain active, a slow wriggle, until—like after a final gasp—life escapes the animal.

Everything falls quiet for a few seconds, until hissing erupts within the crowd, and a man's voice comes in from the doorway—"A morir no hay huir."

The chef looks at the crowd, the browns of her eyes shifting.

"Should have let her go," says the man's voice once more. "Bad luck, it means, killing harmless snakes, expect that a mean one will come around soon."

"Harmless, you say?" the cook responds, clicking her tongue, delivering emphatic sarcasm with her question.

"Not a drop of venom in that garter."

The person voicing these words comes to the fore. It's Rosendo, not even slightly changed since I last saw him—his skin dark, his cheekbones sharp-angled, his moustache bushy and black, not fully covering his hostile lips. Parting through the crowd of pickers, he walks to the dead snake and picks it up with his machete, making it dangle like displayed jewelry from his blade.

"Next time *you* deal with it, snake-charmer that you are," the cook says, pointing at him with a knife, while keeping an eye on her second attempt at my huevos rancheros.

Hissing more laughter, Rosendo teases the prep cook with the body of the snake. She giggles and screams and runs away from him, causing more laughter from the rest of the pickers. When she is well away, Rosendo walks with the snake towards the door, the crowd parting for him again.

"What y'all looking at?" the cook tells the rest of the pickers. "Sit them asses down."

Like scolded children, the pickers walk toward the table, glancing up at me still standing on top.

Carefully, I skip to the floor and decide to eat my breakfast next to the hotline and the cook, leaving the pickers to their seats around the table.

"Pinche Rosendo, mister know-it-all," she says, turning to me while beating three dozen eggs in a large silver bowl. "One shouldn't take chances with bright-colored creatures. Brighter they are, the stronger the venom."

I feel myself nodding. "What's he done with it?" I ask, trying to reflect their dialect, pointing with my eyes at Rosendo, who has now claimed a seat at the head of the table.

"Laid it on a rock," she says, almost whispering, pouring the flood of whisked eggs over the griddle. "He'll skin it later. Shed skin is her soul; a new snake will grow into it."

I look at her, picturing the framed snake skin in my father's living room, and turn to the prep cook, giving away my skepticism but also seeking her complicity. She staves off my gaze, though, assuring me we are not in the least alike, and starts scrambling the eggs on the griddle with a large wooden spatula.

"Viborita esta," the cook says, "she'll be back and about."

"OK," I say, knowing I shouldn't roll my eyes, but surely rolling them in my mind, as I wipe the plate clean of runny yolks with a warm tortilla.

The cook clears my plate before I'm done and hands me a new coffee. "Cafécito, señor, so you're at it up there."

I accept the mug tentatively, already buzzing from my previous cups, wishing there was rye whiskey to pour into it, and bow in gratitude to both cooks, who can't contain a shy laugh, perhaps after witnessing my physical shortcomings, knowing what awaits me in the hills. I'm suddenly left wishing that I had learned the coffee trade better when I was younger, something I couldn't get my hands into when I was shipped off to live with Rose, and which turned me into a writer—if I can even call myself that.

Before leaving, I turn to the cook one last time. "Speaking of viboritas, did you know my mother? Do you know what happened to her?"

She lifts surprised eyebrows, clicks her tongue. Then, shaking her head, she turns her back on me. "No, nada. I've heard about her, but I don't know why she left."

I take my sweet coffee outside and feed it to the grass once I'm out of sight. Skipping over the rocks, I startle at the sight of the dead snake again, thinking it was another one, its ally or the same one returned, back from the dead, out to take revenge.

On a dry spot of grass, the snake's severed head stares up at me, as if in warning.

The rising slope of the hill seemed manageable until I'm halfway up. The altitude squeezes the air out of my lungs and the threaded basket attached to my back makes the climb all the more difficult. The heat surrounding us forms a haze that makes the volcanoes seem far away for a second, then as close as they really are. The rare gust of wind is a passing relief, cooling the sweat washing over my body, combing the leaves on every bush. Once the breeze passes, though, I can taste the minerals of new sweat oozing from my pores.

To add to the discomfort, the pickers seem disturbed by my presence—none of them acknowledge me, walking past and overtaking me, refusing to lock eyes with mine, brushing the coffee leaves aside and tugging on them to get their cherished fruit.

Scattered along the ground, there's a litter of green and red coffee berries, their bright colors making me warier of the ground, looking expectantly for a *gliding movement*, a coiled creature, the soul of the murdered snake after its executioners—*the brighter the color the stronger the venom*. With a cautious pace, I struggle uphill, while the rest of the pickers work faster than me, ahead of me, clearing the trees of the prized berries.

As I'm tugging on a new bush, my basket suddenly feels heavier. I turn to find Rosendo grabbing berries from my load, a wheat stalk arrowing from his lips.

"Uy no, estás chavo," he says. Then clicking his tongue and shaking his head, he opens his palm to reveal green berries with the slightest blemishes of red. "These are not ripe, they're no good." He tosses them to the ground and overtakes me, leaves me to watch the berries roll down the hill until stopped by the thicker grass, fallen branches, and many more ripe berries lying scattered across the ground, good enough to thicken my load and aid my wounded pride.

When I crouch down to collect these ripe berries, he walks back to me, pulls me upright by grabbing the basket on my back, and peers at me with an offended stare rendered through dry, unblinking eyes.

"Pick them berries from the shrubs." He kneels to grab one. "Fallen berries, them death offerings." He flings the red fruit far from reach, and I look away as though taking in the landscape, allowing him to move ahead, and only follow in his path when my palpitations have soothed, watching how some of the pickers are already walking downhill, their quotas achieved, their baskets beaming red. Others reach a plateau where the coffee shrubs end, forming a circle atop, drinking water before the descent.

Rosendo leaves me a tin on the ground with a sip of water, and walks back toward the slope, but I stop him before he paces downhill.

"Rosendo."

He turns, fixes his eyes on mine.

"What happened those days, when my mother left?"

He shakes his open palms from side to side. "No, no, no. Don't ask me about that shit. I know nothing about that." He turns downhill, shaking his head.

I get an urge to fling every coffee berry I've collected in the direction of his head, but I suppress it and let him drift down the hill.

Once reaching the highest point of the climb, I look over Los Confines, over Comala, like a white stain on the earth. I drink the water that Rosendo left me, then kneel on the ground. In the distance below, the pickers emerge from the thickness of the trees, and, after a minute, Rosendo emerges too, making his way through the yard toward the blue house. Behind him, though, the silhouette of a woman paces in the opposite direction, away from the house and straight into the deep shade of the woods.

Heat rises to my face, and I have to blink long and hard to confirm what I've just witnessed—a woman vanishing into the pines.

Haunted by the fear of descending into Comala's ghostly realm— a fear so terrifying because it seems so unlike me, because it requires a certain amount of faith—I spring to my feet, my heartbeat almost audible in my chest, and hurry down the hill, trying to map the woman's trajectory. "Hey!" I yell, but my voice is swallowed by the depths of the forest. *Evelina, Édipa*, I want to scream, but the words, the names, remain in the well of my throat. All I can do is pace ahead, through the empty forest, until I come to the barbwire fence separating Los Confines from the cemetery. The wind rustles through the Fresno trees and the pines, shaking off their leaves, which gently fall upon me. "Mother," I say, but my words are instantly smothered by the wind, which carries straight in the direction of the tombs.

The workday ends with beers in *that* cantina, the one that's always been there—La Eterna de Comala—where the pickers share liter bottles, passing them around the table, while I sip from a shot of mezcal and a can of Carta Blanca I purchased before knowing the extent of the communal act, earning for myself the nickname of *Bebesolo.*

The only other customers in the cantina play endless rounds of Cuban dominoes around a four-seat table, occasionally glancing at a soccer match on the TV. They are smoking up a storm—tobacco clouds swirling upward and gathering against the ceiling.

Once the beers are downed, the pickers leave the cantina and scatter in different directions, except for Rosendo, who has to poke and slap one of the pickers to bring him out of his drunken stupor. Silently, I wonder if this is another one of his relatives, like Fulgor, if Fulgor existed at all and wasn't but one of Rose's literary creations, a character she could just kill off for the purpose of her narrative.

Their sense of kinship, though, soon becomes evident, as Rosendo lands a third slap on the man's cheek, which finally makes him come to his senses.

"Vamos, pinche Toribio," Rosendo says, dragging him off his chair.

When they are out of sight, I try to imagine what Chris would think of this joint, what he'd make of the meat and grease fumes coming from the kitchen, or of the drink menu, which showcases an ample list of only tequila and mezcal, not even the infamous Famous Grouse. He'd try the mezcal, I think, and after performative winces and frowns, he'd zero in on the subject, poignant as always.

"I know what you're thinking, writer," he'd say. "The woman who ran off into the woods. Could it be her? During better days, you'd be scripting a scene from it, as if writing was the device that could finally bring her back. The scene would go something like this"—he readies his voice, which, who are we kidding, has always been utterly mocking: "*Standing in the yard, tequila sour in hand, O watches the coffee pickers ascend the hill. To her left she can make out the volcanoes by memory, and can picture the sun as it moves over the planet, tinting the cliffs a shifting shade—opaque, coppery, golden, pink. She imagines*

this scene as a fast-forward reel, the pickers lunging uphill, beneath the
morning light, then pouring downhill as this edge of the planet dims.
They all seem dead, she thinks, having a swig from her drink, ensnared
in the same day, time and again."

A waiter comes near and leaves a menu on the table. "Will you be eating something today, señor mister Bebesolo?"

Chris laughs loudly in front of me, but the waiter, of course, pays him no attention. I stare at Chris first, then turn to the waiter, wondering if it is actually him who gave me this nickname.

He points to a three-course menu of soup, rice or pasta, and the option of a beef huarache, pork meatballs in red caldillo sauce, or cheese empanadas.

"No," I wave him away, and turn back to Chris, who during the brief exchange, has faced the TV. The soccer match has reached halftime, and there's a newsbreak blaring loudly from the screen. A news reporter is covering yet another demonstration in Mexico City for the forty-three missing students. The throngs, holding up posters with the faces of the missing, are marching straight for the heart of the city, down Avenida Juárez, where the shadow of Hotel Regis would have fallen and what is now only pavement blazed by sunlight. The chanting of the crowd echoes beneath the reporter's voice: "*VIVOS SE LOS LLEVARON, VIVOS LOS QUEREMOS.*"

"Ay, dios mío," Chris says. "Painful reminders everywhere, aren't they, writer?" He turns to me with a shake of the head. "Both the country's motto and yours: *alive they were taken, alive we want them back.*"

"In Mexico, nobody ever dies, right? We never let the dead die," I say, and turn away from him, from the TV, too. I down my mezcal, and ask for a second one before heading back to Los Confines.

When I step into the blue house, my father has carnitas waiting for us on the countertop, the foil sweaty, the pork glistening, the tortillas curling at the edges to the point where he rescues them by overheating them on the pan. We eat together, and I'm wordless because I'm far too hungry to talk, even less to savor the ingredients.

My father feigns terror, and says, "I thought depression killed the appetite." He spoons a generous lump of pork onto his tortilla, perhaps sensing I could eat the whole thing before he even has a bite.

I flip the channel on the TV to the evening news, where there's a story about mothers looking for their disappeared children—they look down wells, abandoned lots, ravines between mountains—without any real help from the police, who often tend to collude with organized crime. One of the mothers is being interviewed as she searches in a field of garbage next to a river, beneath a leafless tree like the one in our yard.

"...this is what my life has come to... I will not rest until I find him... be it dead or alive... there is no calm, no solace, until I do."

My father seems as uneasy as when we watched the story about mass graves, clandestine pits, and the news about the missing students—surely sensing this might, once more, trigger the subject of my mother's disappearance.

"So sad, so sad." He squeezes the juice from half a sphere of lime onto his taco. "Best to not even watch."

He turns the volume down to a hum, while the mothers who have lost their children dig holes with shovels over every forsaken nook of this country. As I watch, some of the innards of my taco escape and land on the counter, which I pinch and bring straight to my mouth.

"Easy," my father says, turning to me, making the word two long syllables. "We're not cavemen, are we?"

"I'm just hungry," the words reduced to long vowels with the lump of food in my mouth.

He frowns. "When your mother felt down, she'd get thin as a breadstick. Seems like you don't take after her that much after all."

My viscera go cold and I have to wait for the feeling to drift, before saying, "Need the food for the picking, don't I?"

We both eye the last bits of pork, probably just enough scattered meat soaked in fat for one more.

"Go ahead, take it," he says, as if expecting to yield nourishment from my resentment.

I frisbee the tortilla onto the sizzling pan, and catch my father biting his lip, fighting back a smile. He then coughs loudly to restore neutrality to his face.

"But remember, if you're to eat like this in this house, you must earn it on the hill."

I keep silent. The flame on the stove emits a grave and continuous murmur, but the sound is overtaken by my father's parting footsteps. The tortilla swells up like a toad in the pan and I increase the volume of the TV, where the voice of the mother returns: *"How can I give up hope if I've found nothing yet to bury?"*

The next morning my stomach is too ruined by the carnitas to burden it with anything more than a coffee, which I slurp down outside the bungalow, letting my toes sink into the morning dew. The pain in my stomach is doubled now, on account of an odd nostalgia for my first days back in Mexico City, since the pain is the exact same as a bout of food poisoning I contracted from a street vendor, one of those with the happy pig enjoying a sizzling bath in the pot, but an illness cured at the time by the elation that was my own studio apartment, a fellowship, and the idea for a novel, all of which has now completely sunk in a sea of cheap booze, to the point, it seems, of never resurfacing.

The day is unseasonably grim. Fires started by farmers to burn excess garbage makes a dark smoke rise from the ravine and smolder the sky, enveloping the day within a haze similar to the pollutants of Mexico City.

The climb is likewise difficult, the pickers walking ahead at their accustomed pace despite the conditions. Toribio is nowhere to be found, though, after last evening's drunken binge.

The mix of my stomachache and the smoke in my nostrils has me in a nauseated state, a voice inside my head, which sounds a little like Chris's, begging me to forget about picking, and to seek comfort in booze, as numbing as it might be.

As I lunge uphill through coffee leaves, running my hands on the frail branches, none of the berries are ripe, all of them are green or grounded.

Having stayed behind at first to talk to my father, Rosendo finally overtakes me, lifting his wheat-stalk sombrero and looking into my basket.

"Uy, no, estás chavo," he says, through barely parted lips.

"I'm doing my best here, Rosendo."

"Remember, pick them berries from the trees. Fallen berries, them death offerings."

I want to ask him if he thinks my mother is dead, or if he thinks she just took off, or if he believes the cartels were after them. Before I can settle on one question, properly crafted—a rhetorical trap to catch him off guard—he has already vanished in the trees ahead, leaving me, as yesterday, to be the last to reach the top of the hill.

Before the final rise, though, none of the speedier pickers are returning downhill. The faint muttering of voices seems to indicate a gathering on the plateau, so I race through the final stretch as clouds swell above the rising smoke.

Gazing uphill at the looming silhouettes of the pickers, my perspective resettles on flat terrain, where in an opening of trees and where more sunlight fights through the murkiness, the smell of rot replaces the smell of the fires and triggers a reflex in my throat. My mouth slacks wide, my eyes water and burn. The trees at this height seem motionless, their shadows mere stumps framing the scene: in the middle of the circle a man lies on the ground, still, and as I walk past the pickers and over his body, I realize it's Toribio.

Short of air, I stare at him, dead and motionless. He doesn't look peaceful at all, his face contorted in fright, which has gone incredibly rigid, with dry blood washed down from a single coup de grâce blotting his forehead. His legs are screwed into the fetal position and his mouth is open like a dead fish. Overhead, the crows and vultures are circling—shadows in motion fighting through the smoke.

The pickers watch Toribio, their faces vacant, unmoved.

"El Narco," Rosendo says, poking Toribio's corpse without much sense of dignity. I want to tell him to stop, but my dropping temperature, the cold sweat, and my goose-bumped skin make it impossible. In my head, at every blink, I see my mother's face superimposed onto that of Toribio's body, the bullet dead in the middle of her forehead.

"Downhill, now!" Rosendo says, and he flips Toribio's corpse with his foot so it lies belly up, like he will be placed in his casket, if he gets that far.

Watching my step downhill; the horizon shifting like during the earthquake, I feel as though I'm running from death itself. Ahead of me, I see coffee berries springing off the picker's baskets and rolling over the ground.

"Slow down," Rosendo orders, and I do, but on account of nausea, not obedience, and see the grass field opening up below.

I leave my half-empty basket in the communal kitchen, and already see my father walking towards us.

"What is going on?" he asks me.

My head spinning, I say, "Dead man," then gasp for air. "It's Toribio," and without more words, he begins storming up the hill until he comes face to face with Rosendo.

Feeling what Rose described in her novel as *"full-body rattles,"* I stay in bed the rest of the afternoon, the light dimming across the shades and beyond them. I peek out at times to try to see what's happening, but can only find my father looking in my direction, which makes me flick the drapes shut.

It takes until the dark of night to see the lights of a police car flashing red-blue into the room and over the land outside, and then there's the unnecessary wail of a siren.

Forensics in fluorescent yellow suits and flashlights finally climb the coffee hills behind my father to retrieve Toribio's body.

Fully bathed in sweat, I adopt a fetal position in bed, not unlike Toribio's on the hill.

ALL AROUND THE COMMUNITY CHAPEL, DÍA DE MUER-
tos celebrations are being prepared. An appalling din of activity
arrives from every direction, the roadside brims with yellow marl-
golds, locally known as Cempasúchil, party tents are erected in back
yards, merry go rounds have been installed in the churchyard, and
the kitsch Virgin of Guadalupe altar at the entrance sits proudly
adorned with pine leaves and coffee berries, and where a starving
mutt sleeps beneath the shrine.

My father and I arrive at six on the dot. He is dressed as always
for the rare social occasion: dark denim jeans, white linen shirt, reed
huaraches, and threaded palm-stalk sombrero. Although a self-proclaimed atheist, a silver cross necklace hangs outside his shirt as he
kicks off a narrative I've heard a dozen times before: "In order to
earn the respect of the locals, I must appear to them as their peer,
and what reigns here is religious belief." He holds the cross steady as
though I hadn't seen it before.

"I'm just glad it's not a golden fish."

He scoffs and shakes his head. "I had forgotten you're a smart-
ass, just as your mother was." He pauses. "She was a real heretic. She
was never liked around these parts."

Is that enough of a reason to leave? I'm on the verge of asking,
but his monologue continues.

He tells me Toribio was in with the cartel, something that is
beginning to feel like a trend, that coffee salaries around Comala—
Los Confines included—can no longer compete with the sordid
amounts offered by drug cartels. The country, its people, chose this
path. He says all this, ignoring the fact that I know he was once in

on *that* business too, that if Rose's novel is taken to be true, he owes all he has to his own cartel—even if he referred to it as a network, operation, or scheme—and which had already taken another one of Rosendo's kin, much like Toribio.

In a sudden burst, I manage to say, "Cartels, yes, I hear they tend to drive people away from their homes."

My father turns to me, surprised, but then surely taking advantage of my opacity, just shrugs. "At least his timing was good—Toribio's—just in time for Día de Muertos. Whether he deserves the celebration or not."

As more people gather around us in the churchyard—some of them wearing carved wooden masks, others with their faces painted as skulls, prematurely wearing their Day of the Dead veils—my father's voice turns into a whisper. "Remember, you're here to earn their respect—play along with everything you see, this is their land, it's their vision, not yours, you're the outsider—you might have become too neoliberal after your time away from coffee country, and so much time with Rose."

"Yes, I know. I've even gone as far as earning the nickname of *Bebesolo* around here."

"*Bebesolo?* Is that because you drink alone or because you're the lonesome baby?"

I'm about to tell him that I don't really know—probably the former, although both descriptions fit the bill—but we are called inside the chapel, a small adobe construction with a foundation that might be made from the blocks of a pre-Hispanic temple, where a woman dressed in a long white tunic is ready to draw ash crosses on every attendant's forehead, a cross with the same proportions as my father's necklace and Toribio's coup de grâce.

Inside the chapel, light sieves through its carmine stained-glass windows, lending the place a hellish feel. The floor is carpeted with rust-colored pine needles and scattered coffee berries. The space smells of burnt matches and pine. There is no Christ claiming center stage. People line the walls, facing votive figurines of saints and Aztec deities, or even the more modern patron saints of organized crime—Jesús Malverde, San Judas Tadeo, el Santo Niño del Huachicol—all rubbing shoulders with their catholic predecessors. Toribio's coffin claims the exact center of the space.

As far as I know, the religious practice throughout the region blends Catholic scripture with ancient Otomí belief, creating a narrative thriving—as Magical Realism does—by way of the acceptance of the unexplainable, and in this case, the supernatural, tales of a half-executed and failed effort of conquest and evangelization—though it ultimately fell hostage to western imperialism and Coca-Colonization. Turning to my father, I suddenly see him as a Pedro Páramo of sorts, and pull my notepad and pen from my back pocket to make a few notes on what I see, trying to capture them in my mother's voice, a borrowed iteration of the register Rose gave her in her novel.

When my father notices, he clears his throat in the way of a cheap drama. "What exactly do you think you're doing?"

I stick both pen and notepad in my back pocket as he points to the middle of the church, towards the sealed coffin, where a chant begins and loudly reverberates across the arched ceilings. Every face in the crowd turns to where the shaman's figure darkens the doorway. She stands there for several seconds before walking into the dim interior light: a heavy woman with black braided hair who could share lineage with the coffee farm's chef, dressed in a black tunic made of lamb fur, Coca-Cola bottle in one hand, live chicken scrambling in the other. Slowly, she approaches the coffin.

"The Coca-Cola replaces the ancient aguardiente; you don't have to look so dumbstruck," my father whispers.

"I know the Coca-Cola for the aguardiente thing," I say, trying to adopt what I've learned of my mother's skeptical voice.

Once the chanting quiets down, the crowd gathers closely around the coffin. The shaman kneels in front of a row of lighted candles and offers prayer in Otomí, swinging her head wildly, her words resembling nature sounds, with long vowels and pronounced hissing, culminating in a deep, far-reaching vibrato. She suddenly falls silent and uncaps the Coca-Cola, causing white foam to rise in the bottle and spill near the candles. The chicken flaps its wings, restless but captive between the firmness of her hand and the pine-covered floor.

The shaman's braids sway pendulously as she prays—silently now—and almost catch fire on the candles. She pours the Coca-Cola over the flames, releasing a swishing sound that vanishes in the smoke.

Right beside me, I catch the hum of my father's low voice: "The refreshment is an offering to the gods, to plead with them, to allow Toribio into their kingdom." He is now speaking to me like a tourist or a guest, not his son and forced namesake, who he tried to raise in this land. It does make me wonder if all that time living with Rose in Cuernavaca and in Mexico City, the adolescent years that shaped me into who I am now, make me a visitor here, at best, or, like my father just said, an outsider.

The chicken flaps its wings again and the shaman lifts it by its neck. A shiver runs through my legs watching the animal's face, as if it had adopted a look of resignation, soon to be an offering and sacrifice—Toribio's ticket to the afterlife.

The shaman twists her wrists, and the chicken's body begins spinning from its neck above the candles—yet another Comala maelstrom.

The shaman's chanting resumes and now the crowd is offering an encore, reaching a swift crescendo, in the middle of which—in what Chris would likely refer to as the *pinch of the dramatic arch*—the chicken's neck snaps and the rest of its body falls to the ground. Blood spews out and the life remaining manifests itself as brief flaps of the wings, expiring reflexes, a gesture not unlike the final gasps of a beheaded snake, its river of blood flowing slowly on the ground, catching on the pine needles and the coffee berries.

From behind me, there is an all-consuming moan of sorrow. Tears stream down people's cheeks. When the shaman turns to face the crowd, she opens up a space of silence. The chicken died to

171

absorb Toribio's wrongdoings, to allow him entry to the next plane of existence. If he returns and presents himself to his relatives, it means he still seeks absolution, hence a chicken must die every fortnight until the blood atones—very much to Rulfo's joy, or García Marquez's healthy finances.

The crowd parts, makes way for the shaman walking to the door, forming a processional line and following her outside, where the dusk, the wind, and the noise are all astounding. The blood-red sun is beginning to sink behind the shadowed hills and stripes of violent light slash at the sky. Looking at them, I can feel a subliminal fear, triggered by all the masks around me, by the people dancing and pirouetting in the churchyard to the music of a band full of wind instruments and percussion. Even the children begin to seem eerie, wearing their masks of painted skulls.

When the coffin exits the chapel, the torturous ripple of the church bells sparks a procession to the cemetery, with six men carrying the coffin on their shoulders, Rosendo at the helm.

The walk is slow due to the coffin's weight, and the mood seems almost jovial now, death suddenly turned celebration, with the band thrumming and blowing out huapangos, rancheras, and el son. The devil dancers prance around the coffin, while others pass plastic bottles of liquor. Behind the coffin, lagging behind the procession, some men and women ride horses and burros, and a few girls at their feet wear crumpled paper wings. The physical body will now enter the ground, now that his soul has escaped the vessel.

When we reach the cemetery's gates, the men carrying the coffin lead the way down a slender dirt path between the tombs, which already boast the offerings for the dead. There's Coca-Cola, pan de muerto, mezcal and tequila, cigarettes, sugar skulls, and coffee berries next to pictures of the departed, all of it surrounded by the brimming Cempasúchil glowering in the dusk. In the distance, Toribio's resting place gapes in the ground, and above it, there's a fluttering cloud barely visible in the final strip of daylight.

"The monarchs are returning for the winter," my father says, but then a heavy silence descends after the coffin thumps against the soil beside the hole. Torches are lighted and roar all around, a sight I now know my mother would appreciate with her affinity for the finality that fire can lend a situation.

A queasiness settles in my gut as I imagine my mother inside such a coffin, so I shut my eyes and follow how the coffin is lowered into the earth, the pouring of coffee berries over it.

The torches are blown out. Pitch dark. The view all around me is like Toribio's black mourning page. His casket is lowered into the ground, swallowed by it, and the only sound left is the metallic clatter of shovels as they dig into the soil.

THE CANTINA IS CLOSED FOR DAY OF THE DEAD; NObody goes to Los Confines either. Constant fireworks blast like expiring puffs of cloud, their delayed sound like gunshots rippling across the sky. People walk along the main road wearing masks, the band plays through its festive huapangos, rancheras, and el son. Everyone, like me—puppets pulled by invisible strings—funnels into the cemetery and its labyrinthine paths, where candles are lighted over every tomb. I imagine it as seen through my mother's eyes.

The marigolds, the food and the drink on the tombs remain untouched, but even so the dead persist. The sugar skulls almost stare back from the tombstones, reminding us of their names. The voices of children playing hide-and-go-seek in the grassy fields. A picture rises in my head of what my mother's altar could look like, superimposed over the tombs I walk past—a mound of dirt, a heap of stones like Pedro Páramo's remains, a cross with her best picture pinned to it, the skin of the dead rattlesnake as offering, glittering over the stone, jugs of tequila sour at its side. Somehow, I find myself enjoying the reverie, but it comes to an end when I arrive at Toribio's resting place, its mound of fresh, dark dirt, recently watered. Next to the cross erected from pine sticks, a woman with a shawl tied around her back with a baby sleeping in it offers prayer. When she spots me, she stands, pats the dirt off her knees, and comes near. Our greeting takes the shape of shy nodding at first, then she extends her hand my way.

"Jóven," she says. "Truth be told, you look just like your mother."

Her words suck the air out of my lungs. "De verdád?"

She nods again. "Same face, same eyes."

"Nobody has ever said that before."

She shakes her head, stares into the distant hills. "I don't think she liked it here. I don't think she was ready to be buried in this cemetery. She still had places to go."

Biting my lip, I stare at her and nod.

"But don't you worry." She takes my hand and squeezes it. "Maybe one day she'll come back, she'll realize this is the place where her family waits for her. I'm sure of it, she'll come to realize that this is her place to rest for eternity."

Behind her, the baby has woken, calmly observing while trapped in the tightness of the shawl. He blinks and smiles, as if he knows something I don't.

All I manage to say is, "Thank you," and walk out through the path of dry grass, past a tuba's low moan, the smell of carnitas and sweet pink tamales floating over the land. Everyone here will spend the whole night with their dead, beside the tomb, "la velada," as they call it. But me, I head back, unmoored, no tomb to tend to.

Beyond the cemetery gates the road is empty, like in the *Pedro Páramo* film, dust so vicious it blows through me, but nobody materializing in my wake.

When it settles back on the road, I turn for a final glance. In the penumbra of the lingering sunset, the cemetery is even more crowded—I can tell by the candle flames that stretch over every inch of its parcel. A few of the soft cries travel on the wind and reach me, the lamentations, and I join in with them—I let out my own ghostly wail.

THE CEMPASÚCHIL DRIED AND ROTTED, ITS PETALS littered down the dusty road, scattered by windstorms come early. The libations atop the tombstones have been drained, the food nibbled at, the pictures of the dead stuffed back into drawers, the dead themselves back in the unstable pit that houses our memory. Me, I still have no tomb to visit here, to weep over a surface greened with moss. Everything has returned to normal, to the machinations of mythical time, spinning in its circumfluence, further unhinged by my recent increase in consumption of booze—the foul mezcal—which is back to its New York and Mexico City volumes, which I shoot back at the end of every workday in the coffee hills, after the pickers share their liter-sized beers and leave for the day—like ghosts of themselves.

I've also returned to my attempt at writing *that* novel, what Chris called the red ink-stained manuscript, now admittedly writing as if I could bring her back, or else grow the courage to kill her off and bury her.

Heading for my now usual table against a column in La Eterna de Comala, I breeze past the table of the four men playing Cuban dominoes, where one of them checks his turn and curses at his partner directly before him.

"If only Mister Bartolomé would come back from the grave, he'd scold you," he says, and, shaking my head, I settle into the haze of cooking smoke, of unrecognizable sounds from the TV, the occasional clinks of glasses and beer bottles, recurrent sounds that, if I didn't know better, might mark the passing of time.

When the waiter lays eyes on me, I bob my head to get my usual pairing of beer and mezcal, as if I was ordering my rye-spiked double espresso at Andromeda Coffee.

"Cerveza y mezcal para Bebesolo," the waiter tells the barkeep, who slouches towards the fridge.

Opening up my laptop on the table, I notice a layer of dust carpeting the red tablecloth. A four-armed fan above provides the only means of ventilation, swaying from its weak grasp to the ceiling, turning the fryer-grease in spirals through the air. My laptop is soon covered in a goop that I can only smear across the screen.

As I click the Word document open, the waiter's footsteps louden behind me. "Señor mister Bebesolo," he taps me on the back. "A few new bottles of mezcal came in today. You want to try a one?"

"Why the hell not," I say, without turning to him.

He taps a pen against the notepad where he writes down his orders. "We have Pechuga, Alacrán, Cascabel."

His final word has me turning to the bar, where the barkeep has displayed the bottles over its chipped wooden surface. While there is a chicken breast smothered in raisins and cinnamon sucks inside the first, and a small scorpion with uplifted claws and a curled telson sitting at the bottom of the second, the sight of the third causes my stomach to contract into a painful knot, or, rather, coiling inside my navel as much as the rattlesnake is at the bottom of the bottle of mezcal.

With cold sweat drenching my hairline, I turn to the waiter, who can't avoid laughing even though he is sternly biting his upper lip.

"Cascabel," I tell him. "Bring it over."

Wide-eyed, he nods, then says, "He went for it, pinche Bebesolo." He nabs the bottle from the bar to hold in front of me, as if he were a sommelier at a fancy restaurant in the city. A few scales have detached from the snake's skin and swim fleetingly in the liquor. The creature's eyes remain open and the rattle, consisting of four conjunctures on the end of the animal's body, floats gallant and slow.

"Go on," I tell him. "Pour me one and leave the bottle."

"A la verga!" he says, impressed, and catches a shot glass tossed to him by the barkeep.

Dust rises and settles after the waiter places the glass on the table, and as he tilts the bottle to pour the foul mezcal, the snake inside appears as though it's positioning for a deadly strike.

The shot glass now full, the smell smoky and pungent, venomous almost, the snake returns to its coiled position.

Fetching me my can of Carta Blanca, the waiter asks, "Will you be eating something, señor mister Bebesolo?" He points to a three-course menu of soup, rice or pasta, and the option of a beef huarache, pork meatballs in red caldillo sauce, or cheese empanadas.

"Are you serious, man?" I say with some hostility. "How long have you had that shit out back?" I wave him away, my eyes still fixed on the diamonds on the snake's back, my fingers slowly creeping upon my keyboard, which are oily like a reptile's skin.

On the white page, the cursor ticks patiently underneath my previous paragraphs. The barren space over which it winks is like a white ghost, awaiting the summoning of a glyph, a keystroke that might conjure her into our world—can a ghost only be brought into existence by the living?

Pushing away from my computer, I decide to test the Cascabel, as if through its taste, its very essence, I could embody my mother's awareness, feel, if even partially what she felt when the snake sunk its fangs into her skin.

The liquor is so strong that I erupt into a full body rattle, conjuring images both real and fabricated—the snake on the kitchen floor, the fangs in the dead snake's mouth in Los Confines, the same snake leaving two bleeding puncture wounds on my mother's leg. My chest lights up to a tingling sensation, a throbbing warmth, as if the creature's venom was, indeed, coursing firmly inside me. My fingers slide across the keys, then peck at the first sentences, hollow and sure.

O walks into the woods, straight into the corridors formed by coffee bushes, pacing through the tall grass. The venom

mingling with her blood, she knows there is little left to fear, and she flicks matches over the coffee leaves, letting them fall, lost amidst the greenery. They won't need much more than the dryness she feels inside to catch fire, for Comala to become as arid as herself, her inner desert. Down below, she spots the blue house through the trees. Her son is there—could she take him with her, free him while including him in another one of her fantasies?

For a second, I raise my eyes, piercing through the snake's in the bottle. Beyond, the fish-eyed image of Chris, sitting on the chair in front of me, is distorted through the glass.

"Hold it, writer," he says. "Leave that shit about snakes and fire to Rose. Have you ever thought you might have been onto something with your own novel?"

A sudden commotion outside the cantina quiets him. A hand of dominoes seems to have come to an end, leading to unintelligible chatter, probably curses in Mexican pueblo slang, followed by the tumble of domino pieces. The defeated pair heads to the bar to fetch four cans of beer, sporting obligatory moustaches, proof of countryside virility. The barkeep accepts a one-hundred-peso bill from one of them, and lets the cans expel a hissing breeze of gas when he opens them, then wipes the drinking spouts with his dirty rag. As they walk back outside, beers in hand, they hold my gaze, and then stare at my bottle of mezcal.

Turning to the waiter, one of them says, "Se va a quedar ciego el pinche vato este," pointing at me with an out-stretched arm that swiftly rises and falls. "He'll end up cross-eyed if he don't bite the dust."

The waiter laughs and shakes his head.

I down my mezcal to stave them off and pour myself another full glass.

The barkeep looks over to me, then to the men, who are already heading outside for their rematch, and then taps the wood of the bar. "Bebesolo?" he asks the waiter, "more like Bebeunchingo."

"Y en chinga," the waiter caps the joke and they chuckle together.

I gulp down half the glass right away, opening my throat, but then walk outside for a breath of fresh air before I hear them chuckling even harder.

Outside, the temperature has cooled under the threat of rainfall, and the tips of the volcanoes are covered by dark clouds.

The men playing dominoes at the outdoor table have begun their rematch, their beer cans sweating. I stare at one man's domino hand, but he seems to shield the pieces even from me. I look ahead, sensing their gazes on me, on the calluses on my hands that coffee picking has given me. Then the church bell tolls and I return inside, where, after swatting at the flies orbiting my shot glass like zopilotes, I sit and place my hands on the keyboard again.

Before I can type even one word, though, Chris's shaky image reappears.

"Remember, writer, don't project, it will kill your scene. O *is* and *isn't* your mother. Seek her in your creativity, not in someone else's words."

His directions have my hands trembling over the keyboard. To stop the shaking, I finish my gargantuan pour of Cascabel, to which the waiter laughs, quite loudly. When he quiets, a prompt rises, magically almost, in my head.

The path leads O to the opening where the cemetery lies. The earth is the depository of the dead, she thinks, in an attempt to rid the suicidal, almost wishful, thoughts. It's this death drive that will make her leave without her son in her arms, that will make her leave him behind, this ancient, gripping desire to become one with dust, or better yet with ash, the ashes of her many fires, the ashes of Comala's dead. It'll be up to him, to her baby son, to turn himself into ash too, at the moment when he pleases. Life is not for me, she thinks, life in Comala is not for me, and she doesn't know if life lies beyond it.

As I finish that very line, I find myself gulping straight from the bottle. Somehow, I can no longer hear the laughter, and I can no longer embody my mother, her bravery, her *come what may* outlook. To add to that, I can't really bring myself to write a scene about her digging a hole in the earth—to bury her and turn her into ash. Why did she leave? Why did she leave me here? No piece of writing will make the answers come forth. With another generous gulp, my lucidity hazes like my eyesight, it ebbs from my body like the stench of the booze, and emboldens me to do what I, perhaps, should have done long ago.

As I'm about to delete my failed novel, the laptop emits one of its cheerful pings. I open my email, where a message from Nayeli tops the list, in bolded black text. I cover one eye for better focus to read her mass email: "Tune in tonight, Channel 11, for a preview of my new book, *Schrödinger's Cat*."

Leaning back in my chair, I shut down my computer and tilt the bottle over my lips, imagining the reality of Nayeli's successes, her books celebrated at bookstores and universities, toasted by Rose and the rest of the intelligentsia, the media fawning over her every word, her every new project—all of it washing down over me like a dark cloak of confirmation: for me there is nothing left to write.

With a sunk stomach, I stand from my chair in a sudden move, startling the waiter.

"Ay cabrón, pinche Bebesolo."

"Torta to go, please. And I will be taking the bottle."

He writes down the order without looking away from me and slides the piece of paper to the barkeep.

The open doorway frames dark moving clouds and streaks of lightning in the distance. The hills are becoming rapidly enclosed in a pendulous mist, and, down below, the first raindrops burst on the dust of the road. Only one man out of the four domino addicts remains at their table outside, petting a shaggy cat with leopard spots.

"They've all gone but you are here," he says, in a tone of voice that people typically reserve for babies, to the shaggy cat, or to me. Beyond him, the rain quickens and its rebounds gather like glass shards on the animal's fur and on the fluff of his sweater.

Stepping into the rain-studded evening light, computer and a warm torta tucked under either arm, bottle of Cascabel hanging weakly from my hand, the drizzle chases me down the dirt road and along the empty gravel driveway to the blue house.

Inside, I set the torta on my lap, the bottle of Cascabel on the counter, and watch the news come to an end. The death count from the drug war is omnipresent, rising, in a bar underneath the news anchor's rants. Over the sound of the rain and the TV, I can make out the whir of my father's Wagoneer somewhere outside.

Dizzy and drunk, the effects of the Cascabel increasing to an eye-slanting lightheadedness, I click the remote over to Channel 11, where Nayeli will be presenting her new book. After a string of info-mercials hyping products to bring your body back from the dead—Life Extension Collagen Serum, Anti-Aging Skin LED Lamp, Live Forever Stem Cell Tablets—the show fades in with an electronic jingle, and there she is sitting on a brown leather settee, in the same attire I last saw her wearing: torn jeans and the t-shirt with the black-ened Mexican flag.

The host of the show, a bald man with a lazy eye, holds Nayeli's new book in front of the camera. The cover is divided in half by a purple line: on one side, there are silhouettes of human bodies standing erect, while on the other, the same bodies are lying on the ground, in postures much too similar to Toribio's on the hill. The title of the book is a fluorescent yellow on the upper edge of the cover, *Schrödinger's Cat,* right above Nayeli's name.

The host welcomes the audience and takes his time with TV pleasantries. I take another swig of the mezcal, straight from the bottle, which is giving me a sharp pain in my stomach.

The torta is already sweaty when I unwrap it, but the sandwich stops halfway to my mouth once Lazy-Eye begins his interview with Nayeli.

"Schrödinger's Cat is a famed thought experiment developed by scientist Erwin Schrödinger." He pauses, stares pensively at the cover of the book. "It tries to explain one of the biggest issues in quantum physics, and its analysis of everyday objects. It is often referred to as a paradox. Well, it is indeed a paradox, and it offers insight into the patterns of thought in the field of quantum physics... although I have been told you are a fiction writer."

Nayeli performs a grave nod and a smug smile, and allows Lazy-Eye to carry on.

"The paradox," he says, "or the thought experiment, or hypothetical scenario, whatever you might want to call it, entails a cat that might be both dead and alive, at the same time. This is explained by what in quantum physics is called a quantum superimposition, a subatomic event that *may* or *may not* occur."

I look around, trying to spot my father, the headlights of his car flashing through the windows, but no sound reaches me apart from that of the TV.

Nayeli intervenes. She shifts in her seat and says, "Correct. Now, the clichéd version of the experiment places the cat in an atomic chamber, a bunker, which will be infused with a radioactive storm— there will be radioactivity inside the bunker, which, as you said, *may* kill or *may not* kill the cat, both are possibilities, and so we must understand that the cat is both dead and alive until we can observe the result." A pause, an uplifted index finger. "But, during that moment in time, when the radiation has been shot through, and we have not yet opened the bunker, the cat is dead *and* alive, simultaneously."

I have another sip of Cascabel, and I'm no longer sure if the cringe that washes over me has more to do with the foul liquor or with Nayeli's words, as they sure sound like an argument Magical Realism could thrive from.

"A period of time," Lazy-Eye says, playing the part of the dumbstruck and confused, "where life and death become simultaneous, one and the same." He runs a hand over the cover of the book, over the images of people dead and alive. "And somehow, you've found this paradox and turned it into a social metaphor."

Nayeli nods, lips pursed. "I know, this sounds totally absurd, right? Of course, one might think that the cat is either dead or alive, and perhaps the idea of a dead cat is somewhat daunting—I'm not here to force images of dead cats on your audience. But what I do seek to demonstrate through this paradox, is the crisis that grips our country. While Schrödinger was only trying to pose a simple question: when does a quantum system stop existing as a superimposition, and when does it become one or the other, albeit using death as a symbol, the question *I'm* trying to pose is one related to our very evident and overly documented civil war, the war against drugs, the one which has not only claimed lives in the hundreds of thousands, but that has also left us with an astounding number of forced disappearances in this country." Another pause, defiantly unblinking eyes. "Wouldn't you say the metaphor is called for?"

While Lazy-Eye nods, extending both the silence and the suspense, I feel a fastening in my throat. It makes me put the torta beside me, push the bottle of Cascabel far from reach. On the screen, Nayeli carries on.

"This country *is* the atomic chamber, this country *is* the bunker."

I feel like I've lost the color from my face and am overwhelmed by nausea. I'm finally recognizing the absurdity of my own pain, the impossibility of finding closure, my endless dwelling in a quantum superimposition, and I'm trying to breathe in deep to the impending and certain arrival of my father.

"Clandestine pits in this country, mass graveyards, *those* are the chambers, and even though we know the outcome, the fate of those inside them, let us imagine what life is like for their relatives, their loved ones." Nayeli's voice has become so loud it is now scratching the old speakers. "Parents, brothers and sisters, friends, lovers. Their life *is* a quantum superimposition, a hell they now live in and that has no end in sight."

I'm breathing out long puffs of air now, the image of my mother clear in my mind. I look at my torta without any real appetite, the nausea coming in strong waves, reminding me I am, too, a body, when my mother's body, on the other hand, dead or alive, is nowhere to be found.

"How does one get closure?" Nayeli asks.

My breath is thick, the mezcal fumes burn my nose.

"How do *they* carry on, when they don't know if they should mourn, or if they should harbor any hope?"

Lazy-Eye seems unsure of how to respond, bombarded by Nayeli's rhetorical questions, and his silence opens up the possibility for Nayeli to close her argument.

"There's this Freudian concept," she says more calmly, face down, "from *Mourning and Melancholy*." She lifts her head again to stare at Lazy-Eye while she talks. "Something about the fact that when someone dies, the grieving one goes through a process where subjectivity can split around the loss, with half of the griever entering the stage of mourning, and the other half still attached to the lost person. The loss never fades, and real mourning can't really begin, because there is no body, which amounts to uncertainty. It's living as though our loved ones who have disappeared were in fact dead, while the slim chance of life, of return, remains... a constant nagging they will feel for the rest of their living days." She pauses. "Resolution is at stake here, for only after the process of mourning, and of a burial, can one be free."

Head in my hands, looking down at my spoiled dinner, I imagine my mother on Nayeli's cover, dead and alive at once, standing on one side, supine on the other.

Lazy-Eye turns to the camera and says, "The book is *Schrödinger's Cat*, and this is Nayeli Ramírez."

There's the sound of canned applause, and once it fades, Lazy-Eye adds, "I hear you have yet a new book coming out very soon."

"Yes, a surprise," Nayeli says. "Let's say we will have to *wait* for it just a little longer."

I lower my forehead to the counter, trying to temper the hot threat of tears. Then the door shrieks open, and, before I can lift my head, my father is behind me, saying, "My word, what's going on?"

Lazy-Eye is still talking onscreen, bidding the audience adieu, perhaps, but I'm no longer registering his words. Even if I was, my father has the remote in one hand, and has just pressed mute. He's got a torta in his other hand, too, and his eyes look like the deep gray of the imminent storm.

"The flutter in my arm is acting up; always does this before a big storm. Come on, let's have our shit dinner al fresco," he says, raising the paper bag and nodding sideways towards the patio. "Might improve it."

He goes outside, switches on the Noguchi lamps on the patio, and when he sees I haven't followed, taps the window with his fingernail. He looks so vulnerable, so old and alone under the yellow light, like a widower with bags under his eyes and creases on his forehead, that it's enough for me to join him.

We sit facing the volcanoes, their sharp edges flickering under the constant forks of lightning. The initial euphoria of the Cascabel is beginning to wane and I feel like I'm lost amidst the thunder clapping inside my skull. Along the road, a man sprints home in the rain, wearing, it seems, black fingerless gloves, sparking a pang dead in the middle of my chest. He picks up pace until the encroaching darkness of evening swallows him whole. The sight of him makes me shiver, and it seems like my father notices my unease.

"You were never from here," he says, opening his arms wide, welcoming a wet gush of wind, as if readying himself for years of constant rain, "that's clearer than ever." He unpacks his torta from the paper bag, which makes me look at my own humid torta in front of me.

"I'm from absolutely nowhere," I say, aware of the whine in my voice, and noticing how the wind is now laced with thicker drops of rain.

"You were raised here. That should be enough to root you to some place, as far as I'm concerned." He pours himself a drink of his top shelf tequila, and the wind ripples the surface as he lays it down.

"What do you like so much about it anyway?" I ask, poking at my torta with my finger.

"How could you not? The land is fertile, generous, and time can stop still. It's Macondo in the hills, forget all the Comala bullshit."

"You do know the place is actually called Comala, right?"

He sips his tequila and coughs out a chuckle. "It just really feels like Macondo to me."

"Except with coffee shrubs instead of fruit groves," I say, doubting if I should mention sativa too, but my father doesn't catch the sarcasm, and just nods with a smile on his face, raising what remains of his torta to his mouth, the wind blowing his napkin from the table.

While I shake my head, my father dusts crumbs from his moustache and says, "Life's like a novel here." He glances up from his food and looks out in every direction, where the raindrops are falling in a slant, as if they were punctuation marks.

"The land is here, but there is no one left," I say, flipping my torta over, trying to find an edge of crispy bread. "And a place is its people. It seems like the only people here have nowhere else to go, the domino guys at the cantina, the pickers... you." Before I take a bite, I sigh, "It's like we're all haunting the place."

My father looks first at me, then at the last quarter of his sandwich. It's hard to know how much of what I've said he's really taken in, but that's nothing new. After another bite, he asks, "Would you please quit it with that awful mezcal and have a tequila with me, like a father and son?"

The smell of his drink rides the buffet of wind all the way into my nose, that tang of dirt and agave, much favored over the Cascabel, almost providing the hint of a subconscious stimulus, as if I could—through the smell of tequila—faintly guess at both my parents' reasonings. Shaking my head, but craving a glass, I say, "Seems like I just drink when I think about death."

He shrugs, then sips his own drink. "Your mother was like that too; she drank when she felt abysmal. This place is not for everyone, I'll tell you that much."

"That's probably why she left." I take another bite of my torta before the last one's fully chewed, more to avoid saying anything else than because it's appetizing, which it isn't.

My father winces and pours me a glass of water. "I can't speak for her. I can only assume she had her motives." His eyes go far into the darkness and I wonder if he's thinking about Toribio, the police, the drug war he was once part of. Or my mother.

The wind is now blowing from every direction, strong enough to take the half-empty glass of water from my hand, but I hold it steady and ask, "Couldn't you have made it easier on her? Couldn't you have let her have a say in your decisions?"

"Maybe neither of us tried all that hard."

"That's not true. She stepped blindly into the unknown to be here, she didn't know anyone, she took that leap of faith to be with you," I say, while in the distance, the roar of thunder is so intense that it shakes the earth under us, vaguely reminiscent of those two September the 19ths.

Once the rumbling fades, my father sighs. "And she never let me forget that. That sacrifice of hers killed us as a couple. Mind you, if she hadn't come here at all, that would have killed us, too." The wind knocks over his snifter glass, but he either doesn't notice or doesn't care; he just hunkers forward on his elbows, the smell of tequila rising pungently from the spill. He shakes his head. "No, there was no going on like that. Trying to make her see we were living a dream, a mythical tale, like I had forced her here—"*You dragged me here, I'm trapped here*"—everything like that." He clicks his tongue, then goes on. "Like I didn't feel the same, sometimes. It's not easy making a coffee farm work, you know. You need someone beside you."

I'm on the verge of making him come clean about the dope, the danger he put upon them, upon our family, but since it's the first time he's really ever opened up to me about my mother, worried he'll close down, I just say, "I really feel like she is dead. Like maybe someone who was after you two finally got to her, like that snake in the living room."

My comment doesn't throw him off. "No, I don't think so, but it'd be easier to think of it that way, as *if* she were dead. Put the whole thing underground."

The most I can muster is a silent shake of my head, the silvery fizz of the rain misting against my skin.

"You have to bury your dead, son," he says, looking straight at me. "Otherwise, you can't move on." He takes a long slug of water to chase his newly-poured tequila. "You want to be like this?" He taps his finger against his sternum, then releases a hissing laugh. "I'd guess not. So, put your dead in the ground. That way, if she ever does come back, there's your novel: it's Macondo in the hills, after all, right? Or Comala, if you'd rather."

On that, he gets up from the table, abruptly, away from the cold mist, as if the conversation was over. "We'll get soaked out here," he says, but somehow his words seem muted compared to Chris's rising in my head.

"This is more than a metaphor, writer,"—and in the sudden zip of wind and rain I hear his pen slashing through another dud paragraph. "Don't you think the notion of burying someone who might be alive is a little too fantasist?"

I nod, looking at nothing but the falling rain.

"But you can bury those who *are* dead, writer, *really* dead."

The dust is now buried under the weight of the downpour, and the saplings are bending almost to the ground. My father is inside the house, but I stay outside, watching the rainfall under the weak light of the Noguchi lamps, the wind and raindrops at such a pitch that it's almost like they're going to wreck his Macondo, its distant landscape revealing itself briefly under the photoflash of lightning.

I stare at the leafless tree in the yard, witness to Comala's circularity. To suppress the onslaught of rage, I try to focus on the rain, on every single drop, letting them push out my every, intruding, windswept thought, until it seems like there are only drops falling from the branches of the dead tree.

Behind me, I catch my father's footsteps growing louder. He's carrying the bottle of tequila, his half-full snifter glass and another empty one for me. He lays them on the table, and as he tops off the glasses the night seems to suddenly glow. My father looks away, into the distance, as if the past was gaining on him.

"For what it is worth, I don't think she's dead," he says. "I really don't, she's just gone."

"Gone, and never to return. I'd be better off searching for her elsewhere, anyplace but here."

"You never once searched for her. Maybe in your writing, but that's all."

I bring the tequila to my mouth, gulp it whole. I let it slide down my throat, its burn washing the inside of my body like the rain did down the bark of the leafless tree. The tequila settling warmly in my stomach, I imagine the tree blooming to life. Turning to him, I say, "Don't you think I deserve to know what happened? That you should at least tell me what you know?"

He lowers his eyes, nods in resignation. A moment of silence passes, and then he turns the tequila in his glass, slow and ominous—as if he were turning back the years.

BOOK IV

Macondo Here, Macondo Elsewhere

1970s–1980s

YOU DO DESERVE IT. BUT IF YOU WANT TO HEAR EVerything, then you need to hear the whole story, the *true* story, not just the highlights.

Here, pour yourself another drink. It'll help you digest what's to come... hopefully... because, well, you know, there's more than just one way to look at what I'm going to tell you. I guess it's a matter of perspective, and how flexible your morals are, if you believe in such a thing.

Your mother stepped into something dangerous, through no fault of her own. A grand idea, mind you, but one that had a sinister end. She arrived in Mexico with books and one change of clothes—an odd change of clothes too—latched on to Rose, following her every move. A real naïve creature, she seemed at first, but what she stepped into had begun a few years before her arrival in Mexico, in the hills above Santa Cruz, Bolivia.

As you listen, I beg of you, try to accept this story as if you were reading one of your novels—a piece of fiction—or else you'll see me with different eyes. Listen to me as if you were reading a character's account in a book, an unreliable first-person narration... is that what you call it? Hell, what I'm going to tell you was supposed to be turned into a book anyway, but I guess Rose never ended up writing it down. Let's just say mine was a book never written.

I had driven down to Chiapas, to Chamula territory, to participate in the production of the film *Juan Pérez Jolote,* based on the novel by Ricardo Pozas.

Do you know that book? No? I guess that's a big hole in your knowledge, then, son. It deals with the Mexican Revolution, just like the book that everyone else has read that takes place in Comala, *you* know the one. Where the dead wander with the living. Different outlook and literary philosophy, though. Shame that one book is so much more renowned than the other.

My friend's father was the film's writer, director, and producer, and he was kind enough to hire us to help around the set. I must admit that I had nothing going for me in my life then, and I was anxious to move out of my mother's apartment. Anything would do.

San Juan Chamula, let me tell you, a wild land if I've ever seen one, and a real ghost town too, never mind this town. The men there were real drinkers, you'd often find them lying on the ground, some of them napping over the brittle dirt upon graves in the old church-yard. I think that town might have been where I first got my drinking habit, draining down all that Pox, the Pechuga de Ángel, and what-not, a drinking habit I'm now pretty sure I've passed down to you, judging by the bottle with that snake in it on the kitchen counter.

That's where I first met Rose. She had been hired as a script doc-tor there, interviewing the locals and revising the lines of the script onsite.

When filming was done and everything packed up to return to Mexico City for post-production, me and my two pals had pockets full of cash and nothing really to return to, other than our dull lives. One of them we called "El Tiburón," and the other "La Rémora," who was, in fact, the director's son. They were inseparable those two, or so it seemed at the time, and, well, I'm sure you can guess at the dynamics of their friendship just by their nicknames.

It was there, in the southernmost edge of this country, son, that El Tiburón came up with what he called a spur-of-the-moment idea, but which we later found out, had been cooking in the fires of his mind for quite some time. We'd drive down to South America, to the highlands of Bolivia, where he would tell us more. And let me tell you, the roads in Central and South America, they're long and winding, not like the bullshit federal road we have here. It took us most of seven days just to make it to Santa Cruz, to its hills covered by clouds, much like the volcanoes in front of you.

Once we were there, it was hard to understand why we'd gone. Santa Cruz! As ugly a place as you'll ever see! A forlorn town! So high up it's hard to even get there, let alone breathe into your lungs. The cold wind blew garbage through the streets. It was hilly and damp, the limestone streets narrow, and all we received were hostile looks.

After a few days there, sleeping in little hostels on the shaded back streets behind the cathedral, we met one of El Tiburón's acquaintances, a wiry, dark-haired man—his hair, I mean—coming out almost from the middle of his forehead, almost merging with the thick bush of his eyebrows, a hairline that will never recede. He had the nose of a condor, too, I remember that well, and his little portico-shaded storefront reeked of leather, that stuffy smell of a freshly cut up cow. The back wall was lined with boots and leather, all dyed in different shades, resistant to the humidity up in the hills.

And don't ask me how El Tiburón found out about this place, about this man, he kept it a secret.

He told us the initial investment had to be done then and there, right in the leather shop. Our pockets were thick with the money from the film, converted into the local currencies. You'll see it multiply exponentially soon, El Tiburón said, and horse crap of that caliber.

We gave him shit about it immediately, sure enough... *We came all the way here, to the highest peak of the earth, to invest in leather boots? Have you not heard of Queretaro, or Guanajuato? There's fine leather there, too, and all that.*

We couldn't quite believe it—La Rémora and I—that El Tiburón's grand idea was leather, and that we had to come this far to get it.

It soon became clear, though, that the real goods he was interested in were located higher up the mountains, in the ever-spreading, shaded fields between them. And green they were, those hills, greener than here, far greener, a green I've yet to see again in my life.

El Tiburón took us to the coca fields a few days after that. The leather merchant was in on the business too, of course, the *connection*, as it were, but also the façade.

During those days, son, Colombia was—of course, as it is now—at the forefront of the cocaine trade, and Bolivia had been mostly forgotten, or never been discovered. Go figure.

The market was there for the taking, if one was willing to make the long trip. The late seventies, let me tell you, an odd time, when freedom was still a thing!

Consumption was huge in the U.S., as it's always been, but you wouldn't really see anyone snorting powder in Mexico until the beginning of the eighties. We were wild about weed then, couldn't really see past it. All that Acapulco Gold and whatnot. El Tiburón saw opportunity and he saw it well. But if there was something he was blind to, it was risk. Some people have no sense of intuition.

And before you save me a spot right next to the devil, son, before you place me on a throne by his side, you better understand that I came from nothing. All the opulence you see around you, if you can call it that, what you were born into, had its beginnings then. Without these murky deals I'm confessing to here, there would be nothing but a grim apartment at El Edificio Chihuahua in Tlatelolco, overlooking la Plaza de las Tres Culturas, a place that is *truly* full of ghosts, mind you, if anything at all.

Search for some empathy as you listen, will you?

And help yourself to some more tequila, top yourself off. This tale isn't by any means a short one, or an easy one to digest, better take the edge off as you listen. And by god, quit drinking that shitty Cascabel, you'll go blind when you get to the bottom of it, as blind as I was then.

Now, to give you some context, the coca fields in Los Altos de Santa Cruz were controlled by los Cerreños, a group of humble farmers with no sense of ambition, harmless too, not terribly unlike Rosendo and the pickers here; just not showing any real sense of menace. They set their prices for their raw product, and all we could do was nod in agreement and then turn whatever we were given into a profit. Dead simple.

Our leather merchant, he turned the leaves into powder in a small room behind his shop, and hid it within packages of leather boots, which we all began to wear.

It wasn't until I was boarding a plane with a huge shipment of leather boots that the fear kicked in. I flew from Santa Cruz to Lima, from Lima to Quito, from Quito to Bogota, Bogota to Panama City, then into Mexico City, and every single time, the fragile little planes struggled and moaned to climb through the southern continent's perennially overcast skies. I was sure I'd die in a plane crash, high in the ridges of the southern mountain chains, like it was the fate I deserved.

Somehow, though, don't ask me how, I landed back in Mexico City every time, and not once did anybody look through those boots. There were bigger fish to fry, or lock up, rather, during those days. It seemed like we had flown under the radar of the established drug trade, and we went unnoticed.

This went on for a year at least, and the next time I was in transit from Mexico City to Santa Cruz, Rose was in the seat next to mine, forever reading her books, and passing along the ones she finished. We were on a Pan Am flight from Panama City to Bogota when she first handed over *One Hundred Years of Solitude,* and as I went through those pages, I knew that this archetype of a paradise, of eternal abundance, lay somewhere out there, in the landscape racing beneath the airplane. Something had turned inside me after reading that book, and my goal in life would be to find that place: my very own Macondo, right? And I wouldn't stop until I found it.

Rose kept saying a writer like herself needed a plan B, financially. Writing is a lottery, she said, like she didn't understand the same thing applied to me, that people who come from nothing, who have no real skills, need a plan A, I told her, to deaf ears.

Rose had already been involved in some sort of scheme in the United States, this thing called the "Love Junkies," which was a tight knit community of writers, playwrights, and performance artists. Early '70s. You paid a membership to belong, and had access not only to private readings, underground plays, and performances, but also your weekly fix. Cocaine, pot, maybe even heroin. But like any American trafficker at the time, she knew supply had to come through Mexico.

By the time she was involved with us, she had already built a powerful web of consumers in Mexico City, both expats and Mexicans. But you know what they say: a web is a home but also a trap.

The money was indeed coming, in bundles, wads so thick they were getting hard to store, which forced us into to re-investing and scaling up the operation.

It sure gave Rose the time to write. And it gave me the time to dream of building a life for myself, maybe even a family, a Buendía-like dynasty like I had read about in *One Hundred Years of Solitude*—but you seem to be the only heir, and don't seem particularly keen to perpetuate.

Like I said, the money was building up. Rose and I even smuggled a few of the boot shipments into her neck of the woods, which is also where your mother hailed from, the first place she escaped. We snuck the coke into California through Tijuana and Tecate, like it was no big deal at all, in the trunk of a car. Rose's American passport and California driver's license worked the magic just fine.

It all went gallantly for a few years, in and out of South America. I managed to move out of my mother's apartment in El Edificio Chihuahua, and took on a suite in a beautiful hotel in La Alameda Central, one that you'll never get to see.

I felt worth something, at last, you know, able to hold my own, and the willingness to keep things that way, the ambition, might have clouded my vision. With these sorts of things, son, it's hard to tell how far you can push your luck, and let me tell you, it sure isn't easy withdrawing the chips when you're getting them pushed back at you in even larger stacks. And what else was I supposed to do? It's not like the money I had then would have lasted a lifetime.

La pinche ambición! Esa sí te acaba.

Here, let me pour you another tequila. The wind tonight, eh? Surreal.

The next time we were down in Santa Cruz—El Tiburón, La Rémora and myself, Rose hadn't come—tensions were boiling over a bit politically, if you catch my drift. The party long associated with los Cerreños was down in the polls, and a conservative faction was sure to ruin their business in the coca fields. You know how it goes, the eternal war waged on drugs, a war that will never end.

And oh my, the tension down there—you could touch in the air.

To make matters worse, our connection, the leather merchant, was nowhere to be found, like he had slipped from the face of the earth.

Was he lying low during times of turmoil? Was there a reason for him to hide, you ask? In retrospect I think there obviously was. He knew exactly what he was doing. And if I remember correctly, he was the first to go down. But then there was us, too. We should've foreseen it in his shuttered portico-shaded store. The time to get out was past us already, slipping farther away.

Like I said, El Tiburón was a blind man when it came to danger, who couldn't see past the bright glare of money. There was no talking sense into that man, and, for reasons I still struggle to understand, we remained there with him.

La pinche ambición!

The elections came and los Cerreños lost. There were rumors about a huge electoral fraud on the side of the conservatives, that people who had been long dead and buried had cast a vote. Nothing could take victory from them. It was sealed and stamped before anybody could file a complaint.

Can you believe that shit? I mean, old tactic and all, and it seems like it never fails: everybody six feet underground and all of a sudden, for crying out loud, alive in the voting booth. You know, that has happened around here too, I think even your mother voted here once: Édipa Más, a foreign national, for the PRI of all parties. It happened long after she had vanished, too, but that's a story for a different time. Money is an evil thing, son. It's blinding like an ingot of gold struck by sunlight. Looking back at it now, I can't quite believe we didn't flee. Somehow, we believed we could strike a deal with the new people in power.

So, there we were, in a humid jailhouse in Santa Cruz with most of los Cerreños, and, of course, the leather merchant, who now didn't even want to look our way, like we were to blame or something.

The jailhouse reeked of piss and shit so bad, let me tell you, I've never encountered such a putrid smell again in my life, and in the middle of all that, we were fed water frogs for dinner, the day's only meal.

That sopping calaboose! I've never felt so far from home. That tiny room at my mother's apartment in Tlatelolco sure seemed like a luxury at the moment, the grim view over La Plaza de las Tres Culturas, forever washed in blood.

The hostilities with los Cerreños was becoming so evident, that we were moved to a different cell. And that is where El Tiburón found a way into one of the officer's ears.

Yes, you're right, that might be a better way of putting it: he found a way into his pocket. He found a use for all the money he had collected: seems like *la mordida* is not only a Mexican concept after all. Works across the globe, in any currency.

El Tiburón was allowed to use the phone, and not just the one time, like noir films will lead you to believe. He was in and out of the cell, and the echo of his boots on the stone floor of the corridor angered los Cerreños beyond belief. They raked the bars and spat at us. Not a single one of them was allowed out.

Don't ask me how, but our food marginally improved, too. The water frogs were replaced by fried yuca, then by silpanchos, and it wouldn't take long before we were getting a banquet with an apple stuffed in the mouth of a full hog, right in our cell. That's the power of money.

Meanwhile, los Cerreños kept eating those water frogs. And El Tiburón kept raising the stakes, adding a bill to the bribe with every passing day.

Next thing you know, come the end of the month, the keys to our cell were jingling our way, clacking the gates open. A few Cerreños were allowed out, too, but rest assured, there were more and more getting locked up every day. Their cell was like a circus, and the time would come when you couldn't fit a needle in that joint, it was so crowded.

Now, believe it or not, the tricky part was only beginning. We thought we were tasting the sweet juices of freedom anew. But, immediately—hell, they didn't even allow a minute for a cigarette, to bask in the smell of fresh air—the few Cerreños that got out with us started casting aspersions our way, and chasing us down the garbage-littered streets. Up and down, we went through those hilly roads, somehow outpacing them.

It's funny how you find a fifth gear in you when you're running for your life, isn't that right? Pure adrenalin makes you an athlete of the highest order!

We took refuge in a shit hotel once we lost them. It's a maze of a town, that one. Once we were hidden in our room, we didn't even turn on the light. We didn't eat for those two days either, and only drank the foul water coming out of the bathroom tap. The few sounds we dared make came in the form of phone calls, El Tiburón offering yet more bribes to a local police officer to get us out of town, trying to arrange a car service to La Paz, where we could flee the country proper, to the farthest place any commercial flight would take us.

Did I mention El Tiburón also had the hotel clerks in his pocket? No? Well, there you have it. Everybody's silence was worth something. And just imagine the cash we had been raking in.

If you ask me in hindsight, with the history book tucked beneath my arm: was it wise to leave all the Cerreños back in jail? No. That was the game-changer. We should have bailed them out, kept *them* in our pockets, cut our losses, if you will. Leave them with somewhat of an amicable goodbye.

I guess survival and getting the hell out of there was clouding any sensible strategy, if there was any strategy at that point. But if you've watched enough TV, you can probably guess the twist in the story, the curve ball any knowledgeable audience expects. You know, son, what all those mainstream TV shows tend to get right is the fact that there's always a snitch, someone with little to lose and always willing to gain a little more than he already has.

Frankly, I have no clue who it was.

Yes, you are probably right. Either the hotel clerk or the corrupt police officer—who else could it be, right?

The days were growing long in the hotel, and I felt like I was going crazy staring at the humid drywall.

Somehow, El Tiburón finally managed to set up an escape. At four a.m. the next morning, we were to step out of the hotel to find a silver Grand Marquis without any license plates waiting for us at the door. It all had to be done in a flash, we were told, or rather El Tiburón was told through the phone. The car couldn't sit there for long waiting without raising suspicions. We would be driven straight to the airport in La Paz, and once inside the terminal, we were to be on our own, solve our own fates, make sure we never went back.

And, sure as hell, come four a.m. that fateful morning, the Grand Marquis was there, like a shining pearl disturbing the darkness of the street. The engine was running, silently, a vague string of smoke pumping from the exhaust pipe, a mirror image of our breath in the chilly air.

We got into the car like the devil himself was after us, and the driver immediately wheeled the car down the street. The windows were polarized, giving the world outside a far darker hue. *Keep your faces down,* the driver told us, or some bullshit of the sort. *Don't draw too much attention.* And so we drove on in full darkness, faces tilted down.

Daylight hadn't crept behind the mountain chains yet when everything began to reek of suspicion. The car began to climb steeper roads.

I can't quite explain the feeling, but there was a sort of logic nagging at the back of my mind. Somewhere deep inside me, I knew that if we were really heading to the airport in La Paz, we should have traveled downhill, then onto flat valleys. I had been in and out of Santa Cruz enough times to vaguely have a sense of the geography, even if only subconsciously.

And then the world started filling with the doom of daylight. As those first beams snuck out from behind the hills, shedding light over the southern continental cone, I knew we had been conned. Sunrays poured over those green hills we once loved, and the car turned onto the dirt roads between the coca fields.

El Tiburón had been sleeping—can you even imagine? I had to land an elbow right into his ribs.

As he woke, I think the driver knew, he knew that we knew, and he started speeding over the cumbrous road.

At the far end of the road, there was already a mob awaiting us, and I swear to you, in the distance it seemed like they were holding machetes in their hands.

Imagine what they felt, los Cerreños, the anticipation. To see the delicious luxury of revenge slowly inching their way, spying the glint of the car in the early morning light, slowly getting bigger as it approached, like we were being delivered on a silver plate.

La Rémora reacted with a face of fear—he went the color of the car's bodywork—but El Tiburón nodded like it was just another day at the office, you know, *los gajes del oficio*.

Before the driver could even yield his gun, which, earlier that morning, had given us a sense of relief, El Tiburón and I were onto him. El Tiburón went straight for his throat and I just remember landing punches all over his body. La Rémora tried to slow the car down, but the only thing he accomplished was getting the car into a minor wreck in the field, crashing against a ravine that was used as a water source for the coca bushes. The driver's face was a bloody mess at this point, like his face had slammed into the steering wheel. He was in a daze, too, groaning like a drunkard on a street corner. We jumped out of the car, adrenalin pumping through our every muscle, and began the dash downhill. From the top of the hill, son, los Cerreños started pouring down like a landslide, and we realized they didn't only have machetes in hand when bullets began wheezing by our sides. They shot to kill, los Cerreños, their bullets fizzed, warming the air all around us.

It seemed like La Rémora had shifted into yet another gear, el cabrón went into turbo mode and was leaving us behind. Far ahead, I could see the length of his lunges, almost floating along the dirt. El Tiburón was lagging a bit behind, though, and I could hear him gasping, making me turn every other second. Los Cerreños's wild roars were becoming louder too, their shots ricocheting closer to us. And then, it struck, son, a sound I'd never heard before.

It was the sound of a bullet tearing through El Tiburón's skin. I don't even know how to describe it. Hell, I even think my conscious mind went into protective mode, and made me forget the sound so that I can only remember it as if it were somebody else's memory.

Then came the thud of his body against the ground. More gasping. The blood streamed out instantly. I stopped. I went to him, removed his layers to see the wound, which was dead in the middle of his stomach. The stench of it, god almighty, hit you like a physical force. The warm lead and torn skin, the smell of human innards. My eyes began watering; hard to tell if it was the smell or the emotion.

La Rémora had turned around, and was sprinting to us, like he was a lone brave Gaelic soldier ready to clash against the byzantine crowd of Cerreños rushing in our direction.

When he got to us, La Rémora pulled me upright, pushed me in the direction of our escape.

I swear I tried to protest, to go against his wishes. But they were getting near, and El Tiburón was surely done. You should've seen the pool of blood under him, soaking through his shirt, his eyes going white. *He would have done the same if that were you*, and all that. He did make sense, La Rémora, but I don't know.

El Tiburón was a good man. I see his face every morning and every night, as much as your mother's, dare I confess.

Yes, son, we ran off, looking straight ahead, and we knew immediately that the crowd was no longer gaining on us. When los Cerreños saw El Tiburón laying there, and us storming away, they didn't fire another bullet.

I can't tell for sure what happened next. But they took him, son, they probably killed him, or finished him off, rather. I never heard anything of him again, of course.

And, you know, the worst part of it is I've never known if I regret it. I only feel confusion when the images come rushing back.

What I *am* certain of, is that if I was faced with the same situation again, I would react exactly the same. I'll do the same in my coming lifetime, and the same after that. I would let him die one million times over, and I know it would happen in exactly the same way.

I understand your silence. Let it sink in. I'll go grab us another bottle of tequila in the meantime. We are nearly done with this one anyway.

There we go. Brand new bottle. Let me top you off. I see you've developed a sturdy stomach during the years you've been away. I just hope you have the liver to match.

Don't you love the smell after it rains? I can't understand why anybody wouldn't love this place and its magic.

But anyway. Cheers. To your health, son. By all means, drink up. The tale isn't over. Hell, I haven't even reached the climax.

And you haven't stormed away either. Good sign. I take it I should carry on then…

Yes, we will get to your mother, show some patience. And yes, we will get to her before we're completely shit-faced.

Once we set foot back in Santa Cruz, it seemed like nothing had happened. We somehow knew that the weight was off our shoulders, like every debt was paid and El Tiburón's blood had fully atoned for our collective transgressions. We even had the peace of mind to look for another hotel room to shower and figure out our next move.

We left the heights of Bolivia forever: one bus to La Paz, then another one, overnight, to Bogota. Once we were past that border, I felt that we were free, absolved. The nightmare was behind us, irretrievable.

La Rémora didn't seem all that relieved, though. He still wasn't quite himself. His teeth kept chattering, and he was shivering all the time.

We had a cup of the strongest coffee I've ever had, then went around the cobblestone streets looking for a hotel. Bogota: a beautiful city, so like Mexico's every provincial pueblo, with the tiled roofs, the colorful houses. I felt like I could stay there for a while. And let me tell you, the money sure would have lasted.

La Rémora couldn't manage, though. Something was broken inside him. He had to leave. Before we could even find a hotel, he grabbed my shoulder and told me he was off. He'd start the route back home, back to Mexico City, forget all this ever happened, put the money in the bank, lay low for the rest of his life. And just like that, he took off down the road. I followed his path, until the distance snatched him away.

Well, you never got to meet him because I never saw him again either. Truth is, he never made it past Panama. Once he landed there, hoping to catch his connecting flight to Mexico City, he was arrested on thirty-eight counts of drug-trafficking, which, go figure, was the exact number of boot-shipments we passed through the border. Rumor has it he's been locked up there ever since.

No, I couldn't really do anything, nor did I find out until many years later. I couldn't have known. Truth is, as soon as he left, I checked into a hotel room in Bogota's historic center, and slept like I had never slept before in my life. For three days straight, trying to cure the images that kept bouncing around in my head: El Tiburón's dying face, him at the mercy of los Cerreños.

I was far from cured, but I did know exactly where I was going next. The one place I thought could save me.

Yes, OK, go take a piss. In the meantime, I will try to find a way to tell you what comes next: a way that won't infuriate you.

Bladder empty now, Aureliano? Feeling the booze a bit? Good. Perhaps it might help you see the magic.

OK, OK, but just hear me out. And don't be so judgmental. I'll tell it as it was, and you can come to your own conclusions.

Realism, yes! I know that's what you're all about. No gallant tales, no perking up reality, no tinting it a flowery pink or a deep jungle green.

Like I said before, ever since I read that stunning book Rose had loaned me, there was this urge inside me to go find it, to seek out everything in it.

Yes, I know, a place is not only a place, it's its archetypes. And don't think I didn't catch the sarcasm in your voice. But all that doesn't mean the *magical place* that exists beyond a sole geographical location didn't begin at an *actual* place. The book referenced the Caribbean and banana plantations, and I vaguely recalled Rose saying Macondo wasn't Macondo in the real world, *Aracataca's the name, or some shit of the sort,* and so imagine the feeling that ran through my body the minute I pinned it down on the map. I can swear, son, just getting there, as soon as I stepped off the bus, I saw a place—how can I say this?—*instilled* with magic. The light there was at once cinematic and dreamlike. It was as if García Márquez had first typed it, and then the world outside had come to fruition.

Do you believe in that, son, writing reality before it even exists? Being the architect of your own life? Can you take that solipsistic leap with me?

I found lodging near the river. Yes, I'll say it, *a river of diaphanous waters*, no matter how condescendingly you roll your eyes. It was in the house of a man whose son had left to complete his military service. How crazy does that sound to you?

In fact, let me correct that, rephrase my previous question: Have you ever felt like your life has been scripted, and you're playing a part? Fate, right? What an odd idea.

The man who offered me the room in his house was incredibly kind. It always seemed like he lived a little distance from his present movements, aware of both past and future, of their convergence. He spoke of himself from different points of view, time-tenses so seamlessly shifting. As seamlessly as one day shifted to the next, like there was no such thing as time. I even thought I was going mad at one point, but, honest to god, I also think I just needed the rest, to be idle. He had the best medicine for me there too, a garden full of marijuana plants, tall as any other plant in that burgeoning land. We smoked together every day, from four different sativa strains, all of which the man had bred, and which, he claimed, were found nowhere else in the world. Those sativa strains, hell, they gave the world an even more supernatural hue. They really lifted you, kept you floating, not like that Acapulco Gold, Zacatecas Purple, Guadalajara Green, Yucatán Red, or la sin semilla no less, you name it. I won't delve into the kind of garbage people smoked in Mexico in those days.

My life became one of an observer, of sensually feeling what I wanted for the rest of my days, the rest of my lifetime.

Goes without saying, I was staring at exactly what I wanted. I wanted no more running. No more trouble. I wanted to be there, heaven on earth, forever circled by that river, dipping my feet in its waters, forever in that town's orientation. I loved that most people were young, and that I never knew where the cemetery was.

No, I'm not drunk, it takes far more than this to knock me out.

And no, I'm not reciting. I've never learned any book by heart.

There came a time when I stopped knowing how long I'd been there for. The mysticism of it fucked with my sense of time. Even if I wanted to keep track of it, people there didn't count the hours and didn't care if the years kept piling up. Days began and ended. Then the night. Day and night until death, I thought, what else could I really ask for? There's a lot of solace in that, whether you believe it or not.

But you know what, son? I think time only ticks on when we allow it to. It's our man-made creation, like a chain, a means of imprisonment. And I made the mistake of letting it wind back to its confining ways when Rose came to find me, in Macondo, the real one, the first one. Aracataca if you'd rather.

You know what's never been revealed to possess the circular workings of time, son? That would be money. There's an infuriating linearity to it. Once it runs out it doesn't reappear. That was the one thing that did not regenerate while I was in Macondo.

Yes, OK, OK, relax, I meant Aracataca.

And Rose was there because she had run out of as much money as I had. The sense of intuition she had, that woman. And when she was there, her questions were endless, too. *What was the deal with El Tiburón and La Rémora? Why had the shipments stopped? Our consumers in Mexico City are aching for a fix.* I tried to explain everything that had happened, that there would be no more coke coming from Santa Cruz, that it was all done, dead and buried like El Tiburón. She took a deep breath then, slowed the hell down. I even got her to smoke some of the weed our host planted in his garden. I gave her that joint because I thought it might set me free of her too, of her nagging insistence. But I guess, in hindsight, yet another mistake in a long line of mistakes.

This is it, she said, or something along those lines. She was hovering too, the color was back on her face, the sparkle in her eye. *Fuck the coke, this is it*, she said shaking the joint, making crucibles of smoke rise and fall in front of me. *And it'll be only you and me, we'll build our own operation. Weed from the magical township of your dreams.*

I still can't believe I fell for all that shit. Writers, how cunning they can be with their proper handling of words.

But now that I think about it, it might've been my own mind that tricked me: the real Macondo would help me build my own, right? And the money would last.

Have you ever felt that? The yearning to have your financial life solved for good? I think that might have been a problem for me, more than once.

No, it's not laziness, I disagree with you there, son.

What can I say? To put it simply, that was my biggest mistake, the one that still burns: leaving Aracataca, the real Macondo. That was the sordid decision that led me to here and now, to my present loneliness, in Comala, if not the real one, then one that is just as dead.

Comala: I guess it's just your poor person's Macondo in the end.

It's my turn to piss now. Enjoy the solitude for a minute. How fast the clouds cleared, didn't they? Enjoy the star-studded night until I return.

Otro tequilita? No? Come on now, don't let your old man drink alone. I don't normally talk this much, but I guess the tequila and the smell of the rain are sparking this nostalgia in me. And you know what? We're coming to the point where your mother comes into the picture, so have another glass, it'll keep you interested.

It did finally happen. I left Macondo trying to hold on to the vision in my mind, trying to daydream how a new one might look, one that I could work my way toward.

Rose gave me three months, *to get my shit together*. Can you believe that? Although I guess you do, you must know her well enough by now. Rose and her jeering tone. She was heading to the United States, to get her own shit together, if you catch my drift, then we'd reconvene in Mexico City, where I should have everything ready to go, our scheme, for yet another attempt at what had almost killed me. Talk about recurrence. It's like there's no controlling it, one can only fall into its merciless arms.

When I was saying my goodbyes to the man who'd lodged me, he sat me down on his porch, lit another one of his joints, which we passed between one another until it vanished. In a threaded pouch, he had packed seeds of each of his sativa strains, *Mire usted, so you take a part of this place with you,* he said, or something along those lines. They have such a proper way of talking, Colombians, such gentle cadence. Little did he know that I would carry that place with me everywhere I went, seeds or no seeds.

Say that again?

You think you have me all figured out, son, don't you?

OK, yes, you are right, guilty as charged. Busted. Yes, I had already taken some of his seeds. I was about to omit that just to give the story a lighter tone, keep a bit of magic in there, for goodness' sake. Isn't that what you writers do all the time? Sculpt by omission?

In any case, the man showed no real emotion as we parted ways. Gave me nothing but a little pat on the shoulder. There I was, moving away from it, Aracataca, Macondo. The world began losing its vibrant color as soon as I returned to Bogota, to catch my flight. There was no going into Panama, that much I knew was true. I swore to myself, too: this was the last time I would sneak narcotics through any international border.

Back in Mexico City, I didn't have as much money left as I hoped, but enough to go straight to the hotel suite on the top floor of Hotel Regis. I stuck those Macondo seeds in four flowerpots, and babied them like you wouldn't believe. Bathed them in sunlight on the terrace, pulled them down under the shade, watered them, hell, I think I even spoke to them.

By the time Rose came back, all four strains were brimming in their pots. They had flowered and we had enough seeds for a first attempt.

With Rose's investment—what she also claimed was the last of her money from the coke days—we took over an abandoned parking lot, sealed it, and started growing our goods there. It took another few months before we could dry and trim them, and begin to learn our fate as sales people. I swear, son, those Macondo strains, they would've grown anywhere in the world, such generous plants; they would have grown in the arctic and in the desert, make any dead place bloom to life.

Rose went back to the States while the plants grew, and would come down via Sinaloa and Guadalajara, see if we could get a network set up in the north and west, such was the ambition in her, but she soon realized that our plan had to be more secretive, highly curated, if you will, and that we would have to find our place in the Mexican market under the radar. Most of the stuff, historically, had gone to feed the demand in the United States, and we thought we could get away by producing our own strains and catering to a wealthy local market only.

We built a web of consumers, in a pyramid-shaped structure, me at the very top, with Rose underneath, establishing extremely high prices in exchange for exclusivity and a sense of belonging, of community.

It worked right away, son. The money was coming in again. My only job was to take care of the plants while it was Rose's responsibility to protect the community, to approve of every member down the structure, and hand-pick who we could trust.

Yes, son, there's always a snitch, I know I said that already, but don't go jumping to conclusions, allow for some linearity, I'm not as sophisticated a storyteller as Rose, or maybe even as yourself.

Around this time, your mother arrived. There she was, in Rose's shadow: weird-looking, and wearing weird-looking clothes too, that damned huge men's blazer she never took off. In they came to the suite, and out your mother went—straight onto the terrace. At first, I thought, shit, we have more weight to carry now, but I think we liked each other from the first minute. Your mother became somewhat of an assistant to Rose, but who in the hell are we kidding, she soon became my partner, within a month of her arrival.

She loved it there—your mother—the city, the hotel, she loved the people, how bodies dissolved into other bodies in the city, sitting and observing everyone in the hotel's restaurant, and sipping agua fresca from styrofoam cups come sundown in la Alameda Central.

She had the best times of her life there, I know, and we could have stayed there forever—in the city I mean, not in that hotel—if I hadn't been so ambitious and reckless. I was still looking for my Macondo, and a hotel suite in the city didn't quite fulfill that dream.

With success, we had to make some important decisions. Our parking lot greenhouse could no longer produce the quantity needed to supply the operation. We had to scale up. It was the perfect excuse, mind you, to search for my new Macondo. We needed land to grow, and this meant life in the country, perhaps a river of diaphanous waters, a land of muted lightning bolts.

What we found was Tomatlán, a ranch called El Comal.

Yes, nearly Comala, I know. You might be right, kind of an omen now that you mention it. But what sold it for me was not just the cheap land, populated with mango and papaya, but that the house on it was painted blue. Blue! Seemed like a more substantial omen at the time, for me, at least. I really felt like a Buendía if you don't mind me saying so. We all have a short-sightedness of some sort, you know, and I fell prey to it then.

What we did, son, was plant sativa under every mango and papaya tree.

Yes, concealment, but also a calculated amount of sunlight, shade, and humidity between the leaves. There was also this huge eradication program, Operación Condor, a cooperative program between Mexican authorities and the D.E.A. Most of what you saw in the news about it were soldiers burning down whole fields of poppies and marijuana, but what they did before that was fly over in helicopters and spray herbicide over the plantations, which, mind you, is a better fate than getting pushed out of those same helicopters and into the Pacific Ocean, like rumor had it during those days. I never saw bodies raining from helicopters in Tomatlán, but what can I say, anything is believable with this never-ending war. In any case, there was a huge bust with Operación Condor, at Búfalo Ranch, so we thought the mango and the papaya could shield our sativa from their bird's eye view.

Yes, Rose had moved to Cuernavaca, a place you know well. She had her own literary pilgrimages, I suppose. Logistically, though, it was perfect for our scheme. During those days, we smuggled our weed from the coast and into the city, stopping by Rose's place in Cuernavaca. It was a perfect cover. With most drug shipments heading for the U.S., no one was really looking into produce trucks going straight into the heart of Mexico City.

I kept me quite busy; it was hard thinking about anything else, like my relationship with your mother. But that's what you do: you work toward what you want in the long run.

On the other hand, it was hard for your mother in those days. She never really settled into El Comal. She took long drives along the ocean road, but there was something missing, I could see it in her face. She sure wasn't sold on the Macondo story, and maybe I wasn't the best at communicating it: how grand our luck was, to have a go at living in our own personal paradise. Your mother never knew, but I was sleepless those days, while building what I thought was an empire, and then the sleepless nights began for both of us when you came along.

It was difficult for her too, having a baby, and having it so young. But there you were, there was no looking away.

It has always been hard for me to understand why you don't like our name. And you're a writer, too. Though it is quite understandable that all you ever wanted was to leave Comala. But, then, here you are. All roads lead to Rome, don't they? Or at least to one's own origin.

You came during a period of upheaval, son, in more ways than one.

We ran into our first problems with the operation during those days. And this is something your mother claimed she was onto for a while. Said she warned me, but that she only found my deaf ears. She thought people were onto us. I guess history proved her right in the end.

One of our associates and main distributor had been taken into police custody. He called Rose from the jailhouse he was kept in. He was in the custody of a judicial police officer named Cancio. God, I'll never forget his face, the face of the demon, more like, with pudgy cheeks, the hair graying at the temples, a nose full of acne, the perfectly trimmed mustache underneath, his blood-red eyes always behind the dark lens of his sunglasses. He was one of the infamous El Negro Durazo's apprentices, the police officer and drug-dealer, prostitution ring master, customs agent, who built himself a Greek Parthenon off the coast of Guerrero. One of the Barbarians of the North. Look him up sometime. It will give you an idea of the sort of danger we were getting ourselves into.

In any case, Cancio was as fond of Hotel Regis and its many diversions as we were, and that is probably where he caught our trail.

But don't let me jump ahead, because I crossed paths with him a few weeks later.

As soon as our associate went missing, I called a meeting at Hotel Regis, in the suite. I rode in one of our shipping trucks, stopped by Rose's in Cuernavaca, and then we carried on into Mexico City. With all the distribution members in agreement, we stipulated that handovers could only happen in our suite, to ensure security. But the worry that kept gnawing at me was this little voice in the back of my head that we already mentioned: there's always a snitch.

I went back to El Comal, to your mother's anxiety. All I was hoping for was peace of mind, no news from the city, hoping the cogwheels of the scheme were turning without interruption. But then our associate, the one who had been taken into custody, went missing. Not even his brother, who was also in on the scheme, could find him.

Was he laying low, had he fled, had he been kidnapped?

I never knew what he got in exchange, but it must have been something good, because he gave us all away, everything.

I called another emergency meeting in the suite, but when I got there, to that top floor at Hotel Regis, the door was ajar, there was banda music playing in the room, and there he was, Cancio, smoking one of our joints, legs spread wide upon the couch.

Yes. Your mother had stayed behind with you.

What came next, son, was the worst day of my life. It made it seem like everything we went through with los Cerreños in Bolivia was nothing but a vacation.

This was a real nightmare, and it began right there, in Hotel Regis, in my beloved suite 705.

Sprawled across the couch, exhaling a dense fog of my Macondo sativa, Cancio invited me to sit in the chair across from him—*Tome asiento, jóven Lázaro*—his voice exaggerated and jovial to the point of being terrifying. Behind me, two other officers, pistols tucked into their pants, stepped into the suite, shutting the door behind them.

There we were, the guards sealing the exit behind me, the only way out. A bloody sunset crept in through the glass doors of the terrace. Cancio waited for me to sit down before speaking again, *I was just having a taste of your magnificent product. What a life you must have! A suite in Hotel Regis, a farm on the Pacific Ocean, a beautiful wife and son. I could get used to a life like yours, jóven Lázaro.*

He went on like this for a while, sarcastic, full of mocking flattery, pointing out how grand my life must have been, when someone like him was tasked with the shit job of going after the people that let drugs rip apart society, creating addicts and violence and whatnot. The fucking charade.

When he ran out of words, out of wit, he abruptly stood, told me we were going for a quick walk, that he'd also treat me to dinner, that he just wanted to have a chat.

The hotel lobby was full of noise and the four of us—Cancio and I, plus the two other officers—walked closely together. *Don't pull anything stupid, jóven Lázaro, lay low, you sure know a thing or two about it,* and all that cheap mordant shit he was giving me. I must have been shooting nervous looks all around the place, like *fucking look, somebody stop them.* Everybody in that hotel knew me for god's sake. But out we went through the revolving doors like nothing was happening.

True, son. You're right. He must've known everyone there too. Plus, who would they be more afraid of: jóven Lázaro, or the corrupt judicial police officer.

Outside, the wind was wet and the trees in la Alameda Central shook lightly. The sun was heavy in the sky. It looked like a red teardrop between the city center's low-rises, making the last of the day's shadows lean precariously over the asphalt of Avenida Juárez.

Independence Day was behind us, but the nationalistic banners still hung over every intersection and Mexican flags still clung to balconies. They led me down the street, then we made a sharp right before el Eje Central, in the direction of el Barrio Chino. I knew where we were going when he made us take that turn. Right on Puente Paredo, we stopped. It was our old greenhouse. By then, the place was empty of course, our lease had run out a good time back, but Cancio leaned on the wall, took out a joint he had rolled in the suite. One of his apprentices, guards, whatever they were, lit him up. Looking me straight in the eye, he exhaled, like he was saying: *I know about the scheme, its every detail.* No words were exchanged, and once he finished his joint, he tossed the roach in the direction of the empty lot, and then we started on the way back, exactly from where we came, north on Calle López, then west on Avenida Juárez, up its river of people and noise. Hell, we went straight back into Hotel Regis like I was just part of the gang, straight into the restaurant, where a table for four already awaited us, right in the middle of the place.

A round of rum and cokes came without anybody ordering them, and Cancio gulped down half a glass with one sip. Then there was a second thirsty sip, and he finished his drink. He was brought a new one immediately, and only then did he come into character again, offering me a toast: *Por sus éxitos, jóven Lázaro, I drink to your success, short lived though it may have been.*

What was I supposed to do? Not clink his glass in return? He had me at his mercy, and all I could do was wait it out, see if he would offer me something, a crack where I could slip out.

Cancio ordered food for the four of us, a lineup of the most exotic appetizers on the menu: escamoles, gusanos de maguey, angulas. But all the pretension came to a halt when the main dish arrived at the table: four plates of fuming enchiladas verdes.

Yes, that's right, that was your mother's favorite dish. I guess you know more about her than I thought. Perhaps you might even have a better guess at where she is or what happened to her than me.

Noticing my fear and confusion, Cancio told me what you just did: *That girl you hang around with, your wife is it, mother of your child? Enchiladas verdes is all she eats. I thought I would treat you to some in her name.*

There I panicked. It was impossible for me to know if you two were OK, if they had gotten to you. Ugly thoughts raced in my mind.

He made me eat the enchiladas too, even though all I could taste was nausea. At that moment, believe it or not, a few members of the network dropped by the restaurant. We were supposed to be having the emergency meeting in the suite after all, and they must have come down to the restaurant to look for me when I didn't answer the door. They all immediately turned away. All that mattered to them was saving their own asses, of course.

No, can you believe that? Rose never showed up, and she's never confessed why. Made up a bunch of excuses. We've never been as close since. Something broke between us then. It was at that very moment when I knew, son, that everything had gone south, that this was the end of it all.

When our dinner was cleared, Cancio ordered a round of cognacs. *Before I forget,* he said, *there is something I must show you.* One of his apprentices pulled out a document, tossed it over the table.

I tried to read slowly, but it must've taken me minutes to get the words to register. In a nutshell, son, it was a warrant for my arrest, providing detailed accounts of our operation, the present one and also from our South American coke days. Hell, that document had details I had even forgotten, some I didn't even know.

Cancio stood, inched closer to me, brought his chair right beside me. *You might be wondering why you're not in handcuffs by now, and why you're getting the VIP treatment. You have a choice to make, jóven Lázaro, but before you do, there's one last thing I want to show you.*

This time we didn't walk out of the revolving doors of the hotel, nor was the sun a spectacular ball above El Monumento a la Revolución. We went out of the parking lot in Cancio's police car, the night already covering the city. Cancio drove us in the direction of Tlatelolco, which was once my home, and which immediately made me fear for my mother, a feeling that somewhat lightened when he turned toward Tepito—you know, where the nooks of the city really show their teeth. He parked outside a poorly lit vecindad and led me to a pretty ravaged house. As soon as Cancio unlocked the door, I could smell the human stench. He flicked the lights on and a murmur travelled through the air. Inside, the room was like a storage building, with no windows or dividing walls. A man in a pair of jeans and no t-shirt, with blood on his lip, was tied to a column. Behind him were loads of cocaine, heroin, and pot, and beside them, was a second bound man sleeping on the floor, blindfolded and gagged.

Imagine what I felt at that moment, son.

Cancio lit a joint. He pulled in a drag. Exhaled. *You have a choice to make, jóven Lázaro,* he repeated. *You can be my partner, or you can be my foe.*

I kept staring at the men. The one that was gagged and blindfolded had woken up, and he could only whine like a frightened dog, oblivious to what was happening around him.

You can cut me into your deals, or you can rot forever in jail, jóven Lázaro.

I couldn't speak. I could not bring myself to say "yes." Working for that fucking asshole.

I'll give you one night to sleep on it, Cancio said. *And you will be spending that night in here.* He pushed me all the way in, but he did not tie me up. That would've been something, right? The universe telling me, *you wanted your Macondo, here is your Macondo.*

Cancio locked me inside the windowless room, but I could still hear his voice from outside. *I'll be back to get you in the morning, jóven Lázaro. I'm sure you will have made a sound decision by then. Meanwhile I will enjoy suite 705 in your name.*

And so it went, son, the offer to join the drug protection racket in Mexico City, led, no less, than by the judicial police force.

I turned off the light to wait for the morning.

No, I didn't untie them—well, not yet. I sat in the darkness, trying to figure out what to say to Cancio in the morning, trying to figure out a way to escape.

But my bladder is acting up again, son. I must release.

Oh, you need to go too? Just take a piss outside while I use the bathroom, will you? Go piss on that tree, see if you can bring it back to life.

You know, son, I never once thought that disaster could also spell salvation. Like it was a calling from up above. Like my Macondo was summoning me back to freedom.

The night I spent in that house brought back the days I spent in the jail in Santa Cruz, only there was no one to bail me out, or to bribe my way out of what I had gotten into. I couldn't sleep all night thinking of that fucking crook sleeping in my suite. The bile simmered in my chest. There were also the men, asking me to untie them, saying we could all break out of there together. But no, I didn't even reply to their calls. I sat there in silence, trying to unravel the knot, devising a way out of this muddle.

Disaster as salvation, son! After it happened, all I could do was fall into another solipsistic loop.

Yes, go on, call it narcissistic, same difference if you ask me, when it comes to practical purposes.

When the first crack of daylight crept beneath the door to that windowless room, I was waiting for Cancio's footsteps, a key in the lock, or what have you. But it was a far different sound that came that morning, September the 19th, 1985. It was an ugly rumble, and before I could really understand what was happening, the shaking of the earth made the house go berserk. Cries of panic rose everywhere, and then the walls started cracking under the trepidation. The roof—which was constructed from a few wooden beams, topped by a sheet of fiberglass—started to tear open. Next thing you know, son, the front wall crumbled like stale bread, and more daylight flooded into the room, along with the roar of destruction. I was caught underneath that fallen wall, it hit me on my left side and took me down with it. My arm was caught under the rubble for some minutes and pinched a nerve or what have you. It gave me this flutter in my arm which hasn't stopped ever since I freed myself from the wreckage. The man who was tied had his eyes wide open, to their full extent, and I couldn't tell if it was fear or just the thrill of the world opening before him. The man that was blindfolded and gagged, well, he could not help but whimper; he could only guess at what was happening around him.

It must have lasted over two minutes son, the earthquake, but it sure felt like longer than that.

As soon as the earth stopped moving, I immediately climbed onto the crumbled wall, trying to find a way out, but the shattered brick, the beams, were too heavy. That's why I untied the men. And let me tell you, son, I was moving as quickly as I've ever moved; Cancio could've been just around the corner, rushing our way.

Once the two men were untied, the rope-burns tattooed on their skin, they thanked me like I was their savior, and not our mother earth, the grand spirit, call it what you may. To me it has always been fate. Like for some reason I deserved another go at it. Don't forget I had a better half, a son, and I was getting the chance to put things right.

The men spoke to me in that lovely Colombian cadence, and then I knew this was a message from up high.

Coincidence? You're free to interpret events how you wish. But I guess this is *my* story to tell and not yours. You'll have to learn to play the part of the audience this time, son.

In any case, we managed to push a hole through the rubble, and discovered that the city outside looked like a warzone. Helicopters, ambulances, terrified wailing, people swarming like chickens without a head. We dashed away, and the Colombians were gone in an instant. I was quite unsure of where to run to, my mind was like mesh, dazed by thoughts of you and your mother, of Cancio coming after me, but also concern for my own mother. I ran straight to Tlatelolco first, and as soon as I got there, in front of la Plaza de las Tres Culturas, my heart sank into my stomach. One of the towers had fallen, like it had been dynamited down. I rushed to it, confused of course, but was ecstatic to find that it was Torre Baja California that had tumbled. Torre Chihuahua stood, almost proudly, which made me confident enough to turn away, to know that my mother was alive, and that she still had a roof over her head. It was enough for me to carry on, in the direction of my own family, you know, my Macondo. I knew your mother must have been worried sick.

All around me I could only catch bits of hearsay, of fallen buildings, and even before I knew it, I had made my way back to La Alameda Central, like my mind was on autopilot, like I was returning to my home in Mexico City, to see if it had withstood the quake. As I made my way closer, strings of smoke rose in the air. I circled Bellas Artes and came to Avenida Juárez. In front of La Alameda Central, the building on the corner of Avenida Juárez and Balderas had fallen, and people stared up at it in disbelief. But then it struck me, son, first like perplexity, then like grief: Hotel Regis was no longer standing, its yellow walls were no more, its once grand illuminated sign lay cracked under the rubble.

There I stood. Looking at it for hours. It was surreal. El Monumento a la Revolución peeked behind what was left of it, watching over the city, a catastrophe in every direction.

The rescue mission carried on all day but all I could do was stare at the fallen hotel, this once mythical place for me. I stared until the sky behind the rubble was cut with a gash of red, until the sunset trailed to nonexistence.

Was Cancio in Hotel Regis when it fell? Was his body trapped beneath the rubble? I think that is exactly what happened. Every passing hour staring at the mess seemed to confirm as much. I never heard a thing about him again, and, if you ask me, that warrant was probably in there too, effaced. I was free, son, I somehow knew it. And now, like there had been in South America, a homecoming awaited me. Macondo at the end of the road.

September the 19th, son. When year after year, people commemorate death on that very date, I commemorate my freedom.

Once it was dark, I went straight to the bus station. The moon hid somewhere in the sky that night, covered by the smog of the city. The bus station was complete mayhem, but I managed to catch a ride out to the coast. Little did I expect, though, son, what I would come to find on September the 20th in El Comal.

I hitchhiked from Mexico City to Guadalajara and then Puerto Vallarta, then took a local bus along the coast. It took me a whole night and a good chunk of the following day to get to you. Once I left the city, the sense of doom had lifted, and life ticked on, continuing its inevitable cycle.

The last stretch of dirt road I had to travel on foot. I had nothing on me, except a yearning to return home. The only thing driving me forward was El Comal, your mother, yourself. I wanted to get there and feel safe again, like nothing had happened. The city was far behind, and so was Cancio, it seemed. I forced myself to embrace my new freedom.

But my *real* freedom, mind you, my idea of freedom, at least, was gone before I knew it. I can't even begin to explain what I saw when I got to El Comal. Behind the hill was black smoke, and as I approached my fears were confirmed. Our rancho El Comal was on fire—or, rather, the fields were, but not the house. The fire was blazing and consumed every tree, every sativa under its shade.

And this, son, I must confess, I have never known for sure. The truth has never fully been revealed. I've never known if it was your mother who burned it down, if it was an accident, or if it was rivaling cartels who were onto us.

That is what she claimed at first, your mother, that cartel people had been there during my absence, and that this was their solution to rivalry. To be fair, the drug wars had turned nasty those days, and violence was on the rise.

In fact, Rosendo—who had already been working for us in Tomatlán—voiced to me his theory that your mother set fire to the ranch. He'd swear to that today if you ask him. And he's not shy when it comes to his theories.

In any case, there it was, my homecoming to Macondo ruined, finished before I even got there. And of course, the fear was still with me. If it was true that cartel people had come over, then perhaps they were related to Cancio in some way. Your mother's story had some credibility to it, that's for sure, so I took her at her word.

Your mother finished packing and I dug out the cash from the spot I had been stashing it, under the soil of the tallest papaya tree in the field. God forbid all the profits burned, too. There hadn't been a drop of rain in months, maybe years. The only kind of rain you saw in that land was shooting stars, *la lluvia de estrellas*.

I still miss that place to this day.

We left as the wind torched the groves. I could see the flames rising as we drove away. You could even say it was a beautiful sight, the flames almost walking over the mangoes, the wind pungent with coal and fruit, the smoke rising in patterned undulations.

We were off, to Manzanillo first, then Infiernillos, or some other god-forsaken town, down the monotonous coastline, its cactuses and its heat, bending through bays covered with dead vegetation, copses of mango and papaya trees. Utterly nondescript land.

We had crossed Colima state lines and then we were climbing inland, past more Mexican ghost towns.

Your mother seemed in her element then, sleeping in motels, drifting along. She knew how to do that, like it was in her DNA.

Me, on the other hand, I knew we needed a place to land. Final roll of the dice, if you will. One last shot at my dream. We had the money and I still kept some sativa seeds.

Your mother felt like we had to leave all that behind, though. Maybe the cartel was in fact after us. We had to become something new, she said, new identities for a new life.

Yes, son, that's when it happened. That's how you and I became namesakes. Lázaro was done and buried.

Yes, OK, maybe you're right. I was forcing it a little, but cut a man some slack. That can happen when you actually think you're living out a novel.

And can you believe it, the randomness of it all? The place we landed was Comala. Here of all places, son.

Driving into town that first time, there was a feeling I had never quite felt before: awe, but also fright. Deep in the hills it was rainy and misty, spooky. As we arrived in Los Confines, guided by Rosendo, darkness had completely encroached. A deep darkness, son, inaccessible. The road seemed to be trapped in some sort of space-time warp, like driving into a mind-boggling loop. No matter how long we drove, the road kept winding, going up, up, up, through the fog. A glaring crescent moon came in and out of sight through the rain-soaked woods, stabbing at the nebulae like a newly sharpened scythe.

That's how we arrived here, son. Home, right? And all your mother wanted was to leave, from minute one, if I recall correctly.

Me? Let's just say I thought of myself as able, at least, to accept this damnation, transcend it even. Perhaps if we just kept at it long enough, the place would bloom into the Macondo I was seeking. Maybe we could find some sense of pride, for accepting where time and chance had taken us.

A place is not a place but a state of mind, isn't it?

This, I'm sure you know yourself: one day here seems exactly like the last.

There are views of sunlit valleys between the volcanoes. There's the gathering of clouds at the volcano's foot. There's wild wind and torrential rain. Today has been the perfect example.

No, I don't mean exactly that, not every single day one after the next, but you know what I'm getting at. In the poor Mexican provinces there's a day's work, and then it happens again the very next day; people tend to say the same things at the same hour, day after day.

I think your mother needed more excitement, like there was for her in Mexico City. She was young, too, and with a child already. She must have known a quiet routine in an anonymous place was not going to be enough for her. And credit to her, for mustering the courage to leave, to slip out when she thought she could.

I think she found it cliché of me, the whole business of planting more sativa under the coffee bushes. She couldn't understand why I couldn't let it go, or maybe how I couldn't fathom a different way to live.

And, unfortunately, both you and I know of the cycle that engulfs the country. It was present then, too. A circle drawn with blood.

During those days, the leading cartel around these parts was asking for derecho de piso, something they ask for to this very day, something I'm ashamed to say I diligently pay. They charged a fee just to let us get on with our work. The coffee, I mean—god knows what they would have done to us if they knew about the dope.

Your mother nearly went crazy every time the cartel swung by to collect payments. That was around the time she had a painful surgery, and she turned to drinking. Oh my, was she sinking.

Rosendo swears that your mother even tried to burn this place down, too. That is, if she ever burnt down El Comal, as well. But you know Rosendo, he's a lunatic in his own right.

In the end, the dope operation in Comala never played out. The network was no longer in place after the racket collapsed in Mexico City. The pyramid had crumbled, too, on that fated September the 19th. We uprooted the sativa. That side of Macondo, I was able to let go. I wasn't about to get us all killed in the name of turning my past into my present.

For a moment, I thought your mother would've been delighted to know that the whole dope thing was finally finished. And even though it wasn't easy making a living on the right side of the law, I was trying to stay positive. *Look,* I'd tell her, *we're doing good with coffee as well. This is a prosperous place,* but she was far too deep in her mind already. She was already gone even though she was here still, wasting away, in the drink, watching TV, putting reality on hold, or something to that effect.

Doesn't it feel kind of obvious to you that one day she just disappeared?

Yes, there was that incident with the snake, when she was bit. She had been deathly afraid of them ever since I met her. It seemed like her fate had been slowly slithering its way to her. Hell, after growing up in a place full of rattlesnakes, she gets bitten in Comala!

No, I don't think the snake bite put her over the edge, to be honest. She had made up her mind already, if you ask me.

For her, there was a certain nobility about fleeing, it was a brutal habit, her life was marked by it from a very young age. Her own mother left her in a similar manner, to be raised alone by a father.

Yes, son. That is all there is to it. She vanished. Just like that. And you and I remain in this country warped by loss. The ghost of Comala had been foretold.

I'm sorry you grew up without a mother. I'm sorry that you've also made it a reason to wage this war against yourself. In some ways, I'm glad Rose was willing to take you in, because, god knows, I had no more answers.

It pains me that you're not at peace. But you have to make this an old wound, like I have. Learn of closure. Like I said earlier, son, you have to bury your dead, but also, you have to find the joy in living. Your life is there for you, even if your loved ones may have gone. Live your life like it's worth something.

BOOK V

An Open Book

2017

DRESSED IN MY MOTHER'S BLAZER WITH THE RATTLE-snake pin, hung-over, I step out of the bungalow and onto the rain-swept grass midmorning, duffle bag over my shoulder, knowing that my hope of finding anything about her fate here was nothing but a tough ask—Comala, where there's nothing to be solved; you leave it knowing no more than you already did.

In front of me, there are patches of sun over the meadow, the hardly oscillating shades of trees, butterflies gleaming as they flit in the sunlight. Steam is lifting from the rooftiles of the blue house as the sunlight pours over and the sweet smoke of roasting coffee beans is rising beyond it.

My father is already in the kitchen when I step in, standing behind the counter with two cups of coffee in front of him. He laughs with resignation at the sight of my attire and shakes his head.

"Your Lungo is nice and steamy," he says. "Long day ahead, I reckon."

I sip the coffee he made me.

"Colombian," he smirks. "Just in case you were wondering."

I nod and sip again, and raise my cup as though offering a toast. Beside him, the TV is still on, only this time it's white noise that is crackling on the screen.

"No signal," I point to the black box.

"Storm screwed it up last night." He lifts his cup to his mouth. "My arm finally gave me a rest after the storm. I think the tequila helped."

I nod. "Don't you want to turn it off for once?"

"I would." He sips and licks his foam-flecked lips. "But how will I know when it's back on again?"

"I don't think it'll come back on just like that, by way of magic."

"Just forget it's there for a second." He waves his hand at the TV. "So, where exactly are you headed?"

"Bury my dead," I say, picturing Chris sitting at Andromeda Coffee with his red pen in hand.

My father nods, finishes his coffee with one long gulp and leads me out the front door to where a mild breeze flows through the leafless tree in the yard, whose branches are still bare despite last night's downpour. The forward motion of the wind lends the illusory impression that Comala's time vacuum has begun to tick on, a temporary fissure. I only need to slip out, quickly—like my mother once did—to escape the trap that is closing around me, before one day becomes the last, before my father's stiff embrace, before he puts on his sombrero and sits down to watch me go, butterflies dancing around him, before I glance up to the tips of the volcanoes capped with snow over a low embankment of clouds—the past, like he thinks, forever on the verge of recurring.

ONCE ABOARD THE FLOODLIT AEROMEXICO RED-EYE, the honeyed sting of an overpriced Jack Daniel's gets me cruising long before we rise through the clouds, and by the time the plane levels off, I'm half-in, half-out of a dream about Chris as a news anchor wearing his fingerless gloves. He is counting the number of forced disappearances in the country next to a picture of my mother. The red ink-stained manuscript is sitting in front of him, only this time it's really red, as though the markings were made in blood.

I wake with a start as the plane enters a turbulent zone and check my bag underneath my seat for the crumpled pages. Why am I still carrying these with me? I no longer know—there's nothing in them, just as there's nothing in Rose's failed novel, much less in my father's sensationalist tales. Perhaps it is my manuscript, too, that must be buried.

I take a gulp of the drink hoping to wash away the aftertaste of the dream, but it only transports me further down into the realm of even more eerie images: my mother pacing around my fellowship studio in Mexico City, kneeling down to hold a finger against the vein in her ankle, where the rattlesnake sunk its fangs, then Chris again, running his hand through Rose's pages. The next time I jolt awake it's because the plane is beginning its descent, making me feel like I left my stomach at cruising altitude. From the oval window of the plane, New York City glows like an electrified mockup, it's bridges wildly illuminated, but with dark patches where the cemeteries in Brooklyn lay like deep holes in the earth.

From the airport I make my way to Andromeda Coffee, the words *bury your dead* loud in my mind like an involuntary mantra. The cab ride has me in and out of sleep as morning breaks over the river and strengthens into daylight.

The large window with the words Andromeda Coffee in faded letters reflects a distorted version of myself, as though Giacometti had drawn me. When I push the door forward, it creaks knowingly and cruel. The interior fan blows out immediately while the heating post clinks and rattles next to the door-side tables. I place my usual order with a bob of the head, to which the barista winks back. When I turn to Chris's usual table, though, it is my mother that's sitting there, removing layers of clothing. I'm surprised at how normal it all seems, and I go straight to her. Her hair seems freshly dyed, glimmering a tar-like black. She bobs her head to the barista just like I did, and then places a red pen on the table. I stare at her, finding it hard to talk—I'd think I'd have so much to ask her—and she even widens her eyes, as though saying *out with it,* but I can't. Her latte and my spiked double espresso arrive in the barista's freckled hands, a gentle peck escaping as he lays the mugs on the table, but underneath that sound, there's a louder peck: it's the cab driver knocking on the window, right on the corner of Hudson and Jane, pulling me out of the skewed workings of my unconscious, my duffle bag already sitting on the sidewalk.

When I get out and adjust to the brightness of a satiny silver sky, I check for the pages of my manuscript inside the bag, then pay the driver. On the sidewalks and parks, most trees have already lost their leaves. My heart is rattling swiftly as I turn towards Andromeda Coffee—where I wrote the first full scene of this manuscript, where I last saw Chris, where he last butchered my work—but I can't seem to find it. On the glare of what used to be its large window, there's not the suggestion of the barista working behind it, rather only a version of myself before the words "Space for rent."

Andromeda Coffee is gone, wiped off the corner of Hudson and Jane, and turning every which way, staring at the lonely streets, making sure that I'm on the right corner, I decide to walk west, to the river, where the Hudson River's surface is transformed by a strong gust of wind.

The room I booked at the only hotel I found overlooking the river is not yet ready when I arrive. Check-in begins at five in the evening and not a minute sooner, as clearly stipulated on the confirmation page of my booking agreement. The woman behind the desk circles the check-in time on a printed page, adding unnecessary pressure with her red pen.

"Seriously?" I ask, no longer sure if I'm thinking of the room or her gesture.

"Yes, *seriously*. But we can take care of your luggage, until you come back later today." The smile on her face seems forced, strained, but instead of arguing further, I fish the manuscripts from the bottom of my bag and walk out to the sight of wind ruffled trees on the sidewalk losing what is left of their foliage.

Looking to kill time before the freckled barista's bartending shift at Widow's Walk, I wander the city like the ghost of my recent past.

On my way to Widow's Walk, the wind is cold on my face, lending me a pleasant, almost drunken feeling. Walking in the neon daze of East Village streets, I feel like the ghost of my former life is slowly becoming a person again, like I might bump into myself on the sidewalk walking in the opposite direction.

Once I reach the dark recesses of Alphabet City, I pull open the door of the restaurant and shove the velvet winter curtain aside, becoming instantly enveloped by the warm interior. The hostess is covered in tattoos, but the one that catches my eye is the one on her left shoulder—a baroque crow like the one calling upon my mother's form, which also is, I can now admit, O's specter.

Deeper into the restaurant the space is dim, shading the walls a hue at once golden and mysterious. The sound is similar to what Rose or my father would describe at Capri: the stringed voices, their communal utterance.

Once at the far end of the restaurant, I catch sight of him behind the circular-shaped bar, Andromeda Coffee's barista pouring drinks, working the job that actually makes him some money. I give him a shy wave, but he doesn't spot me right away, so I claim a stool facing the restaurant's back wall.

With his sight toward the opposite end of the circle, he slides a cocktail menu in front of me, and blindly pours me a glass of tap water. "Good evening," he says.

I have a sip of water and clear my throat, letting my stiff muscles adjust to the warm interior, and watch him prepare a cocktail with an egg white in a tin glass, shaking it mightily, high-pouring it into a cobbler topped with a dense froth, and placing it in front of the customer directly opposite me.

He then turns to me, "Start you off with a drink?"

His casual, disinterested manner, makes me force eye contact with him.

His face pales, and he doesn't seem to be able to blink. Once recovering from the initial surprise, he says, "Look at you," exits the round bar and wraps his thin, sweaty figure around me. He looks the same as the last time I saw him: hair tucked behind his ear, slim and gracious, feminine almost, forever dressed in tight black clothes, which makes me think of how accurately I rendered him in all those daydreams.

Once he is inside the circle of the bar again, he rests a soft hand on the metallic surface, his freckles lost in the weak light. "Let me buy you a drink," he says, and once I have it before me, he adds, "Man, I can't believe you're here."

I nod while sipping the ice-cold drink, breathing in the scent of high proof rye whiskey, at last.

"Man, oh, man," he says, "it has been a long time."

"Andromeda Coffee went under?"

He slowly nods. "Rent was untenable, you know how brutal this city can be." He quiets, hesitates, as if he was going to say more, that it went under, perhaps, after losing me and Chris, the only two regulars of the joint. On that, though, two customers arrive and sit at the opposite side of the bar. "Sit tight," he tells me. "I'll buy you dinner, we'll have a chat, I'll pick out your food too, tons of new specials," and then he makes his way to listen to their requests, fix the overcomplicated drinks.

In the meantime, the mind wanders, aided by my favorite booze, and this time I try hard to fabricate the presence of my mother sitting beside me. Her image though, crystal clear for no more than one second, morphs into that of O's, with her freshly dyed bangs glimmering in the low light. Her food would have arrived before mine, and she would have been taking sips from what would be the barista's version of a heavy-handed tequila sour. She'd breathe out long after putting down the drink and would turn to her food. "You don't mind if I start, do you?" already slicing through her enchiladas verdes.

"No, go right ahead."

"So many places I could've gone, yes? I loved the city, but I always longed for the desert, too. I grew up there, after all."

The barista turns to me with a plate in hand, sliding it before me. "Pulled pork crostini, munch on that," he says, and he turns to the other customers and half mixed cocktails in stirring glasses resting on ice.

I dive into the dish that looks way too similar to Mexico's carnitas, and as I'm taking my first bites, O has already finished her meal.

"You know" she says, a wicked smile bending on her face, "I once thought you had come to be the one boundary to the future…"

A cold feeling sinks in my gut and I try fending off her eyes with a few mouthfuls of my own food. The flavor of Mexican food stalls comes around as I eat, but I keep going until I'm done. My plate is instantly removed when only breadcrumbs are left on it.

"Look at me," O says.

I meet her eyes just as my second course arrives—"lamb sausage cooked in its own blood," the barista says—but his voice is soon overtaken by O's.

"I told you one day I would be back for you, come what may."

I breathe in the scent of sacrifice rising from my dish. "And when exactly might that be?"

The barista shoots me a worried look and fixes me a quick and careless Old Fashioned. "Interior monologue you have going on there," he says. "The true writer, always at work."

"I don't know about *true writer*," I say, then have a bite that I wash down with the newly-made cocktail.

Our exchange has made O vanish from the scene—a peculiar ability of hers. Only this time I treat it as if she had gone to the bathroom.

When I'm done with my food, the barista removes my empty plate and takes it back to the kitchen, where a flambé desert fuels rising flames in a pan, which briefly catch on the cook's shirt. O seems to take the flames as her cue—she exits the bathroom, lays eyes on the flames, winks at me as she walks away, past the hostess with the crow on her shoulder. "Bury your dead, come what may," she says, and waves goodbye before vanishing, yet again, this time beyond the velvet winter curtain.

It takes two more double servings of rye whiskey paired with the flambé crepes with notes of ash, charred fruits, and burned fields, for the restaurant to empty.

The lingering customers sitting at the bar have food and drinks before them by now, so the barista has time to talk. He prepares us two rye-loaded double espressos and leans forward on the bar.

"Shedding the old skin?" He nods at the rattlesnake pin on my lapel, making me cringe while my mind unravels images of snakes, like the one framed on the walls of Los Confines, like the one in the bottle of Mezcal Cascabel.

"I'm supposed to bury my dead," I say, startled at myself for cutting straight to the point, for once.

The barista's wide-eyed grin turns into a troubled wince. He drinks again, downs his coffee, the gulp passing thick through his gullet. He grimaces and exhales. "You were not there."

"That's why I'm here now."

He pours more rye straight into his cup and leans forward, as if preparing an accusatory sentence, but fumbles the bottle. The spilled rye streams over the metal surface of the bar around the small glasses holding ambiance candles, like Coca-Cola did in the Comala church, like my father's tequila during the storm.

"Fuck, sorry." He wipes the spill with a rag.

"It's a tradition back home," I say, and allow a moment's silence. "I need you to tell me where his grave is."

He rubs his face. "He's at, well not he, his fucking grave, at Green-Wood, lawn four, plot seventy-one." He pauses, swallows. "Fucking burned in my memory."

I finish my drink, thinking of leaving soon, but he tops my espresso cup again.

"To Chris," he says, raising his libation.

Nodding, I raise the cup and we toast. "To the burial of the dead, come what may," and we finish our drink in one quick gulp.

"Go on, then, get there." He comes round the bar to bid his goodbyes. After a quick hug, he pats my back and slides a flask into my coat pocket. "Chris's favorite rye, you can pour some over his grave, quench his thirst."

I nod to him and start towards the door.

"Lawn four, plot seventy-one," he says. "You can't miss it, it's an open book."

My eyesight hazy, I exit past the crow on the hostess's shoulder, like O, or my mother, did moments ago, while thinking about how I can only do this with Chris's grave and not with her, because with him at least there is a body.

The subway train jolts, heaves to a start, and the station begins to rush by, quickly blurring behind the windows' grime. Once the train has cleared the station, the sight out the windows becomes completely dark, and I meet my reflection in the glass, isolated from the people around me.

Deep into Brooklyn, as the F train takes to the elevated exterior track, I have a first swig of rye, stealthily, trying to shield the flask with the lapels of my mother's blazer. The speed of the train and the winking lights on vanishing lampposts become something like stains, ink white and black washing over the city.

When I reach Prospect Park and exit the station, I find a glove vendor at street level, Brooklyn's version of a Rulfian apparition.

"You have to be fucking kidding," I tell him. "Go on, give me a pair."

"Ten dollars, señor," he says, and I slide the black fingerless gloves over my hands.

When I reach the cemetery's front gate, the liquor in the flask swims at mid-level. Past the threshold, there is the cawing of birds nesting in the uppermost part of the gates. The slope begins its rise and the lawn spreads out before me in the dark. The night is cold and blows a Comala-like wind with Manhattan shimmering at the far end of sight, factories on either side fuming out a smoke whiter and thicker than the powdery clouds above.

I walk through the paved trail in the darkness, the red ink-stained manuscript rolled in my hand, faintly catching sight of the flat gravestones sinking in the grass, just like the memories of the names on them, their epitaphs—the dead's final characterization.

I try to imagine Chris's appearance on the day of his vigil, the day I nearly drank myself to death in his apartment rather than mustering the courage to get *here*, see him groomed and pumped with chemicals, his Daliesque moustache perfectly combed for his final farewell. Did he wear his gloves inside the coffin? Are they slowly dissolving beneath the ground?

Lawn Four is massive, spreading over the first rise. Plot seventy-one is situated on a swell of grass, overlooking Manhattan, mostly downtown, stretching the imagination, perhaps, into the West Village and what once was Andromeda Coffee.

Bury your dead, my father said, so I come across plot seventy-one a real internal wreck. The tombstone is an etched slab of marble in the shape of an open book. As the wind suddenly wheezes, my first idea is to leave the red ink-stained manuscript as an offering, a coffee berry of sorts, but the manuscript still holds my mother, the possibility of her return, so I grip the manuscript tightly, holding on to the sight of smoke from factories in the distance, suddenly catching a whisper of the wind again, but this time through the grass: Is the wind reading out the words on his epitaph, or the words my father spoke, or the descriptions in this red ink-stained manuscript, descriptions I might actually be feeling in my body, *the place begging for an outsider presence, my chest short of air, my lungs full and out of breath at once?* I put these questions to the darkness, and soon the darkness takes the shape of Chris, sitting on his tombstone, sardonic grin on his face, his dense moustache, twisted at its ends, underlining the sharp angles of his cheekbones. He is dressed all in black, too, fingerless gloves like mine on his hands, while his legs dangle over his book-tombstone, blocking part of his epitaph from my sight.

"Ah, so you finally came, writer. The best way you found to honor me was nearly drinking yourself to death."

"Seemed poetic at the time." I lift my gloved hands. "I can use these every day from now on, instead."

He smirks and nods towards my gloves. "Still the cheap man you always were. You got the real shitty kind too."

"Yeah, but look at you, a book for a tombstone. What the fuck were you thinking?"

He shrugs. "Everyone will forget about it soon enough anyway." He hops off his grave and lands noiselessly on the grass next to me. "You want to tell me why you're here? Funeral was a while ago."

"I need some good old literary guidance," I say, breathing steadily in hopes of keeping him there next to me.

He runs a fingertip over the rattlesnake pin on my lapel. "Seems like you've been receiving guidance and that you know more than you knew before."

I shake my head, wordless.

"What are you stuck on then?"

"It seems like the story, no matter who tells it, always comes to the same dead end."

"If I can be honest, writer." He runs his hand along the marble book himself. "I was never fully convinced there was a narrative in there. There was always something missing, too many loose strings. And stories need actions your characters can perform. Forget all that Rulfo and García Marquez bullshit. There's no such thing as characters returning from the dead, especially when you want to read the work with a realistic eye."

I can only nod, slowly.

"Look, writer." His face turns serious. "The reason you can't write this novel is because you don't know what happens. Magical Realism is convenient in the sense that every loose end can be tied up neatly, it only requires bringing the dead back, or just revealing they were dead all along."

A cat meows in the distance, chased by the otherworldly cawing of a bird.

"You will always have loose ends with your story," Chris says. "What happened will never make sense. The only possible ending for you is to kill her, kill O, be done with it already."

I turn to him and watch his face morph into an eerie grin.

"Bury your dead," he says.

I shut my eyes to find the black of mourning behind my lids and lean my head on his grave. The marble is cold on my forehead, the grass ticklish on my uncovered fingertips. After having a final sip, I pour the remaining rye whiskey from the flask over the letters spelling his name.

Like a helpless vagrant at the end of the road, I finally arrive to my hotel at the city's end.

They apologize. My room is not yet ready. They thought I wasn't checking in after all, but they are fixing a room for me *as we speak.*

"A free drink perhaps?" I say, through a tired whine.

They decline, but I nonetheless claim a stool at one of the corners of the bar at the lobby, and place the red ink-stained manuscript over the polished, beer-soaked wood. In front of me there's a rusty old mirror behind the lined bottles. Of what I can catch of my reflection there, I seem like my own corpse struggling to come back to life—I feel weak and sick and can barely register the clatter of high-heels under the low bass of house music.

"Hey there," the barkeep approaches, her curls bobbing, her hoops swinging.

"Cheapest rye on the rocks," and, after she nods, a few ice cubes clink into a glass and liquor washes over them.

With the initial burn of the drink pungent on my tongue, the low lights are dimmed even further, in a quick, almost dreamlike, transition, making Chris's red markings less noticeable on the manuscript, a change of light that seems like it might transition into one of my Magical Realist fugue states, with Chris at the center—but nothing, he is buried underneath Green-Wood's grass by now.

I keep drinking, noticing how parts of the liquor are still warm and others chilled as they swim around the ice cubes, and drink myself into a stupor like I did that night after his death—second and third servings a bit more generous, the level of the drink near the lip, only with less ice: a fuller, darker amber, the barkeep's demeanor friendlier once the other customers leave.

"What's it about?" she says, tapping the red ink-stained manuscript on the bar.

I look up with eyes that are surely swollen and bloodshot, and stare at her before I slur, "You don't want to know."

When I'm almost dozing with my head against the bar, yet still poised to order another shot of Cascabel from that waiter in La Eterna de Comala, I'm finally escorted to my room by a bellboy dressed in a fine black suit.

"I like the pin on your lapel, sir," he says, holding me for balance, and adds that I'm allowed to take my glass of diluted rye with me, that it will be charged to my room, where he is leading me through a soft, carpeted floor oozing the scent of smoke and humidity—something like the halls of the fallen Hotel Regis.

The tap of a card on the door activates a winking green light and then there's the opening click of the electronic lock. The view out the window is all too similar to the one in Chris's apartment, with city lights wavering over the Hudson's surface. The room also has a desk, a modern task lamp that might bear some resemblance to a pouncing snake, its cable coiled all the way to the floor. Behind it, a metal door gives way to a small balcony, where the air wheezes past cold and timid. All the glasses of rye I've downed tonight have, to quote my father, "instilled the place with magic"—the water of the Hudson holds its gleam and ripple, and the night lights of the city burn through it. I finish the last of my drink and shut my eyes, waiting for Chris's voice to flutter into my consciousness again. His voice doesn't come, though, not even with the Hudson River's sound of lapping water.

BOOK VI

Waiting for More than One

2017

THE NEWS CAME LIKE THE SWIFT STRIKE OF A RAT-tlesnake, and the poison streamed slowly into my consciousness, quieting everything else around me.

By then, I was looking for a place to live in New York, looking to spend the rest of the fellowship's money on a studio apartment and then take it from there, maybe get a job pouring drinks at Widow's Walk, but above it all, just make every day seem like the last—a new life, having buried my dead.

All was going well—riverside walks, daily rations of coffee with only the slightest dash of rye, notes in a new notebook: the closest thing to a blank slate. I was trying to keep New York City like a safe haven where I could roam endlessly, and be followed not by ghosts but only by my own shadow.

But the news struck, arriving by way of long-winded emails from the Under the Volcano's fellowship account, which, for a while, I had been treating as spam. The quick piling of message after message, though, managed to pin my attention to the screen.

Bit by bit, forensically, I pieced the story together: After the publication of her latest book, titled *Waiting for More than One,* a rendition of Samuel Beckett's *Waiting for Godot,* only reimagined—or rewritten, rather—in the context of the Mexican drug war and its crisis of forced disappearances, Nayeli set off on a long-awaited, country-wide book tour. The play—in the words of one of the reviewers, "a generative act of plagiarism and appropriation"—has two mothers who search and wait for their missing children, who they believe have fallen victims of organized crime. After searching for them down rivers, wells, waste-lands and mass graveyards, exhausted and lacking answers, the mothers remain in a state of waiting, which is at once chronic and existential. Confrontational as she tends to be, not only in person, but with her writing, Nayeli planned for her book tour to take place in nooks of the country that have been famously ravaged by the war on drugs, as she notes in one of the interviews linked to in the emails: "A play like this one serves little to no purpose if performed for the elites in comfortable venues where they can watch the nightmare engulfing the country while sipping on fine glasses of wine. To be politically active, the play must reach out, graze the settings of actual violence and its actual victims." The location of the play, much like Beckett's original, is set in something of a no man's land—in this specific case, a dirt road in the Mexican countryside—and a tree with bear boughs—which Nayeli first found in the town of Aguililla, Michoacán, during the month she spent scouting the conflicted areas of the country. The place she found ticked all the boxes—marred by conflicts between La Familia Michoacana, Los Zetas, El Cartel Jalisco Nueva Generación, and the famous self-proclaimed Autodefensas; she even found the location of a dying tree before a brick wall spray painted with the cartel's insignias. There was no argument to be had, the first performance would happen there, despite security threats, disagreements with the local police, and the lack of collaboration from the local government. The play's contingent set out to Aguililla: production team, documentation team, a languid private security team, a group of cultural journalists covering the event, and a performing cast of five—Rose playing the role of one of the mothers.

Employing the ever-convenient vantage point of hindsight, one of the tabloid pieces linked to in the emails states that there were warning signs ignored, but nonetheless, in the feeble lighting of the makeshift stage, the play opened with Nayeli narrating the first stage directions, off-stage, like a distant omnipresent voice: "A dirt road in the Mexican countryside. A tree. Evening. Dolores sitting on a low mound, is staring at the crumpled frays of a missing person poster. She brings it close to her face, squints. She gives up, tosses it to the ground, stares away distantly, picks it up again." Rose, playing the part of Dolores, entered the stage, not knowing that by stepping onto its unstable wooden planks, she was stepping into cartel crosshairs. The bullets that flew into the crowd whistled in surprisingly. "So surreal," another article notes, "that it seemed like the bullets were part of the play." The crowd was slow to react, and so was everyone around. The bullets tore into Rose's body long before she could utter that famous opening line of dialogue, as ominous in the original rendition as much as in Nayeli's—"Nothing to be done."

The attack killed two members of the audience, one bystander, one journalist, and left Rose fighting for her life.

I left as soon as I finished reading the thread of messages, and barely made it on the next flight to Mexico City, taking off just before midnight, knowing the full moon imprinted over the Hudson's waters would follow me all the way—to here and now——leading me to the endless stream of lights in the hospital's corridors, where a sleepy receptionist directs me to the ninth floor while she combs her hair. Upon finding the only elevator out of order, I rush up the stairs, past more late night hospital vignettes: a junior doctor in white scrubs and white tennis shoes erasing chalk markings on a blackboard and writing in the coming day's schedules, or a senior doctor in a gray suit with a stethoscope hanging from his neck lecturing a nurse in the middle of the coiling stairs, tapping his pen against a bulk of paper. In the final stretch of the climb, a few people I vaguely recognize from the fellowship crowd the space outside Rose's hospital room. The fellowship advisors lock eyes with mine, but we decide to ignore one another. There are a few whispered "hellos" and raised eyebrows on anonymous faces, and then I'm into a small waiting room, where Nayeli is sitting. Her face seems lost and her eyes shoot up at me, loaded with guilt.

I sit right beside her and match her silence. The only sound around us is the beeping of machines, those inside Rose's room, marking the beats of what remains of her life.

When we are finally allowed to see her, the open door to Rose's hospital room sets off a thrumming sensation in my chest. The beeping machines keep at it, but gain in volume once I enter, marking time and Rose's gravelly breathing. Lying still on the bed, an oxygen mask covering her nose and mouth, Rose's arms lay still at her sides, her white hair combed back, in a style she never wore before. Already, it seems like there is no fight left in her, she is giving out, just lying on her back, her breathing composed of lengthy pauses, then returning with a pant and a snort, her face mostly relieved of its gestures.

Nayeli steps into the room behind me and goes straight to Rose. She runs a hand over Rose's forearm, and leans her head on the railing of the bed.

"The doctors say she is still with us because her heart is so strong," Nayeli says.

I purse my lips, keep silent.

"But if you ask me," Nayeli adds, "she was probably just waiting for you to be here, so she can finally let go."

Staring at Rose, an image of my mother lying like this comes to me, her arms in the same position, the still eyelids. The heaviness in my chest and the welling in my throat makes me turn away from her. Behind the glass window and the diminishing fog of my breath on it, the shyest suggestion of light sparks across the horizon. The moon is still there, but it's beginning to pale, announcing its withdrawal.

Behind me, I hear Nayeli's voice again. "This should be me. It's like my written words were every bullet that went into her body."

My heartbeat goes cold in my chest, while, through the window, and far beyond the city, the sun begins to rise in an orange haze behind the buildings.

After a short nap in Rose's room, I wake to a thick coat of plaque on my teeth. Through the half-open door to the waiting room, I can see Nayeli is also sleeping.

Staring at Rose, at the gaps between her breathing, I wonder if what is about to happen to Rose is what I sought with my own writing: the knowledge that mortality *is* mortality, the end.

The rise and fall of Rose's chest looks like the operations of the machines around her. It's all too terrifying to watch, so I write down what I'm seeing to put a scrim of language between myself and the brutal reality of what's occurring—an old, one would think, useless habit: *Her breathing from the waiting room*, I jot down. *Her breathing follows me wherever I go*, and after writing this down I walk to get a cup of the worst coffee, which squirts from a vending machine— Americano, Espresso, Macchiato, Latte, Mocha. Even though the letters come out funny against the rugged surface of the coffee machine, I jot down more. *There is no such thing as distance, only long, troubled gasps followed by temporary silence.*

After scalding my tongue downing my espresso, I return to Rose. Nayeli has woken and is sitting on the couch inside the room, paying close attention to Rose's breathing. There seems to be a new air of worry, but it's hard to tell whether it's only Nayeli's high-strung energy.

Rose's breaths seem more agitated, though, every gasp seems like her last.

There is another roaring breath, its rasping exhalation. But the parenthetical pause where everything sits still, where there is no breath, has me approaching the bed, laying a hand on Rose's.

Another breath.

One more, her chest swells, contracts. I cover my mouth with my hand.

"Let go, Rose," Nayeli says.

Rose's breathing, clinging to life.

Air in her mouth, a painful expression, air out of her mouth.

Did my mother go through these last agonizing breaths? Is she still breathing?

Did Chris experience these long, drawn-out seconds, or did he die at the moment of impact, after leaping off that window looking over the Hudson River?

Rose's pale skin seems to pale further, like the moon did hours ago in the polluted sky.

The wrinkles in her skin sink deeper with every troubled breath. Her face goes still.

Is our movement our life? I write.

A wash of fear runs through me, like I'm sensing the touch of death coming into contact with me—death grasping at my hand. I turn to Nayeli.

"What?" she says, her eyes fixed, unmoving. Rose breathes out, lazily it seems, and Nayeli takes my hand and squeezes it. "No, no," Nayeli says.

And Rose's breathing does not return. It flat-lines on the machines. She seems to deflate rather than die, and the little snore of trapped air escaping signals the exact moment of her life leaving her body. A great sorrow courses through my own body, driving me back to the world of death, of darkness, but hopefully of closure this time.

Hands on my head, I turn toward the large window, the only apparent escape: behind the glass, both the moon and the sun are lost behind the clouds, and the sky is utterly grim, bled-out.

WHILE ROSE'S BODY IS BEING CREMATED IN EL PAN-
teón Francés de San Joaquín, thunderstorm clouds swell over the
city. The corridors between graves brim with fallen leaves, some dry
and sallow, others damp, well in the trajectory to decomposition,
broken apart and dissolving. Cemetery cats scamper in and out of
sight, vanishing behind the crypts. Are they alive and dead at once,
ignored by the living and only alive amongst the dead? They are silent cats, too, the only people who pay them any mind are the children playing between tombstones, who try to coax them near with
open palms, kissing noises, the clicking of their tongues and the repetition of the word *kitty*. None of them dare go too near, though,
and after they give up trying to persuade them, the kids return to
their cemetery picnic, where their parents munch on tamale tortas
and gulp from a pear-shaped, family-sized bottle of Coca Cola next
to an open crypt—the wounds of their grief healed by now.

The wind is beginning to quicken, like a prelude to a Comala
storm, ridding leaves from tree branches—towering trees that long
outlive people, casting shadows over the crypts.

Nayeli has stepped into the crematorium, waiting for Rose's
remains, while I continue staring at the smoke rising out of the
chimney's crown, hoping this process is another rung on the ladder
of my emotions—first Chris's grave, now crossing the actual threshold from life to death, through the witnessing of a dead body now
turning to ash. The smoke coming from the crematorium darkens
all of a sudden, and so does the sky, which is completely filled with
encroaching clouds.

The picnicking family pack up, wrapping their food within their large checkered cloth and ramming everything into the trunk of a car to the tune of "Ahí viene l'agua."

The sky is about to blow up, the first instance of shy rain rattling over crumbled tombs at the far end of the cemetery, pearling on the asphalt around me.

Glancing up, it's harder to tell whether there's smoke still petering from the crematorium's chimney, not only because there's less and less of Rose's body with every passing second, but also because the rain thickens and lashes down in denser beads. All around me there's a crackling sound and hail is beginning to bounce off the tombstones, pinging against the roof of every crypt. Within this downpour, I feel something nagging at my throat, my own sure and impending grief. The hail around me beats off the warm ground, the steam like molecules of past lives rising everywhere in sight. Taking cover under the crematorium's portico, the wetness streaming down my face is a mix of tears and rain, and I sit on the steps facing the glass doors. My vision transforms into images of people dying on pale-white hospital beds, so all I can do is turn away, to the rows between tombs, to the accumulation of hail between them reminiscent of melting New York snow.

Once the rain is reduced to a patter, Nayeli steps out of the crematorium, ash urn in hand. Rose's name is engraved on it, like on the cover of one of her books. Nayeli places the urn on the ground and sits next to me on the wet steps. I find myself trying to look away from her, to shield the traces of my tears, but it's too late.

"It's fine," she says, "it's always safe to breakdown in a cemetery."

I look away.

"Rose told me about your mother," she says, and I can feel her gaze on me, magnetic. "It will be different this time, you'll see." She forces the urn onto my lap. "Maybe it can help you mourn your mother, too."

I shake my head and hold the urn in front of her, asking her to reclaim it.

"She was your aunt, and your godmother," she says with a broken voice. "Keep the urn, let it sink in. Just don't scatter the ashes anywhere. We'll be going on a trip in a few days. You'll hear from me when it's time." With that, she stands, skips down the steps and looks up at the sky, like she's weighing the potential for more rainfall. "I'm sorry I brought all this pain," she says, returning her eyes to me. "But I promise we will make this right. We will honor Rose and we'll put everything at peace, even if the same can't be done for the rest of the dead people in this country."

She walks away toward the gates of the cemetery, past the wet moss on graves, past a few branches that have fallen and split over the tombs, over streams of melting hail flowing in an unbroken, glassy flow.

A taxi without license plates takes me down Río San Joaquín and Reforma, as far as my fellowship studio, and as we're approaching la Plaza de las Tres Culturas, night is falling over the city. Against the darkening backdrop between buildings, tamale steam escapes pewter pots on street corners, mimicking the factory smoke on either side of Green-Wood Cemetery.

Rose's urn tucked under my arm, I descend on Calzada de los Misterios, where the site of the fallen building has been cleared and is now a lot for sale. Crosses made of brass remain as remembrance for the victims, although city grass is growing well over them.

In front of the door to the studio, scattered on the floor, are envelopes with my name on them. Before stepping inside, I sort through them—credit card offers, comida corrida menus, brothel flyers, but also a letter from the Under the Volcano Fellowship, informing me

I've been expelled from the program. This makes me try the keys to the door, but of course they don't fit in the new lock. I peer through a window to find freshly painted white walls inside and the space completely empty, waiting for the next fellow in line.

Helpless, I throw the rest of the correspondence against the door, but as the envelopes fall to the ground, I find one with Rose's name on it, clearly printed with her unmistakable longhand.

Something like an electric jolt goes off in my chest, then infuses the rest of my body, making me break into a sweat. I stare at the urn with her ashes, then at the piece of paper beside it. One of the lines in Rose's manuscript circles back to me: *in this country the notes telling us a relative is dying arrive long after they're dead, that's why people think we are a ghostly folk.* Though it might only be the time-warping delays of Correos Mexicanos.

Rose's note, illegible at first under the feeble street lights, becomes somewhat decipherable under the light from my open flip phone— *bailing on the fellowship doesn't mean stop writing,* words trapped dead in the middle of the glaring white of the page.

My own version of her idea, skewed to a Rulfian tone, repeats itself in my mind: *the dead, even if lost, will keep on nagging, they'll find a way to tell us that they're still among us, through words, or even through the eyes and grins of others, of those who are still alive.*

I make my way from Tlatelolco to La Alameda Central, the city, in its provisional stillness, sliding by me at my tired pace. I follow the same route my father did the morning of the earthquake—around Bellas Artes, up Avenida Juárez, to come face to face with Hotel Regis's ghost. I stay there for several minutes, staring blankly at El Monumento de la Revolución behind it, its glaring copper dome dim in the grainy night. There is something like the sound of the seismic alarm in the distance, and though it sets off my heartbeat, I know it must be only another one of the city's unebbing noises.

Lacking other ideas, I check into the hotel closest to me, a tiny colonial building, where even though I seem like the only customer, I have to argue for a room overlooking La Alameda Central.

Once inside, I leave Rose's ashes on the only table and open the window to stare out at the park as dark as the Pacific Ocean at night. Lights blur on every side of the park while the city rests under its violet haze. I stay there looking out the window, through my mother's eyes, my father's, even through Rose's, until our eyelids flutter, until they give way, until they're lost to the mourning page-black of the darkness behind them.

NAYELI DOES COME CALLING, EXACTLY A WEEK AF-
ter Rose's cremation—time I've spent mostly dozing in hammocks
on the terrace of my hotel, or looking off its balcony toward La
Alameda Central, at times going over Rose's failed novel or my father's tales in my mind, again, trying to resurrect their descriptions.
There was the occasional walk around the nearby vicinities, to Puente Paredo Alley, where the place that might have been my father's
greenhouse has been repurposed back to its original intent, a parking
lot with dust-covered cars. Rose's ashes haven't moved an inch since
I checked in either; they remain on the table, holding down the pages
of her manuscript and mine.

It's precisely the ashes that Nayeli wants to talk about. Are they
still there and inside the urn? Is the urn still in my possession?

She only explains her worry further after my insistence: Rose's
final wish was that her ashes be scattered over the Wirikuta Desert,
during a peyote ceremony, a habit she had taken on later in life, and
which had purportedly cleansed her of all the ill and suffering drugs
had wrought her in her youth.

"I know she would love it for you to be there, the only family she
had left."

Trying to ignore the stab brought about by her comment, I agree
to journey with Nayeli, to meet her at La Estación Central del Norte
at midnight.

After she hangs up, there remains that feeling, the odd one that
has lingered with me since as long as I remember, and which she
so lucidly articulated: the split subjectivity of my loss: is my mother
dead, or is she gone? Could the news of Rose's death bring her back,

finally spark her return? Is there a link between them, a single person other than my father and myself who might deliver the news?

On the desk, the urn remains over the pages, whose corners lift with the soft push of the wind.

AFTER ANOTHER OVERNIGHT JOURNEY AND WHAT seem like endless dirt roads, we reach the far ends of the Wirikuta Desert.

Traveling this far under the burning sun makes the journey feel like a reel of connected déjà vu cuts: the clock next to the bus driver beaming 6:00 AM in a bright blue light; waking up in the void developed by the body's memory, feeling alone, looking under the seat for the folded pages of my manuscript and Rose's; or exiting the station into the cold air of dawn.

Around here, the shamans are called Maracames, and the one that Rose used to visit drives a black Chevrolet Silverado pickup truck, and wears a suede hat and a metallic-blue Dallas Cowboys zip-up; a man with dark skin and a bird-like nose, who hugged Nayeli with stiff arms outside the station, and then stepped on the gas, racing first through Matehuala's every-pueblo scene of kiosks, street carnitas, and domed churches, and once we were free of the low adobe buildings divided by thin cobblestone streets, the pickup turned onto the two-way federal road and powered to the desert, through its thorny vegetation rising from the dusty ground, first to a small community made up of two shanties to pick up logs for the fire—all amidst the preoccupied skimp of chickens, shaggy mutts among the dusted shoes, the plaintive bleats of lambs in the distance, a little girl named Mariposa wearing a yellow t-shirt in and out of the indoor shanty shade—and where the Maracame asked his son to select and catch the lamb we'd be sacrificing, then to tie him up by his legs despite the pellets of shit shooting from his rear, to load him onto the back of the pickup truck, and drive us to the place where we are now.

Every cloud has since dissolved, even the cloud of dust that rose behind the departing Silverado with the Maracame's son behind the wheel.

I stare out at the horizon, as though searching the path from where we came, while behind me, Nayeli and her new friend—a man wearing a poncho that we picked up while purchasing mezcal for the ceremony—pile wood next to the bleating and squirming lamb, Nayeli already sunburnt, him, as clean-shaven as when he emerged from the abandoned village on our way here, a close neighbor to Rulfo's Comala, where Nayeli sought her bottle of mezcal and vanished into dusty serpentine streets, behind a row of deserted houses.

"He'll come with us," Nayeli said when she returned with bottle in hand, a scorpion floating inside the spirit. "Alone and in that town, he's surely a good omen we should heed." The man wearing the poncho took off his hat before all of us as greeting.

Dry tumbleweed rose and sat back on the ground as we drove along the dusty path crisscrossed by roadrunners, past abandoned adobe houses— not a voice, not a sound other than the clang of our engine in the hollow. The mystery man rode with us in the back, his gaze fixed on the town he was leaving behind, petting the lamb's head, the threaded ends of his poncho swirling in the draft.

"We all have our demons, don't we?" he asked in a soft, almost feminine voice with a passing glance at us, the sky cloudless, the landscape without patches of shade.

With arms folded, peeved, standing next to the fire, my rear sore from sitting in the back of the Silverado for so long, I fear I might not be able to hide the fact that I'm resistant to what I agreed to, not even in Rose's name.

Mounds of peyote buttons stare back at me from a bucket, once sticking out from the dust, now cleaned and shimmering after a rinse, all a slightly different shade of pastel green.

The fire we built struggles at first, but soon gains force—flames leaping and flailing in a manner that my mother would appreciate.

The magical realist character that walked out of the empty town with Nayeli is appointed "Guardian of the Flame," and while he tosses more wood and blows at the red-hot center, the Maracame changes into his millenary attire, fitting his wide torso into an embroidered shirt of complex patterns and fiery colors that extends over his Levi's jeans. Tossing the Dallas Cowboys zip-up aside, he puts on a woven hat that boasts the same patterns as his shirt, and grabs a bouquet of exotic feathers with bells attached to it. He circles the fire three times while shaking his bouquet, having us introduce ourselves before the flames and adding a cleansing motion with his bouquet following every speaker, running the feathers down everyone's face. Afterward, Nayeli passes chocolate and oranges around the circle, which I refuse.

"It'll taste like hell if you don't," she says, and sticks one piece of each in my hand. "Eat as many buttons as you can stomach," and she removes a segment like one does with a tangerine. "Really chew on it, so it releases its fluids." She sticks it in her mouth, her face twisting in disgust, to which the Maracame grins behind her.

Biting off a chunk from one of the buttons, I can't fight the frowns that come with the taste, its bitterness pulling my jaw back with every bite.

Above us, the blanket of night folds open over the sky, and, one by one, are bright eruptions of stars alongside puffy nebulae.

After four full peyote buttons, the taste becomes unbearable, and I have to take a swig from Nayeli's mezcal, the scorpion pirouetting inside the bottle as I put it down. There's a flash of lightning in the distance, Comala-like, although there are no clouds in sight, and I have to return my eyes to the fire.

The Maracame rises from his seat and begins a dance. He invites us to join in and the Guardian of the Flame is the first to rise from his log, followed by Nayeli, who shoots a demanding look my way. Her dancing seems out of place, less of a ritualistic millenary dance like the Maracame's, and more of a move befitting cumbia tunes at a *Miércoles de SOMA* literary party.

I remain sitting by the fire, its flames sparkling orange against Nayeli's shifting profile, shadows from the other dancers moving across her face, the coals crackling and animating figures that can match any resurrection of the unconscious, such as the shape of a woman morphing into a bird.

Nayeli keeps turning to me as she dances, and, in a last-ditch effort to avoid her, I lay down on my back and stare at the sky, where the stars reveal the connections among them, bright lines like the diagramed constellations in a text book, only animated. The Maracame sits next to me, has a sip from the mezcal, looks up, and runs his fingertip midair as if scraping it against the surface of the sky.

"Look," he says, drawing lines across the night. "That's the crab, and right next to it, the scorpion, right?" He lifts the bottle of mezcal with the creature inside. His finger movement parts the nebulae around these constellations. "That's the minotaur guy, maybe, but who knows, and if you eat enough buttons, you might even get to see the blue stag we worship."

The sparkling links between the stars are set in motion, occasionally cut by shooting stars that leave a cosmic tail. Standing and walking back to the fire, the Maracame leaves me with another peyote button. I bite off a chunk and chew it down. The connections between the stars flicker like luminous laser beams in a nightclub, under which Nayeli continues to dance. I can't contain a rush of laughter, a feeling of pure and unapologetic joy I can't fully recognize or ever remember feeling.

Nayeli returns and sits next to me. She's looking for something in her bag, and eventually pulls out Rose's ashes, placing them on the ground beside us.

Behind the fire, the lamb screams and bangs his tied legs against the ground. His bleating and his stomping make the images in front of me quiver, while the sound ripples through my body.

The cold air stings, the closest thing to Hudson-wintry yet, its sudden gusts making the flames sway, shrink and grow, while the Guardian of the Flame dances and feeds more sticks and dry leaves onto them.

"It's only nine o'clock." Nayeli's voice reaches me from behind, a swath of time that had seemed far longer. It dawns on me: looking at the clock is as futile as it is panic-inducing. Only a few minutes have elapsed in this eternity, and I no longer have a sense of my own pulse—heartbeats, clock hands, they seem to belong to a different universe. Is this a place really outside time, like Comala and Aracataca claim to be, another dislocated Macondo?

Nayeli lies down in her sleeping bag and shuts her eyes, while above me, the constellations continue their dance, but fade in color and intensity, as though running out of batteries. I see myself wearing my mother's blazer, contemplate the rattlesnake pin on the lapel, then I stare down toward my hands, partially covered by fingerless gloves.

I return my gaze to the fire, where the Guardian of the Flame's and the Maracame's faces have morphed out of recognition.

"What was I thinking," the Guardian of the Flame mutters, and swigs the mezcal, "having a kid?" His voice has gently transformed into my mother's, and as I close my eyes and sense movement around me, a brushing against my blazer that could well be the wind or a person, searching around me in the darkness, I can almost make out a female figure. Is the Guardian of the Flame ventriloquizing her, a literary device that walked out of the ghostly township so I could finally be closer to her?

Beside him, the flames are elusive arms reaching out, teasing me in, then withdrawing, and I watch them until I sense a bird flying overhead, like the shudder of wings or a puff of air flying past me, also lost in the darkness, so I shut my eyes, trying to listen to its shrills, but the only sound is the crackling of coals, around which two bodies are covered in dust, kneeling, rolling on the ground, the thick film of dust now hiding their features—no more birdlike nose, no more clean-shaven cheeks. Do they have black bangs that resemble the wings of a crow, or is there espresso foam that could cloak an outgrown moustache? The two of them dance around the fire like ancient spirits inhabiting the same realm, as one of the figures— whom I'd like to imagine is Chris—sings like the Maracame did, songs of endless vowels and seamless conjunctions, senseless to my ears, while dust slowly clouds over the star on the Dallas Cowboys zip-up lying beside him. "We must keep on feeding this fire," says a feminine voice, and, as I listen to it, something inside tells me it's my mother, the figure she embodies throwing more wood onto the fire, blowing directly at its core, making the flames rise. I get up and walk to her—thinking this might be the only chance to have my specters available to help my present condition—and I find myself distraught at my inability to do so, for it seems I'm not in control of my body. I feel lucid even though my confusion only throbs, dissolving every grain of my assurance. The effect, somewhat comical and somewhat magical, is, above all, deeply unsettling, and in my mind— only in my mind—I feel as though I have to veer around the figure of a sleepless rattlesnake to get to her. When I do, I can see that her hair carries patterns of feathers under the dust.

Face to face with me, she wets her lips with the mezcal; it runs easily down her gullet like a tequila sour would.

I sit next to her, and as she notices my presence, she shakes off some dust. She peers at me. "You came," she says. "Not everything is helpless for those who know what to do with their loss."

I nod, but then turn to the brushing sound of the sleeping bag behind me, where Nayeli sits up, her eyes half-open slits releasing thick tears, surely having caught some vision in the glowing embers. Immediately she lays down again, Rose's ashes tight against her body. She shuts her eyes, adopts the same position Toribio did the day he died in the coffee field, which inspires me to lean my ear against her mouth to confirm she's breathing, even if the air out her nose comes in waves, systoles and diastoles similar to Rose's the day she died.

Is she accessing Rose in the gaps of her breathing? Is she mourning Rose with her tears? Or is she becoming Rose, yet another character in my personal amphitheater of the dead?

Pushing myself upright, my body cramps, my eyes sting as they are hounded by the fire.

"This is the place where we all exist, the place of perpetual present, an ever-changing apocalypse," my mother says, as Chris's ancient mirage sings in unreal tones, the onomatopoeic language in which words resemble the sounds of toys, that light up shapes like incandescent bulbs in my head every time I close my eyes, if only for a second. "See all this ash gathering here," my mother says, running a hand through the fire. "They could well be my ashes, or Chris's, as much as Rose's."

The bird soars above us in the darkness again, making me crouch to the ground, and, jerking myself upright, I see myself holding my manuscript and Rose's, our attempt at writing my mother's salvation, or her actual return, and as I'm holding the pages over the fire, I turn to my mother like I'm asking her approval.

"You've made it here. Let it go," she says. "Pages of mourning, are they not?"

What could be Chris or the Maracame begins a brief loop of song, only to return to spoken words. "Now is the time to say goodbye," and he lets a pinch of ashes from the fire drift through his fingers.

Coming closer to the fire, I toss the manuscript pages onto the flames. They crash and scatter with a loud whoosh over the embers, sending sparks midair. The pages curl at their corners, the burning bits detach, the rest of the pages catch in the fire producing burn marks like blobs of black ink descending over the white, over Chris's red marks.

"Finally," my dust-mother says, as if it had taken me a lifetime to do this, to abandon the hope in my writing: a burial, a step forward.

I stare deeply into her eyes and she smiles back at me. "See, it's here, it dawns," and out of the deep blackness around us, the sky lightens. The fire instantly weakens against the brightening backdrop. The Maracame stops singing and opens his arms to welcome the morning like my father welcomes his Macondo wind.

The manuscript, and everything it held, is gone, and I walk around the vicinity, admiring my own breath, suddenly catching a movement of the earth, as if it were breathing with me, swelling and contracting.

The Guardian of the Flame and the Maracame sink deep into personal prayers, while Nayeli is now up and standing over the lamb, whose bleats are weaker, whining, as if it was out of air.

Underneath me, the earth, too, pulses, as does every object attached to it. I lean against one of the rare, tall trees, finding it hard to recall my mother and Chris, their faces, as if they were indeed gone. But, head down, a feeling of dread comes over me, as it seems like the earth is taking my breath from me, sucking it from my body to breathe itself, air leaving me through my feet and into the pulsating ground. Could I be dying, too? Or am I, like Juan Preciado, a dead man already?

The shuddering desert weeds are like the pasture of my breathing. They are taking the shapes of snakes, swarming toward me. I am the memory of everything, all in one moment, and the thought makes the air thin in my lungs. I try to look out to calm myself, to restore my breathing, but the vastness of the desert, my mother's and now mine, fails to deliver any assurance.

Beyond us, the Maracame walks towards the Guardian of the Flame and the lamb. The Guardian of the Flame restrains the lamb against its final attempt at escape, its instinctive fight for survival, his hands on both sets of the animal's tied legs.

Blade in hand, the Maracame points the knife in all four directions, the glint of the early sun catching on the gleam of its metal. He then kneels, runs his hand over the animal's face, and sticks the knife in its throat, flaring the ends of every nerve in my body.

The bitter smell of the animal's blood fills the air, and a liquid feeling monsoons within me. The animal lets out a final jolt, while the Guardian of the Flame collects his blood in a silver tin. Some of the blood, though, washes over the dust, grows like a flash flood in the desert, the rivulet streaming all the way to the ashes beneath the fire. Right then, Nayeli tosses Rose's ashes to the ground, over the remaining, dying flames.

At once, the earth ceases throbbing, and a flux of warmness comes over my chest.

The flames die, the fire fully reduced to ash, and in the distance, the Silverado approaches, lifting a new cloud of dust.

Before we leave, while the lamb is loaded onto the pickup truck, I collect ashes from the fire, bits of desert, bits of my writing, bits of them all—realizing now that I am made, too, of their absence.

Back in the shanties, we rinse our faces under the gush of a hose while the Maracame's sisters cook the sacrificed lamb.

There are chickens wandering across the dry ground in their skimp, shaggy mutts among the dusty shoes, the plaintive bleats of lambs in the distance, a little girl called Mariposa with a yellow t-shirt in and out of the shanty shade, and I feel as if I'm waiting to start everything over.

Sitting in the crooked shade cast from the desert hills with an icy Tecate in hand and a plastic cup with the last of Nayeli's mezcal, I keep a close eye on the ashes I collected, and spot the Maracame approaching me, leaving Nayeli behind to help his sisters with the cooking.

"Hijo," he says, and pats the back of my head. "Feeling better now?"

I nod, take a sip from my Tecate, then say, "This morning, everything I walked by took on the shape of a snake."

"There must be a bit of snake within you," he says, running a hand over the rattlesnake pin on my lapel.

His comment suffuses a warmth inside me, a long-forgotten sense of calm. I turn to him and nod, even though I want to tell him more. Instead, I raise my beer bottle and clink it with his, knowing the calm I feel inside is the only thing I need at the moment—what might actually be closure.

The Maracame finishes his beer. He winks at me, and returns toward his shanty, leaving me there, alone—adrift and asunder as ash blown by the high desert wind.

WE SLEEP IN THE ABANDONED TOWN, LIKE WE ARE hosted by Rulfo's characters themselves, in an adobe house with thresholds but no doors, where there is no drinking water, and where the blankets prick at our sleep—all the while willing time to tick on, hoping the past stays put.

After Nayeli falls asleep in the cot beside me, my father's face keeps returning to me, the only relative I have left, someone I still don't have to bury—a vision that persists in and out of my sleep.

It drags long, the night and its profound darkness, but for a second morning in a row, sunlight arrives unannounced, premature almost, this time through the gaps between the curtains.

After a timid whistle beyond the doorway, we know it's time to leave, to step out into the dusty street, where the Maracame is back to his everyday civilian attire, this time wearing a zip-up of the Mexican National Soccer Team.

As the sun shyly peeks behind the desert hills, burning off the daily overcast, the Maracame drives us to the bus station in Matehuala.

Nayeli buys her ticket back to Mexico City, but, somehow, I can't seem to buy mine. Standing at the ticket counter, letting the people behind me move ahead, knowing I have nothing left to pursue in the city, let alone nothing waiting for me, I decide to take a different route, to travel cross-country, like my mother and Rose once did, on a string of buses, watching the cooking smoke rise from villages, with only the green road signs mapping my ten-hour long trajectory—Zacatecas, Aguascalientes, León, Guadalajara, Sayula, Los Encuentros, even Rulfo's birthplace of San Gabriel, before arriving at Colima, where there are no more buses departing to Comala, the place I've never longed nor yearned for, but that I might now have to accept as the closest I have to a home.

At the station I get a rental car and drive the remainder of the route, through the maniacal landscapes around my hometown, its gorges, its steep, darkened cliffs, the bends in the road opening to cloud-filled valleys besieged by hills that look like petrified waves of the Pacific Ocean, and where eventually the volcano gently wheels into the scenery, gradually growing vague in the day's weakening light.

Closer to Los Confines, the longest night of the year descends, like a crow's wing shrouding the land, smothering every suggestion of light. It calls for resolution, a fade out of sorts, ink-black like the mourning pages we need in this country.

The car rattles as it veers onto the dirt road, but I press on a little too fast, kicking up a cloud of dust that chases and overruns me when I slow down for people coming into my path. Once the dust dissolves, my drive continues, straight toward this new version of Los Confines, where my mother no longer exists, where she only existed in the past, where her ghost is the manifestation of a TV set that is never to be turned off, or of seeds left for birds on feeders forever littered with expressionist droppings.

Out of the darkness on the side of the road, more and more people come into my path, like a parade of the living dead, with stares on their furrowed skin, with their buckets brimming with coffee berries, like apparitions that come out only at night to walk their former land, and which keep me rooted in the same spell ever since I left the desert, wondering which people are people or only dust-people rising from my mind.

The cemetery slides by behind lined posts and barbed wire, suggestions of color in the flowers over tombs caught by the running lights. Pouring out of the cemetery's open gates, and then right in front of me, a stampede of sheep like a low travelling cloud.

I hit the brakes again, the wake of dust flooding over the windshield, flowing towards where the sheep run on, to where the man shepherding them whips their backsides to guide them away. Behind him, a hunched woman comes into view, pushing a wheelbarrow full of animal bones. Their images drift before my headlights, and then they are out of sight.

Setting the car in motion again, the black spears of the gates at Los Confines light up in front of me, the halogen lights lending them a waxy appearance.

Beneath the dark sky, the inside of the blue house is dimly lit— perhaps only the light from the TV weakly flooding into every other room, bathing the windows throughout the house.

On the patio, for an instant, my mother is sitting beneath the weak light of the Noguchi lamps—a sight I know only I can see.

The wheels crunch onto the gravel path and I bring them to a halt in front of the leafless tree, whose taller branches are covered in the impressionist patterns of hibernating monarch butterflies. My father opens the front door, sending a flurry of butterflies all over the patio, and peers with inquiring eyes in the direction of my rental.

I step out onto the shifting gravel, now knowing that the goal— the finish line—is one's origins.

The leafless tree's texture is as rugged as ever and my mother is running a hand over its bark, beneath the gathered butterflies, but my father can't see her, and even though I can't really see her myself, she's somehow walking past every window, vanishing behind every corner and behind every ivy-clad blue wall. The feeders in the back-yard are heavy with crows and my mother is filling them with seeds.

Little by little, I begin registering the rest—there is no wind, no sound, not even the far-reaching voices from the TV. The sky is deep and obscure, empty.

My father says, "Hey, you're back," but I don't say anything in response because I'm looking for my mother again, racing after her, even if I know I'll arrive at the same absence, that I'll be forever left with wandering eyes, eyes that search for her, that sometimes see her—just like the many others in this country who keep on waiting for those that they have lost, those that are nowhere to be found: all those who have disappeared.

Two Dollar Radio
Books too loud to Ignore

ALSO AVAILABLE Here are some other titles you might want to dig into.

A HISTORY OF MY BRIEF BODY
ESSAYS BY **BILLY-RAY BELCOURT**

⟶ 2021 Lambda Literary Award for Gay Memoir/Biography, Finalist.
⟶ **"A Best Book of 2020"** —*Kirkus Reviews, Book Riot, CBC, Globe and Mail*
⟵ "Stunning." —Michelle Hart, *O, The Oprah Magazine*

A BRAVE, RAW, AND fiercely intelligent collection of essays and vignettes on grief, colonial violence, joy, love, and queerness.

THEY CAN'T KILL US UNTIL THEY KILL US
ESSAYS BY **HANIF ABDURRAQIB**

⟶ **Best Books 2017:** NPR, *Buzzfeed, Paste Magazine, Esquire, Chicago Tribune, Vol. 1 Brooklyn, CBC* (Canada), *Stereogum, National Post* (Canada), *Entropy, Heavy, Book Riot, Chicago Review of Books* (November), *The Los Angeles Review, Michigan Daily*

⟵ "Funny, painful, precise, desperate, and loving throughout. Not a day has sounded the same since I read him." —Greil Marcus, *Village Voice*

NIGHT ROOMS ESSAYS BY **GINA NUTT**

⟶ **"A Best Book of 2021"** —NPR

⟵ "In writing both revelatory and intimate, Nutt probes the most frightening aspects of life in such a way that she manages to shed light and offer understanding even about those things that lurk in the deepest and darkest of shadows." —Kristin Iversen, *Refinery29*

⟵ "A hallucinatory experience that doesn't obscure but instead deepens the subjects that Nutt explores." —Jeannie Vanasco, *The Believer*

SOME OF US ARE VERY HUNGRY NOW
ESSAYS BY **ANDRE PERRY**

⟵ "A complete, deep, satisfying read." —Gabino Iglesias, NPR

ANDRE PERRY'S DEBUT COLLECTION of personal essays travels from Washington DC to Iowa City to Hong Kong in search of both individual and national identity while displaying tenderness and a disarming honesty.

808S & OTHERWORLDS ESSAYS BY **SEAN AVERY MEDLIN**

⟶ **"September's Most Anticipated LGBTQIA+ Literature"** —*Lambda Literary*
⟵ An elegant mash of memoir, poetry, tales of appropriation, thoughts on Black masculinity, Hulk, Kanye." —Christopher Borrelli, *Chicago Tribune*
⟵ "Purrs with variety and energy, with riffs on Black masculinity, anime, gaming, rap, gender identity, and dislocation in Phoenix's western suburbs." —Michelle Beaver, *The Los Angeles Review of Books*
⟵ "Gives a voice to queer Black rap enthusiasts." —*Teen Vogue*

BORN INTO THIS STORIES BY **ADAM THOMPSON**

⇢ The Story Prize Spotlight Award, Winner.
⇢ Readings Prize for New Australian Fiction, Shortlist.
⇢ Queensland Literary Awards – University of Southern Queensland Steele Rudd Award for a Short Story Collection, Shortlist.

← "With its wit, intelligence and restless exploration of the parameters of race and place, Thompson's debut collection is a welcome addition to the canon of Indigenous Australian writers." —Thuy On, *The Guardian*

SHE IS HAUNTED STORIES BY **PAIGE CLARK**

⇢ Readings Prize for New Australian Fiction, Shortlist
⇢ 2022 Stella Prize, Longlist
⇢ 2022 Barbara Jefferis Award, "Highly Commended"
⇢ "A Best Book of the Year" —The Guardian

WITH AN UNFORGETTABLE VOICE and exuberant wit, She Is Haunted is a masterful debut exploring issues of identity, connection, and loss, told with remarkable grace and assurance by Chinese/American/Australian author, Paige Clark.

TRIANGULUM NOVEL BY **MASANDE NTSHANGA**

⇢ 2020 Nomo Awards Shortlist for "Best Novel"
← "Magnificently disorienting and meticulously constructed, *Triangulum* couples an urgent subtext with an unceasing sense of mystery. This is a thought-provoking dream of a novel, situated within thought-provoking contexts both fictional and historical." —Tobias Carroll, Tor.com

AN AMBITIOUS, OFTEN PHILOSOPHICAL AND GENRE-BENDING NOVEL that covers a period of over 40 years in South Africa's recent past and near future.

THE WORD FOR WOMAN IS WILDERNESS
NOVEL BY **ABI ANDREWS**

← "Unlike any published work I have read, in ways that are beguiling, audacious…" —Sarah Moss, *The Guardian*

THIS IS A NEW KIND OF NATURE WRITING — one that crosses fiction with science writing and puts gender politics at the center of the landscape.

THE BLURRY YEARS NOVEL BY **ELEANOR KRISEMAN**

← "Kriseman's is a new voice to celebrate."
—*Publishers Weekly*

THE BLURRY YEARS IS A POWERFUL and unorthodox coming-of-age story from an assured new literary voice, featuring a stirringly twisted mother-daughter relationship, set against the sleazy, vividly-drawn backdrop of late-seventies and early-eighties Florida.

Thank you for supporting independent culture!

Two Dollar Radio
Books too loud to Ignore

ALSO AVAILABLE Here are some other titles you might want to dig into.

THE BOOK OF X NOVEL BY SARAH ROSE ETTER

→ **A Best Book of 2019** —*Vulture*

← "Etter brilliantly, viciously lays bare what it means to be a woman in the world, what it means to hurt, to need, to want, so much it consumes everything." —Roxane Gay

A SURREAL EXPLORATION OF ONE WOMAN'S LIFE and death against a landscape of meat, office desks, and bad men.

VIRTUOSO NOVEL BY YELENA MOSKOVICH

← "A bold feminist novel." —*Times Literary Supplement*

← "The book's time and action are layered, with possibilities and paths forming rhythmic, syncopated interludes that emphasize that history is now." — Letitia Montgomery-Rodgers, *Foreword Reviews, starred review*

WITH A DISTINCTIVE PROSE FLAIR and spellbinding vision, a story of love, loss, and self-discovery that heralds Yelena Moskovich as a brilliant and one-of-a-kind visionary.

WHITEOUT CONDITIONS NOVEL BY TARIQ SHAH

← "*Whiteout Conditions* is both disorienting and visceral, hilarious and heartbreaking." —Michael Welch, *Chicago Review of Books*

IN THE DEPTHS OF A BRUTAL Midwest winter, Ant rides with Vince through the falling snow to Ray's funeral, an event that has been accruing a sense of consequence. With a poet's sensibility, Shah navigates the murky responsibilities of adulthood, grief, toxic masculinity, and the tragedy of revenge in this haunting Midwestern noir.

THE REACTIVE NOVEL BY MASANDE NTSHANGA

→ **A Best Book of 2016** —*Men's Journal, Flavorwire, City Press, The Sunday Times, The Star, This is Africa, Africa's a Country, Sunday World*

← "Often teems with a beauty that seems to carry on in front of its glue-huffing wasters despite themselves." —*Slate*

A CLEAR-EYED, COMPASSIONATE ACCOUNT of a young HIV+ man grappling with the sudden death of his brother in South Africa.

THE DEEPER THE WATER THE UGLIER THE FISH
NOVEL BY KATYA APEKINA

→ **2018 *Los Angeles Times* Book Prize Finalist**

← "Brilliantly structured... refreshingly original, and the writing is nothing short of gorgeous. It's a stunningly accomplished book." —Michael Schaub, NPR

POWERFULLY CAPTURES THE QUIET TORMENT of two sisters craving the attention of a parent they can't, and shouldn't, have to themselves.